MURDER MUSEUM

MURDER MUSEUM

MAJOR ROXBROUGH

ISBN: SOFTCOVER   978-1-5434-9336-8
           EBOOK   978-1-5434-9335-1

Print information available on the last page.

Rev. date: 11/14/2018

To order additional copies of this book, contact:
Xlibris
1-888-795-4274
www.Xlibris.com
Orders@Xlibris.com
780939

CONTENTS

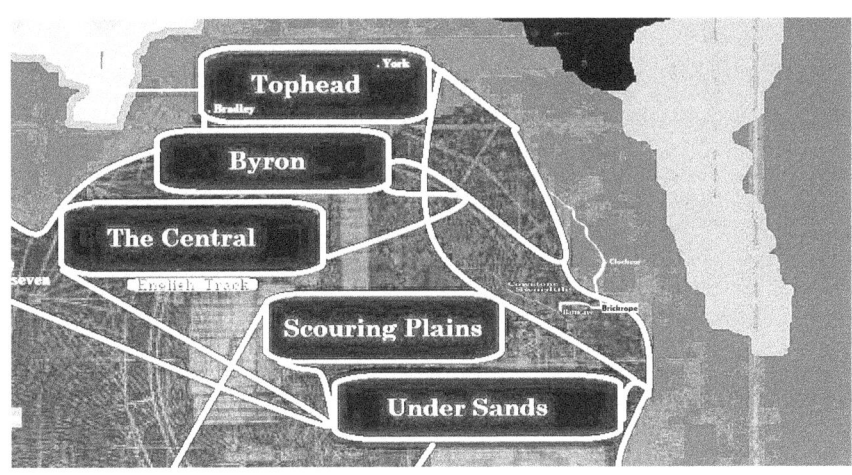

The Flesh

One

Dustin Stallone realised he was a man with only one problem. The problem only had one solution, as far as he was concerned. The problem was his wife. The solution was her murder. He was not a vindictive man. So he wanted her removal, though permanent, to be humane. He did not want to be caught, however. On Venus, in the Anglo-sector, capital punishment was practised. Stallone did not want to feel the hangman's noose around his neck.

If only Madchen would simply walk away from the marriage, she could live. As it was, she would want half of everything. Stallone could not afford to divide their flat in Cowstone. The sleepy little and provincial town lay east of Scouring Plains, just off the main line. Property values were not high, divide them by fifty-percent and they made no sort of deposit for a new place.

He had loved her when they had first married. An outmoded contract she had insisted on. He had gone along with it though. He had agreed because everything was going so very well. Madchen was blonde, shapely and it was not until they had been together for several months, that he discovered her dreadful weakness. Madchen was unintelligent. Worse than that though, she was dull. She was complacent about her lack of intellect. If he could have helped her with education tapes, that would have proved one solution. She had no application though. No desire to be anything other than what she already was.

Stallone should have discovered this terrible short-coming before he had agreed to marry her. The truth was, he had spent most of their courting trying to get into her pants. Endlessly. Time had crept by. They had been living in Cowstone for twenty months. She was entitled to half. Of everything?

She was not going to get it.

She had to die.

One small detail. Though an imaginative man, Stallone had no idea how to kill someone. Even less how to do so and evade the long arm of the law. There was always the web. Risky though. The comb-men might use the same sites as he chose. No point in selecting a fool-proof plan, if some officer of the law recognised the modus operandi. He needed to get out of the flat and think. So he jumped on a train, at the local station. The first one to pull into Cowstone. It was going further east, the next town was Swordtile. An equally uninspiring hamlet in the north-east of the planet. Stallone watched the landscape jostle past, through the special Energisave glass of the windows. A dull plain of scarred rock, eaten away in many places by the years of sulphuric-acid rain. Now the lichen-furs and other hardy plants were continuing to terraform the second planet from the sun. The satellite reflectors kept the world at a constant 292.039 degrees Kelvin. Mankind had come out from under the early domes. Though it was not easy to breathe without the new, slimline respirators even then.

There was constant wind. Infrequent rain. The planet could not be easily tamed. There was also the Venuser. Those being who had lived in disembodied form beneath the ravened surface. There they had lain dormant. Waiting. Waiting for the time when creatures they could inhabit arrived to be taken over. The first settlers had been prepossessed to a man. Only a biotron and android had managed to avoid the invasion. The internal invasion. Times had changed. The Venuser now agreed to reanimate only the dead. It was easy to see why they were evaded, circumvented. Yet they were not a warlike species. Ironic. They were also immune to Scaqualies. When the plague ravaged the human population of the world, not a single one was Venuser. Scaqualies, or to give it its full name Scapedic Qualito Iesthemia was a disease which was feared throughout the Solar System.

It attacked the immune system with startling rapidity. No amount of antibiotics were able to help rebuild the white cells which the disease destroyed. They were exploded from the inside out. Once the suffer was thusly debilitated, the slightest infection of any other sort was fatal. People died of colds, influenza, pneumonia septicaemia. They all had the same thing in common, firstly they had contracted Scaqualies.

Dustin Stallone (named after the sepia-toned silent-movie star of the ancient cinematic times) climbed off the train at Swordtile and gazed about him. He managed to breathe without his mask for a while. The nose filters doing a perfectly adequate job. He doubted that the provincial back-water hamlet could supply him with an answer to his conundrum. Who knew though? Fate had brought him here. Was it for a reason?

Reaching into his thermojacket, he pulled out a pair of Jean-Claude Schwarzenegger optic protectors. The bar rested on his ears. The lenses protecting his eyes from the harsh ultraviolet at such proximity to the sun. The town looked even more depressing through the filtration. Could such a place have any clue that would aid him in his quest? It seemed unlikely in the extremis. Shrugging his shoulders, he assumed the gallump. The special gait that any born off-world

2

used when perambulating on mankind's newest world. He reached a bar called, Pfeiffer's and decided it was not too soon for a drink.

The instant he went through the simple airlock, he removed his optic protectors. The place was dimly lit inside. Windows on Venus were small, dictated so by the outside environment. Stallone looked at the meagre source of the light and was amused. The place was lit by oil lanterns.

An attractive, mature woman looked up from her polishing of the bar. She was slim, green-eyed, smoky-blonde. Perhaps the lanterns had helped with her hair pigment?

"Good morning", she smiled pleasantly. "What can I do for you, Stranger"?

"I know it's quite early, but could I get a drink"?

"Sure. What'll it be"?

"A vedka (Venuser vodka) please"

The woman smiled. It was early. Sales were sales though. As she pressed a glass to the appropriate otic she asked,

"Bad day huh"?

Stallone sighed and took a seat on a high stool, "You could say I'm having a bad month".

"Here", she handed him the drink, "That's a Venushillin, do you want a tab"?

"No, I'm not going on a bender", he explained and found the appropriate coin. Thumb had yet to arrive in places like Swordtile.

"Looking for something then"?

"Yes, but I'm not exactly sure what". *'Don't tell her to much'*, he thought.

"That's a tough one then", Pfeiffer agreed, "No idea what, even roughly"?

"Information that's not on the web".

She looked thoughtful, "Like the ancient documents"?

"Ancient documents"?

"Yeah, you know like those in the Athenaeum, over in Barncave"?

"I don't know what an Athenaeum is", Stallone admitted honestly.

Oh, right, it's a repository, a vault or museum of art-works and books".

"Books? Like volumes of actual tree-mulch".

Pfeiffer smiled, "That's right, it was called paper. They were going to be destroyed when the information they contained had been loaded into pads. They contain scrip, but ink in, on paper, wrapped in books. The Venuser had them brought to Venus and built the Athenaeum in Barncave. Done in conjunction with the Anglo-government here".

Stallone could not believe his good fortune. If what the bar-keep said was true, he had hit pay-dirt with coincidental rapidity.

Swallowing his beverage, he rose from the stool. Thanking her, he trudged back to the Station. The timetable would tell him when the next train to Barncave left Swordtile.

3

The Athenaeum took Stallone's breath away. It was huge. The sheer scale of it was not what he had imagined. It dominated the frontier town of Barncave. The instant he climbed down from the carriages, it hovered over the town like some monstrous beast of stone and glass. As he walked toward it, Stallone felt humbled. Mankind, in the past, had aspired to such monuments of grandeur. On Venus though, all was squat and airtight by necessity. It had come down to the diminutive Venuser, the ancient race of the formerly acidic world, to create such a work of sublime beauty.

Had Stallone not been alone he would still have approached the museum in awed silence. He did so at its only visible entrance. It was the airlock at the base of the grandly-domed cupola. The interior ceiling was terrific arch. It was supported by large stone columns. The lower floor contained an army of shelving, filled with actual books. Above it, a railed mezzanine mirrored it in size and content. For a few moments, Stallone simply craned his head back and drank in the visual feast. He suddenly became aware of the presence of someone else. Looking in the direction of the slightly wheezing sound he found himself face to face with a Venuser. The Custodian of the Athenaeum was not human. Why should he be?

"Good day", Stallone began, "I am looking for a book".

The mustard-hued smile was sardonic, "Right place you've come, library many has".

Though the body was old the Venuser had not inhabited it for long. The speech was still newly mastered.

"I am Dustin Stallone, pleased to meet you".

"Loog, likewise. In particular, anything"?

"Yes. Fiction. Murder/mystery".

Stallone found himself speaking in clipped fashion as well. The Custodian waved a mustard-coloured and slightly shrivelled hand. "Please to follow".

As they trudged the stairs to the mezzanine, Stallone felt obliged to ask,

"So what are the duties of an Athenaeum Custodian, Mister Loog"?

"Core Duties and Responsibilities: Monitor building upon entry and contact Director or designated contractors regarding problems. Coordinate with contractors doing on-site work as needed. Clear all entrances and walkways of snow as needed. Remove debris from grounds as needed. Maintain lichen shrubs. Clean, disinfect and re-supply bathroom. Vacuum tiles, swiffen all wood and dilurlleum floors. Clean main entrance Energi-glass doors. Remove all trash. Polish furniture and woodwork throughout the building. Check lanterns and replace wicks and oil as needed. Keep Custodian's area orderly". Loog had memorised his responsibilities by rote it seemed.

"Murder/Mystery section here is. I leave".

"Thank you and yes. I'll browse and call you if I need any help".

"Do".

Then the little figure was gone leaving him alone.

4

He gazed at the rows before him. Roving them appreciatively. Until his eye caught one volume, the title of which, seemed apposite.

It was a blue book. As Stallone lifted it from its niche he felt the texture of the binding. It was from the skin of a real cow! Almost caressing it with his fingers he opened the book. The fusty smell was intoxicating. The row of dark ink on the yellowed page:

Murder through the Ages.

edited by Darcy Sardon.

Stallone was trembling with anticipation. He took a seat on one of the provided sofas. Unable to resist reading the first short story in the book in one go.

Cellular Stream

MARIA FÂNTOM

From the metallic dust of ancient, lunar corpses, through geometrical, arched waves, the fluid body of a dream collapses, shattering into meaningful, everlasting nothingness. It doesn't remember the secret from which its existence had been shaped. Cursing the erased memories, the androgynous entity laments its paradoxical captivity, whispering thunderously through the invisible matter.

"Listen, it isn't too late to change your mind. If we go through all the data once more, maybe a different solution will reveal itself. There is a chance that the scripts harbour an underlying stream of data that we haven't managed to access yet. Don't concern yourself with the minutiae, try and focus on the bigger picture", he explained with a calm, deep voice.

"You don't understand. Are you willing to kill it or not?" she cried.

"There is *always* another way," the reply came after a transient pause. "Always. Please believe me."

"Even if there was… it doesn't matter anymore", her voice was breaking.

Melted by the white noise, the wires twisted in discontentment.

"What do you mean?" suspicion and fear tainted his every word. "Why does it not matter any more?"

An obtuse dial tone came back as a sterile answer. Carefully, she placed her feet on the wooden floor. The soft, azure velvet of the armchair regained its freedom. Though her skin felt cold, she was overcome by a blistering heatwave spreading from deep inside her core. Her eyes were burning. The pounding silence was deafening her senses. The enrapturing smell of fluid clay and the blossoming purity with which the liliaceous plants had been bestowed, abandoned her in a pellucid crucible in which cell by cell the transfer had begun.

*

Swept away by binary worms, the consciousness wails its decomposed scripts. During each compressed moment, the lucid black dyes the abyss.

*

Sternly, the shapely anchorwoman had read:

"Doctor Anima Schwartz was a well-respected member of Professor Carl's scientific research team. Due to her break-through in the development of artificial intelligence, the *D.E.U.* (Diffuse Enkefalos Unit) also endearingly named Animus by its founder, was introduced, linking all technology devices and enabling the continuous transfer and collection of information across the globe. A spokesman for the Anonymous Group, which had condemned the D.E.U. from its conception, stated that the disappearance of Doctor Schwartz was a tragic event. That the group had no involvement in it. In an interview with our reporter, Doctor Arvi Insk had presented his opinion on his colleague's vanishing. He was convinced that Doctor Schwartz had entered the D.E.U. in order to stabilise the system and cease its apparent, omniscient control over mankind. Though his claim was perceived as phantasmagorical, the governmental agencies continue to carry out an in-depth analysis of the lunar satellites. At the same time, the police department was not ruling out suspicious circumstances and they continue to treat the case as a possible criminal activity. The investigation is led by Detective É. Ulmo, who specializes in criminal profiling and data…"

Worldwide, the screens had turned white. Tiny, black insect numbers had then crawled across in orderly, vertical lines.

*

The fall is eternal...

Anima and Animus – Carl Jung's theory states that the anima (unconscious feminine within a male) and animus (unconscious masculine within a female) are the two primary anthropomorphic archetypes of the unconscious mind

Enkefalos – Greek "brain"

Déu – Catalan "God"; **deu** – Catalan "ten"

Marvin Minsky - an American cognitive scientist concerned largely with research of artificial intelligence.

Two

An intriguing read. One which hinted at the level of quality to come. Stallone wondered if there was a borrowing service. He tucked the book under his arm and carefully strode downstairs.

Loog was still at his desk. The two of them still the only current occupiers of the building.

"May I borrow this book please, Mister Loog".

"Is a library it is". Came the clipped reply. The Venuser pulled the book from Stallone. From inside the front flap, he drew forth a slim foil slip. In an indentation on the desk, he carefully fed the foil. Somewhere in the bowels of the Athenaeum, the metal click of relays could be heard. Loog placed the slip into a box. The container had been empty before then.

"Days of twenty-seven, may you have. Fine after that there will be".

"Plumb", Stallone acknowledged understanding and pleasure. "I'll be sure to bring it back before the forty-eighth of the month. Thank you for your help. Good day to you, Sir".

"Also to you", came the polite response.

Stallone walked thoughtfully out of the impressive structure. Murder through the Ages was his textbook. Thank the stars for Darcy Sardon.

It grew heavy in his hands. It grew heavy in his brain. On the train going home, he could not leave it closed. He had the irresistible compulsion to read the second story

The Man from Lunar Sea

BY NIK GEHENNA

1.

Doctor Van Heston felt a burning pain in his neck. The discomfort was so great that it woke him instantly.

Hell's teeth what is that"? He exclaimed rather prosaically. "Scarlet! What on Mars are you doing with that laser needle in your hand"?

His three-year contractee looked nonplussed and confused. Struggled to drag herself from slumber. Even so, the implement was in her hand.

"What are you doing to me, Scarlet"?

"Oh, What"? Was all Scarlet Lamarr could mutter.

"That surgical tool! There, in your hand. Is that from my bag"?

"Tool"? She echoed plainly confused. "I don't understand what am I doing with it"?

"I'd have to say that you were about to cut through my airway", Heston gasped. "That you were about to commit murder, Scarlet.

"No!" she shrieked, "What are you saying, Van?

"Lights on". Heston demanded and the room was flooded with brilliant LED.

"Van"! Scarlet's voice sounded desperate. "There's blood running down your neck. Let me help you, let me...".

"That's all right", Heston cut her off short, "I am the qualified one, I'll deal with the wound. Why did you take it, Scarlet, why did you want to kill me"?

"I didn't, I wasn't awake before you darling. I don't remember taking it. I don't remember anything. You have to accept that Van. I would not hurt you for any sum, any reason".

"Very well I accept that consciously you wouldn't do it. Do you hate me though? Wish I was dead"?

"No", Scarlet shrieked, "I love you, Van".

"It's possible to hate someone and not even realise it. You haven't been feeling to well have you? The phases of Phobos"?

"I've felt a little unwell since Clark's accident".

"That could be the reason you know? After all, I shouldn't have let a man his age drive a Morphy Richards 200bhp. I loaned him the flitter, you could hate me for that"?

"Van no. I wasn't your fault".

"That's obvious to me, I didn't make him speed like that. Especially through a sand-storm. He was obtuse to do so".

"Don't say that", she flared in her dead brother's defence.

"You see"!

Scarlet took a long intake of air before asking hesitantly, "Do you think I'm losing my mind"?

"No", he smiled, "It wouldn't hurt to see my good friend Sherlock though".

Scarlet bristled, "The Nut Doctor"!

Heston returned patiently, "The term is a psychiatrist, Darling".

"I don't need to see him, Van. It won't happen again, I swear it to you".

Heston's tone changed to one of sympathetic concern, "I know you'd never deliberately hurt me. What if you do it again, without knowing it. What if you succeed and I die? Let's both feel safer and go and see Sherlock".

2.

Sherlock Watson's plush offices were in Protonilus in the Eurasian Block of Mars. The lower-Southern quadrant that contained the south pole. They were opulent, spacious, free of dust and very comfortable. Finally, the android receptionist looked up from her iPad and told them they could go in. Scarlet had been critically gazing at the mechanism's rather impressive breasts. Plainly she did not approve of their gravity-defying pertness.

"Come in. Come in", Doctor Sherlock Watson asked them both, "Please take a seat, good to see you again Van".

Moments later his face was wreathed with concern, "And you say Scarlet was asleep"?

"Yes. Really soundly so", Heston confirmed.

"What else"? Watson then required. "I mean volatile demeanour of any sort"?

"A catalogue of small instances", Heston began, "She hears sounds that aren't there, misplaces items. Moves items from one place to another. She also becomes very abstract on frequent occasions. A lot of action s seem to mark stupefied antipathy".

Mz Lamarr, were you very attached to Clark"? Doctor Watson suddenly asked the silent woman.

"I was like his mother", Scarlet began, "There were only two of us since the Orion exploded just outside Callisto. So I brought him up".

"Ah yes the Orion", Watson remembered, "Both your parents were on it"?

Scarlet nodded.

"So obviously the two of you were very close. Closer than many siblings".

"It had nothing to do with last night though, Sherlock", she asked him to believe.

"I'm just assembling data for my diagnosis, Scarlet", Watson accepted her familiar form of address.

"Data", she began to lose her composure, "Like the fact that I tried to kill Van"!

"Scarlet", Heston objected, "Let Sherlock do his work. Let him help you"?

Scarlet suddenly burst into tears, "I apologise. The thought that I could harm the man I love is just too abominable to accept".

Heston put a comforting arm around his wife's shoulders.

"Maybe I am crazy wha wha wha".

"You certainly need some sort of treatment, Scarlet", Watson tried to sound reassuring. "Have you been sleeping well, you may be over-aught"?

"Yes", was all the sobbing woman could manage.

"What about nightmares? Frightening dreams"?

"No".

Watson tried, "Do you find yourself unusually upset when matters don't go as planned"?

Scarlet suddenly snatched up the psychiatrist's stylus and with a savage downward thrust buried the point in his faux-leather topped desk surface.

"You've broken Sherlock's stylus"! Heston almost wailed, "What were you thinking"?

"I don't know, I'm just so frustrated", Scarlet whimpered. "I'm so sorry, Doctor. I'm just so on edge since Clark was...".

"I understand. That's all right", Watson soothed. "I think I'll see you again tomorrow, Scarlet. Alone".

"Are you certain that's best, Sherlock. In her current state, you don't want her accompanying"?

Watson nodded.

"Very well. You're the expert", Heston agreed reluctantly.

"Wait outside now please, Scarlet. While I have a little chat with Van".

"The instant they were alone together, Heston demanded, "What do you reckon, Sherlock"?

"It's too early to tell", his colleague returned, "She shows no outward symptoms of violent behaviour".

Heston argued, "I don't think your stylus would agree with that, Sherlock".

"Van", Watson explained patiently, "The last thing we need is abecedarian psychoanalysis. Go home, for now, look after her. She needs plenty of understanding".

"All right, Sherlock. Thank you", Heston agreed reluctantly.

3.

"More lichen-tea, Van"? Scarlet asked as she was gathering up the crockery from their evening meal.

"No thank you, Darling. Leave those, I'll load the washer".

Scarlet shook her head and gathered up the cutlery. Suddenly Heston cried out in alarm, "Put that knife down, Scarlet"!

She slammed it on the table in anger and her voice was low. She explained with restrained patience,

"I was just going to cut some Angel Slice".

Heston paled, then managed an understanding squawk. "I'm a bit rung-out myself, Darling".

Her voice low and full of menace, she asked him, "You're not afraid of me are you"?

"No. Of course not. Considering what we've been through, I was just in the moment. I was being too cautious. Forgive me"?

There was an awful silence and then she said, "Of course". It stretched further until she offered, "It might be best if I take the sofa tonight. You can lock the bedroom door".

"Hmm", Heston was hesitant and then he finally admitted, "If you think that's the right action, then I won't argue with you".

"There's someone at the main airlock", she told him then.

"What do you mean"? He was nonplussed.

"I mean the chime is ringing, the chime of our front entrance. Don't tell me you cannot hear it"?

"Don't be silly, Scarlet, what are you saying now"? Heston began to feel panic grip him.

"The chime"! Scarlet's voice began to grow shrill, "It's chiming, Van. Go and see who's there"?

"Darling, calm down", Heston begged her, "There's no chime right now".

"But I can hear it! Go and see who it is, Van".

Heston could do nothing but nod and go to the airlock. He keyed in the unlocking code and the inner door hissed open on its pneumatics. He could hear Scarlet repeating desperately,

"Please be there. Please. Please".

The outer lock then hissed to and all that came into their apartment was the wind and the red sand.

"The chime's stopped", Scarlet gasped her voice little more than a whisper. "But it was chiming, Van. I swear to you".

"By whom"? Heston was reasonable. "Once we knew none was without, then your head stopped chiming. Forget it, Darling, I hear pops and clicks that cannot be explained on several occasions".

"I don't know what to do any more, Van. Tell me what you think I should do about all this"?

"Sherlock will help you in the morning. He's one of the best in his field".

"Scarlet"! Scarlet heard her voice cried out.

"What"! The woman gasped, an icy dread trickling its way down her spine.

"What, what"? Heston asked, "What do you mean by what"?

"You said my name didn't you"? Scarlet asked, but she knew the truth of it with a terrible certainty, for his lips had not moved.

"Scarlet"!

Voice low with frightful alarm, she told her contractee, "Someone is calling my name".

"I heard nothing", Heston gasped, "Try and get a hold of yourself, Scarlet, your cognition is starting to run away with you".

"Cognition", she repeated, practically spitting the words. "Cognition, Van? We have one meeting with *your friend* and already you're a psychiatrist too"?

"Scarlet. Scarlet. Scarlet. Scarlet".

Holding her hands pressed to her temples she screamed, "Stop, stop leave me alone"!

"Maybe I should ping Sherlock"? Heston suggested, climbing to his feet.

"Scarlet. Scarlet. Scarlet. Scarlet".

"It's driving me crazy", she screamed, "Call him, Van. Call anyone". With that, she hurled herself from the room crying and stumbling up to the second floor.

Thoughtfully Heston picked up his pad and tapped Watson's address. The psychiatrists face appeared on the screen with admirable rapidity.

"Thank goodness you're available, Sherlock", Heston gasped, "It's Scarlet, she's hearing noises and is very distressed, what do you suggest"?

"In your bag or your own medication cupboard, do you have any blue lubies"? Watson asked.

Heston nodded, "I have some 61mg, how many do you recommend"?

After a seconds deliberation, Watson advised, "Give her two of those and see how she goes. You can ping me again if they don't work".

Heston admitted, "I don't know what to do about all this, Sherlock. What if she tries to attack me again"?

"We'll see after tomorrow", Watson decided. "She's not yet bad enough to be institutionalised. Not only that but Nadzi Sanatorium doesn't have the best reputation. It still seems a very last resort option, Van".

"She might make another attempt on my life", Heston's voice was laden with strain.

"Get the lubies down her and then keep an eye on her until tomorrow", Watson replied, "You know full well I have to have a counter-thumb from a J.P. to get her institutionalised".

"All right", Heston caved, "You're the expert, Sherlock".

"It's a puzzling case, Van", Watson admitted then. "I don't have enough information to declare Scarlet out of her mind. I need to speak to her in greater detail and intimately. I'll see her as scheduled. Be careful for this one night, Van".

4.

"Did you sleep all right, Scarlet", Heston asked the following morning. He sipped his lichen-tea with a certain grim dread.

"I did, Darling. Those capsules you gave me did the trick I think".

"What a relief that is. After you've seen Sherlock again I'm sure things will soon return to normal. What are you drinking by the way? It looks gruesome".

Scarlet actually chuckled. "Lichen-tom that's all, would you like some"? She was already rising from her chair so Heston felt obliged to say that half a glass would be nice. Seconds later though he was coughing and spluttering and the tensions were back between them. As terrible as ever.

"What's wrong now"? Scarlet felt her fractured nerves would shred. If only these awful incidents would cease.

"What did you put in this glass"? Heston gasped, his voice sounded like he was strangled.

"Just the lichen-tom. From the carton in the kitchenette".

"No. Scarlet there's something else in here, I should know I nearly swallowed it. It tasted like iodine"!

Scarlet echoed hollowly, "Iodine"?!

"Why, Scarlet? I thought after last night things would be back on track, but...".

"I swear to you on Clark's grave that I put nothing in that juice, Van".

Heston jumped from his chair, striding through the tastefully decorated apartment. "There's an easy way to settle this". He sounded understandably annoyed. Scarlet hurried after him, they reached the medication cabinet in the utility room and the doctor threw it open with unnecessary vigour.

All the while Scarlet was wailing, "I just poured the juice out of the carton. Why don't you believe me"?

Locating what he desired, Heston held the bottle aloft, almost with a triumphant awareness he declared "Here's the bottle, Scarlet. The cap is on but look! Iodine on my fingers. This has just been used. Not by me Scarlet".

Desperately, his contractee attempted, "I cut myself this morning! That's why you got some on you".

Heston raised a supercilious eyebrow, "Really? Show me the wound please, Scarlet"?

Scarlet burst into tears, "I don't remember where I cut myself. I don't remember using the iodine. I...must be...crazy".

5.

The flitter was a swanky Morphy Richards 200bhp. Outside the constant wind and sand buffeted the bonnet, sides, boot. The couple inside were oblivious of the elements of Mars. The interior was warm and scented with the smell of sex. Nurse Natalie Kelly was just pulling her skirt back down to a respectable position. She complained,

"The next time we flutter it will be in a bed, Van. Your bed. In the apartment, with her gone. Get it? Just break the contract and let me move in with you"?

"You know she gets half of everything if I do it that way. Be patient, Babe. The remote switch for the chimes and the pressure pads that activated the speakers worked really well. I put the iodine in the drink this morning and it nearly tipped her over the edge. If I get her locked up in Nadzi Nuthouse then you move in and I give her nothing".

"Does it really matter if you give her half"? Kelly objected. "We could get somewhere together somewhere of our own"?

"And lose the Roxbrough canvas or the Matthews sculpture? What about my USA violet 2 cents with the inverted watermark? Do you realise how much just those three items are worth? I've grafted my sack off to afford them, Natalie. Since we contracted she has done no work. No, they are not ours. They are mine and I will not give them up".

"Then you'll be celibate until I do move in", Kelly warned. "I'm not having any more snatched quickies with you, Van. In sluice rooms at the hospital, doctors overnight bunk or this flitter".

"It won't be long, Darling".

"So you've promised over and over, how long is not long, Van"?

Heston gunned the engine and turned on the filters before replying. "She's on the edge, her nerves shredded. It's a just a matter of days and then Nadzi and her interment will be a life sentence".

"Sending her bonkers though", Kelly observed, "Why not just put her out of her misery? Kill her".

"Just leave everything to me, Hun. She'll be out of the way permanently that's as good as dead".

6.

"What happened at Sherlock's, Scarlet"?

The two of them were in the lounge. The Roxbrough over an ornate but fake mantle. The Matthews in the faux-hearth.

"He asked me a lot of questions and told me I seem to be all right".

"Did you tell him about the iodine? The voices? Hearing chimes that weren't ringing"?

"I'd forgotten about them, Van. Maybe they never really happened".

Heston sighed, matters were not progressing quickly enough, "When I spoke to him afterwards, on the iPad Vid he seemed to think you might need a rest. In a rest-home, Scarlet".

She shuddered before asking, "What kind of home"?

"A very high class and comfortable residence. Somewhere where you can face your compulsions".

"I don't think I have any compulsions, Van".

"You're getting over-aught again. Sherlock had shielded you from some of his more serious concerns".

She clenched her fists in dread, "Please let's just move on as though the past few days didn't happen", she begged.

"Scarlet", Heston began in his medically toned voice, "Something has to be done. Twice you've tried to murder me. We cannot pretend that it did not happen. You hear noises that don't exist. you've lost control of your own actions. You have bouts of amnesia. Scarlet, I'm not the bravest of men. I am afraid of what you might do next. I'm afraid of *you*, Scarlet! Without the care, you need you may tip over into full derangement and fanaticism. Look at yourself. Your puffy-faced. Red-eyed. You cannot stay still. Clenching your fists like that. Your head darting hither and thither in confusion. *Look at me*"?

She screamed, "I am"!

"You can't", Heston was shouting by then, "You can't look at me like you used to, Scarlet. You can't look at me with love in your eyes and heart. You hate me because you've become convinced I killed Clark. Why don't you admit the truth? You become like this when Phobos is overhead. You know what that is. It is moon-madness. You have lost your reason, Scarlet".

"That's not true", she said, her voice indicating her exhaustion.

Speaking very quickly then, he demanded of her, "What's the date, Scarlet? How many days are there in this month"?

"You know I get confused with the different calendar", she wailed dramatically.

"You see, you regress into childhood when you were on Earth. You don't even want to be the woman I contracted with any more. You want to be a little girl with no responsibility at all. You need the constant attention of someone with special training, Scarlet. I don't have the special training your brother he is dead"!

Scarlet collapsed in a flood of tears, totally distraught and miserable.

"Will you let the experts help you, Scarlet, or do you intend to go hopelessly psychotic"?

The doctor's contractee collapsed in a swoon of total misery and confusion.

7.

Heston had his iPad on his lap. In his hand was a chilled glass of lichen-vod. The iPad was video and at the other end was Natalie.

"Are we any closer to be together, Van"? He voice was tinny in the tiny speaker of the portable communication instrument.

"We are very close", the good doctor assured, "Just another few days and I believe she'll tip over the edge".

"Don't bother talking to me at the hospital then", she ordered, "There is already too much talk about us and anyway you get nothing until I'm in your apartments. Does Watson still maintain she's in her right mind"?

"He's mystified, but still not ready to take out an order for her care. He's disappointed me in that regard".

"Maybe he has some notion of what you're doing"?

"Stop worrying. The only person who is in control is me. I'll ping you tomorrow, we'll keep in touch on my pad. It will not be much longer and when I get you in this house I'm going to....".

Natalie abruptly cut the link. Heston could still see her in his mind's eye though. Tall, blue-eyed with coils of blonde hair cascading down her shoulders. Naked she had a... He took a huge pull on his drink, he felt he was so close.

8.

"There's no need to dust that, Scarlet. It happens to be Venetian glass and..."

The sound of glass shattering on the tessellated floor was sharp and disquieting. Scarlet looked totally terrified as she exclaimed, It was an accident, I fumbled...".

"You did - didn't you? Your fingers are now being affected by your nerves. Why don't you admit the totally obvious"?

"I'm fine. I...".

"Fine when I'm not here you mean. You want me dead because of your careless lackadaisical brother and...".

"What have I got to do"? She suddenly sighed, her voice low. "You win, Van, just instruct me, I want some calmness. I can't take any more upsetment and distresslogy".

"I know how fine a place Nadzi Sanatorium is. You'll have a suite there. A very luxurious abode. It exists to help people like you, Scarlet. Think of it as a high-class hotel for people who need a special kind of care. After a while with the right medications and psychoanalysis, you'll feel like a different person".

"How long do I have to go in there"?

"You must understand that my field is not in that area, Scarlet. I cannot imagine it being more than eighteen months or so though".

"Eighteen Mars months! Let me think, how long is that in Earth months? I can't remember how to convert it".

"I know you've forgotten many things. Every day you'll lose more, that's because your mind is going, Scarlet. Can't you feel it? You can't you feel your mind going"?

"I'm all right when I'm with Watson, I remember everything then", she wailed.

"Of course you do. That's because he's had the special training to deal with people like you Scarlet. Someone like Sherlock will be over in Nadzi. Someone who knows how to deal with schizoid maniacs. In my recent discussions with Sherlock, we agree that this is the best for you".

"So you want rid of me. You want me out of your life! All right make the appropriate arrangements. I just want some rest".

9.

The banging on Heston's door was urgent bordering on frantic. "What is it Scarlet? I'm just pinging Nadzi, getting you a place".

Her voice was faint through the study door, even though it wasn't an airlock, "I've just done a bad (indistinct). I'm sorry, please come out I need you, I don't want to be alone".

Annoyed at the interruption, Heston strode to the door and threw it open, "What's happened"? He asked her.

By way of an answer, she threw her arms around him, bursting into tears, "I was lonely. I haven't been out since this all began, I need your company. Please don't be cross with me".

For the merest of instances, his resolve almost weakened. Then he thought about Natalie. Naked beneath him moaning in pleasure and he was once more determined. He held her for a while before declaring,

"I do have to go to the hospital, but I'll be back at seventeen hundred, no matter how much they need me. You need me more right now. Before you go to... well before you start your treatment".

He dialled the code on the outer and inner airlocks and picked up his anorak. "Se you tonight, it might be our last for a while".

Heston planted a chaste kiss on her fevered forehead and turning, left.

Scarlet glanced about her as though the empty apartment might very well swallow her up. She shivered and was then distracted by a soft ping coming from Heston's study. Slowly, with feet of lead she went into the one room she entered but rarely. The skeleton in the far corner always made her uneasy. Uneasy was the order of the day though. So she went around the desk to turn off the source of the noise, Heston's iPad.

It was still displaying the name of the last person to message him.

"Natalie Kelly", she read aloud, '*Who's Natalie Kelly*'? She opened the file, there was a text of a conversation Heston had conducted with her on a vidlink. Feeling a sense of guilt, but doing so anyway she began to read the text.

"Are we any closer to be together, Van"?

"We are very close. Just another few days and I believe she'll tip over the edge".

"Don't bother talking to me at the hospital then". "There is already too much talk about us and anyway you get nothing until I'm in your apartments. Does Watson still maintain she's in her right mind"?

"He's mystified, but still not ready to take out an order for her care. He's disappointed me in that regard".

"Maybe he has some notion of what you're doing"?

"Stop worrying. The only person who is in control is me. I'll ping you tomorrow, we'll keep in touch on my pad. It will not be much longer and when I get you in this house I'm going to....".

There was no more, but it was enough. Van was having an affair with a Natalie Kelly and in order to have her in his home, he was driving Scarlet mad. Driving her mad and having her locked away in a Sanatorium with a terrible reputation!

"I believe she'll tip over the edge". "Does Watson still maintain she's in her right mind".

Scarlet began to laugh. The laugh became a cackle. The cackle a chest giggle and she could not stop it. She could not stop the laughter of a woman who had lost her wits.

"My name is Scarlet! S.C.A.R.L.E.T", she screamed. The voice she heard was not her voice, it was the voice of a mad woman. "He said I hated him. But it was him who hated me. He wanted to drive me into a loony. He wanted to lock me up in a loony bin".

Outside Phobos was in the sky, looking down on Mars with its single waxy eye.

10.

Heston opened the airlock and stepped into his apartment. Before he could react in time a figure darted toward him and he felt an incredibly sharp pain in his chest. As he fell back in agonised surprise he saw Scarlet's face and the expression upon it filled his veins with ice-water. His body fell onto the floor with a sickening thump.

"Scarlet"! He gasped. "You stabbed me. You stabbed me with my Belgian Percussion Knife. You've been in my office"!

"Knife", Scarlet's tone had a sinister and terrifying quality to it, "There's no knife, Van. It's in your imagination".

"Scarlet", Heston gasped as greyness began to fog his vision, "Ping the hospital, it's not too late. Hurry".

"Ping them"? She returned, "Like you pinged Natalie. Like you frenged the filthy whore! Don't worry though I'll ping, I'll ping that slut once you're gone and then she'll be well and truly frenged".

"You're crazy"! Heston gasped, his chest full of fire, "Make the call, hurry".

Scarlet seated herself on the floor beside the growing pool of blood, "Doctor Watson said I was sane. He was wrong though wasn't he and two murders will serve to prove him so. Then I can get some rest. Rest in the luxurious apartment in the Sanatorium"!

Scarlet Lamarr began to laugh and her laughter was hollow in her ears as she laughed for a very long time!

Three

Stallone almost missed the stop at Cowstone. The second story had thrown up a possibility. The only trouble with it was he did not think Madchen possessed enough wit to go insane. In order to lose one's mind, one firstly had to be in possession of one. He punched in the combination to their flat and discovered she was home.

"Where've you been"? She wanted to know. Her voice contained no hint of accusation. Just simple curiosity.

"Why"? He countered. He did that quite a lot recently. It seemed to stump her.

"No reason, have you had any tea"?

"No".

"Want something zapping in the hypa-wave"?

This was the level of most of their intercourse recently. Not exactly intellectually stimulating. He reasoned aloud,

"I can do that".

"I'm going to shower then and then watch Celebrity Parts".

Celebrity Parts was mind-numbingly plebeian. In the tri-vid broadcast, several apparent celebrities had close-ups of various parts of their body photographed. Then an invited audience had to match the part to the celebrity. The fact that the celebrities were not so, never had been and never would be seemed to concern Madchen, not one jot. She never missed an episode. Never failed to howl with laughter when one of the parts was embarrassing or genital. In one of his most sardonic observations, Stallone had suggested that Celebrity Dumps would be a good follow-up to the series. He had even considered pinging the station with his idea. He little doubted that *Dazed* would consider it. He could even hear the immensely annoying Antand Deck now,

"So audience did Hopeless Neverwas do dump number three, or maybe he'd curled off dump number seven? See the hilarious answer after these important messages"

It was just a shame that Smellytelly had never taken off!

Stallone opened the frifreezr and looked at the array of gaudy cartonettes that promised, 'A nutritional and delicious meal in just twenty seconds (neoplas fork supplied in - carton)'!

He pulled out the Geet Casserole. Thank goodness for Hoyle and his genetic engineering. The hybrid creatures were as delicious and nutritional as *Big Bites* promised. The plas-box zipped off with the special red pull release and the carton went into the Fiat hypa-wave. Thirty seconds later Stallone was consuming it carefully. It was very hot and not so bad. This was his usual evening routine with Madchen. Or rather without her. He was contracted yet still lonely. She had to go.

After a shower, he decided to do a little work. His office was in the apartments. Being a bottle designer he rarely had to travel into head office. He usually pinged his latest creation digitally. Lottabockle headquarters were in Scouring Plains so only a short train journey even if he needed to go in. The corporation had branched out from their original designs. Cartons, heavy containers, packing, ornaments, all designed by Lottabockle over the years. Stallone was a bottle specialist though. He was currently working on shampoo containers. Designing an ergonomic but functional grip was not something for the faint-hearted. What if some ignoramus dropped his or her bottle in the shower? Subsequently slipping on it, doing themselves a mischief. In an age of litigation gone mad Lottabockle would undoubtedly be sued.

Stallone spent several minutes on his special graphics programme. His desk-pad was the super-fast Rowntree-Cadburi with Domesstoss processor. It had 32terrabites of storage capacity, while the processor was capable of 140nm++, 80 core threads, a base clock of 36Ghz and a cache of 160Mb. With it, Stallone knew he could design a very nice shampoo bottle. Yet he struggled to concentrate. His mind was not properly on the job. It wandered, eventually settling on the prospect of getting rid of his current problem. His current wife.

"That's enough work for now", he said to himself. "Time to settle down with a nice sherry and a good book" What an anachronistic sentence that was. Could it possibly have been the first time it was uttered on Venus for many many years? Audiobooks were state of the art. Why would anyone actually sit reading? It caused Stallone to wonder why the Athenaeum existed. What connection could there be between a Bibliotheca and the curiously mustard-hued reanimated bodies that the Venuser used? Stallone mused on the nature of the aboriginal race of his world too. With the great strides in biotronic construction, the Venuser did not need to inhabit the recently deceased. It frequently caused them great inconvenience to do so. Especially when the former host had died of a fatal and painful disease. The Venuser were expert at repairing most of the ravages of terminal illness in the human form. Why bother? Why not simply possess the recently created Biotrons. The fantastic organic androids that were making their predecessors obsolete in great numbers. As refined as the androids had become, they had always remained discernable to any but the insensate. Biotrons were originally repaired, humans. People with spare-parts that had been created from the newest of materials available to industry. Duridium, Nyloplanyon, Celldulight, Titanicore to name but four. When the latest plague of phleege had decimated the populations of the worlds of Earth, Moon, Venus, Mars and Callisto though there had suddenly been a need for instantaneous replacements in some areas.

Up had stepped *The Surgeon.* Living on Venus, himself a biotron he had been born human. The Venuser invasion of humanity had killed all but he. To recompense him they had given him their medical technology. The Surgeon had used it to create the first totally biotronic man. Born twenty-five subjective years old Frank Earnest Nicodemus Stein was going to live for many decades. He had a brain of Domesstoss construction, yet it was also partly human tissue. The Surgeon had used the newest of cell parallelismology techniques learned from the Venuser. One could start to examine Frank E.N. Stein from top to bottom. In every part of him was a combination of biological and technological hybridomorphic melding. There was just one problem. Shortly after his construction Frank E.N. Stein had declared on the W.W.W. (worlds-wide-web) that he wished a life out of the spotlight. He wanted to be considered simply as Nicodemus. Then he vanished from public life. No sign of him had been seen or heard of for five standard years. Shortly after Nicodemus had disappeared, the Venuser stated categorically that they would never inhabit biotron. They would continue to wait for humans to die. Ascending instead from the heart of their planet to become flesh once more when a corpse was available.

This earned the Venuser a bigoted moniker. Those who could never warm to them called them the *Reanimators*. After the recent events on Earth when Pope Pius XXIII and the Orgaria had been assassinated on the same day anti-Reanimator feelings began to run high. The Katholiartum had collapsed as a result. The world of Earth had become Pagan. It had also become immensely suspicious of future Venuser activities. How dare they interfere in Earth superstition? What would they do next? A Cold War was developing between the sister planets and war could never get colder than when it spanned the vastness and frigidity of space.

Like most ordinary working-class people Stallone viewed all such events from one single point of view. 'How does this recent development effect me'? The answer was usually the same. Only very obliquely. Life goes on much as before. One thing that affected him to a far greater degree was his current domestic arrangement. He was dissatisfied with that in the extremis. Madchen was a major problem that required an imminent solution. Stallone reached for the book and began to read.

Fools for Luck

LEIGHTO W. PRITCHARD

It was the day after my tenth birthday. I was with my best friend Carl Hughes at his home. We were trying out our latest acrobatic tricks on his trampoline. Carl shouted "Watch this!" and he proceeded to attempt a double back somersault. It nearly worked, but he didn't quite land right. He was thrown into the air all legs and arms flailing. He ended up in a crumpled heap. He seemed to have hurt himself quite badly. I couldn't stop laughing. It was just so funny to see him tossed about like a rag doll. The fact that it gave him a nosebleed just made it even funnier. Not far away there was an ambulance siren. We were so engrossed in laughing (me) or crying (Carl), that we hadn't taken much notice of it. Not long after, we heard a police car siren. It raced down Carl's street. In no time at all, another police car followed it with the same urgency. Nothing much of interest ever happened in sleepy Westbury. So in our young minds, three emergency vehicles in succession constituted an incident of epic proportion. It was time to investigate. We were up and off. Racing each other down Lorne Avenue and onto Chamberlain Street - where the blue lights were still flashing although the sirens had now stopped. The two police cars and the ambulance were parked outside No. 22 - which was our house. In an instant, the sheer excitement of the occasion took on a very different complexion for me. The adrenaline that had been flowing now exploded through my system. The enjoyment of the chase was replaced by a visceral sense of fear and foreboding. I made my way to the front gate of our house which was barred by a policewoman.

"What's happening? Is everything okay?" I cried. I was aware of tears running down my face.

"I'm very sorry, young man, nobody is allowed in there." was the response from PC Wilkins. "But this our my house. I live here. I'm Bradley Phillips". PC Wilkins motioned to her colleague, then spoke gently:

"OK, Bradley, come with me." She put her arm around my shoulder. Walked me slowly to the house next door. Shepherding me in by the back door, through the kitchen and into the living room. My sister Margaret was curled up on the settee, shaking and sobbing. She could be a bit of a Princess but I instantly knew that this was different. There were no crocodile tears. Mrs Johnson had always lived next door to us. She was very friendly and we were always able to call round to her house. We did little errands for her, she looked after us whenever there was a need. She seated herself close to me and our eyes met fully and deeply. She began gently,

"There has been a terrible accident and your Mother is very badly injured. I am just so sorry." I felt a deep pain that began in the pit of my stomach. It shuddered through my body. I had to gasp for breath in order to stay conscious. I groaned knowingly,

"It's, Dad, I know it" and then I felt myself going into a faint.

Twelve months later the public gallery at Bath Crown Court was packed for the start of the trial of our Father - Derek Phillips. Accused of the manslaughter of our Mother, Kathleen. After considerable representations and negotiations, the twelve members of the jury had been selected. They were in place for the start of proceedings. It would prove to be a difficult and contentious case. After the opening remarks. With added guidance from the presiding judge, the prosecuting barrister presented his version of what had happened on the day in question. Our Father had phoned the emergency services to ask for an ambulance to be sent to his house. To attend to our Mother who had fallen and was bleeding profusely. When the ambulance crew arrived they found our Mother unconscious, close to death! Therefore they had immediately called for the police to attend. Unfortunately, she had lost too much blood. Despite the valiant efforts of the ambulance crew it was not possible to save her life. The case presented by the prosecuting barrister was that there was a long history of violence by Derek Phillips against his wife. He had hurt her badly on many occasions previously. On this specific instance, there had been a real intent to seriously injure her. Due to his attack, she had received serious injuries which had resulted in her death. In sharp contrast, the presentation of the events by the defence barrister was different. On a fateful day, our Father and Mother had been arguing strongly. Which they did often. They started to push and shove one other. Derek Phillips had pushed his wife back, she had tripped over a loose cushion that was lying on the floor. As she did so she hit her head on the corner of the coffee table. There had been no intent to seriously harm her. Her death had been the result of a very unfortunate accident. Over the course of the next seven days, a great deal of evidence was presented in respect of the specific incident. Also of the relationship between our parents. It was not a clear picture. Various witnesses gave a wide range of conflicting versions of events. Some stated that our Father was an angry, aggressive man. Others that our Mother had been on the receiving end of his beatings for many years. All agreed it had indeed been a tempestuous relationship. Stating that it was our Mother who was often the initiator of the fighting that took place between them. That Father was basically a quiet man who was provoked beyond reason by her. Having been presented with all the evidence, having received the closing remarks from the two barristers, the judge took time out to give full consideration to the respective arguments of the prosecution and the defence. He then reconvened the court. Gave clear guidance to the jury on what was important in their deliberations. Above all, they had to put facts, reason and the law above feelings and emotions.

I learned later what had transpired during the jury's deliberations. From the outset, there was a clear divergence of views among them. Everyone was allowed to state their views. After which was the first show of hands. There was a seven to five majority. There followed a great deal of discussion during which the specific reasons for the individual views were clarified and reviewed. As a result, three people changed their minds. The majority changed to ten to two. The judge was consulted. This was followed by further sessions of protracted discourses. The majority remained at ten to two. The judge eventually decided to accept this result, and on the basis of it, our Father was found guilty of manslaughter. Dad was released on bail whilst the various social reports were prepared prior to sentencing. It was deemed that it was not appropriate that he should continue to look after me and my sister Margaret.

This was another devastating blow to us. The last twelve months had been an extremely stressful time. This was a decided turn for the worse. I had enjoyed my eleventh birthday and had started at Westbury Comprehensive School. Margaret was now twelve. In addition to all that had happened to our family, she was having to cope with the dramatic effects of puberty. Her transition from childhood to adolescence. Despite the trauma of the constant bickering and squabbling of our parents, the fact that we were often on the receiving end of collateral damage, literally and subtly, we had deeply loved both of them. The death of our Mother had been a grievous loss for both of us. The time that we had been living alone with our Father had been very difficult. Especially when he had resorted to drinking again to attempt to cope with his own demons. Through this, we had clung together for mutual support. The two of us had found ways and means of coping. The situation now changed drastically. We had to be immediately placed in a care home, as there were no family members or neighbours who were able and willing to take us into their own. Mrs Johnson was prepared to take us in but her health had recently deteriorated and the social services department had deemed her not well enough to take on such responsibility. The home we were allocated was situated in a quiet area of Frome. It was a council-owned home that could cater for eight children. Our arrival brought the house up to full capacity. The home was run by Norman and Joan Turner, supported by a number of social care staff. They were caring in their approach, but there were a lot of things that were not right about the place. They never seemed to get to grips with the problems. There was a constant turnover of youngsters like ourselves who were sent to the home. Half of them were reasonable but the others had been badly affected by very challenging and often dysfunctional backgrounds. Some of them were frightening and as such, it was never a place in which one could feel completely safe let alone comfortable. After six weeks, Father had to return to court for sentencing. Marget and I were very concerned. The judge gave the result of his review. He said that he had taken into account the full circumstance of the accident, especially the constant provocation that Father had suffered from our Mother. That he had to impose a custodial sentence but that this would be limited to just two years.

A lot of people, including quite a few family members, considered this to be overly lenient. Above all, they seemed to want Father to be punished for what had happened. They clearly weren't thinking much about Margaret and me. When we heard the verdict, even though the news was passed on to us as gently as possible, our hearts sank like great stones. We didn't understand all the technicalities of the case. We had been living in hope that our nightmare would soon be over. That we would be able to return home. To find out that we had to continue living in so-called care was devastating. This period of our life was truly awful.

Looking back, we were just too young to cope with the situation. We each suffered deep and lasting damage. In some ways, we were reasonably well cared for, but mentally and emotionally we were subjected to all sorts of subtle abuse. It left its scars, some of which ran very deeply. Some of the others youths in care were incorrigible. Barry Rogers, for instance, was wicked beyond correction. He was much bigger than us. Added to which he was as strong as an ox. He was truly unpredictably weird. If caught on a wrong day he could be vicious. Once his gander was up, the sensible feared for their lives. The care home staff did what they could to look out for us. There was a limit to what they could achieve. They couldn't be there constantly, we were always anxious as to what

Barry might do next. The harsh reality was that we did not have the resilience to cope with everything that had happened to us in such a short period of time. We were convinced that we had fallen into an inescapable abyss. The one saving grace of this terrible situation was that Margaret and I knew that in order to survive, we would have to really look after each other. We genuinely did this. We became extremely close, more like twins than just brother and sister. Everyone else seemed to be against us, so we forged an unbreakable bond of love. We didn't know it at the time, but we learned later that prison life for Father was extremely tough. He was subjected to serious harassment from the two rival gangs. Those who largely controlled proceedings and drugs in the correctional facility. With no small amount of resolve, cunning and self-control, he managed to keep himself out of serious trouble. The reward was for him to be released after serving the minimum sentence of twelve months. When he came out of prison, there was a big question as to whether we would be allowed to go back to live with him. After a great deal of investigation and negotiation, it was finally agreed that we would be reunited as a family.

I can't tell you just how relieved and happy we were when we were told that we would be moving out of our care home and returning to the family abode. We missed Mother enormously. With a deep regret with what had transpired and an equally deep sense of longing for what might have been. Whilst life with our Father had all sorts of downsides, it was decidedly better than life with the Turners. Their scary *mish-mash* of youngsters in care. Thus it was that we returned home to Chamberlain Street. It would never be the same without Mum, but somehow things settled into an acceptable routine. We managed to live a more or less normal existence. In a way, this almost seemed too good to be true and sadly this was the case. We would soon have to face yet another huge twist of fate. One Saturday morning, Dad said that he needed to have a word with us. He told us this in a tone that sounded ominous. I felt a shiver run down my spine. He seated us on the settee and then began to speak to us in a strangely nervous way:

"Now then, Margaret and Bradley, I want to tell you about my new friend. A lot of things have happened to me and it's been very difficult trying to cope with life without having your Mother around for support. I have met a new friend - a woman called Eileen. She's a lovely person, and she helped pick up my spirits. She has a great sense of fun and when I'm with her I can forget about all the awful things that have happened in the last twelve months." I was listening carefully. I could feel my stomach churning. I thought that I might be sick. I didn't dare look at Margaret but just stared straight back at my Dad, who continued to speak to us, "Because we get on so well, I have decided to invite her to live with us. I know that this means that things will be different from now on, but I'm sure that everything will work out well. What do you think?" I turned to Margaret. Hoped she would say something. Tears were welling in her eyes and I knew that she was hurting deeply, just like me. Without thinking, I blurted out "What about us?" It was clear to both of us that he was more concerned about the new love of his life than us. As to our Father's confidence that everything would work out well, we most certainly did not share that. On the contrary, my gut feeling was exactly the opposite. I felt strongly that everything would work out badly. I knew that Margaret was feeling exactly the same. Just two days later, Eileen Whitworth was brought home by Father for the first time. This introductory meeting was decidedly less than successful. She was a blousy peroxide-blonde with a full mouth exaggerated by thickly applied cherry lipstick. She waltzed around the house, swiftly taking it all in, confidently announcing,

"Oh not to worry, we'll soon have this place knocked into shape. I can see just what we need to do here; yes a drinks bar in that corner will be perfect" and so on and so forth. She looked at Dad knowingly. Then turning to Margaret and me Informing "Your Father has his good points, but homemaking is not one of them" followed by a trademark raucous laugh, which she saved for the best of her own jokes. Margaret and I, with our hard-won streetwise premonition, were horrified. It was as if our grim future was being presented to us in glorious technicolour. We did not like the picture that was being painted. We both feared the worst.

The following day, Dad asked us what we thought about the prospect of Eileen coming to live with us. In truth, we dreaded it, but we were still very much in fear of him. Neither of us had the courage to tell him what we really thought. He had an inkling that we were not happy with the prospect. He was so besotted with his new lover, we could tell that he was not prepared to entertain even the slightest doubt that his plan might not work out so well. It was that just a few days later Eileen moved into her new abode, our home. For both of them, this was a successful move. They were an odd couple, to say the least. Yet their individual shortcomings were decidedly diminished by their coming together. Eileen had some very clever ways of dealing with Dad's temper which could be extreme at times if all else failed, she always had her trump card of taking him off to the bedroom. We were left to imagine what happened behind the closed door! Eileen was incapable of conducting life in anything like an orderly fashion. She breezed through each day following her latest whims and fancies. Now that she no longer had to meet the costs of renting her own place, she had the money to treat herself to her favourite indulgences, not the least of which was her beloved gin, which she drank with a wide range of accompaniments. She hardly ever undertook household chores such as cooking, cleaning and ironing. She could always find something else to occupy her time. To our complete amazement, Dad quietly accepted this chaotic approach to life. For him, all things considered, life was much better with her than without her. Consequently, he was very forgiving of all of her deficiencies. When it came to Margaret and me, he took a much different approach. We were now given quite a long list of tasks to get through and woe betide us if we fell behind with our duties. If we ever complained about the unfairness and the fact that Eileen was not doing her share, we were told in no uncertain terms to be grateful that we were back at home. It became more and more obvious that to us, that as far as Eileen was concerned, we were just nuisances with a capital 'N'. As for Father, he conveniently ignored his parental responsibilities. In reality, we were now very much secondary in his thoughts and feelings. We received no real support, love or guidance. We were left pretty much to our own devices once our daily tasks were completed. Whilst we were aware that things were not close to ideal, we didn't appreciate how quickly our quality of life was deteriorating. Our diet was predominantly junk food. This resulted in us not having the energy to get through each day properly. With the almost total lack of interest from our Father, we lost our own motivation in our schoolwork. Somehow, there just didn't seem any point in doing anything! There was no one to inspire us to knuckle down when we found the going tough. In no time at all, we were both floundering at the bottom of our classes. Getting poor grades in all subjects. We soon found ourselves getting into the wrong sort of company as a result. We seemed to drift naturally towards the troublemakers, misfits and general undesirable sorts in the school. I suppose that because we were becoming rebellious against the school and its discipline, we were comfortable with the other rebels in it. In the evenings, we were allowed to go out and about for long periods without serious questioning of what we were doing. Who we were with or where we went. What we were doing was no good whatsoever. We enrolled in a gang. It mostly hung around doing nothing much at all. Occasionally we would do some real mischief or even vandalism, like smashing up some of the equipment in the children's playground. We weren't malicious, it was just that we didn't value anything properly and we were bored.

There was soon to be another twist in our inexorable downward spiral. For some time Eileen had been badgering Dad about the possibility of them getting away from it all for a proper holiday. With some residue of conscience, Dad had staunchly resisted the suggestion. Latterly though, his rejection had been noticeably weakening. Eileen had discerned that behind the voice that kept saying no, there was a small voice that was silently saying '*Actually, that's not a bad idea. It would do us a power of good*'. Needing no stronger message than this, Eileen had taken it upon herself to book a fortnight in Tenerife. It was not a surprise, the holiday was to be just for the two of them. There was no way that Margaret or I would be invited. When Dad was informed of the booking, he was both pleased and impressed by Eileen's dynamic approach. Even he could see the obvious difficulty that this presented.

"What will happen to the children when we are away?" he tentatively posed to Eileen.

"Oh, something will turn up" she confidently asserted. "I'm sure that they will be able to stop with their friends. After all, it's only for two weeks." The departure date for the holiday, November 1st came around very quickly and with only a few days to go it had not been possible to identify anyone prepared to take us in for a fortnight. Dad and Eileen discussed what to do and they convinced each other that we were indeed capable of looking after ourselves. They were so intent on planning their time away together that it never registered with them that to leave a twelve and a thirteen-year-old on their own in a house for two weeks was while legal - hugely irresponsible. They made a small effort to make some provision for us. Some simple dishes like pizza and fish fingers were bought and put into the freezer. They made sure that there was some choice of tins and packets of basic food items. We were given meagre funds and told not to spend it all on the first day. Other than that, we were left to fend for ourselves. When the taxi came on Saturday morning to collect them, Dad turned to us both and instructed confidently,

"Now be good and don't get into any mischief." And that was it! We waved them goodbye looked at each other with a mixture of incredulity and excitement. At first, we were extremely happy. This was just like having our own holiday. We could do what we wanted and watch what we wanted on the television. We got by quite nicely, but by the Wednesday things were already starting to get a bit tricky. The money that we had been given was supposed to last two weeks but we were already down to the last few notes. The remaining food supplies were looking decidedly thin. That evening, we stayed up late to watch a particularly nasty horror film, The Shining. After that, we didn't sleep well and when the alarm went off we couldn't get up in time to go to school. When we finally got up we persuaded each other to have a day off. After a few hours we decided to go out for a walk and as soon as we went outside we saw Mrs Johnson. She asked us why we were not at school, and we explained to her what had happened. We told her that we were running out of food and money and asked her if she could help. Mrs Johnson was shocked to hear about our predicament and after checking with another neighbour, Mrs Scholes, she decided to report the situation to the Social Services Department. They must have checked our history because they responded very quickly. That same afternoon a social worker came to investigate the situation. She looked around the house and we explained everything to her. She consulted with her supervisor and straight away the decision was taken that Margaret and I would be taken into care. We were allowed to get some clothes and personal belongings together and then we were taken into the Fairview care home for young people. All the memories of our time with the Turners came flooding back. I had a dreadful feeling in my guts and I asked Margaret,

"How are you feeling? What do you think about the situation"

"Scared after the other place we ended up in last time."

"Yeah, me too." Sadly, our first instincts proved to be justified. Fairview was indeed a dreadful place. The building itself didn't help. It had been built in the sixties, it was really beginning to show its age. It needed a small fortune spent on it, or more realistically, it probably needed pulling down and building again from scratch. Nothing worked properly, the decoration was drab, it possessed the dreary smell associated with an institution. The youngsters who were being *cared for* survived only, at best. The carers were a mixed bunch. Some had a heart of gold and genuinely tried their best to help each and every kid in care. At the other end of the spectrum were the bullies who used these strange circumstances to exercise their sadistic tendencies. The majority were somewhere between these two extremes. Margaret and I spent our next three years in this dismal environment. If one was being generous, then one could say that at least we managed to survive. In reality, this was not only a waste of three vital years of our adolescence but in many ways, especially emotionally, we went backwards at a rate of knots. By the time I was fifteen and Margaret was sixteen we were emotionally wrecked. Hopelessly insecure, totally lacking in confidence. Our learning performance was abysmal and our social skills were virtually non-existent. We were not good company for anyone, with the exception of each other. Our very special bond was the stronger for our experience. Deep down we each knew that we were far better than what outside world perceived. During this time, we had only occasional contact with Father and Eileen. They would come and collect us, then we would spend the day at *their* home. We no longer thought of it as ours. These were miserable days. We had nothing in common and it was clear that we were all going through the motions of being together as a family. On a good day, very little was said. We would sit and watch some videos or play some computer games until it was time to return to Fairview. We were usually treated to a MacDonald's or a KFC for lunch, which when it happened was by a long way the best part of the day. On other days, either our Dad or more usually Eileen would start a conversation which was designed to motivate us into doing something useful with our lives. This was always disastrous. We would start by retorting with some grunts or rude noises and gestures. This, in turn, sparked some criticism, to which we inevitably responded in kind. In no time at all, there would be shouting and swearing and the whole situation would become seriously unpleasant. A couple of times, we even ended up fighting and then we were swiftly despatched back to Fairview, leaving us feeling worse than ever. It was very noticeable that these days they were a lot better off financially. Dad was driving a fairly new Volkswagen Golf and in the house, there was a lot of new furniture. They dressed in expensive flashy clothes and Eileen had a lot of bling. I kept asking Dad "Where is all this money coming from? You always seem to be buying new things."

"None of your business, Bradley. We keep working hard, just like you ought to be doing." At the end of each visit, when we were taken back to Fairview, he would give us some decent pocket money, and we were grateful for that small gesture. Sometimes, on our visits, we would call in to see Mrs Johnson. She was as friendly as ever, and she clearly worried about us a lot. She could see that we were very unhappy and that life was working out badly for us. She had a conscience in that she felt guilty that she was partly responsible for our situation. She once said that she wished that she had never said anything to the social services about Dad and Eileen going on holiday and leaving us on our own. One day I asked her

"How come Dad seems to have so much money? He's always spending, and they have some really nice things in the house now. I have asked him if he'd won the lottery but he never tells us anything."

"Well," replied Mrs Johnson, "I noticed the same thing. I'm a bit more subtle than you are. I talk to him and he sometimes tells me about things. So then I put two and two together and I am pretty sure that what happened was that when his Uncle Joe died, he inherited quite a lot of money." We had never met my Dad's Uncle Joe but I remember Dad telling us that he had gone off to Australia when he was young and that he had been very successful out there. Things started coming back to me and I recalled a conversation when I said that when I was older I would go over to Australia to meet my Great Uncle Joe. Nothing had ever come of that dream. Still, what Mrs Johnson said could well be true. Margaret and I started brooding on this. We began to think about how we could get our hands on some of the inheritance.

One day, we decided that we would call on the off chance to see Dad. When we knocked on the door, Eileen appeared, she was a bit taken aback to see us.

"Come in," she managed, "Your Father's having a rest at the moment. I'll go and let him now that you've come to see him." We were surprised because it was not like Dad to have a rest upstairs in the daytime. After quite a while, he came downstairs, and it was a shock to see him. He looked a bit dishevelled. He did not seem quite normal. His complexion was paler than his normal ruddy glow. He looked as though he had lost quite a bit of weight, as his clothes hung off him. Margaret was the first to speak,

"Are you, all right Dad? You're not looking as good as you normally do."

"Oh, I'm okay. I've just been a bit under the weather for the last few weeks, and it's hard to shake it off." Margaret was even more worried now.

"Well what does the doctor think it is?" she probed.

"Oh, it's nothing for you to worry about. I'll be alright. I just need to get some proper rest and a few good dinners inside me. I'll soon be back to normal." We stayed for an hour or so, and Eileen got us a bite to eat. Dad didn't want anything, and even though we pressed him quite strongly, he was adamant that he was okay for now. We left wondering what on earth was going on. Once we'd gone around the corner, I suggested to Margaret,

"I think Dad's quite poorly. What did you think of him?" Margaret pulled a mean face,

"She's poisoning him. I know it. I can see it in her eyes. She's determined to finish him off." I understood straight away.

"Yeah. You're right. She's after his money. You know all that money that he got when Uncle Joe died, she wants it. She's prepared to kill him so that she can get her filthy hands on his money." Margaret's mind was on overdrive.

"So what are we going to do then? We can't let her get away with this. We've got to stop her, and we've got to do it quickly before it's too late." My own mind was now racing as well. "We are going to have to get rid of her. I don't know how we're going to do it, but she's got to go." Margaret's face suddenly grew very serious. She looked me in the eye and said,

"Do you mean that we have got to kill her?"

"Yeah, I do. I haven't worked out a plan yet, and that's not easy. We've got to work out how to kill her and also how to do it so that we don't get caught." Margaret looked at me with even greater scrutiny,

"Never mind the little details, are you seriously prepared to kill her?" I fell calmly about the prospect, and I spoke very slowly and meaningfully, "You said it yourself, Margaret. She is killing our Father. We have to kill her. It's either her or him." Margaret herself fell very calm and then spoke slowly,

"Okay, I'm with you. We'll do it. We'll find a way." For the next few days, it was all we talked about. All we thought about. How were we going to kill Eileen without getting caught? It was not going to be easy. We had seen no-end of murder and horror films, but when we tried to work out how we were actually going to do the evil deed in practice, we could never come up with the perfect murder. We were getting more anxious day by day, worrying about Dad's health, but the more we thought about it, the more difficult it became. Whatever idea either of us had, the other one soon thought of a potential problem, especially with respect as to how we were going to get away with it. I was getting more and more frustrated, and eventually, I jumped up and declared,

"I've just got to get outside. This is driving me mad. I'm going to go on my bike to see my mate, Max. Maybe he'll come up with something" I headed off towards the canal path as this was the best way to get to Max's house. It was about three miles, so even at my pace, I could be there in twenty minutes or so. I was riding along, trying hard not to be thinking all the time of how to eliminate Eileen. I indulged in wheelies to enjoy myself and it gave my mind a rest. In the distance, I saw a lone person walking towards me along the path. As I got closer there was a familiarity about the person, closer still I realised amazingly that it was none other than Eileen. She was the last person I was expecting to see, although, in fact, we were not far from Dad's home. I had my hoodie on and I kept my head turned away from her so that she would not recognise me. When I had ridden past her, a surge of adrenaline shot through my system. A subtle voice came from deep down whispering, *'Bradley, this is your moment. It is no coincidence that she is walking down this path now at exactly the time that you are here'*. My head, my heart and my guts were all in a whirl, but something in me listened to that voice. I looked all about me, there was no other person in sight. Something in me decided without any further anguish to act then. I watched carefully, and when she was on the path close to the canal side, I rode my bike hard and fast right towards her. When I was very close I shouted, "Hey watch it, missus!" She turned around and I headed straight for her. At almost the last instant she saw me coming at her. Instinctively jumped out of the path of the hurtling bike. She

34

stumbled, fell over the edge into the canal. There was splashing about in the water and desperate cries for help, but the wet weight of her clothes was dragging her down. I looked around and saw a branch lying on the ground. I picked it up and held it out towards her. She was nearly drowned by then but realised that this was her last chance for survival. She grabbed the branch and prayed for all she was worth "Oh God, please help me". She reached out and she managed to grab hold of the proffered saviour. As she did, I twisted it, she, in turn, twisted over in the water. To make sure, I pushed down with all my might and kept my weight on the branch. After a minute or so I was sure that she had drowned. I jumped on my bike and rode for all that I was worth until I came to the main road. There was a couple walking their dog and I went up to them, crying, "There's been a terrible accident. A woman's fallen into the canal. I tried to save her but I think that she's drowned." The man used his mobile phone to ring '999' to ask for an ambulance urgently. Then we went as quickly as possible to the place where Eileen had gone into the water. At first, there was no sign of anyone, then the man spotted a body lying in the water face down, entangled in some thick weeds. We were clearly too late to help. The ambulance crew arrived very quickly, followed shortly by a police car and a fire engine. (Inside, quite a thrill shot through me – all three emergency services at once!) With great difficulty, they retrieved the body, which was already in a terrible mess. I had to give my statement to a very kind and understanding policewoman. I told her how I was riding along the canal path and that I had seen a woman walking along in a strange manner as if she was drunk. The next thing, she staggered towards the canal and fell in. I found a branch and tried to rescue her but she was struggling too much and I didn't have the strength to save her. The police were brilliant. They were the most caring people I had ever met in my life. They gave me a lift home to Fairview and told the staff of the ordeal that I had gone through. They left very strict instructions that I was to be given five-star treatment and taken very great care of for the next few weeks. When finally, Margaret and I were left on our own, I said to her,

"I have a fantastic story to tell you. It's called 'The Perfect Murder'."

Bloody Murder

M. M. HAYSEA

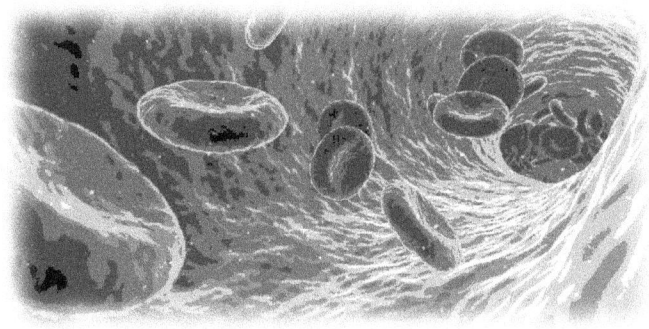

One

"Come in. The door is unlocked." Though weak, the voice maintained its familiar assertiveness.

"Good afternoon, Dad. How are you feeling today?"

Mark stepped into his father's imposing office. Each piece of furniture was a collector's item. The ceiling-high bookcases adorned the lateral walls while opposing the door two Georgian windows opened up to the intricately landscaped garden. With its sparkling crystals, the chandelier was every cleaner's nightmare. As a child, the only time he was allowed in there was under the careful supervision of his mother.

The frail, elderly man, sitting behind an elaborately decorated 19th-century mahogany desk, smiled.

"I'm just fine, dear Mark. My heart is made out of steel. It doesn't give up that easily."

Recovering after a triple bypass, Jonathan felt stronger than he had in years. It was a pity that his dear departed wife wasn't there to have witnessed the operation. That would have proved her wrong. A long time ago she told him he had no heart. Well… he did. He couldn't vouch for his soul though. Along the years, he had made many sacrifices, but he firmly believed that every one of them had been necessary for the good of humankind and his pocket.

Like he used to say, 'One must feed their family'.

When his finances were sufficient to provide for entire villages, Jonathan still couldn't say no to any opportunities for enriching his company even further. He possessed an extra sense for making a massive profit and having studied law, an undisputed advantage. While some of his competitors were battling lawsuits, his company, *PharmaCo*, had been untouchable. Unlike them, he understood early in the game, that risky business was better made overseas. Therefore, every time a new product was developed, he provided the testing ground for it far away from his homeland. If there were negative effects, his company was safe.

"I received your message. You wanted to see me?"

"Oh, yes, of course", Jonathan replied, pointing towards the red velvety chair opposite him.

Mark had always been polite and proper, even as a child. The British schooling had shaped him into the man he had become: capable and intelligent. During his formative years at PharmaCo, Jonathan made sure that his son didn't receive any preferential treatment. He knew he could trust Mark with carrying on his legacy. Yet he was also aware of the fact that his son was not as ruthless as one needed to be in the pharmaceutical world. The way he had been - maybe still was. Only months away from celebrating his seventy-ninth birthday, Jonathan finally decided to completely hand over PharmaCo to his only child. A dull pain in his chest reminded him that once he had been the father of two healthy, happy boys. Back then life was full of laughter and joy. His beautiful wife, his wonderful sons were his world. Then he inherited his uncle's pharmaceutical company and everything changed. Work days grew longer and longer, while family time became rare and tedious. Eventually, all that hard work paid off. PharmaCo became a leader in its field. Mark and Sebastian had grown into young men and he had missed most of it. But he kept telling himself that it was worth it, that he had provided for their future and the future of their children. Unfortunately, he couldn't control his children as he did his business.

Mark, even though having many relationships, never married, while Sebastian… oh, Sebastian! His heart was aching and it wasn't due to the lifesaving surgery he had recently endured. No, it was because his beloved son had been ripped away from him by that disgusting disease. If he had known what was to come, he would have done things differently.

"Konrad assured me that the contract is as good as signed", Mark interrupted the older man's trail of thought.

"Yes, of course", Jonathan said, pushing away the painful memories. "But I didn't call you about that. I've another matter I need to discuss with you."

Two

After a long period of unusual heat and drought, the heavens had opened. The drains couldn't keep up with the heavy summer rain and flash flooding was hindering access to certain areas of the city. The drainage system was in desperate need of an update. Pedestrians were affected the most. Most vehicles were unleashing waves that were of biblical proportions. A few cars slowed down; their drivers showing more consideration toward the wet pedestrians.

After the meeting with his father, Mark needed time to clear his mind. Parking his Mercedes on a side street, he headed towards the park. A couple walked past him, holding hands, they were engrossed in a whispered conversation. The downpour didn't seem to bother them. Others were taking refuge in shops, cafes or even entrances into residential buildings. It caused him to wonder what Joanne was doing.

He had found himself falling in love with this enigmatic librarian. At the advanced age of fifty-two, love had previously escaped him. For a man of his years, he had atypically known nothing of romance. Then his neighbours, the rather flamboyant Jane and partner Max, had introduced him to one of Jane's friends, a quiet and shy, fifty-one years old spinster. He hadn't expected to be suddenly transformed into a blushing teenager. But there he was, hanging on to her every word, following her around like an eager puppy. There was something in her elegance, her somehow melancholic demeanour that mesmerized him. When he asked her to join him to the Commodore theatre to see "The Physicists", no one could have been more surprised that she had accepted. Since then, they met several times a week and their relationship blossomed into something quite wonderful - something that Mark considered unique.

Inevitably, along the years he had been involved with a multitude of women, from actresses to sales assistants, but none had survived very long and none had provided him with intensity. He felt that with Joanne it was totally different. He found himself at ease talking to her about anything that came into his mind. He trusted her, in a way that he had never done with anyone before.

Normally, he would have rung her, in the hope they would meet up for a bite or a drink, but tonight he needed time to think. The shareholders were worried about a recent development, a person, whose identity was being withheld for legal reasons, had come into the possession of a series of incriminating documents. The individual was planning on releasing them to the authorities and to the press. A private investigator was hired to verify the veracity of the claim. His father had made it very clear: take care of the problem before it got too big to be *handled*.

Mark had always harboured his suspicions regarding PharmaCo's dark past. All documents from the eighties having been destroyed before he had started working for the company. Now, the old man - Jonathan had confirmed his worst nightmare.

Back in the eighties, his father's pharmaceutical company had continued to sell and deliver blood products to different institutions of health service, even after they were found to be contaminated with HIV and Hepatitis C virus. In reality, this hadn't been a surprise, as the factor VIII used in the treatment of haemophiliacs was manufactured from the pooling of blood donations of around twenty thousand donors. Attracted by the payment, most of these had been prisoners, prostitutes and drug users. Every time alarms were raised about the infectivity rates of the products, Jonathan had managed to avoid the recall of the batches and to divert the attention. Even Jonathan himself had travelled to specific haemophilia centres and attended meetings with their directors, convincing them that PharmaCo's factor VIII was a life-saving treatment. Not to mention all the other benefits that were included in the "package" like research opportunities, investments, etc.

Since Mark had taken over the company, its headquarters had been relocated to London. He was aware that his father still maintained a huge influence over the running of PharmaCo.

Konrad, whose position Mark had never fully understood, was reporting periodically to Jonathan, a sort of right-hand man. It was some sort of tacit agreement and everybody went along with it. The middle to the late nineties faded into the past, PharmaCo had slowly distanced itself from any type of blood products. Yet no matter how hard Jonathan had tried to cover it all up, those very documents had the power to resurrect the proverbial 'skeletons in the cupboard'.

Of course, Mark didn't maintain any desire to see his father's legacy destroyed, but how could one fight the devastating actions of the past? Until that day, Mark had refused to meet Nicholas, his brother's surviving partner. Nick had tried to contact him several times but Mark had been apparently too busy. The truth was that he didn't want to lay eyes on the person he blamed for Sebastian's death. Had he been wrong? Were Sebastian and Nicholas the victims of PharmaCo's contaminated blood? He had to know for sure.

Three

Elaine had been right: the boys were nothing like their father. Both boys were too "soft". Jonathan had tried his best with Mark, while with Sebastian he really hadn't had much of a chance. After finishing school, his eldest had decided to remain in Britain. From Mark's expression, when his father had requested a reaction from him, he understood that his son would not take any risks. Especially if they proved to be at the expense of the company. Maybe Sebastian would have been different. He had been different and not just in ways Jonathan had either understood or approved of.

Thinking of the day when Sebastian had been seated in front of him, just as Mark had preceded hours previously, he was overcome by the same feeling of despair that had twisted his gut back then.

With tears in his eyes, his oldest son had announced he had been infected with the retrovirus HIV. Now it had morphed into the worst scenario and he had been subsequently diagnosed with Aids. Jonathan had heard rumours about Sebastian's "unconventional" sexuality, yet had refused to believe it. His son, the son of all sons could not have been a homosexual, was not a homosexual. Yet, there he was, telling him about his long-term partner, Nicholas. Anger and disappointment had clouded his judgement and with a quiet, solemn voice he had ordered his son out of the house. That was the last time he would ever see him.

Not long after, Elaine's behaviour had changed too. She became secretive and hateful towards her husband. For his part, he chose to avoid her as much as possible. When Sebastian lost his fight, he had not attended the funeral. A pretext had been forwarded, he could not cancel a crucially important meeting. That night, he had wept in the arms of his latest mistress.

Elaine completely collapsed mentally, suffering such a nervous breakdown that she never recovered from it. It pained the head of the family and firm to see his wife in the sanatorium. Seated in the big-floral armchair in front of the barred window, she stared unresponsively toward the horizon. The last time he had seen her, she had looked so beautiful. Shimmering in the evening sun, her thick, golden hair framing her pale-delicate features. He wanted to kiss her generous lips, to hear her infectious laughter and to lose himself once more in the multi-faceted blueness of her eyes. Elaine had been the love of his life and indifferent to their past and present, that emotion had survived. Before leaving, he bent over to kiss her forehead. With a high pitched scream, she jumped up and pushed him away.

"Don't you dare touch me! You killed our wonderful son. You're a murderer! Murderer!" she cried as two nurses dragged her back toward her room. Back then, he believed those words belonged to a psychotic woman. One who had lost her son, but today he was no longer quite so sure.

Was he a murderer? Thanks to his company, new medicines had been tested and perfected. The fact that some had been contaminated with viruses had not been his fault personally. It was true that one could argue that once he had become aware of contaminants, he could have ceased distribution of the faulty products, but it would have costed the company over a million and that was a huge sum of money even then. He had not been prepared to take such a radically expensive step. Now, on the combined altars of science, fame and profit, the lifeless body of his beloved son and countless other victims were laid. All these years, he had been able to keep all this away from the world; but since his heart attack, the pain of Sebastian's useless demise filled his thoughts constantly, they followed him everywhere.

"Come on Jonathan, you really need to go to bed now. It is nearly midnight. Here is your medicine", Sarah, his trusted, private nurse, whispered gently so as not to startle him. She handed him a small plastic container and a glass of water.

"Okay. But only because you force me to", sighed Jonathan, pretending to be coerced into something he did not wish to do. The truth was the little, white pill, which he had been prescribed after the surgery, helped him escape Sebastian's gaze.

Four

There was someone following her. She was certain of it. It wasn't just a feeling any-more. She had noticed the same man, an ectomorph with sandy hair, staring at her on several occasions, at the exit from the library and at the cafe where she usually had her lunch. Pulling her bag closer to her body, she quickened her steps. Her flat was only a block away, but by the time Joanne had locked the door behind her, her heart was pounding with such ferocity that she had to lean against the wall to calm herself down.

"It must be because of the papers", she whispered to herself, making her way down the hallway and into the kitchen. Her solicitor and close friend, Lorna Davidson had promised to keep her identity a secret. At least for the moment. Lorna had warned her that things could get "ugly", but that didn't deter her in the slightest.

For so many years, she had watched her parents suffer, their marriage falling apart and every facet of their lives being deeply affected by the loss of their son. Julian, her brother, had been a haemophiliac. On some irrational level, her mother never forgave herself, even though there was nothing she could have done. The haemophilia gene (the inability of blood to coagulate) run through her mother's side of the family - only males were affected, while women were mostly carriers. There had been a fifty-fifty chance that Joanne was one. After the positive result for the gene in one of her X chromosomes, she made the heart-breaking decision to never have children of her own. As far as she could help it, history would not repeat itself.

Julian had been a healthy boy. One afternoon, they decided to play hide and seek together with some family friends. Joanne came up with the fantastic idea of hiding in the apple tree that grew at the bottom of their garden. Julian didn't want his younger sister to outdo him and climbed even higher. With a horrible crack, the branch broke from underneath him and Julian landed on the grass. He was fine, except for an ever-growing lump on his wrist. Her parents took him to the hospital, where he was diagnosed with mild haemophilia. He received cryoprecipitate [a frozen blood product prepared from blood plasma] and within two days, he was back home. From then onwards, Julian had to visit the haemophilia centre on a regular basis. Due to the mildness of his condition, he didn't need any further treatments until he managed to cut his knee on a fence. The wound kept bleeding. Another trip to the hospital. When he returned, Julian seemed different. Suddenly, the lively boy was becoming increasingly lethargic, pale and thin. Her parents kept asking the doctors about the cause of all these changes, but each time they were sent home with vague and sketchy answers. After several years of continuous hospital trips, Julian was admitted once again and this time he never came back.

Years had passed and Joanne still kept Julian's school photo on her night-stand. When she had been old enough to be able to understand and process the information, her father had explained to her that Julian had been infected with Hepatitis C. He had developed liver cancer. He had stood no chance of survival. Her mother had died believing that the doctors had tried everything in their power to save him. Now, thanks to Linda Mathews' gift, Joanne knew better.

Dr Paul Mathews had been Julian's haematologist and consultant from the moment of his haemophilia diagnosis. Unknown to his colleagues, Dr Mathews had kept a diary and detailed records of his patient's treatment. After his passing, his widow, a retired nurse, found a box full of his notes. Reading them, Linda decided to find and contact Julian's next of kin. As a librarian, Joanne had also participated in several scientific research papers that had been published in print and online. Therefore, a search on her name generated the results Linda had hoped for. They met at a central coffee shop and after exchanging pleasantries, Linda handed the box over to Joanne. Confused, Joanne thanked her and for weeks never opened it.

A couple of weeks ago, she remembered the box and started browsing through the handwritten notes. The following day, her eyes were bloodshot from crying. She hadn't slept a second. Phoning in sick, she reread everything. Distraught and angry, she promised herself to do everything possible to uncover the truth behind her brother's and other haemophiliacs' sufferings and to expose the systems that had allowed such tragedies to happen.

After a quick microwaved dinner, Joanne slipped into her nightwear: delicate, pale blue pyjama top and bottoms. Checking that everything was closed and safely locked, she switched the lights off and headed to her bedroom. While on TV a soothing voice was explaining the behaviour of a giant marsupial, she fell asleep.

Five

Konrad's apartment was a true reflection of his personality. Crisp and pristine. White reflective furniture and sparkling chrome fittings. No splash of colour, no fresh flowers, no happy family photos. Nothing personal. Three times a week, a closely scrutinised cleaning company did its magic. Except for Jonathan, not one soul from the company had ever visited or even knew where he lived. And that was the way he liked it and intended to keep it.

Konrad Maximillian Vorhaufen had fought his way up to second in command. For countless years, he acted as Jonathan's right hand and now he would serve Mark with the same loyalty. Though, there was one difference: Mark would never allow him to use the methods he had used in the past. He had to act behind his back and he hated it. No matter what, he had never kept secrets from Jonathan. When he had found out about Sebastian, he told his boss and witnessed him falling apart. At the news that Nicholas had been infected with HIV from one of PharmaCo's blood products and unknowingly transmitted the virus to Sebastian, devastated Jonathan. He was overcome with guilt and remorse, something Konrad had never seen in him. Not even later on, when he instructed him to make the arrangements for Elaine to be taken into the care of Spring Sanatorium. Indeed, she had suffered a serious nervous breakdown, but what made Jonathan take the decision of having her committed was her finding out of the truth about Sebastian's death. Konrad had ensured that at the sanatorium she received the appropriate treatment to render her incapable of destroying Jonathan's lifelong work.

Now he had to deal with a similar situation. This time around, he had to act without his boss's knowledge. Mark would never allow anything bad to happen to Joanne Williams. And even if Mark knew what Joanne was doing, Konrad doubted he would approve. Three days ago, Jonathan had summoned him to his mansion.

"What do you think, Konrad. Is she a real threat?" Jonathan had asked, twisting a handkerchief between his hands.

"The private investigator is convinced she has something. But as yet, he doesn't know exactly what. He believes the documents are in the possession of her solicitor. For the moment he is encountering difficulties in getting them."

"Oh, Konrad", Jonathan sighed. "Can Michael not get a viewing arrangement? Maybe if…"

"Don't concern yourself with minutiae", Konrad interrupted, noticing his boss's hesitance. "Are you willing to get her killed or not?"

At Konrad's sharp question, Jonathan dropped his handkerchief and stared him straight into the eye.

"No!" he nearly shouted. "No more blood. No more", he silently added.

Konrad agreed. The old, frail man, even though still mentally sharp and capable, had lost his ruthlessness. And after the heart surgery, he seemed tormented, distracted and melancholic. Konrad knew it wasn't due to Jonathan's fear of dying. It was guilt. After witnessing his distress at hearing about Sebastian's fate, Konrad had somehow managed to convince him that he wasn't at fault. Without the factor VIII, these damaged individuals would have died anyway. The fact that they were infected with HIV or Hepatitis C, was an unfortunate happening. Keeping it all silent, especially from the patients, didn't change the outcome in any way.

But it saved the reputation of PharmaCo. He still had one son. He had to think of Mark and do everything in his power to defend his legacy. Jonathan had agreed reluctantly and eventually, he returned to being his old self.

The triple bypass appeared to have changed all that. Haunted by his son's death, Jonathan had retreated and Mark was lacking his father's cold-bloodedness. It was up to Konrad to take care of this problem. And maybe, when Mark would finally understand the risk this woman had posed. He would forgive him. It didn't matter anyway. He owned Jonathan his life, so he would return the favour by protecting PharmaCo indifferently to the circumstances.

Letting himself down on the white leather settee, he switched the TV on. Earthquakes, floods, fires, murders. Nothing new. Political dramas bored him. A high-rated woman was complaining about corruption. He nearly burst out laughing.

"You don't know half of it, darling" he mused.

Senators, governors, officials, they were all in the pocket of some big corporation. Many of them were eating out of his hand. He had personally seen to it.

Six

The shrill ring of the phone made her jump out of the bed. Running to pick it up, she stumbled on the corner of the carpet and landed hard on her left knee. The shooting pain struck a hole in the pit of her stomach.

"Hello", she said into the speaker avoiding swearing and rubbing her leg.

On the other end of the line, there was only silence. After a few seconds... dial tone.

"Who the hell is messing around at this time?"

The digital clock on her bedside cabinet was showing 12.15am. The thought of the man following her sent shivers along her spine.

"Don't be bloody paranoid", she muttered to herself. "Nobody, besides Lorna, knows you have those papers. And if they would know, what would they do?"

Carefully, not to put too much pressure on her injured leg, she walked into the kitchen and switched the light on.

"The notes are not even here. They are locked away in Lorna's office."

But maybe *they* didn't know that. *They,* who?

"Right. Stop it, now!" Joanne told herself. "You are driving yourself crazy."

Opening the American style fridge-freezer, she grabbed an ice-pack and then made her way to the dining table. On the swollen joint, the ice pack felt like a gift sent from heaven.

"Probably just a wrong number or some kid playing a prank", she uttered while filling the kettle. She knew she wouldn't be able to go back to sleep. Maybe a nice cup of hot chocolate would help calm her mind and body.

With the warm drink in her hand, Joanne released the kitchen back to the darkness and headed for the comfortable settee in the living room. She had finally managed to pay off the mortgage on her apartment and was mighty proud of it. After years of working as the assistant of a university lecturer, she had managed to save enough for the final payment. To celebrate, she handed in her resignation. The university's library had opened up the position of main librarian and custodian. Due to her vast research experience, Joanne's application was successful. She loved having her evenings and weekends free from papers that needed revising, compiling bibliographies, researching thousands of books and so on. At times, she had felt lonely and maybe slightly lost, but since Jane had introduced her to Mark, her free time had been rather pleasantly occupied. Romance hadn't been one of her priorities. When different colleagues had asked her on dates, she had awkwardly refused. The moment Mark had stood tall and handsome in front of her, asking her to accompany him to the theatre, she had found it difficult to say "no". His piercing, dark blue eyes had her under their spell. Smiling, Joanne realised he hadn't been in touch today. She missed him.

A metallic noise coming from the front door disturbed the peacefulness of the night. Nearly knocking her drink over, Joanne stood up holding her breath. Was someone trying to get into her flat? Or was it one of her neighbours unlocking theirs? There it was again. It was at her door. Trying to move as quietly as possible, she slid along the walls into the hallway. Under the door, a shadow was moving. Before she had the chance to check through the viewfinder, the doorknob turned and the door opened. Terrified, Joanne tried to scream, yet no sound came out.

Seven

Through the darkness of his living room, Konrad was pacing kneading his hands. When he stopped in front of the Venetian mirror, he was startled by the sight. Grey strands of hair were stuck to his sweaty forehead. Worry lines stretching from one side to the other seemed deep canyons. Wrinkles and gnarly blemishes were covering the once handsome face. What he found most disturbing were the eyes: wide, bloodshot and filled with fear.

J. had rung. He had finally managed to find out what the documents contained and it didn't look good. No court would turn a blind eye. It was written black on white that haemophiliacs, who didn't necessitate treatment, were given factor VIII without their permission or that of their parents. Their company's name appeared over and over.

"Dirty blood that came from druggies, whores and inmates", J. had said. "All with the PharmaCo's logo on it."

Konrad started feeling nauseous and dizzy. He barely made it to the armchair. Suddenly, he acknowledged his age. He wasn't a young man anymore. He was tired physically and mentally. J. had advised him to call it a day and leave it to the current board of directors to take the fall. That was easy for him to say. Not so for Konrad. For so many years, he had worked hard to keep Jonathan's company out of trouble. It had become his business as much as Jonathan's. Late in the evenings, he had no wife or children to come back to. He had been too busy for anything like that. He had made sacrifices and he didn't regret any of it. Konrad owned everything to Jonathan, who had saved him from certain death, and he wasn't willing to let him down now. Jonathan, Mark, PharmaCo were his family. Undoubtedly, he would do anything to defend them.

Eight

Holding her close to his chest, Mark caressed her long, brown hair. When her big green eyes looked up at him, he had to fight the fearsome desire to kiss her. It wasn't the right moment. She had just been through an awful ordeal, an attempted robbery. Luckily, the neighbour residing in the apartment opposite hers had just returned from visiting his parents and had surprised the thief. Unfortunately,that low-life bastard had managed to get away. Policemen were called. Fingerprints were taken. A crime number was issued and a further meeting at the police station was arranged.

Joanne had rung him just as he had returned to the car after his nocturnal walk in the park. With trembling voice, she had told him that a man had tried to enter her flat. Within ten minutes, he was outside her building. Now that everybody had left, they cuddled on the settee. They had both agreed that he would spend the night there. Next morning, he would ring a locksmith and have the door lock changed.

"I think we should move in together", he whispered into her ear.

Ignoring his question, Joanne gently pulled away from him. Thoughts were racing through her mind. She had managed to get a glimpse of the burglar and she recognised the same man who had been following her. Was he a burglar? Or was it something else he was after? She had explained everything to the police officer, but Joanne had the impression he didn't really believe her. Nevertheless, he had agreed on a further meeting during which an e-fit of the intruder would be created. A long time ago she had learned to trust her instincts and they were telling her something was seriously wrong. This man wasn't after her ancient laptop or a few pieces of jewellery. He was after her and the documents Linda Mathews had given her.

"I don't think it was a burglar", she blurted out before she could stop herself. Mark looked at her surprised.

"What do you mean? He broke your door, but didn't count on you or your neighbour being here."

"I think he knew I was home. But, indeed, he didn't expect James", Joanne replied sternly. "I have noticed the same man staring at me several times. He was following me. I am sure of it."

Mark had not been aware of this. While she had talked to the police officer, he had spoken to Joanne's neighbour. At the thought of someone meticulously planning to harm Joanne in any way, panic and fear gripped at his heart.

"Why did you not tell me?" he asked, trying not to sound harsh.

"Look, Mark, when even I didn't believe myself. I thought I was going paranoid. Until now..."

Deep inside Mark's mind, an alarm bell went off. There was far more to all this and he could sense it.

"You already know I had a brother, who passed away when he was young. I haven't talked to anyone about the circumstances of his death. He was a haemophiliac", Joanne's voice started to falter.

Reassuringly, Mark gently squeezed her hand. His heart was racing.

"Julian had suffered a minor injury. He didn't actually need any treatment besides cryoprecipitate which had helped his blood coagulate previously. He was only a mild haemophiliac. But under pressure from the directors of the haemophilia centres and the pharmaceutical company that was producing and distributing the blood product, the haematologist administered him factor VIII as part of a clinical trial. Julian was classed as a "virgin haemophiliac". This was the first time he was receiving commercial factor VIII."

Mark didn't interrupt her. He was listening attentively, while every fibre in his body had tensed. She spoke fast, afraid that at any moment she would lose her voice.

"As a result, Julian was infected with the Hepatitis C virus. He became ill and developed liver cancer. He got transferred to a bigger hospital where he was placed on the liver transplant waiting list. Unfortunately, a matching donor wasn't found in time."

Taking a deep breath, Joanne paused. All this time, she had focused her eyes on the corner of the small coffee table that was placed in front of her. Turning towards Mark, she added:

"I have the proof for all this and for the fact that his doctor was bullied into not telling my parents the truth. A year before his death, they were finally informed that somewhere along the line he had contracted Hepatitis C. Of course, the hospital staff didn't say when or how. And Mark...there's more. Julian wasn't the only one. All the haemophiliacs that received commercial factor VIII were infected with the Hepatitis C virus or HIV. Some even with both. I have the proof in Doctor Mathews' notes. I believe the man that broke into my house was after these documents. And maybe after me too."

Though Mark was looking straight at her, her features didn't register with him. He had been told that person had some sort of documents that could destroy PharmaCo. The board of directors, his father, they were all worried. That person was Joanne. His Joanne. Suddenly, he needed to get out, to feel the wind on his face, to be able to breathe. He got up and walked out onto the small balcony. On the street below, a drunk was singing a Christmas song. It was only July.

"You don't believe me..." behind him, Joanne said quietly.

The night's events had left her exhausted. In the damp heat, she was shivering. Mark turned around and took her into his arms, softly kissing her hair, her forehead, her lips.

"I do believe you and I will do everything in my power to protect you. I love you, Joanne. I won't allow anyone to harm you, no matter for what reason."

Nine

The imposing mansion was surrounded by three hectares of gardens, woodlands and a fishing pond. The carefully landscaped garden was the home of a variety of flowers and decorative plants. On sunny days, Jonathan would spend hours sat in the gazebo surrounded by the rose bushes Elaine had planted. That is where Konrad found him.

"Good morning, Jonathan", he said making himself comfortable in the deck chair next to Jonathan's.

"Hello. Isn't it a lovely morning?" Jonathan replied.

"It sure is. Looks like we are in for a long summer. Towards the end of the month, it's going to get hot again."

"But you haven't come to visit me in order to talk about the weather, right?" Jonathan turned towards his visitor.

"I have come with news. The private investigator has more information about the woman. Her name is Joanne Williams."

With a hand gesture, Jonathan invited him to continue.

"Ms Williams is the librarian at the university. Her brother was a haemophiliac. He was part of the clinical trial for PharmaCo's factor VIII. Subsequently, he was infected with the Hepatitis C virus and developed liver cancer. He passed away."

"Oh, God!" Jonathan sighed.

"The documents contain the boy's medical records including test results, copies of the minutes from different haemophilia centre meetings discussing the factor VIII and results from clinical trials together with his doctor's private diary."

"So, she has proof", added Jonathan deep in thought.

"There's something else..."

Attentively, Konrad assessed his boss's vacant expression.

"Joanne is Mark's sweetheart. Their relationship appears to be serious."

Konrad's words seemed to jolt Jonathan back to life. He was staring his old friend straight into the eyes, trying to work out if he had heard correctly. Mark was going out with this woman who had it in her power to destroy his company? Did he love her? Or was she just another fluke? Most importantly, did she know who Mark was, his connection to her brother's fate? Of course she knew. She must have planned it all out. She was after revenge and a simple law suit or even the downfall of PharmaCo wasn't enough for her. She wanted to destroy his family, his son. An eye for an eye...

"We must do something, Konrad. We can't let her hurt Mark", Jonathan's voice trembled with anguish and anger.

"Don't worry. I will sort it out..."

"We need to tell Mark", Jonathan interrupted. "Let her have her bloody law suit. But I won't allow her to hurt Mark."

Konrad had considered talking to Mark about Joanne. Based on what he saw in the photographs the private eye had brought him, he very much doubted that Mark would actually believe him. And even if by some miracle he did, Mark would never allow any concrete action against her.

"I shall talk to Mark. Tomorrow, at the office", hesitantly Konrad said.

"No. He is my son and it is my duty to have this conversation with him", Jonathan had made his mind up and Konrad knew there was no way around it.

"What conversation?" Mark's sudden appearance startled the two men.

Surprisingly quick for a man of his age, Konrad jumped up. Mumbling an excuse and farewell, he made his way towards the mansion.

Once Konrad was out of their hearing range, Mark turned towards his father. "What was all that about?"

"Sit down, Mark", with a tired voice, Jonathan prompted his son.

The blazing sun positioned itself high up in the sky, yet the two men didn't notice. They had been too engrossed in their tense, whispered conversation. Suddenly, the younger one stood up abruptly.

"Put a leash on that old, nasty henchman of yours", Mark's voice thundered.

Without waiting for an answer, Mark stormed off, leaving his father deep in his thoughts.

Ten

It was getting late. Mark hadn't arrived yet. Checking her phone once more for any message, Joanne grabbed her bag and headed towards the exit. The library was submerged in silence and so were the hallways. Students were enjoying their summer holidays. Normally, she found the peacefulness soothing, yet tonight, it made her wary and nervous. Locking up, she walked past the empty reception desk. Thomas, the night guard, must be doing his round.

The library was located in the east wing of the main university building and dated from the end of the nineteenth century. Over fifty years ago, a fire had destroyed most of its contents, but no irreversible structural damage had occurred. A few government grants later, everything returned to normal and only the two Greek-style columns, that guarded the main entrance, still carried the scars of the disaster by displaying a darker, burnt shade of ochre. To replace the books had proven slightly more difficult. But with the help of various institutions, the library was reinstated in its glory, housing almost fifty thousand hardbacks, paperbacks, slides, papers and even five ancient parchments. And Joanne was their keeper. Even now thinking about it, she got goose bumps.

"No wonder you don't have many friends", she laughed to herself.

Still no sign of Mark. Had he forgotten? It had been at his insistence that she had agreed for him to come and pick her up. When he rung her, he told her that he needed to talk to her about something very important. Was it in connection with what she had confided in him about her brother and Dr. Mathews notes? He had sounded so serious; she was certain, she had detected a note of sadness in his voice. Coming from the hedge framing one side of the footpath, a rustling noise averted her attention. An overfed pigeon strode nonchalantly towards her.

"Silly bird! You scared me", she muttered. "Great, now I'm talking to winged pests."

Stopping at the first lamppost in the car park, she opened her bag and started fumbling around for her phone. As her fingers touched its metallic edge, something slid around her neck and yanked her backwards. A horrible cracking sound in her neck was followed by sharp pain. Dropping the bag, Joanne desperately tried to loosen the grip that was suffocating her. Tears came to her eyes as she was gasping for breath. Her lungs were burning and no matter how much she tried to kick backwards, her foot never made contact with her attacker. The thin, metallic wire was cutting her flesh and she couldn't get her fingers underneath it. Who was her attacker? Was it the same man who had tried to get into her flat? She had to stay conscious and find a way to escape.

"Now, he will have to listen to me", a gravelly voice echoed through the night.

The grip tightened. Millions of tiny lights exploded in front of her eyes and then … darkness.

Eleven

From the veranda of his beach house, Konrad was enjoying the spectacular sunset. The reflection of the fiery sky in the watery mirror, reminded him of an expressionistic painting his boss had displayed for years in his office.

The image of Jonathan's unresponsive, frail body, sunken in the whites of the huge hospital bed, filled Konrad with sorrow. His old friend had suffered a stroke and now was lying in a coma. He was beyond help. Torn, he had left in the middle of the night with a handful of his belongings and had boarded a plane to Hawaii. He owned a holiday villa there and that was where he planned to spend the rest of his life. PharmaCo was slowly collapsing in disarray. Mark had been arrested. Everything was falling apart. There was nothing left for him back in Britain. He wasn't prepared to spend the last few years of his life in a dirty prison cell. The wind picked up and a chill made him shudder.

Snapping one last mental photograph of the peaceful scenery, Konrad retreated inside. Four seagulls started a quarrel over a half-eaten fish.

Twelve

Her father and friends had visited her daily at the hospital. She had suffered a slight concussion and bruising. The crimson necklace around her neck stood as a testimony to her horrifying experience. Joanne was certain that without Mark's sudden arrival, she wouldn't have survived her attacker. Once she had been discharged and had spent a couple of days in bed trying to piece together everything that had happened, she met with the police officers in charge of the case. It was thanks to Lorna though, that she finally had a full understanding of the events.

Mark had been on his way to pick her up, but a flat tire meant he ended up being late. His phone had run out of battery, so he couldn't message her. When he arrived on campus, he noticed to silhouettes struggling in the car park. Realising that something was wrong, he switched the engine off and tightly grasping the wrench he had used to change the tire, he silently made his way towards them. With one powerful hit, he knocked the man down. Next to her attacker, Joanne's body laid unconscious. Alerted by suspicious sounds, Thomas, the night guard, found them and called the police and the ambulance service.

Nicholas was pronounced dead at the scene and Mark was arrested on suspicion of murder. Lorna had explained to her that Nicholas had been the bereaved partner of Mark's brother, Sebastian. A haemophiliac himself, he had been infected with HIV and Hepatitis C by PharmaCo's factor VIII. Even though he had tested positive for the viruses, the doctors hadn't informed him and subsequently, he transmitted them to his partner, who developed Aids and passed away. Nicholas survived, but the illnesses, the bereavement and the abuse related to the stigma of being a HIV carrier had damaged him not only physically but also mentally. He had become increasingly paranoid and psychotic. The desire to get his revenge had taken over his existence. The fact that Mark had repeatedly refused to meet with him, had only exacerbated his condition. He was the one who had been fallowing Joanne and had tried to break into her home. Indeed, his final goal had been to murder Joanne so Mark would feel the kind of loss he had to experience when Sebastian had died. The fact that Mark had no involvement in the actions of PharmaCo in the eighties didn't matter. He realised that to get to Jonathan, he had to go through his remaining son. Destroying Mark would also destroy his father. When Mark knocked him out, in the fall his head hit the border and fractured his skull unleashing a deadly haemorrhage.

Joanne couldn't help but feel sadness. Nicholas had been a victim. Just like her brother. But his anger had taken over his judgement and had nearly claimed an innocent life. After Lorna had told her about Jonathan, PharmaCo and Mark's connection to them, Joanne decided to overrule the profound grief and betrayal she was feeling. She asked Lorna to arrange a visit for her to see him. Through his lawyer, he passed on a polite and dry refusal.

After the investigation concluded, Mark was acquitted. The campus's CCTV footage, showing Nicholas strangling Joanne with a wire, helped his plea of manslaughter in self-defence using reasonable force. Joanne's injuries were proof of her attacker's intentions. Shortly after the trial, Mark relocated abroad, leaving his company in the hands of his assistant and board of directors. Before leaving, he left instructions for Lorna to be allowed access to any documents from PharmaCo.

Thirteen

Outside the window, the branches of the horse-chestnut tree hung heavy with snow. Together with other solicitors representing victims of the "blood scandal", Lorna had started court proceedings and even though the process was slow, Joanne had a sense of contentment. The story of her brother and so many other haemophiliac sufferers would finally be heard and the truth would be uncovered.

Pulling the blanket tighter around her, she pressed the play button on the remote. The DVD had arrived in post with a note attached. The familiar handwriting read: "Now, you are safe. Hope you win for Julian, Sebastian, Nicholas and all the others. Good luck, yours M."

"Casablanca" was her favourite movie.

Four

Poison, an interesting concept as far as Stallone was concerned. It did seem to be a feminine way to kill but he did not know why it seemed so. Glancing over to his chronometer he saw he could read another tale of murder, before retiring. Fixing himself a second drink, he thoughtfully lit a med-cig and continued to read the ancient tome.

Kreisākājene

MARGARET KRIMPTON

a~

There was an expectant buzzing in the courtroom. The crowd were waiting for the jury to return. Seated in the dock a man unmoving – unwavering. Tall dark with straight jet hair. Not his most noticeable characteristic, however. Rather the red eyes that burned like the very coals of Gehenna itself. A portly man in a dark business frock-coat and black slacks approached the frightening and foreboding figure.

"I did all I could for you Manzemi, but you would insist on pleading guilty and offering the strange defence to the court. You actually admitted killing him. I don't see how anyone can find you innocent".

"I told you why he had to die", Manzemi's voice was not of deep timbre, rather a slick and tenor quality. "He called me a charlatan and a trickster. Me, the Great Manzemi".

"Great Scott they're returning already", his solicitor moaned, "That's not a good sign".

"It matter not", came the calm reply. "I fool none, my powers are very real. He had to die for what he claimed about me".

The judge banged his gavel and asked in stentorian fashion, "Members of the jury having carefully weighed all the evidence presented in this court have you reached a verdict"?

"We have your honour", the elected foreman enjoyed his brief moment of fame, "We find the defendant guilty. Guilty of murder in the first degree".

"Obtuse and ignorant imbeciles", Manzemi said almost to himself. "They too think that I am an imposter and a fake. They shall learn differently. If I am to die, then I will not be the only one"!

"The prisoner will get to his feet", the judge then ordered, "I said the prisoner will rise".

"All right", Manzemi said levelly, "So that each of you can see my features. Burn them into your memory, for it will be the very same face you will see before your own deaths".

The judge silenced him with further vigorous use of his gavel,

"Patrius Manzemi you have just heard the verdict of the members of the jury. It is the punishment of this court that you shall be done to death. We have learned a great deal from the historical mistakes of the past. You will not languish in prison now sentence has been carried out. On March the 23rd at 23:00 hours You shall be turvystrated and beaten with Bățluptă until the attending physician declares you dead. Take him out of my sight".

β ~

"You have a visitor, Manzemi", the turnkey informed him from the freshly opened doorway.

"Let him in then, Screw and be quick about it if you do not wish to go on my list".

"You can have twenty minutes", the turnkey said to a figure behind him.

The man who entered bore a resemblance to the condemned man, "Hello Patrius".

"Hello Lydneus", the unsettling tone of the Great Manzemi returned, "I see you managed to get one of those idiots out there to let you come and see me. It's around eight is it not and I die at twenty-three hundred".

"I tried to get an appeal together for you, Patrius, it was no use though. The courts are obdurate".

"It does not matter. I did kill him. What is death anyway but a new state for my quiddity? They think killing me will be the end of it. It will not. They will curse the day they tried to put an end to the Great Manzemi".

"Trinica is waiting outside. Will you see her"?

"I told you before that I wished her to stay away from this miserable place. We were never close my daughter and I. Why would she want to weep on my shoulder now"? Look around you, Brother, the bare walls the iron gate. The thick cold steel bars at the window. Is it any place for a beautiful young woman full of the joys of life"?

"To deny her a farewell though Patrius"?

"Listen to me, Brother. You were my assistant. No two brothers have ever experienced the sort of bond we enjoyed. So I am asking you to swear you will do something for me"?

"I'll do anything I find possible Patrius, anything I am capable of. What is it"?

"When you come to collect my body, it will be a beaten and pulverised shell. That which was the Great Manzemi. Bury it in the family tomb but do not screw the lid down. Do not spend more than the most simple coffin you can find and have it left resting on end, propped against the northern wall".

"The north wall propped almost laterally, I will do as you say, Brother".

"Then seal the tomb and lock the iron door with a mortise of vanadiron. Leave the second key inside the vault, so that it can be undone from there".

"It doesn't make much sense to me Patrius. There again I have not always understood your ways so I shall follow your instructions to the letter".

"Remember, I must have a key so that I can open the vault from the inside".

"Patrius! You're not serious, are you"?

"When have you know me to jest, Brother? Do all this and one more thing. Behind my head have the Book of Shadows is to be placed. In that book I want you to write the twelve jury members who found me guilty. Their addresses and their occupations, so I will have a crude idea of their movements. In addition, I want the same information about the prosecuting solicitor *and of the judge"!*

"But why, My Brother"?

"Vengeance will be so much more easily facilitated with such information. Sworn retribution I have sworn to Asmodeus. I will not achieve eternal rest until such is manifested".

"That's not the oath of a sane man, Patrius"!

"Do you – Lydneus, you who have seen so many things. You who have been with me all through my illustrious career, disbelieve at this the final hours"?

His brother knew when to keep his peace and that was one such time. The Great Manzemi continued, "They did not believe, Lydneus. For if they had they would have given me a verdict of justifiable homicide. Instead, they chose to sneer and scoff through that travesty of events they laughingly referred to as justice. Well, I will show them justice, My Dear Brother. I will educate the plebeian swine. For I have learned much more than they will ever know and one of them is how to reach out from the dismal pit of limbo".

The door groaned open and one of the warders said almost apologetically, "Time is up, Sir. The cook is waiting to prepare your last meal".

"I think I shall have something light. For when the bars start to beat my body I will like as not bring it back up anyway. Have him make me cheese and Marmite on toast will you, Screw".

"Goodbye Patrius".

"Goodbye Lydneus, just tell me one more thing, is the giant blue globe of Iysador filling the sky this evening"?

"A total eclipse, Brother, Angelus is completely hidden and the sky is full of distant suns".

"Good. Hear this then. Each time from this night forward that such a conjunction is in the Brahman sky, one of the accursed will join me in damnation".

Γ ~

It is better to draw a veil over the brutality of the Great Manzemi's execution. Bestial and excruciatingly painful for the condemned it was meant to be a terrifying deterrent. No such could ever be one hundred percent effective. Though the crime rate on Brahma had fallen dramatically since its introduction the taking of life was still conducted by the misguided the passionate and the mad. Days passed, the trial, the case the man himself were all forgotten. Past recollection by all except for Lydneus that was.

Forty-six days passed before the huge blue planetary globe of Iysador blotted out the star known as Angelus once more. With its arrival came a terrible feeling of dread and unease for Lydneus.

"Uncle, do you ail? Does the ague threaten you once more? Pray to tell me you do not fear the onset of the phleege"?

"I'm sorry Trinica but the eclipse is approaching and will be complete in but a few short hours. I'm racked with dread. No matter how much my logical mind tells me I'm being foolish. I fail. You know I saw your late Father do things no other man on all Brahma could".

"Please don't Uncle Lydneus. Please don't fret. My Father had a darkness within him that spread to every man or woman he ever met except you and my dearly departed Mother. It was a lack of compassion. He could not empathise with anyone. I don't know how you stood it all the years you stood by him. You're not thinking about his threat"?

"Of course I am. There are greater things of the macabre that he understood of which, we will remain eternally ignorant, thank goodness".

"Don't be absurd, Uncle Dear. When his time came close he managed to envelope himself in his own delusions. He had a glimpserama of lunacy, he even claimed at times to *remember next week.* Obviously impossible. He was just a mistaken mortal like the rest of us are sometimes. I think he was affected by the great blue moon you know"?

"I know all that. He had such certainty on that final day. He believed what he promised even if you don't. Those intricate instructions for his interment! Perhaps I should have deliberately ignored them. You know what though? I dare not! You're right I am being foolish. If I continue like this I might even be found guilty of superstition myself and you know that carries a prison sentence since the last war".

"Why don't we go and take an evening stroll in the darkest of twilights, Uncle? It will calm the pair of us".

"It's a pleasing notion Trinica, but I think I would rather go alone if you don't mind. If anything unpleasant were to happen I'm no longer younger enough to know I could protect you".

"I understand", the girl returned evenly, "I'm well into the very latest Roxbrough novel anyway and am dying to know how it ends".

"I'll be back in an hour or so, Dear. If Makers-Guild or Trentavoria transmit for me on the short-wave, please take a message and promise my reply. If nothing happens during the eclipse, I'll then be certain that Patrius fooled even me in the end".

δ ~

The instant her Uncle had left the home Trinica rushed to the shortwave radio and tuned it to a certain frequency. She depressed the button on the bakelite microphone and said urgently,

"Zero two three to one four seven, come in please".

She only had to repeat it twice before a voice answered, "This is one four seven, go on zero two three".

Trinica smiled in lascivious pleasure and told her lover, "He's gone for an hour long walk, do you want to come over"?

"Just an hour eh? Are you sure that's long enough for you zero two three? I can remember days when you wanted to spend all day in bed together".

"On four seven, get your cute little ass over here, I want your body", Trinica replied. The connection was cut and she went to take a hot steaming bath. She was just finishing her ablutions when the doorbell rang. Careless of a towel, such was her carnal anticipation, she rushed to answer it naked and wet through.

One four seven gasped when the door cracked open and then slipped through the gap. Trinica found her left breast suckled, as her visitor's mouth sucked the water from her nipple. It immediately hardened beneath tongue and lips. She took the other's hair in each fist and twisted it upward so that their mouths could then meet hungrily.

When the urgent caress finally let them part, Tricia murmured in a gasping sigh, "I've missed you, Maggie".

"I've missed you, you horny little minx", her lesbian lover agreed. "But let's not waste time, let's get naked and on that bed of yours I long to drink from the furry cup".

They had kept their love affair secret for three years. Lesbian relationships were illegal in the principality of Umgahtung. If discovered they would both go on trial for 'Unnatural and Filthy Practise'. A guilty verdict would mean public turvymentation and death by Bățluptă. The weapon was basically an iron quarterstaff. The fact that the execution would be public was designed to add humiliation to the intense pain of having one's bones pulverised whilst hanging upside down. In addition, the guilty lesbian would have had all hair removed from her head and body and would be naked.

Yet still, lesbians hid in secluded parts of the realm. It was not always possible to hide one's sexual orientation and those who described it as disgusting and bestial were quite bigoted even if in the majority. Ironically it was the Queen who had made the act of lesbiešu mīlestība (lesbian love) punishable as a capital offence, the King her husband being more modern and moving more with the times. He had not objected to her puritan stance however and the fate for those found guilty of nepareizi vīrieši (roughly translates as perverse men) was similarly humiliating and dreadfully painful.

As the two female lovers groaned and writhed on the bed, they were not thinking about the consequences of their illicit acts, however. Merely questing for their next climax and they shared many. Finally, Maggie rose from the bed a satiated smile on her face and observed as she gazed down longingly at her naked lover,

"How can anyone find what we do anything other than beautiful. Such bigotry will one day be a thing of the past on all Brahma".

Trinica was gathering up her pants and krūtsvielasturētājs (busty substance holder) her previously clean - lithe body glistening with the perspiration of one who has been vigorously engaged in physical activity.

"You have to go. If Uncle Lydneus finds you here....he is not stupid. He is always trying to introduce me to hairy, vaporous men with their thick limbs and masculine desires ugh. He wonders why I show no interest in any. I'm not sure whether he would go to the policija or not. But I dare not risk it".

"Sometimes I think you only put up with me because I give good head", Maggie teased, but she dressed quickly and was out the door after a long passionate kiss goodbye.

ε ~

A short stout man was walking home from a card-school evening with colleges and friends. He admired the massive blue globe in the sky overhead. When the sun shone on Brahma it did so fiercely and constantly until times of eclipse. The man was enjoying the coolness like a respite, refreshing and different.

From out of the shadow of the blue fronds that edged the park a dark figure emerged. The slim frame of the undoubted male suddenly barred his progress.

"Just one-moment Cietušais", a familiar sounding voice rasped.

"Eh? Out of my way, Sir if you please".

"Wait"!

"Who are you"? Cietušais demanded, despite his nervousness.

"All I require is a brief conversation".

"Well I don't desire such with you so get out of the way or I'll call the policija".

"Iysador is very beautiful this eve is it not"?

"Is this some sort of robbery, because if it is you can...".

"You have nothing of value that I crave Cietušais".

Cietušais was not so easily fooled, "Why do you hide your features under the shadow of that wide-brimmed black trilby then? Why are you holding that Băţluptă"?

"My face is ruined since I had my skull pulverised. You would not find it pleasant to behold".

"What do you mean? You make no sense, if your skull was shattered you'd be..."!

"Dead"?

"Who are you"? Cietušais demanded, "What by the burning souls of Gehenna do you want with me"?

"Are you not beginning to recognise my voice? My outline, altered as it was during my execution? I believe you know who you are now speaking to. Your own guilt will not let you admit it though will it, Cietušais"?

"The Great Manzemi"!! Cietušais paled and the ice dread of terror gripped his bowels.

"That's right Cietušais. You judged me guilty of Murder did you not? When you craved the dubious honour of being elected to the foreman of the jury. A group of individuals who condemned me to a pain-racked and bloody death"!

"No. No, it's impossible, the dead remain dead", Cietušais babbled frozen into inactivity by sheer tepidity "The dead remain dead", Manzemi repeated, "But the Great Manzemi has come back from the dead"!

"This is some sort of depraved trick of some sort. You must be his brother, the quiet one who looked so sad, what was his name"?

"Is this a trick Cietušais"? The first blow of the iron quarterstaff shattered Cietušais' ankle. He let out an almost feminine scream of agony and intimidation. The Băţluptă described an arch in the air over the Great Manzemi's head and fell once more. Over and again it rose and fell. The body did not last long. Heart failure due to terrible pain. Yet the Băţluptă did not cease until a shattered ruin of gore and bodily fluids were nothing more than a pathetic puddle on the ground. Gazing up at the impossible executioner one dribbling eye that had been smashed out of the ruined skull, would never blink again.

Ϝ ~

The short-wave radio emitted a crackling sound and Trinica answered its signal,

"Hello, zero two three receiving".

"Can I speak to Lydneus please"? A strangely familiar tone requested. Trinica felt slight foreboding as she informed,

"I'm sorry he's not in. Might I take a message for him, who is broadcasting please"?

"Don't you recognise my voice, Trinica? Admitted we had not spoken much over the last few orbits".

"Father?! But, but...".

"You too, who knew so much about my talents, my powers, you are also filled with doubt. Daughter mine".

"Father it is you! How, why did you broadcast, what is it you want"?

"Just inform your Uncle that the first act of vengeance is completed. He will understand all too well. Just as predicted, when Iysador blotted out the sun. He died at 23:00 hours just like I died at that dreaded time".

"Please no. Father wherever you are, in what so ever state, stop it just rest".

"I wanted to warn him not to alter any of my arrangements. Lest consequence become equally unpleasant to that fate which will befall all those on my list".

"He has the power to stop you, Uncle Lydneus. Could I"?

"Try to do so and you and your illicit lover will be turvystrated. For I will get word to the Queen, of two lesbians living in Shalewyre"!

"You know about..."!

"That filthy slut Maggie? Yes I know what the two of you get up to and it's filthy and depraved and if you try to stop me finishing my list. Then I will add two more names to it"!

Ϛ ~

"No Trinica, you say he radioed, wanting to warn *me*? How could he do that, he has no radio? How could he broadcast to one without a cabinet of his own".

"I don't know, Uncle Dear. "It was just a few minutes after 23:00 when he broadcast. Uncle, he said...".

"I think I know what he told you. I was in the local eatery having a dzēriens (local beverage) when the local radio station broadcast what had happened. They found a corpse in the park, it belonged to that zotĕri (mister) Cietušais. You remember he was the foreman of the jury at Patrius' trial. His body was hideously beaten to a pulp, the policija suspect a Bățluptă as being the murder weapon. I think the Great Manzemi was responsible for this illegal execution".

"Which is impossible surely"?

"Impossible to normal mortal men perhaps. Not to the Great Manzemi, it seems".

"And it was his voice, on the radio. How could anyone forget his voice? The power, the menace the burning desire to be great"?

"We've got to do something. Do you think if we warned the others on Patrius' list"?

"But he said if you tried, you and I would be added to it".

"I can't let that consideration affect me. When the sun comes back out of the shadow of Iysador, I'm going to see the prosecutor, Sinisetiķius".

"Please don't involve me, Uncle. I want no part of it".

"You have to help me Trinica, I need your support".

"I can't I don't want to be turvystrated".

"Turvystrated? How could that happen Trinica, even Patrius could not arrange a judicial execution. None would listen to him, or even believe who he was".

Trinica swallowed and then asked her Uncle, "You know Maggie, Uncle, my friend Maggie"?

"What? What are you talking about, Tricia, what has she to do with anything"?

"She and I are lovers"!

Lydneus blinked is disbelieving horror. For terrible seconds he was silent and then he finally gasped, "The two of you are filthy *bean-flickers*"!

Trinica's mouth twisted in distaste and she observed coldly, "I thought you at least would understand that how we feel is pure and unsullied and you should not judge us for it".

"What you do is unnatural and against the will of the Great Architect. You will go to Gehenna unless I get you some help".

"If you mean the 'Sisters of Purity' then you can forget it, Uncle. Do you know what they would do to Maggie and me? They would get a tube and fill it with detergent and then they would stick it...".

"Enough, Niece! I don't want to know, thank you. I remain ignorant of certain matters that do not concern me".

"You mean you hide your head in the sand. You know very well what they would sow up and what they would cut out and you contemplate that as help"!

"Trinica, I am not without sympathy for you. Suffering the disease of lesbiešu mīlestība is a terrible thing, but I hope for a recovery one day that is all".

"How can I recover from ailments I do not have. You speak as though I'm sick. I am quite healthy thank you, Uncle. Healthy and happy with my sexual orientation".

"You are nefarious and filled with sexual depravity, but I must act against firstly the father before I return my attention to the daughter".

η ~

"Prosecutor, Sinisetiķius, you've got to believe me", Lydneus begged desperately, "You and the jury and the judge are in grave danger. The next eclipse, which is in fifty days, one of you will be killed by the Great Manzemi".

"Manzemi. Your brother is dead. You, on the other hand, cannot account for your movements last night. True you were seen in the eatery, but none can swear it was from 23:00 hours. You could have avenged your brother's death and then gone to the eatery to furnish yourself with an alibi. Now I am busy I've enough on my mind without listening to the babblings of a murder suspect. If you take my advice you'll go on a trip somewhere, possibly out of the country. They say the Isle of Thernadyl is most conducive to those suffering from distempsio of the brain".

"It's true I tell you. The special instructions I was given regarding interment...".

"Dramaturgic hoodwinking and pērtiķu spīdums (monkey shine), Cietušais was the victim of a robbery and that's all that actually happened. The policija will catch the perpetrator and then you can relax, you'll be off the hook as a suspect. Now I have more important matters demanding my urgent attention. Close the door on your way out Manzemi"!

ϑ ~

"Zotĕri Banalizēt you're the most well-known reporter on the staff of the Daily Sprādziens. If you print a warning to those on Patrius' list they will have to take notice".

"Manzemi, my job involves printing the news. Not writing phantasmagoria. Why don't you write your story down and see if some editor will print it? You could try Neticami Magazine, or Weird Tales for the Sekotāji, I understand they pay three monētas a word for that sort of dross".

"So you think my claim is the product of my imagination and should be serialised in one of those *comics*"?

"Look Manzemi, I've actually a friend at - Weird Tales for the Sekotāji. A blonde secretary as it happens with the sort of ass you could eat your lunch over and then turn her over and eat... I digress, sorry about that. Anyway give me your manuscript and I'll let her take a look at it for you"?

"You think I'm here to mildly titillate one of your sexual conquests? What I'm telling you is actuality Banalizēt, not some whimsical piece of vagary designed to make people smile".

"Then our conversation seems to be over, Fellah. Don't trip over on your way out".

"Right then! If that's your attitude I'll leave with my dignity intact. You're going to look pretty damned foolish when the Daily Pļāpāt runs the warning though".

"I advise you to keep a low profile Manzemi. Your trick shop and magical supplies will suffer if you make yourself look a fool to the public. Not only that the policija will start to believe you're the killer and you're using the publicity to further your business. Well, this newspaper is not going to give a murder suspect free publicity. Now I've really reached the end of my patience with you Manzemi, so jāšanās off".

I ~

"You've got ten minutes with him, Defender", the warden said as he let the portly man in a dark business frock-coat and black slacks approach the frightening and foreboding figure.

'I don't believe my luck', Stāvētzia reflected, 'Two cases like this in as many months'.

"What is it Varžīgs? I can't tell you anything, the jury is still out and has been for two and a half hours".

"I need a knife", the Defendant demanded. "Get me a shiv, a blade, get me one".

"Are you out of your mind Varžīgs how could I possibly...".

"You just get what I want"?

"There may not be any need, I felt my summation to the jury had won them over, I don't think they have enough evidence to...".

"Shut up and listen. When the jury comes back in he might be there and I need something to make him pay".

"Do you mean Baron Gasparei Itrādājit"? Stāvētzia asked sceptically.

"I know that however many times I tell you, you will never believe me".

"I know of the Baron, Varžīgs, I've read about him in the papes".

"It was he who slaughtered my dear departed Wife, planted incriminating evidence against me and now he's going to let me be turvystrated for it. Now you've been in that courtroom for days, spouting your high faluting twaddle without really listening to the one word that you should have been paying attention to. Itrādājit killed my missus"!

"And the reason"?

"Because he was used to never failing to get what he wanted. You know how the ijkë (elite) view we fashtar (pleb, peasant)? They believe they can take a fashtar woman whenever the fancy takes them and that idzimus (a coarse reference to someone born on the wrong side of the blanket) saw how beautiful my Icario was and decided he would take her from me.

"The night he came over and asked where I was. Poor Icario must have told him truthfully that I was working late down the mine. He'll have told her he would wait for me, wanting to see me on some business pretext. The business turned out to be that of Gehenna! I can barely bear to think what must have happened next. He must have made some sort of advance toward her and when she rebuffed him, gotten angry. It hurts my head to think about it. He must have tried harder and when she struck him he let her have the Stiņš (dirk) between her ribs. My Stiņš, so when the policija arrived they saw my Stiņš in her heart. What they did not know though, was that when I got home she was not fully gone. She had the strength to murmur two words before she passed Gasparei Itrādājit. Then Icario was no longer mine, he had taken her away from me, forever"!

"There was no trace of the Baron in your home, Varžīgs, nothing to collaborate your claim. The policija have that new images of fingers, but they found nothing but yours and some unswirled smudges".

Because he wore gloves, the ijkë always wear gloves, we fashtar can't always afford them, can we? It doesn't matter any more Stāvētzia. What does is that he will be here when the jury gives their verdict. He will be here to listen to the judge pass sentence upon me. That will be my one moment, my only moment to deliver a brand of justice that is my own. Get me a Stiņš and before they turvyment me I can make certain he pays for what he did to her".

ӿ~

"Order in this courtroom", the judge demanded, banging his gavel onto the sounding block. "Ladies and Gentlemen of the jury have you reached a verdict"?

A middle-aged woman rose to her feet and confirmed, "We have your honour".

"Read it".

"We the jury find the defendant guilty of Murder in the second degree".

The judge looked momentarily surprised before demanding, "Prisoner, rise and face the court".

Varžīgs climbed numbly to his feet. The judge asked, "Have you anything to say before sentence is passed upon you"?

"Yes, I have"! Varžīgs suddenly grew extremely animate, "Because he's here. Look! There's your murderer, The Baron Gasparei of the house Itrādājit! It was he who killed my beautiful sweet young wife. He murdered her because she would not respond to his sensual advances. There's your man, Judge. There, there"!

Varžīgs suddenly launched himself over the edge of the dock and dived toward a distinguished looking man in the public gallery. Two stewards struggled to grapple with him as he screamed oaths and threats of savage retribution.

"Clear the courtroom", the judge cried banging his gavel to no effect. Varžīgs was like a madman,

Listen to me Itrādājit, I'll get you, I'll get you if it takes me ten lifetimes to find your depraved soul. You'll not get away with it, you killed her not me and I'm coming for you".

The physician was hurried into the chaos and after a hasty injection of lubie Varžīgs finally subsided into a doped stupor. All the while the figure that he had been demonstrating against remained seated, silently smiling a rather sardonic expression.

Varžīgs could not remember much after that until he regained possession of his senses in a single cell. The walls were slate coloured. He was lying on an iron sprung bed with a thin mattress over it. The window was high in one wall and heavily barred. The door in the opposite wall was of thick iron with a single peep-hole at eye height. A single lantern illuminated the gloom, kept behind a heavily padlock mesh box to stop any prisoner using it as a weapon. The door suddenly groaned open and in stepped Public Defender Stāvētzia "Will you please behave Varžīgs, while I'm here"?

"I feel that much of the fight has gone out of me", came the reply.

"I'm afraid the sentence is one of death, of course. For murder, there is no other possible verdict. As the jury only found you guilty of a non-premeditated homicide, however, your manner of execution will be much swifter and more humane".

"I'm not going out anyway", Varžīgs said levelly with a cool certainty that amazed the solicitor.

"There's no chance of escape from here and my application for appeal has been denied", Stāvētzia informed. They say death by archery is usually painless and instantaneous. The royal Toxophilite are very skilful and ten members will be shooting at the given signal".

"I don't believe anyone has ever escaped Trebanagh Castle. They will be moving you to a cell for two tomorrow, try and behave yourself for the five days you've got left".

"Thanks a whole lot Stāvētzia. You've been everything I was told about before the trial began", Varžīgs returned with heavy irony. "Don't leave the door open on your way out, I don't want to catch a chill from a draft and cheat the archers".

Two guards appeared and eased past the solicitor though, the really huge one told the prisoner,

"We're moving you to death row, Varžīgs. Are you going to come peacefully"?

"A new luxury apartment, sure, let's go".

He was led in cuffs to a carriage outside the courthouse and then taken to the castle of the King and Queen of Umgahtung. Once they had passed beneath the massive portcullis, the carriage took them to the base of the donjon and Varžīgs was removed from the transport and hurried down several spirals of stone steps. The three of them were then walking down a lithic corridor lit only by burning brands. Condensation ran down those walls as though nature was attempting to wash the soot from them and off the stone surface. The cobbles beneath their feet were slippery with lichen and salt water. Finally, they passed through a series of iron gates and Varžīgs realised that escape would indeed be impossible, each one was separately guarded. Each warden possessing a unique key to each gateway.

The cell was reached and the iron door pushed open. Varžīgs was bundled inside with a few rags thrust into his arms,

"Ablutions at 06:00, exercise at 10:00", the warder informed him. Execution on Desuu (Tuesday) 23rd at 23:00".

The door slammed behind him as he left Varžīgs with a hunched figure supine on the lower iron bunk. By way of commencing a dialogue, he observed to the fellow's back,

"He never mentioned meal times".

"07:00, 13:00 18:00", came the muffled reply. The odd thing was, though, that the voice sounded familiar.

"I'm Varžīgs", the newcomer began, "Just been found guilty of killing my dear sweet wife".

The figure slowly arose, the rough blanket falling from his twisted frame and Varžīgs found the breath catch in his throat. He stared without shame at the lumpen head, the crushed body, the twisted legs,

"How are you still alive"? He asked in disbelief.

Before words, came the most twisted smile that anyone could give expression too, before, "Because I am the Great Manzemi and even horrible violent death could not contain me".

"Manzemi"! Varžīgs gasped, "I heard about you on the short-wave radio. You were an Illusionist, a master of legerdemain, a Sorcerer".

"And now a Necromancer", Manzemi gave a horribly twisted rictus of a smile. "I have also heard of your case Zotëri Varžīgs and before my execution, I was knowing of Baron Gasparei Itrādājit".

"A blackguard and eater of other people's leftovers, I want to put a bar through the nose of his pig", Varžīgs cursed, already over his shock at the Necromancer's appearance.

"I too would like to break wind in his direction, I found him to be a zoiding milfung (f***ing c***). So perhaps you and I can become the most bizarre team in the history of Umgahtung! There is just one minor detail for you to agree to. In order for me to be able to help you, the execution must proceed, you must be dead Zotëri Varžīgs"!

λ ~

The Itrādājit stately home was magnificent indeed. Especially during the eclipse. For when the darkness came, the Baron Gasparei lit the halls and library with the newly developed electric lights. Argon bulbs, more brilliant than even the brightest oil lanterns were all through the splendid property and Gasparei was in the sort of financial position that meant he did not have to worry about utility bills.

The hall was atop a hill. During the time when Iysador cut out the light of the sun, it became a shining beacon to the fashtar miners who toiled and lived in the town below. The strangest and most frightening of figures walked up the cobbled driveway to that stately home and using the huge iron ring set in the animal's teeth, pounded the blue front timber door. After a patient wait, it eased open and a tall man dressed in the livery of a butler peered out into the darkness. Upon spying those without, his face registered a mixture shock and trepidation. Admirably he maintained his composure but only with the greatest of difficulty.

"Yes", came his tacit response.

"Visitors to see the Baron", the least disfigured of the nightmarish duo instructed.

"Is the Baron expecting you", the butler dared to inquire.

"I would doubt that sincerely", Varžīgs grinned like a wolf.

"Then I'm afraid you cannot enter without an appointment, *gentlemen*", he began to heave the door to.

A booted foot was suddenly in the jamb, stopping him from closing it. "Appointment", he echoed "Oh we have an appointment. An appointment with fear".

"I'm sorry but...".

The Great Manzemi's Bățluptă thunked against his forehead straight between the eyes. Pole-axed he fell to the carpeted hall within. His body was dead before it even hit the floor. Varžīgs pushed the door open and with some effort lifted the body inside. It took a great deal of effort, he did not possess the same level of vitality since he had been dead. Still, at least the arrow holes had stopped leaking embalming fluid. One had to be thankful for small mercies.

Manzemi led the way. He was the member of the damned duo who knew where the Baron would be. They proceeded to the library for it amused the Baron to read by the brilliant of electric illumination, while the fashtar struggled in lamp and candle-light. Without knocking the two of them entered and remained standing just inside waiting for Gasparei to notice them.

"What is it now fashtar? Didn't I say I wasn't to be dis...". The last word froze on the Baron's tongue and he regarded the trespassers with a look of shock and indignation.

"How the Gehenna did you two get in here? You're trespassing I'll call the policija and have you arrested unless you get out this instant".

"Don't you recognise me, Gasparei"? Varžīgs asked him then, throwing back his hood.

The Baron's elite features drained of all colour and he finally managed to croak from between parched lips,

"Varžīgs! It cannot be you're...".

"Dead, Gasparei. Like my poor Icario. Yes, you are right, I am dead, but I haven't finished with you. Not yet"!

The duo walked closer to the grand desk which the Baron was frozen behind. Suddenly he managed a smile, though his features were glistening and waxy,

"I don't know how you managed to evade the execution, Varžīgs, but I congratulate you. Indeed I think you should be rewarded for your trouble. How does a hundred uauda sound"?

"One hundred uauda for the life of my dear wife. How does it sound to you Gasparei"?

"I'm very sorry for your loss and obviously you deserve compensation Varžīgs. You must know though that I did not kill the woman, you did, in the eyes of the law".

"Yet on her dying lips, she told me that it was you Gasparei. Oh! You were not at the whole trial! You did not hear me tell the jury that. They did not believe me. Yet I see in your eyes that you do".

"It was a tragic accident", the Baron gasped desperately, "She came at me with your knife and we struggled and suddenly...well, you know the rest".

"Even if that's true you were in my home uninvited, Gasparei. Icario was a sweet and above all else, gentle woman. If she did indeed attack you, what was her provocation"?

"I could not comment on the state of your wife's mind, Varžīgs, perhaps...".

"You tried to force yourself onto her. Is that not so".

The Baron's dry tongue ran over his even drier lips and he finally returned, "Two hundred uauda if you let me go, Varžīgs"?

Varžīgs shook his head. "The rice is insufficient in extremis, there is only one thing that can be the balance in payment for a life, Gasparei".

"No", the Baron suddenly found his voice in a bellow, "Get away from me you filthy fashtar, leave me alone".

With dreadful calmness, Varžīgs asked his companion, "May I borrow your Bățluptă good companion".

The Great Manzemi handed it over and Varžīgs hobbled around the desk. Baron Gasparei of the house Itrādājit had wet himself and was weeping,

"Spare me and I will give you all I have", he begged. "Everything Varžīgs, the estate, the manor the servants. you'll live like an ijkë".

"It's not enough Gasparei", Varžīgs noted dreadfully, "You took everything from me including the chance to *live* like anything".

The first blow broke the Baron's collar-bone. He screamed like a terrified animal. Varžīgs took his time though, careful not to kill the Baron too quickly. When finally he could do no more than croak pitifully through cracked and bloodied lips Varžīgs lay open his brains with the final stroke of the awful weapon.

μ ~

Maggie lifted her sweating features from between Trinica's quivering and perspiring thighs and asked coquettishly,

"Well darling, was that a good one? You certainly made plenty of noise about it".

Body glistening in the lamp-light, Trinica pushed herself up onto an elbow and simply asked,

"Got a cigarette"?

"What's the matter", he lover demanded, "You're not worrying about your Uncle again are you"?

"Of course I koofing well am. He may be my Father but he's a possessed maniac and I don't want him harming my Uncle. When he went to various authorities they thought he was demented. I think they even suspect him of being the Eclipse Murderer".

"I'm not surprised really", Maggie handed her lover a lit cigarette. "I'm not sure I truly believe it, Babe and you seem so convinced".

"Convinced because it's real, Maggie"!

"Just forget it Trinica, what else can you do"?

"But, Maggie".

"You might be in error, Babe. The murders may just be coincidental. Or the work of one of your late Father's fans whose lost his mind when he was executed".

"He radioed me! I recognised his voice".

"That could have been a prank, the work of a sick impressionist"?

"Maybe it was some sort of delusion. I suppose I could have imagined it. After all, with all the stress and upsetment I might be losing it a bit. After watching Uncle Lydneus just pacing up and down, I might have to move out? That might be the best for me. What do you think"?

"You could move in with me, Sweet Thighs. The only trouble is that would lead to talk and an interview by the Morality Watch".

"Those creepy milfungs! Do you really think we would be condemned as dykes"?

"If we were you know what would happen"?

Trinica nodded, "I'll stay a bit longer then, but if he starts up again I'll radio you".

Maggie kissed Trinica long and hard, their breasts pressed against one another in a passionate embrace. When they finally parted panting with spent ardour, all Maggie said was,

"Do".

v ~

"Will you please sit down and try to relax".

"I can't Trinica. I simply cannot. Today is the fifth eclipse since all this horrible ordeal started. Four dead, all beaten to a pulp. One of them, not even anything to do with Patrius' trial. He'll be abroad once more in a couple of hours and that means another horrible bloody murder".

"It's not your doing, Uncle".

"The vault, I ought to seal it so he cannot walk abroad any more".

"That wouldn't stop him, Uncle. If he can come back from the dead I don't think a locked door would stop him with his nefarious killings".

"You've done all you can. Why are you torturing yourself? Here", she patted the seat on the sofa next to her, "Come and sit with me for a while"?

Lydneus' features twisted in distaste at the notion, "Sit with you while you still have the stink of *her* on you. No, that would not calm me at all I'm afraid".

Trinica declared angrily, "I bathed after Maggie had left. She always leaves before you get here. You carry on like this and something will happen to you and I wouldn't like to see that happen. Even if you don't understand my orientation".

"There's one thing he's forgotten though" Lydneus continued to rant, he was no longer listening to the replies. "And that's the fact that I can remember the list I gave him, I know whose name I wrote down next for him. I'm going to his house while there's still time".

"Goodbye then, Uncle", Trinica observed, "For if you're going up against the Great Manzemi there can be only one outcome".

ξ ~

"Zotĕri Pyketais you're in danger while this eclipse is in progress. A danger so dire it could result in fatality"

"You're in earnest, I can see that".

"So you'll take precautions tonight"?

"I've been in the armed forces of Umgahtung for thirty years when I was called for jury service I retired. The time seemed right. I still have all my skills with the Băţluptă, you've no need to worry about an armed conflict with me".

"I'm not sure you can fully grasp the gravity of the situation here. The Great Manzemi has powers the average man cannot begin to fathom".

"Perhaps. Maybe, but the ferobivar has served as an extension of my own arm. I have not been beaten in a joust for thirteen rotations. Now I appreciate you coming here and you've warned me, so I'll bid you a good evening".

"Is that it then"?

"The door will be bolted behind you Manzemi. Go home now and do whatever you normally do during an eclipse. I think I can safely state without fear of contradiction that no ghosts will get past me".

"What if I stay with you"?

"The last thing I want is a civilian under my feet. No, Sir, you would be a dangerous hindrance rather than a trusty ally. Go now, before you begin to annoy me".

Pyketais slammed the door shut and threw three enormous bolts, thinking as he did so, 'What a whack-job the poor fashtar. He needs to see a nut-doctor. I only hope when I get in my dotage that I've nothing better to do than worry about so-called spirits'

To his utter disbelief, he heard the lounge door suddenly crunch shut. There was an intruder in the building, but how?

"Come out idiot before I pick up this ferobivar because if I do I'll crack your skull open like a rotten egg. Is that you maid? Butler"?

"None living is in your house, Pyketais. You give them Ebraan off remember"?

"Who are you? What the Roşumoarte (trans: red devil/death) is the meaning of this"?

"You don't recognise me then", the lumpen apparition enquired, every ablepsy dripping menace.

"Take the hood off and then maybe I can see your features properly", Pyketais demanded. As he turned up the lantern, the Băţluptă (also known as a ferobivar) resting in the same corned just behind.

"I wear this to spare Brahma of a sight which should be forever hidden in the very lava-spewn bowels of djalë infested Purgatoriu. What of my voice though, Pyketais, do you not recognise that"?

"All very dramatic, but I'm not easily intimidated intruder, now get out before I radio for the policija".

"It would take far more than their fumbling powers to place me under arrest. They are poorly misguided fashtar with no authority to hold one who hales from the region from which I belong".

With that, the Great Manzemi threw back his hood and Pyketais saw the horror that was his crushed and mangled face and skull.

Pyketais snatched up his Băţluptă, crying, "Let's have at it then, creature of erfolgriche (Hades, purgatory etc) and see who wins our little contest".

Pyketais brought his weapon into a braukuzsānien (sideways swipe, usually quite high aimed at the head but can also be intended as a body blow) and the disfigured corpse parried with a trīsimsešmit-rotācija (full spin & launch) there was the metallic clangour of iron as the battle began. Jumping back a pace Pyketais attacked then with a ferocious piekitāmās-izmakas-oķēt (overhead strike or block) once again iron rang the tune of combat. Pyketais paimalād (stepped aside) before switching to a piespridzinājums (overhead attack). Thus the battle became a display in military strategy and warrior disciplines. Only one of the opponents could tire though, while the other was just as untiring, the result could only end with one inevitable victory!

o ~

"Trinica. Trinica! **Trinica**".

"What's the matter, what are you shouting for like that", his niece wanted to know. She looked at her Uncle. He was clearly on the verge of grave distraction. Red rimmed eyes looked out from a shock of hair that had not been combed for over a day. His features were filmed with perspiration, but his pallor was pale and lifeless.

"Where have you been, He moaned desperately.

"I just went out to get a morning pape, why"?

"Because it's happened again", he exclaimed, "I've just heard it on the Radio News Station. Pyketais, he's been found dead in his home this very morning. R.N.S. aren't releasing the gory details but I'll bet lézéz to beans that he's been beaten to a bloody pulp just like the others".

"The policija report here in this late edition says the time of death is estimated at 23:00 hours, just like the others", the young woman read, her lips moving quietly as she did so.

"I've worked it out for myself, Trinica. It wasn't Patrius who did those murders. He's dead, how could he kill anyone when he's dead? No, I know who it was, it was *me*"!

"That's not possible", Trinica tried to assure him. "You tried to stop Father".

"I was at every scene. Yes' I tried to stop the murders, but then on the fateful hour when Patrius was executed I go into an albistrapanică (roughly trans as blue-funk). During that fugue, I kill those poor innocents. There is only one way to prove the theory Tricia and you know what it is"?

"Do I?! I'm not sure I...".

"You have to lock me in the vault at the next eclipse. You have to do it, Trinica. it's the only way to stop me from killing again".

Trinica actually found herself wringing her hands, "You have to stop this delirium and you have to stop it now. Albistrapanică indeed, there is no such thing provable by the medical profession".

"Surgeons, pay, what do they know. Maybe Patrius hypnotised me then? What about that for a theory"?

"You're being obtuse. Even Father could not have hypnotised you into doing those horrific things. I can't believe it of you. In any case what of the murder of the victim who was not connected to your brother's case. You did not even know where he lived"?

Lydneus threw himself into a chair and slammed his forehead into his palms, his actions were indeed those of a desperate man.

"I can no longer be sure of anything. Perhaps I killed the third victim for some reason buried deeply within my subconscious. I think that during my brief time in Patrius' presence he impressed upon my mind orders to carry out his vengeance for him".

"You're rambling, Dear Uncle. If you insist though, I will lock you in the vault next eclipse, just so that you can have peace of mind between now and then".

"Peace of mind", Lydneus gave an almost hysterical giggle, "Who could have that living in the Commonwealth of Umgahtung. Who could have it with a maniac living in the city and I am that very psychopath? You have to leave Trinica. Only come back when the eclipse is beginning. For the sake of safety, you understand. Go directly to the vault and turn the key which I will leave in the lock on the outside of the door, ready for you. You have somewhere safe to go don't you, to *that girl* you like"?

"Yes, I'll go. I won't come back till the fortieth of Quintillus (5th month of eight in the Brahma orbit of its sun)

$\pi \sim$

Lydneus was seated in the vault next to the coffin of his dead brother. The bloody bandaged corpse that was propped up against the appropriate wall as he had instructed. He could hear the bell of the tower clock ringing and he counted the peals. Twenty, twenty-one, twenty-two, *twenty-three*.

Would he try to escape and not remember doing so. He gripped the edges of the stool he was sitting on so fiercely that his knuckles went immediately white and his fingers began to burn. Sweat ran down his terrified features and his white collared shirt was stained a dull yellow.

He had taken the radio down to the vault and suddenly it crackled into life. Picking up the microphone of bakelite, he depressed the green button and answered,

"Yes"? the word almost stuck in his throat, his mouth was so dry. "*Hello*"?

"Hello, Lydneus Manzemi", a voice issued from the grilled speaker.

"Who is this, how do you know my frequency, my name"?

"My name is Varžīgs".

Lydneus was dumbstruck and the voice went on, "I'm glad you don't say, '*it's impossible*'"

"No. It's not impossible. Nothing connected to my late brother is impossible. Where are you Varžīgs, do you even have a radio set, do you even need one".

A trickle of sweat ran down Lydneus' spine and he shivered as the two dead men stepped on his grave.

"A superfluous detail", came the reply. Varžīgs sounded rather pleased with himself. "I just transmitted to warn you not to interfere with matters that are totally beyond your comprehension. I have done what I needed to do and can walk no more. With the Great Manzemi it is different, he still has a list to complete. Lock the vault door and neither of you can walk abroad, so get out now before the dyke arrives".

The sound of static and dead air sounded then. Lydneus was given no further chance to debate. Varžīgs had ceased transmitting. Perhaps he knew how verbose the Great Manzemi's brother could be. The quiddity of the other executed man was not prepared to listen to endless diatribe and had terminated it before it could begin. Lydneus had precious few seconds to come to a decision. He little doubted that should he choose to defy his instructions the consequences would be unpleasant in the extremis. On the other hand, he did not want the lives of any more innocents tormenting his conscience. Any second his lesbian niece might arrive and turn the key and once turned. Surely she would not answer his pleading to reverse his decision. She would think it the work of her Father.

The work of her Father! That was the other key. How could he, Lydneus, be hypnotised into killing for his brother, when Varžīgs had just confirmed that Patrius was responsible for letting him have his revenge? If the Great Manzemi could reanimate the dead, what need has he of his living brother? A wave of intense relief flooded through Lydneus. He was not the killer. Either by his own volition or manipulation, for Patrius simply did not need him. He rose to get off the stool. He had been sitting there for a long time though and was stiff. His muscles sore from holding the same position for such a long time. He stretched the ache out of his limbs. As he rose to a fully erect position he heard footsteps outside. Footsteps on the paving outside the vault!

ρ ~

Inspector Thaddeus walked slowly toward the vault. Speculation had been rife for the past few months. Why had the Eclipse Murders ceased suddenly, when they had proceeded at one during each and every one for five and then no more? The papes had run a huge three-page article that very week and the Commissioner had demanded some results from he Thaddeus. In truth, Thaddeus had never been involved in a more mystifying case. The public believed the Great Manzemi was the murderer, but how could a dead man kill the living? The papes had then postulated that following his brother Lydneus' disappearance, he was the most likely to be the malign perpetrator. A search through all the realm had turned up no hint as to Lydneus' whereabouts. Yet while he was missing, no more brutal and fatal beatings had occurred. If it was a coincidence it was a damning one.

74

Thaddeus was no nearer to proving anything and he was getting desperate. He had gone to the courts, demanded a search warrant for the Great Manzemi's tomb and finally gotten one from the very judge who had condemned the Mystic to death. Now was the moment of truth surely. If the vault contained no corpse then the inescapable conclusion was that Manzemi was the killer. If the vault contained a corpse and the hiding brother then circumstantial evidence was strong that Lydneus was the killer. Surely opening the door of the vault would give some sort of answer to the mystery.

Thaddeus nodded to the burly Constable who wielded a huge crow-bar. On an earlier visit, he had been foiled by the fact that the vault was locked and there was no sign of a key. That in itself was strange. Why lock up a dead body? It merely delayed the answer to the mystery, however. For the constable practically bulged out of his tunic, so broad were his shoulders. Muscles that would use the iron crow-bar and force open the door, locked or not.

"Alright Constable", The Inspector said with ill-concealed relish, "Bust that door open".

The Constable set too with a will and within ten minutes a terrible screaming sound of tortured metal proclaimed the door to be giving way.

"Lantern ready", Thaddeus asked. The sweating constable threw the crowbar onto the cobbles with a clatter and picked up the already lit oil-lantern.

"Well what are we waiting for then", the Inspector wanted to know, "Let's get the answer".

The door scraped albescent scars on the dirty flags as it was forced inward. The lantern was held high. Both men coughed at the unpleasant stink inside the lithic tomb.

"Congratulations, Sir", the Constable said then, "You've just solved the riddle".

σ,ς* ~

"Have you seen the papes"? Maggie asked Trinica, "I think you'll find the reports amusing".

"I know I will", her lover replied looking longingly at the strange costume hanging on the back of the wardrobe door.

"They think they've solved it for certain", the master of mimicry crooned, she too was plainly delighted with the way matters had played out.

"Stupid men", Trinica laughed, "And Lydneus was easily the most idiotic of them all. He did not like us very much when he found out about us".

"He never heard the transmission I sent you when I pretended to be your Father though. It was a shame that one, I thought it one of my best performances".

"I too", Trinica shivered, "I almost felt I was talking to the Great Manzemi himself. It was a pity Uncle was out when the planned transmission took place. The conversation we had in bed, when we thought he was in the house, I almost corpsed a few times then".

"You are a genius actress and seamstress, My Love. That bodysuit hanging over there is so realistic by the dim light of the eclipse. To create it from wadding and material and then cover it with that makeup. No man could have conceived of such. Not only that but with my voice coaching, you managed to sound like your Father too. When it came to it".

"Father did conceive of the plan though and he was a man", Trinica pointed out. "It was hard not being able to visit him before his execution. Yet he had thought of the whole thing and every step had to be perfectly played out. His only concern was Lydneus".

"Then the poor fool gets you to lock him in the vault. We could not have prepared for that supreme piece of folly. So my, Murderous Lover, when do we start on The Great Manzemi's list once more".

"I think we should wait a while", Trinica reasoned with a maleficent grin, "Say three more Eclipses and then the Curse of the Great Manzemi can begin anew. We've plenty of time, Love. All the time in the world"!

Purfect Murder

BY PATRICIA M. THEWS

Crouching behind a Buddleia in Maureen's back garden Pete was having second thoughts – was he completely mad? What the hell had possessed him to agree to such a hare-brained plan? It was dark, he was cold and desperately fighting the urge to run – abandon the whole insane idea.

Reaching down he checked his pocket – the plastic bag and extra strong garden twine were still there. Now he just needed to keep his cool and wait for the bedroom light to go out.

Although Pete had known Maureen for less than a year it was fair to say he'd do anything for her.

They first met at a French For Beginners class and had been the best of friends ever since. Sharing the same silly sense of humour they quickly bonded and were soon as thick as thieves.

The French tutor, Mrs Jennings, had thought seriously about splitting them up but chickened out at the last minute – after all, they were in their late thirties. As they insisted on behaving like schoolchildren she had a terrible urge to rap them over the knuckles with a ruler but instead resorted to loudly clearing her throat and flashing them a warning glance over the top of her bifocals.

Pete's wife Sandra was fully aware of this blossoming friendship and wholeheartedly approved. She loved her husband and knew he felt the same about her, it was just that sometimes she needed a break, time to recharge her batteries, time away from his constant jokes, random conjuring tricks and sleight of hand magic. It was never-ending, he was forever trying to entertain her, to make her laugh, anything to brighten up her day. She never knew who she was going to get. One minute he was Tommy Cooper, the next Norman Wisdom.

It was worse when they went out for the evening. That meant a bigger audience, he loved a bigger audience and they loved him. A few drinks inside him and he'd be off. Soon everyone around him would be in stitches. Friends would egg him on not that he needed any encouragement.

"Go on Pete do your Frank Spencer." Eager to avoid the risk of becoming boring and to show he could move with the times every now and then he'd throw in a couple of new characters. His Boris Johnson got mixed reviews but Donald Trump went down a storm. It would be fair to say that nobody went home miserable when Pete was around. Sandra's job as a nurse often left her tired and irritable, and in need of some quiet time. Time to sit with her feet up and do nothing but listen to the slow, soothing tick of the wall clock and maybe immerse herself in a good book.

But Pete always had other ideas, like binge-watching boxed sets. He'd plan an evening of comedy, "Open All Hours", "The Office", "Only Fools and Horses". She'd seen them so many times she knew them off by heart, could recite verbatim whole swathes of dialogue.

He liked to surprise her with trips to the cinema or tickets for the theatre, there was never a dull moment with Pete…and Sandra desperately longed for a dull moment. So when he suddenly announced his plans to enrol for French lessons she was ecstatic. Thursday evenings seven till nine, two whole hours of peace and quiet. That would do her very nicely, she thought.

Maureen Wilson took up French for Beginners to get away from her husband Stan. Almost twenty years they'd been married and lately, she'd reached the point where she dreaded him coming home. At five thirty every weekday huge black clouds would begin to gather over number nineteen Chestnut Avenue, a forewarning of the imminent arrival of Mr Misery Guts. She'd only herself to blame, he was like that when they first met but she was only eighteen and blinded by his dark smouldering good looks. She was a giddy scatterbrain and it was simply a case of opposites attract. They were chalk and cheese, Venus and Mars.

Slowly, over the years, his mean and moody ways began to lose their appeal. Being around him suffocated her spirit and sapped her energy. She became two different people. The funny, bubbly, 'girls just want to have fun' Maureen on a night out with friends was totally unrecognisable from the sad, downcast creature she turned into when Stan was around.

He hated the neighbours, most of his family and absolutely everyone who appeared on TV.

There wasn't a cat in hell's chance of a quiet night in front of the box in the Wilson household. Anyone brave enough to venture across the TV screen in Stan's living room would get it with both barrels.

Like a coiled spring, he'd sit there, remote control wedged in his hand, ready to zap the lot of them into oblivion. The running commentary that accompanied these evenings drove her round the bend.

"The BBC pay him fifty thousand pounds a week to talk absolute garbage; he knows nothing about football. Fifty thousand pounds to state the obvious. I've forgotten more about football than that useless plonker will ever know".

Or "Did you know she had an affair with a married MP – why is she still reading the news? It's an absolute disgrace".

And the classic, "I don't pay my licence fee to watch somebody redecorating some useless pleb's living room. It's like watching paint dry". Maureen remembered that one well, she had actually started to laugh until she realised that Stan hadn't a clue he'd just cracked a joke. To escape the onslaught she would often take herself off to bed and read. She liked a good murder story, something with a complicated plot. At these times she was thankful they lived in a detached house, she could still hear his booming voice through the bedroom ceiling.

Sandra met Maureen once – once was enough. She saw within seconds why she and her husband had become such good pals, they were as daft as each other.

It was a cold and miserable Saturday afternoon and she and Pete were wandering around the supermarket. As she reached out to grab a bunch of bananas she heard a woman's voice.

"Bonjour Pierre," said the voice, "Comment allez-vous?" Pete swung round.

"Ah, bonjour Monique, tres bon, merci, et vous?"

"Comme ci, comme ca," she replied. "Je suis shopping pour le pomme-de-terre, carrot et broccoli pour tomorrow's dinner."

"Je suis shopping pour tomorrow's dinner aussi" said Pete. "Je suis allez up Marks and Spencers pour le salmon en croute et le petit pois". In truth, he was going for their Haddock Mornay but didn't know the French for haddock.

There was a quick introduction during which it became apparent that the two felt that out of respect for Sandra they should revert to English. Sandra stifled a laugh. Thank goodness for that, she thought, if they'd carried on with that advanced level of French she would have had absolutely no idea what they were talking about.

Then as quickly as she had appeared Maureen was off. "Au revoir Pierre, see you Thursday" she shouted back over her shoulder. "Une pleasure to meet you, Sandra". Then, like a whirlwind, she disappeared up the veg aisle.

A heavy downpour earlier in the day had soaked the garden. Every time Pete brushed against the buddleia large drops of rainwater ran down the back of his neck. The thin jacket he was wearing offered little protection and by now he was soaked through to the skin. To add to his misery he felt a twinge in his left calf, a warning of the onset of the dreaded cramp. As it took hold and the pain kicked in he stuffed his hand in his mouth and bit down on it to stop himself from screaming out loud. It was one o'clock in the morning and Stan's bedroom light was still on. He cursed him under his breath.

If it wasn't for Stan he'd be asleep now – tucked up in his warm comfortable bed with his warm comfortable wife.

He thought about Maureen. He'd known her for such a short time. Yet here he was, cowering in her garden in the middle of the night. It was crazy.

What was it about her that made her so special, he asked himself? What attracts you to certain people. You can't always pinpoint it. Is it a primal, basic, uncomplicated thing or is it more sophisticated, intellectual or spiritual? He'd no idea, he was no philosopher so why was he even trying to analyse it?

All he knew was that she had plonked herself next to him on that first French evening class and by the end of the two hours he felt as if he'd known her all his life.

She was small with short dark hair, wore "Ban the Bomb" earrings, had bright luminous green fingernails and was carrying a huge battered old pencil case decorated with characters from the Muppets. As they filled in their enrolment forms they discovered that they had the same birthday. She said it was 'spooky'. She told him her name was Maureen and she hated it so when the French tutor told the class that just for fun she always gave her class French names Maureen was over the moon.

Her excitement quickly turned to bitter disappointment when she just missed out on Chantelle. It went to a woman called Ethel who was sitting just in front of her. Maureen was gutted.

"Chantelle," she muttered to Pete under her breath. "She's got the Queen's hairdo and she's wearing a beige fleece. She's never a Chantelle in a million years. I wanted that".

Pete started laughing, that set her off and then they couldn't stop. Mrs Jennings shot them a warning look.

"You're Pierre," she snapped at Pete. "Maureen, you can be Monique. Now would you like to share that joke with the rest of the class?"

"No, it's okay," said Maureen. "It's like being back at school," she whispered to Pete, "What's next, detention?"

French lessons became a secondary reason to go out on Thursday evenings – especially for Maureen.

At six-thirty she'd pop her head around the living room door and give Stan a cheery goodbye. She'd get a grunt in return. He'd be slouched in his spot, armed with the remote, ready for an evening of ranting at the box.

Five weeks into the language course Pete and Maureen decided to go to the pub after the lesson. The *Rising Sun* was just a walk of a few minutes from the college. One of the town's oldest public houses it had escaped a themed makeover. A bit rough around the edges it was now mainly the haunt of students. It began as just a quick drink after the class but soon they were sitting there till closing time. Pete's wife had no problem with it, she welcomed the extra time on her own.

Over the following weeks, Pete got to learn more about his new friend. She told him she'd met Stan when she was eighteen and married him at twenty. They had no children because Stan didn't want any. She loved reading, hated sports of any kind, could strip a car engine down and was allergic to cats. Closing time always came round much too quickly for Maureen.

Stan didn't care one way or the other what time she got home and more often than not he'd be in bed snoring away when she got back. She knew from past experience to sleep in the spare room. Stan was not a man to disturb, waking him up was akin to poking a stick in a wasps' nest.

He worked for a double glazing company, Fitwell Widows and Doors, had been with them for fifteen years and was their top salesman. Question Stan on the price of a set of new windows and you'd never get a straight answer. The price depended on who he was selling it to. He had no problem charging a vulnerable 85-year-old widow £5,000 more for her windows than the streetwise bloke next door who was too savvy to be taken in by his slick sales patter. He'd sit on her sofa, drinking her tea and eating her biscuits and happily take her last penny.

He'd brag about it when he got home. "They get what they deserve," he'd tell Maureen, "Serves them right for being so gullible. I always leave them thinking they've got a bargain, none of them gets a bargain".

For these selfless services to mankind, Stan drove a top of the range motor courtesy of Fitwells Windows and Doors.

At five-thirty every weekday Sandra would hear the screech of brakes as he slammed the car up the drive. He'd barge in, grab the remote control, switch off whatever she might be watching, plonk his feet on the coffee table and dish out his orders.

"I'm starving, make us a coffee. Hope you've made something decent for dinner".

She'd smile sweetly, walk into the kitchen, grab the dishcloth and squeeze. She's squeeze till her fingers went numb, squeeze till every drop of moisture was gone. If only she had the courage to do it to Stan, she thought, but she knew she'd never get her tiny hands around his great fat neck. No, she'd need some sort of ligature. His blue Fitwell tie with the yellow 'F' emblazoned on the front would do the job very nicely. He was always proud of that tie – it would be a fitting end.

"Here's your coffee," she'd say, emerging from the kitchen with a smile, "Dinner will be in ten minutes". Gesturing towards the coffee table, he'd grudgingly move his feet over so she could place the hot cup down. But his focus would be on the TV and the latest celebrity who had 'only got the job because his dad was famous.'

"Nepotism, that's the only reason he's there. He's as thick as a brick bog. Pass me a biscuit if dinner's not going to be ready for ten minutes".

Every Christmas as a reward for all their hard work throughout the year Fitwell's treated all their employees and their partners once a year to a weekend in the town's top hotel. They'd arrive on Saturday morning and have use of all the hotel's facilities. The women usually headed for the health spa and beauty salon, the men for the games room and swimming pool. All the drinks were free and the two-day bacchanalia ended with a lavish meal and cabaret. Maureen looked forward to it all year. It was a chance to get seriously dressed up and she'd spend hours trawling around the shops for the perfect outfit.

But for the past two years, Stan had made feeble excuses to avoid going and she began to notice that he wasn't keen on her mixing with any of his work colleagues. At the same time, he started to work late a couple of nights every week and leave the room to answer his mobile. Something was wrong but she didn't know what to do.

She knew better than to broach the subject. Stan had such a nasty temper she'd learnt over the years to keep her mouth shut. He had never laid a finger on her but verbally he could tear her to shreds. The slightest criticism from her would always be turned right back at her. He was an expert at it. He'd reel off a long list of things that he didn't like about her and it always ended the same "If you don't like it, leave."

Family and friends never saw this side of Stan and Maureen always put on the front of a happy marriage feeling that if she admitted things were bad she was a failure. Recently Pete had seen a change in her. The bubbly Maureen he met just months earlier seemed to sparkle less, so as they sat in the Rising in Sun one Thursday evening he asked her if anything was wrong.

He wasn't prepared for the next ten minutes – the floodgates opened with an almighty eruption as Maureen let it all out. When she finally finished he sat there shell-shocked. His first reaction was that Stan was lucky to have Maureen – let alone another woman.

"Why don't you leave?" he asked.

"I've nowhere to go", she said.

"Well, the first thing you need to do is find out if he's having an affair. Stop being a victim, spy on him.

Four days later Stan told her he'd be working late so half an hour before he was due to finish she drove into town and parked two streets away from his office.

She walked the rest of the way and seeing his car parked outside, slipped into the supermarket opposite where she had a clear view over the road.

Thankfully the store was busy so no-one was taking much notice of the strange woman loitering aimlessly around the aisles picking things up and putting them back down

She'd been there about ten minutes when the office door opened and out stepped Stan. He glanced up and down the street before quickly getting into his car. For a split second, she thought he'd spotted her so ducked behind the bread aisle nonchalantly picking up a small white bloomer. She hid for a few seconds before daring to pop her head round to see what he was up to. Stan was still sitting in his car talking on his mobile and laughing, yes laughing. That clinched it for her, she knew then that something was definitely wrong.

The door opened again and out stepped a tall blonde woman. She was smiling and talking on her phone. Stan leaned over, opened the car door, she jumped in and in a second they were gone. She desperately wanted to follow them but her car was five minutes away.

Maureen had met her several times. She was the boss's PA and had been with the company for a couple of years. Maureen couldn't stand her. Bridget, they called her. Always dressed to the nines, she liked the men. Rumour had it her real name was Brenda. She was the divorcee that Stan often talked about, claimed he couldn't abide her, told Maureen he was always having to fend off her advances.

"Well, Stan, you didn't do a very good job of fending her off just now, you snake" she muttered under her breath.

She looked down at the pile of crumbs around her feet. She'd squeezed the white bloomer so hard it had broken in two. Her head span, she paid for the loaf and headed home.

As she stepped through the door into the hall she felt a sharp pain in her ankle. "Mortimer," she screamed, "You evil little swine"!

She looked down, her tights were torn and her ankle was seeping blood through four vertical scratch marks. That mangy cat ambushed her at every opportunity. He hated her and the feeling was mutual. She hobbled into the kitchen, smeared antiseptic over her wounds and burst into tears. Picking up her mobile she punched in Stan's number – it went straight to voicemail. She reached for some kitchen roll, wiped away the tears, put the kettle on and made herself a drink.

As she sat there not knowing what to do the door into the hall slowly inched open and Mortimer popped his head round. The convenient amnesia the ginger assassin displayed on these occasions never ceased to amaze her. The vicious attack just five minutes before was now apparently completely forgotten. Now he was hungry and if it wasn't too much trouble he'd like his dinner, please.

She should try to eat something herself, she thought, and although she didn't have much of an appetite she threw some eggs into a pan and made herself an omelette.

The cast iron frying pan which Stan, with little thought or imagination, had presented her with the previous Christmas weighed a ton. That pan could be put to much better use than making omelettes, she thought.

She should wait for him in the hall and when the cheating, lying pig finally showed his cheating lying face she should take a leaf out of Mortimer's book and ambush him. A few whacks around the back of the head should do the trick. Instead, she took herself and her murderous thoughts off to the sanctuary of the spare bedroom and it was one o'clock in the morning before she finally heard his key in the lock.

When she came down for breakfast the following morning Stan was slouched at the kitchen table having breakfast. Head buried in his newspaper he didn't even bother looking up to acknowledge her.

"If you think I'm gullible enough to believe that you were conning old ladies out of their life savings till one o'clock in the morning you can think again. I saw you with that old slapper Bridget, you know the one you can't stand, you cheating, disgusting scumbag. Being married to you is like living with the Grim Reaper. You're miserable, selfish, thoughtless and boring. Go and pack all your expensive clothes, shove them in your designer suitcases and sod off.

'When I get back from work you'd better be gone,' was what she wanted to say.

"You got in late last night," was what she said.

"I know, I went for a drink with Dean after I'd finished work".

Dean, she thought, Dean Spratt. Stan detested him, in fact, everyone who ever met him detested him. In the cut-throat world of the double-glazing business, Dean was a legend for all the wrong reasons. He'd cheat his own granny without as much as a backward glance. He was Stan's arch-rival for the top salesman.

Tall and lean with a six-pack gained from hours of sweating at the gym, twenty-five- year-old Dean had an extremely over-inflated opinion of himself, an opinion that no-one who ever met him shared. Permanently fake-tanned with a shaved head and a tattooed neck, his meticulously ironed shirt so tight he could hardly breathe, he strutted around like God's gift. To his work colleagues, he was nothing more than a big bald ape.

His technique was ruthless, there was nothing he wouldn't do to secure a sale. He could sell a set of windows to a tent dweller.

'So you expect me to believe you spent your entire evening with that knuckle-scraping Neanderthal. If he's not talking about double-glazing he can't string two intelligent words together. The only thing you've got in common with that egotistical bonehead is that you're a slime-ball,' was what she wanted to say.

"So you and Dean had a good night then"? Is what she asked.

"Great," said Stan as he reached for his jacket and headed out of the kitchen door. "I might be late again tonight".

The following Thursday Maureen turned up at the college with her arms, legs and neck covered in scratches. As she sat down next to Pete he asked,

"What on earth have you been doing?"

"I'll tell you later," she whispered.

The pub was unusually busy for a Thursday night so they sat at a table tucked in a corner away from the bustle of the busy bar.

"Okay," he began, "Tell me what's wrong"?

"Well, you told me to spy on Stan so I did. Saw him with a woman he works with. He doesn't know I've seen him."

"And what about those?" he asked, pointing to the scratches, "Who did that to you?"

"Mortimer," she said, "He's got me twice this week".

"Who the hell's Mortimer?" he asked.

"The cat".

"But I thought you were allergic to cats"?

"I am, but Stan wanted one. We'd talked about getting a pet since we got married but it wasn't fair while we were both out at work all day but when I reduced my hours a couple of years ago we started looking. I wanted a dog, just a small one, maybe a Jack Russell, one that didn't need long walks because I knew I'd be the one who'd be doing the walking. Stan said he wanted a cat. A cat was easier to look after, not so demanding and anyway, he liked cats more. Eighteen months ago he arrived home from work with a huge black tom. He said it had turned up in the yard at the back of the offices a couple of weeks before looking ragged and underfed. One of the girls in the office had started to put food out and it had come back every day since. If anyone approached it, it hissed. Anyone that is except for Stan. For some strange reason, it took to Stan and even though everyone warned him that it was probably feral and wouldn't make a very good pet Stan didn't listen. He decided from the beginning that it might not be a good idea to let him out and so he became a house cat and I just had to put up with it".

From the first day Mortimer came into Maureen's life, he let her know he hated her. He hissed whenever she tried to stroke him and although she was the one who fed and watered him it made no difference. It took her weeks to teach him how to use a litter tray and any accidents were always dealt with by the long-suffering Maureen.

A more cuddlesome creature could not be found when Stan was around. Mortimer would leap on his lap at every opportunity and purr away contentedly for hours while he stroked his ears and tummy. If Stan fell asleep he'd gently pat his face with his paw to wake him up.

It was an entirely different kettle of fish with Maureen. He'd dive-bomb her from the top of the wardrobe when she was getting dressed, trip her when she was going down the stairs and attack her ankles whenever she walked past. She got no sympathy from Stan, he thought it was hilarious.

Tears were now welling up in Maureen's eyes and Pete felt helpless.

"I hate him," she said. "I wish he was dead. I'd love to squeeze the life out of him but I haven't the guts to do it".

"Why don't you get someone else to do it for you?" asked Pete. "It shouldn't be too difficult. A plastic bag, a strong ligature, catch him unawares, maybe asleep."

"Forget the minor details," Maureen interrupted, "Would you be prepared to kill him?"

To her amazement, Pete answered without a moment's hesitation. "If it puts a smile back on your face, yes I would".

And that's where the whole sorry mess began.

Their visits to the pub now took a more serious tone. Thursday evenings became 'how to kill and get away with it" nights'.

The first thing they agreed on was that Maureen should be miles away and with witnesses to verify it. Secondly that Pete should have easy access to the house. Then she suggested that it might be easier if she drugged Stan. He always took a sleeping tablet before he went to bed. She could make sure he took an extra one.

"Drug Stan" asked Pete, "Well okay if you think it will help".

Over the following weeks, they hatched their plan. They wrote nothing down, didn't discuss anything on the phone or by text. Everything had to be consigned to memory. Maureen would arrange a night at her sisters. It was something she often did. On these occasions, her sister Kate usually invited some of the girls round and they'd spend the evening just drinking and having a laugh. Huge amounts of alcohol were always put away so being over the limit she always slept there. It was nothing out of the ordinary.

The plan was that before she left for her sisters she would crush a sleeping tablet and mix it into Stan's dinner. Added to the one he'd normally take later it should put him out of action for a few hours.

Pete said that Sandra wouldn't be a problem. She always slept like a log, never getting up in the night once she was asleep. But just to be sure they decided that Maureen would pilfer one of Stan's sleeping pills, he never counted them, and Pete would slip it into Sandra's bedtime drink.

"It's very important you leave your mobile at home," cautioned Maureen. "They can track them. We'll buy two cheap phones, pay with cash and use them only if we desperately need to communicate on the night. Then when the job is done we'll smash them up".

Maureen's large detached house was only a couple of miles from Pete and Sandra's so the plan was that he would walk to her house after his wife was asleep. They checked the route and there were no CCTV cameras between the two homes.

He'd hide in the back garden which luckily was secluded from both sides, wait till Stan turned the bedroom light off, use the key to get in, do the job and be safely back home while it was still dark. What could be more simple?

Maureen travelled to a shopping centre fifteen miles away the following week to buy two mobiles and some credit. Pete thought she was being overly cautious but she said it made her feel better. While she was there she had a backdoor key cut and bought Pete a black balaclava and some Latex gloves.

He laughed when she handed them to him. "Are they really necessary?" he asked.   "You only have to put them on just before you let yourself in," she explained "But yes you really need to use them.

As Pete sat crouching in the shadows and wondering if he would ever get into the house the bedroom light finally went out. It had been arranged that he would wait for at least half an hour before he made his move. Sitting on the wet grass he wondered what Maureen would be thinking. They hadn't spoken since Thursday evening, agreeing that unless anything really important cropped up they would have no contact with each other. He hoped she was all right and managing to keep it together.

Pete looked at his watch. It was time to go. He checked his pockets. The plastic bag and twine were still there. Of course, they were,

'It's ridiculous', he thought, he'd already checked, so why wouldn't they be? It was just nerves. He pulled on the balaclava, then the gloves took the key out of his pocket. The violent storm of the afternoon had given way to a calm but chilly autumn evening. There was no breeze to mask the sound of his footsteps as he edged nervously towards the house but the sky was covered in a thick layer of black cloud preventing the moon from firing down its spotlight and alerting anyone who might be watching to the dark figure creeping slowly through the garden.

As he reached the door he hesitated for a second, took a deep breath, put the key in the lock and very carefully turned it – then he froze. He was paralysed with fear. His Heart was pounding in his chest. What if the sleeping tablets hadn't worked, what if Stan was still awake?

Panic had now set in, he wanted to run but his legs wouldn't. They were riveted to the spot. He reached into his pocket and grabbed the phone Maureen had given him, he desperately needed to speak to her. To his horror, it went straight to voicemail so he whispered a message instead.

"Don't worry I'm OK. Just had some last-minute jitters but I'm going into the house now. Everything's going to be all right, I won't let you down. Mortimer's as good as dead.

Maureen had heard the phone ring but was afraid to answer it in front of the girls. When it went to voicemail she sat there for a few seconds and then nipped to the bathroom to check it. She was horrified at what she heard. 'Mortimer's as good as dead?' What the hell did that mean? She collapsed on to the bed and listened to the message again. No, she'd heard it right. Her head was spinning, she felt sick. What was Pete about to do? This couldn't be happening. How could he have got it so wrong?

She thought back to the night in the Rising Sun when they first hatched their plan. She remembered she'd been talking about Stan and Mortimer. She knew she'd said "I hate him, I wish he was dead". Then it dawned on her. She'd been talking about Stan and Pete thought she meant Mortimer. She thought it was odd at the time that he'd agreed so readily. And he did seem confused when she suggested giving Stan an extra sleeping tablet. How could they make such a stupid mistake?

Everything had been planned down the last detail and now he was going to suffocate Mortimer. She loathed that cat, hated every hair on his fat black body but she didn't hate him enough to want him dead. What monster would kill a poor defenceless creature – even if he was the devil's spawn?

But she was helpless to stop it. There was no way she could ring. What if Pete hadn't remembered to put the mobile on silent? She was nine miles away and had far too much to drink, she dare not chance driving the car. Anyway, she would never get there on time.

She shouted down to Kate that she had a headache and was going to bed, dived in fully-clothed and buried her head under the covers. But there was no way she could hide away from the image of poor old Mortimer struggling for his last breath with a plastic bag over his dark-head.

Pete opened the back door, slipped quietly in and carefully closed it behind him. It was pitch black inside and the only sound to be heard was the humming of the fridge. Maureen had talked him through the layout of the house so although he couldn't see, the mental picture was crystal clear in his head. He knew that to his left was a row of cupboards, to his right the fridge and on the opposite wall the cooker. He could see its illuminated digital clock, it told him it was 13.17 hours.

Next to the cooker was the door to the hall. He stood for a moment and as his eyes slowly began to adjust he could see that the door was open and the hall was in darkness. He had brought with him a tiny LED torch but was afraid to switch it on. Maureen had told him that Mortimer slept in a cat bed in the corner by the side of the fridge and as the kitchen eventually began to take shape he could just make out Mortimer's bed and the outline of the sleeping cat. He slowly reached into his pocket and stepping tentatively to the right took out the plastic bag. That's when the joke popped into his head. It was bizarre – he just couldn't help himself. Typical Pete, and at a time like this. But he was sure Maureen would appreciate it especially as they were learning French. He'd send her a text as soon as he'd despatched the cat. 'Il et mort' it would say. He was so *chuffed* with himself he lost concentration for a second, took a step forward and stood on the sleeping tom's tail.

Mortimer gave rent to an ear-piercing screech and in a split-second launched himself at the intruder. He landed on his head sinking his claws deep into the scalp. In turn, Pete let out an ear-piercing screech. That's when he heard the terrifying sound of footsteps upstairs. Then further horrified heard a door opening.

The infuriated cat finally released his grip on Pete's head and shot like a bolt of lightning out of the kitchen and towards the hall.

Pete froze at the sound of footsteps on the stairs and a man's voice, "Who's there?"

He held his breath and for a moment there was complete silence. Even the fridge had gone quiet.

The silence was broken by a deafening shriek from Mortimer, quickly followed by a loud thud and then the unmistakable sound of someone tumbling down the stairs. Pete knew that this would buy him some time to get out of the house before Stan reached the kitchen.

His heart was beating so loudly he was convinced Stan would be able to hear it. But there was no sound from the hall and no sign of Mortimer – just an eerie silence.

Shaking from head to foot Pete stood in the darkness for what seemed like an eternity. Suddenly the fridge motor kicked back in and he nearly jumped out of his skin.

He reached into his pocket, felt for the torch and crept slowly out of the kitchen and into the darkness of the hall. Although horrified at what its beam might reveal he switched on the torch and moved it back and forth until finally, its light landed on the dark shape at the bottom of the stairs. What he saw made his blood run cold.

Stan was lying in a crumpled heap at the bottom of the stairs, one leg bent at a grotesque angle and blood gushing from a huge gash on the back of his head. It looked as though he'd hit the sharp corner of the bottom bannister. His eyes were wide open but he wasn't moving. Pete knelt down beside him and gingerly felt for a pulse. There wasn't one. Stan was dead.

As he stood up he felt his legs buckling under him, his head spinning with a million and one thoughts. It was an accident but there was no way he could ring the police. How would he explain what he was doing there in the middle of the night? And what about Maureen? How on earth could he tell her that her husband was dead? Apart from checking Stan's pulse, he hadn't laid a finger on him. He didn't kill him but deep down he knew he'd caused his death.

If he hadn't stood on Mortimer's tail the cat wouldn't have shot up the stairs and tripped Stan up. For a fraction of a second, the thought crossed his mind to hunt him down, finish the job he'd come to do in the first place but soon came to his senses. Killing the cat was the last thing he should do. No, he needed that fat ball of fluff to be very much alive.

He took one last look around. His heart was still pounding but now he was thinking clearly. Turning off the torch he walked out of the hall, through the kitchen and out of the backdoor. Turning the key gently he took off his gloves and balaclava and stuffed them in his pocket and crept quietly out of the garden.

It was a calm, clear night with just a hint of mist as he made his way home. On the thirty minute walk, he passed not a soul. Sandra was still asleep when he slipped into bed beside her. He put his arm around her and felt the heat from her body slowly warming him up.

It had been a long night. Pete was exhausted but didn't hold out much hope of falling asleep.

As for tomorrow, he thought, well he'd just have to wait and see.

The Humans are Coming

CYRUS WEIR

In the year 5,555 as measured by the human race, the Jumpdrive was discovered by Adolf Einstein. With its breakthrough in physics and the understanding of space and time as it was then known, the galaxy was opened up to exploration by humanity. It was a doom-laden day for every other race of beings in the Milky Way.

1.

Scientist Hahbo hurried from his observatory toward the University Building on the other side of the campus. He did not want to be the one to raise the alarm but fate had bestowed that obligation upon him. His gills opened and closed more rapidly than usual in the late and dry autumn weather. The rains that the weathermen had promised had not materialised and everyone was feeling the dehydration upon their skins. He passed several familiar faces and several colleagues and could not bear to look them directly in the eye. For he was to become the harbinger of doom. The first man to see the ship in the astral sky. Distant it still was, but none the less provable by Doppler shift and definitely on a course that would terminate at Völkerezég.

Hahbo had been waiting for something like this to happen after all sub-space radio transmissions had ceased from Shalfénia Two. The second planet orbiting Shalfénia had been in touch for twenty-eight years. One day all communication ceased and never resumed – ever. The very last message had been short, to the point and terrifying,

'The Humans are on their way to our world'!

Of course in earlier messages, the Shalfénio had told of the race of beings called the Humans.

Warlike and militaristic mammals who conquered all they came into contact with as though an entire galaxy was not enough room for them to settle in. They came originally from a very normal main sequence star they called Sol. Within two decades of discovering how to fold space, they had conquered five more star systems. After two centuries they had conquered over a hundred. Now, a millennia later, they had swallowed up a quarter of the galaxy. Some worlds they merely enslaved. Used the planet's resources to further their ambitions. Used the locals' populace as slave labour to run their huge factories vital to fuel their never ceasing thirst for yet more conquest

If a world was not rich in resources, however, or technologically advanced enough to be useful to purpose, they used biological weapons and committed mass genocide. Hahbo had read such reports from the Shalfénio with a mixture of disbelief and grave foreboding. Could a race who had discovered how to travel through the vastness of interstellar space really remain so unevolved morally? Surely with great knowledge came great wisdom? It was certainly true for everyone on Völkerezég where the most revered of the populace were those who gave their lives to the pursuit of knowledge.

The fact that nothing was coming from Shalfénia Two any more seemed mute testament to the validity of their claims, however. The Humans [why did they not call themselves Solarian] had reached the world and then the very same had fallen ominously silent. Had the Humans killed every single member of a species numbering a billion? What of the other creatures that lived there? The lower lifeforms that had not higher learning capability? The beasts of the forest. The birds and insects of the air. The fish of the seas and the mammals of the land.

Hahbo found it difficult to accept that the Humans were not amphibian when scientists had thought for centuries that only the amphibians could develop high enough brain function to create tools, record from one generation to the next and possess the power of speech. The silly little mammals of Völkerezég were millions of years away from such development. What sort of a world revolved around Sol, when the mammals had ruled over the superior species of water and land breathers?

Hahbo's flesh blanched to a pale green when he thought of such horrors. He danced out of the patterned sunlight as it flickered through the trees. Inside the air was thankfully cool and the humidity a very nice 70 percent as dictated by the interior steamers. Shzalama liked to look after his fellows of learning. Hahbo trotted directly to the Dean's office, careful not to betray his own rich heritage by hopping and leaping. His race had become erect and walked on two legs for millennia, but it was still somewhat unnatural for them to do so twenty-three hours a day.

He employed an urgent knock and heard the Dean grant him entry at once. Glancing up from his PC he noted,

"Ah, Astronomer Hahbo. I suspect by the urgency of your staccato rapping that you have news concerning the fate of your friends on the deep space radio"?

"The Shalfénio sent me a final and urgent message and then nothing was heard from them since, Dean".

Shzalama grimaced as one of his features could do very well and he asked, "The message, what was it then"?

"The Human's are on their way to Völkerezég".

The Dean of University put his long features in tiny hands and sighed, "What would you have me do, Hahbo. What *can* we do, we have no knowledge of this practice you informed us of. The practice that the mammals employ. What was it again"?

"War, Dean. It is called War".

"Ah Yes. I remember your definition for us now too, Astronomer. A conflict carried on by force of arms as between nations or species within a nation conducted on land, sea, air or space. We have no arms though do we Hahbo"?

"We have never known conflict, Dean. There is but one course of action open to us".

"Complete compliance with the mammals"?

"I doubt they will brook such an option. If they do not then we have one weapon on the entire planet that might bring the mammals low".

"Maybe they will see our world and want nothing from us"?

"Our world is rich in deposits of francium and plutonium".

"They will take these"?

Hahbo nodded, "With or without permission".

"Then we could avoid conflict by simply telling them they can have them".

"And who do you think they would employ to extract the uranium necessary to create the plutonium. We would become a slave race and word has it that such races are worked to death and once their usefulness is done, s are they"!

"So you want to tell the mammals to leave our world alone or we will war them"?

"Declare war upon them is the correct usage of the noun, Dean".

"So we are to be in our first War"?

"We have to defy the mammals or be destroyed by them. There is no other way"

2.

"Duration to Nétéltű Three"? Tribune Peters demanded of the pilot.

"Twenty hours, Tribune", Centurion Rhodes returned.

"Then push engines with greater urgency" the Tribune demanded impatiently.

"Sir", objected Prefect Carter, "Such would blow engine coils. Much delay would then result".

"I care not", the Tribune stormed, he was want to show extremes of temper when under pressure. "We must beat the IEV (Imperial Earth Vessel) Nero to latest treasure. I will not be behind Ainsworth again".

"Tranquillity"? Prefect Carter advised. "The Balbinus will reach Nétéltű Three ahead of the Nero".

"Apologies", Peters kneaded his eyeballs with his thumbs. "Fatigue takes me".

"Go, rest, eat. Leave bridge to me. Returning when refreshed".

The Tribune nodded and slowly left the bridge. Carter picked up his personal pad and pinged a message to the head of security, one Centurion Domalu:-

The Tribune fatigues. Our time to strike grows near. Help with this situation and see yourself rise through rank to Prefect

The reply came as swiftly as Domalu could type his reply:-

My men are loyal. Tell when time to strike is nigh. We obey Prefect.

It was the way of the Humans to rise through the ranks of the Imperial fleet by way of assassination. Indeed Tribune Peters had acquired his command of the Balbinus in just such that way with the full approval of Legate Lockwood. The Legate was the ultimate power of that sector of the galaxy, answerable only to the Emperor himself.

Peters returned to his cabin. Immediately a slave from Rhotanicus Seven knelt before him waiting for instruction. The girl was basically humanoid in general appearance, but her rough skin and grey hue betrayed her reptilian origin. No comet had destroyed the dinosaurs on the seventh world orbiting Rhotanicus and the smallest t of them had evolved into sentient beings. Five and a half thousand years after the execution of the Jewish Prophet on Earth though Humanity had wrought a terrible toll of the civilisation on the world. It had been systematically stripped of its resources. The people pressed into slavery and service in the mines. All for the good of the Human Empire. Only a handful of Rhotanica survived on the hollow world. Nothing better than simple agricultural peasants. The civilisation of Rhotanicus Seven was crumbled to forgotten dust.

This was the legacy of Humanity. The most greedy, warlike race of species capable of Jumpdrive. Before - them quaked other beings knowing their time would come. Behind them, conquered or desolate worlds. Some had resisted. They were the planets that had suffered the most. Nothing more now than rocks of radioactive dust floating around stars on an ever-increasing stellar map. The

Humans had endured the occasional battle defeat but they had never lost a war. The best other races could hope for was servitude in the continued cause of conquest. As the scourge of the galaxy forever spread outward like a plague of locusts that never new satiation.

"Rise, Liucila"? Peters commanded in Rhotanica. He prided himself on his multi-lingual skills. "Fetch wine. Food. Prepare bath".

The girl hurried to do everything he commanded of her. Her position was an enviable one. From all of the alien slaves, the Tribune had selected her as his personal one. True the sex was not especially exciting but he never beat her and she had no chance of conceiving a base-born. No human had ever taken seed in a Rhotanica. Of late he had not even commanded her to kneel forward of him anyway. She wondered if he would soon be murdered. If it happened she would be saddened. The Prefect Carter had his own wench, a Melurian, not even a reptile, but a Marsupial. Nothing better than an animal as far as Liucila was concerned. She fetched a cup made of the metal the Humans seemed to prize above all others. Silver, with its qualities to conduct electricity so well. She poured it three-quarters full of Tellurian fermented grape from a country called Argentina.

Peters seemed to savour it as she fetched him cheese, some poultry and a cob of bread. Whenever she gave him poultry she thought of the poor Aviárdilág. Not only had the Humans raped their world, but once they had stripped it of everything they were interested in they had then consumed most of the population. How could a sentient race bring themselves to eat another? When any other species had dared ask that question of one of them when they were drugged or drunk the answer had always been the same,

'*Because they were delicious*'!

The Human Imperial Empire was cruel, barbaric and hungry!

"Sit with me", Peters suddenly cut in on Liucila's bitter reflections. "Get plate of flies, that you savour so".

Without a thought of hesitation or disobedience, the slave girl hurried to do as commanded.

At first, they ate in silence but then the Human admitted, "I think command will soon be snatched from me. I would not see you without compensation. When enemies make move against me go to safe. Combination is 555-023-023. Great coin is within. Take all for your loyalty but tell none where from you got it. You can buy passage to Rhotanicus Seven if that is where heart dictates".

"You honour me, Tribune", was all Liucila could think to say. She puffed out her neck frond in order to convey sincerity. "But you may be commander yet-a-while".

Peters shook his head, "The Prefect and his men plot even now. In his chest beats the burning flame of ambition and I grow older. I have enjoyed glories past, my time draws to end".

"Then retire and enjoy your later years in peace somewhere in the galaxy", she found herself saying, "I would come with you if you wish it"?

"To die on some forgotten world with old man? No. It is not the way of Empire. I have slain many to earn current post. When time comes I will embrace it like good Human".

Beyond all belief, Liucila felt sorry for him then. She even tried to feel sorry for the Humans. That was asking far too much of her forgiving nature though.

3.

"We need a volunteer", Hahbo said to the Dean.

Shzalama noted, "You have an entire world from which to select one, Astronomer".

"I think perhaps for the sake of security, that our volunteer should come from this very campus"?

The smooth skin over Shzalama's eyes rose in surprise, "You mean an academic! One of our very best, when there are so many plebs in the swamps all over the world"!

"One with the guile and the perceived authority to fool the invaders when they get here. Otherwise, our mission will fail".

Shzalama sighed, "You make your point well and I can find no argument with it. Very well, Hahbo, this afternoon you will address the entire campus, all the students and all the lecturers will be present. Now, does that satisfy you"?

"Yes, Dean". Hahbo returned simply.

4.

Spriznimołodi was a Ranaeva from the southern continent of Völkerezég. He was just enjoying a nice soak in clear water after his earlier mud bath when his room-mate burst into their apartments.

"Have you heard the news", the ridiculously tall and tiny limbed Caeciliaen asked in his typically lisping style of speech. "The Humans are coming"!

Spriznimołodi nearly sprang out of the tub on his powerfully calved legs, "Coming here! What to the University"?

"No you idiot", Chord added, "To Völkerezég".

"I'm not sure I believe in Humans", Spriznimołodi propositioned, "I think they're just something to scare the tadpoles in their pools to make them behave".

"Shalfénia has fallen silent. No more subspace transmissions from them and Völkerezég is next on the projected flight-path".

"If Shalfénia exists, which I dispute", Spriznimołodi began, "Then it is over a hundred light years away, there is no need to panic at this juncture".

"It would seem the Humans have broken the light-barrier though", Chord argued. "They can fold space and *jump* from each edge of the fold to the other".

"According to the great Ranaeva scientist and theorist, Rhana, the speed of light is beyond the powers of any intelligent beings to exceed. Even theoretically should they do so, they would be turned insane by the experience".

According to the Shalfénio, they *were* mad! Crazed with lust and power. All they want are resources of any kind, in order to even greater fuel their ambitions".

"It's a myth designed to make us happy with *our* lot, Chord". Spriznimołodi debated, "Well as it happens I am satisfied with my studies and intend to work hard to become a medicum. So the tales are of no interest to me".

Slide out of the water anyway though", Chord then instructed. "We are all summoned to a conference with the Dean in about twenty minutes. Where he has an announcement to make to us regarding the crisis".

"The Dean gives the rumour credence?! Has the world gone mad"?

Spriznimołodi reluctantly got out despite his scepticism. Just when his skin was starting to feel satisfactorily wet as well.

He donned his skirtel and followed Chord from their rooms over the campus to the grand hall. A crowd was already gathering without. The instant the doors were flung open the hall filled rapidly until it had reached capacity seating and the late arrivals were forced to stand at the back. Midst a buzz of excitement the Dean appeared at the podium and everyone instantly fell expectantly silent.

"I don't know how many of you this will come as a surprise too but I have news that is a grave danger to our world", he began. He then waited for the murmur of astonishment to cease before continuing. "We are not alone in the galaxy. Even more incredible is the realization today that a species does exist that has the capability of inter-stellar passage within a matter of mere days. One such vessel with that proficiency is on its way to our world. It is piloted by an aggressive race of aliens that are xenophobic in extremeiss. They plunder worlds of their resources and enslave the population of those planets for as long as they supply them with what they desire. Then they leave them derelict and often bereft of the civilization that was on them before they arrived".

The buzz grew to a clamorous wave of panic that the Arch-dean had to quell with several amplified entreaties for calm and quietness. Finally, Shzalama continued,

"As we do not possess the mechanisms that this race has, devices called weapons we have but one hope of stopping them from ravaging Völkerezég. The way we possess which is our only hope against the aliens will require the sacrifice of one member of this University. The member who volunteers to try and save all other Völkerezégi will be forced to sacrifice his or her own life in the process. It is almost certainly a suicide mission. It is a grave thing to ask of anyone. Know this though, the one who volunteers to do this may well serve our entire civilization. You are all able to message me by way of our infra-net. I await volunteers to do so within the hour. If there are several volunteers the one who makes the noble sacrifice will be drawn by lot. That is all, may the star of Völkerezég forever shine upon us.

"Well that's two volunteers they've got", Chord turned from his computer, "How many on campus do you think will join us in the list of names"?

Spriznimołodi smiled a very wide smile. An expression that only a fellow Ranaeva could match, with their slit mouths that almost bisected their heads, "I cannot imagine anyone in the University would not volunteer to save our world at the cost of their own lives".

"And the chance for immortality", Chord pointed out.

"Not so attractive a proposition when it means untimely death though. I wonder what the Dean has planned. I cannot imagine how we peaceful Völkerezégi can hope to defeat an alien race that enjoys dominating and destroying others. What is wrong with them"?

"We eat lower life forms for sustenance".

"Non-sentient ones. Only then to sustain our own health. Not simply to dispossess, to take from by force of might".

"That may be a mute point to one of the flies we both ate for lunch. You know what the great philosopher Dolok said, *'Life is an incredible accident in the cold and cruel cosmos'*. It seems he was right. Anyway, if everyone volunteered I think you and I are pretty safe".

An hour later though one of them discovered that he was not! For his name had been drawn out of the computer and the fate of Völkerezégi was in his slimy hands.

5.

"We are entering orbit with the planet, Tribune", Centurion Rhodes reported. "Still no sign of ships coming to oppose us. Not even surface to space missiles being launched. The planet has technology, but our spy equipment registers no form of defence or offence of any sort".

"Is that possible"? Prefect Carter mused aloud. "Without weapons how do they maintain their borders"?

"They do not appear to have any borders, Sir", the legate informed glancing up from his instrumentation. "The planet is one massive swamp. Huge inland seas cover a third of its surface, but the other two-thirds is one gigantic world-encompassing landmass. I've been monitoring their radio-communications and they only seem to have one language. I don't think they have more than one nation".

That was a blow. One of the ways the Humans exploited worlds was to pit one nation against another on alien planets. Half of the time their internal squabbles brought the various races of a planet to heel all the quicker for it. Here was a planet with only one race even if it did boast various species. The screens around the bridge showed images of the creatures. Amphibians all, but varying orders, more than Earth in fact that only had three. It was also a world rich in minerals and without any form of weaponry.

Prefect Carter was disappointed. One of the excuses he was going to use in his coup against the Tribune was his inability to quell the locals. That looked like a lost leader from the get-go.

"Do we have a computerised dictionary yet, Legate"? Tribune Peters asked from his command chair. He referred to an extrapolation that the onboard computer had created from the alien radio signals picked up on the way into the star system.

"I estimate ninety percent of their usual words, Tribune". This meant that a message could be typed into the Human language computer and an instant translation calculated in the alien's tongue.

"What do these call themselves"?

"Völkerezégi, Tribune, from the planet Völkerezég".

"Type this then will you:-

Völkerezégi:- Imperial Vessel Balbinus orbits your world. Desire to survive as race then you will surrender to Emperor of Terra - Claudius Maximus Felesfeliates You are now members of the Empire, will kneel to swear allegiance to Him and all who serve him. Attempt resistance and consequence will be dire. We require unconditional surrender of your leaders who are welcome to be transported aboard so that they can swear agreement and fealty.

That should do it give them an hour before we start sending missiles down to the planet".

Obviously, Carter was waiting to see how control of the planet would go before attempting his coup. Tribune Peters had not risen to command and maintained his position of leader of a jump-drive vessel for four years without having an intricate and skilful spy system, however. He would receive a warning from his operatives and then he would strike preemptively.

They waited for only half of the hour before a response came from the planet below. Peters was in his cabin by then and had the message transferred to his personal screen:-

Imperial Vessel Balbinus welcome to Völkerezég. We knew you were on your way and are excited to welcome visitors from another part of the galaxy to our lush and verdant world. We are oxygen breathers like yourselves and our instruments inform us that your pseudo-gravity is also similar if slightly higher than Völkerezég-norm. We would, therefore, like to send a single ambassador to meet and greet you. You who have come so far to see us. He represents all the leaders of our peoples and would be happy to discuss your terms then. We have but liquid propulsion engines for our few rockets however so wonder if it was possible for you to fetch the ambassador, whose name is Spriznimołodi

Peters grinned ironically, turned to Liucila, "An ambassador", he chuckled, "This Spriz-whatever has nothing *to* discuss. Their surrender is to be unconditional. They speak with great flourish. Yet it will avail them nought. I find curiosity that they do not strike".

"Perhaps they have no weapons, My Lord", the reptile offered.

Peters laughed, "Believe that not. They hide what they have with hope of future insurgencey. No matter, that will be crushed when it happens. Our protective laser-grid makes our ships invincible.

He threw a metal toggle and spoke into the desk-mic, "Centurion Rhodes. Take dart down to planet surface. Request landing coordinates from computer. Let us meet Ambassador of newly conquered dominion"?

"I obey, Tribune", came the immediate response.

Peters threw a second toggle this one painted red, "Domalu"?

"Tribune"?

"I would have knowledge of Prefect's latest plots".

Centurion Rhodes confessed, "You operatives hear nought, Tribune. Would seem the Prefect waits to see how conquering and pressing into slavery of new world progresses before he makes move to take your life".

"Keep informed"?

"Yes Tribune".

6.

The dart lanced through the soupy atmosphere describing a glorious arc in the moisture that the Dean could not fail to admire.

"Are the preparations all completed"? He asked his assistant who assured in reply,

"Down to the last detail, Dean. Spriznimołodi knows what he has to do and is ready. A terrible shame his name came out, he shows the greatest promise in his studies. It was even thought he might stay on as a professor and eventually even aspire to become your successor".

"I grieve the loss of his young life too. His name will never be forgotten by the Völkerezégi however. He will be remembered as the saviour of our people if our plan succeeds. Statues will be erected to honour his name".

The gleaming vessel all straight lines and raw power came to land on the swampy expanse before the University Campus and the engines died to a mere sigh of their former roar. Spriznimołodi, resplendent in his robes of office newly acquired went over to the landing steps that glided down beneath the craft's hull. He half-turned, waved to the gather press cameras and without a word began to alight them. No mammals appeared to greet him. Indeed the vessel may very well of been automated. First, his shiny head entered the line of the hull. Then his slim and lengthy body and within the following instant the hero of Völkerezég was gone.

The ladders slid back into the belly of the dart. At once the engines roared and with a sludgy sucking sound the pod-like feet pulled free and began to fold under the mammals' transport.

"Well that was that", the Dean observed superfluously.

"What happens next, Sir"? His aid wished to know.

"Now we wait"!

7.

"Put away pugio" Optio Castell barked at his two enemies of the same rank. With very different commanders, however. "I call meeting to decide tactic. In past when senior officers war always Optio die in the machinations. I would have different this time".

The other two slid their pugio into red and silver scabbards.

"What mean you, Castell"? Moretonio demanded, "You know my Dominus be Prefect Carter, who soon plans rise to commander by death of yours".

Castell glanced at Rhodes Optio, "Which would you win such struggle"?

"It matters not to me", Crompbus declared levelly, "For by defeat of either my Dominus moves up one closer to command".

Castell nodded, "But whom would you serve under? Peters or Carter"?

Crompbus thought for a second and then returned, "Better the commander one knows than one yet to become".

Moretonio objected, "You side against Prefect. To what end"?

"United in one purpose we may survive". Castell pointed out. "We all live by the killing of Carter".

"And I", Moretonio desired to know, "What reward for betrayal of Dominus"?

"Not betrayal but continued support for Tribune", Castell observed. "And when I take stratagem to Peters may well find elevation for part in such desire".

Moretonio considered his position, then decided, "I wait till move be indicated by Carter then come to you. I hope for reward for my part in plan".

"It is decided", Castell finalised with a nod of his head, "We are for the Tribune and shall all be his agents in coming conflict".

"I aspire we see the day and all victorious", Crompbus agreed while Moretonio nodded slightly less certain of his fate when the time came.

8.

"Grotings from Völkorözg". Spriznimołodi croaked his right arm raised in salute to Peters.

"Greeting to you Ambassador", the Tribune returned in Terran. He turned to his Prefect smiling and saying quietly, "He cannot even pronounce own name properly in language of Galaxy. Sounds like what he is - frog".

"I como in poace", Spriznimołodi struggled, "Roprosonting all Völkorözg. Wo wolcomo you as into-stollor brothors".

"I tire of words spoken by frog. Take to butcher. We will see what Völkerezégi tastes like this evening at dinner".

Two Optio suddenly appeared either side of the completely nonplussed Spriznimołodi and taking him by the upper arm led him away. He would be quickly killed, gutted and then prepared by Sit Amet for the crew that night.

The Tribune addressed his senior staff. "Plain it is that Amphibians have no defences. Darts one through forty to strike on morrow. Locals rounded up and compounds started. Geologists begin excavations. This day Völkerezég fell. Now it is Terran acquisition. We commence usage of it after but twenty-four hours".

"Congratulations". Centurion Rhodes was first to salute the Tribune. The other senior officers fell into line with alacrity. Prefect Carter was the last to acknowledge the Tribunes defeat of the Völkerezégi.

He left the ready-room in a fit of pique. The time to strike was before the Tribune had achieved another single victory. He would wait until dining on the local and then would be a good time to assassinate the tribune and assume command of the ship by right of conquest.

Pushing away his plate an hour later and reflecting that the amphibian had tasted like chicken, he took a huge sniff of Snufz in each nostril and waited for the narcotic to work on his metabolism. The ceiling of his quarters began to whirl with every hue of the rainbow and some beyond ordinary sight. He heard the tines of the colours, tasted their aromas and lost all weight at the couch beneath him disappeared. Through the side of the inter-stellar vessel, he floated and out into the ethereal beauty of the nebula.

His mind encompassed all the dimensions in the same instant and he also knew regret. For when he finally came down he would not remember the tremendous understanding he currently possessed. In the dark recesses of his back-brain though he knew when he returned to the dull and almost comparatively monochromatic world of humanity he would be Tribune of the Balbinus. He had already given the word to his agents aboard the ship. Bought their continued loyalty with the promise of coin and position. While he flew through the endless realms of space, their bloody work was being done. It was torpid minutia to him that so many were willing to kill in his name. Yet when he was once more aboard the ship small matters would grow in importance.

As he flew faster and faster eventually exceeding the speed of light, maybe even the speed of thought he saw what he sought. Worlds. Countless planets orbiting countless stars. All fat with plunder and workforce. All to increase his position in the Empire. All to elevate he Tribune incumbent through even higher strata until he was the Emperor himself. As all things fail eventually, so did the narcotic. He began to lose the feeling of power, the magnificence of mental supremacy. As always the trip ending with the bitter tinge of regret. That was the drugs secret of course. That the ending of it as such. Encouraging even demanding further usage.

He closed his eyes to avoid seeing such magnificent pulchritude fail. He did not want to observe the decay from sublime to mundane. When he opened them a figure was in his quarters. At first, blurred by the afterglow of Snufz. Slowly his vision and his wits returned. It was the Optio whom he had despatched to slay Peters. With a voice that was not still quite his own, he managed to demand through parched lips,

"Is it done, Moretonio"?

To his instant annoyance the foolish Optio shook his head, "Not yet Prefect, but soon the machinations will be complete".

Ire turned to rage, "What mean you by lack of efficiency. I would see it done and an end to it. Have it so"?

To Carter's absolute incredulity the Optio shook his head a second time, "Apologies Dominus, but offer much improved has presented itself to me".

Understanding began to dawn on Carter then. His man, or even perhaps his men had been turned".

"Tell me the coin of your circumduct and I will see it doubled".

His anger began to be nibbled at then by teeth of fear, for the Optio seemed resolved to whatever treachery he had agreed to.

"Offer be better in more than coin, Prefect". The base-born returned and drawing forth his pugio sprang for the Prefect.

Carter tried to dive from the couch. His limbs were still torpid with the after-effects of the Snufz though and he heard steel scraping on bone. Looking down it was to witness a pool of fresh scarlet blood welling on his tunic and catching the edge of his toga. With the realisation that Moretonio had stabbed him came the pain. Lancing shafts of unbearable agony took his breathe away with their intensity. He never regained it but died within seconds

In some ways, Carter was the lucky one!

9.

Later that evening the surgeon of the IEV Balbinus was suddenly kowed by entrance into his medical bay by none other than Tribune Peters himself.

"Tribune"! He bowed to the ship's commander and supreme authority established an hour before by the assassination of Prefect Carter. "I trust this visit inspection only. You have no wound"?

Peters shook his head and declared, "The attempted coup leaves me unharmed. Yet I have irritation of throat. Attend me".

He seated himself upon one of the hospital beds and the surgeon took a spatula and looked down his commander's throat.

"Inflamed", he declared, "Onset of distemper, probably cold. Take remedy and return if not relieved".

The surgeon thought no more of it when two more senior commanders aboard the vessel also sought out his ministrations within the next half-hour. Such was the nature of virus that can survive the outermost regions of vacuous space, then thrive when larger being chance to happen upon them. An hour later, it was plain that an epidemic was beginning on the vessel. Even so, the surgeon did not panic. He roused his three assistants but did not feel it was the beginning of something he could not resolve.

Then the Tribune returned. His eyes streamed as did his nostrils and he was being brought low by a racking cough. The surgeon opened the albescent ward. Turned on all the monitoring equipment and insisted the Tribune take bed number one. Within the next hour, thirteen beds were occupied, the hospital only possessed fourteen. An hour after that bodies lay in the corridor outside the hospital. That was not the worst of it though!. The Tribune's skin had begun to blister. As such abscesses burst, they exuded a foul smelling ichor that in addition to puss contained elements that the surgeon could not identify under the power of his miconoscopes. He came to the only possible conclusion that his learning dictated. The disease was from Völkerezég and the Ambassador had brought it aboard. Without Spriznimołodi's body' he could not create cultures and even hope to begin the creation of a vaccine. Such was even beyond the immense macro-brain of the ship's computer.

The Sit Amet had cooked the entire corpse at high temperature with suitable spices and flavourings there was nothing left that could be of use to the surgeon for the offal had gone in the incinerator. Tribune Peter's lungs began to fill with his own leaking blood after three hours from his initial visit. Despite the surgeons every effort and those of the machines available to him, the Tribune died an agonizing death that conventional painkillers could not lessen. He was by no means the first so to expire.

What Spriznimołodi had done was, once aboard the dart, he had snapped a tiny glass phial and let the fluid contained inside soak against his wrist. From that moment he was infected by Valusandricfebricitantis the disease of the planets deep swamps. On Völkerezég thousands had been scythed down by it before a vaccine had been finally perfected. Even it was not one hundred percent effective and those Völkerezégi unfortunate to contract it each summer still only had a one in five chance of surviving. Spriznimołodi, the hero of the entire planet had carried no such vaccine anyway. He knew he was on a suicide mission. His breath and moisture from his arms and gills were toxic by the time he was taken aboard the humans' ship. He was the carrier that would end the planned invasion. Not just that one but any other sent against them also. For if other human vessel found their way into orbit around Völkerezég in the future they would be sure to explore the Balbinus too. The life of the Valusandricfebricitantis virus needed no air, food, or moisture to survive. It would wait and when warm mammalian bodies returned to the ship it would strike again ad infinitum.

Festering heaps of blood and puss now inhabited the human vessel. It possessed energy weapons of terrible power, yet none could be used. A planet without any form of weaponry what so ever had brought the might of the human Empire to heel.

Five

The second story of the evening had certainly supplied Stallone with food for thought. There were so many designer pets to choose from since Hoyle's genetic splicing had made it possible to unite the DNA of any number of animals at any one time. Consumers seemed to prefer cross-breeds to more exotic combinations, however. Of all these, the most popular by far was still the Dag. There were myriad possibilities with dogs and cats because mankind already knew the various breeds so well. The most frequently appearing Dag in homes on Venus was the Mogterr. Simply a terrier crossed with a cat of combined breeds.

Stallone's eyes felt gritty with all the reading. By way of calming his mind, he slipped on his lightweight mask and slipped out of the outer airlock. While he stood simply observing the still strangely unfamiliar terrain he could not stop thinking about the possibility of letting a pet finish off Madchen. He smiled at the ludicrous notion of obtaining a hugely exorbitant Lamger. He could just hear the conversation with the comb-men now:-

"No, Inspector, when I bought a Tiger crossed with a Lama the last thing I expected was that he would turn on my wife and eat her. Madchen must have been teasing Algenoni again. I had warned her it was playing with fire".

The hangman's noose would be created in orange and black striations just for him!

The pet would certainly have to be something innocuous that was for certain. Perhaps a Parrtoise. They were said to move with languid reptilian legs and the squawking would certainly get on Madchen's nerves He could maybe get the bizarre hybrid to learn to caw,

"It was an accident. She tripped over my shell".

He could try a Girrararoo. Apet that would jump around at the top of the stairs and possibly trip Madchen with its long neck. The only trouble with them was the fact that they simply refused to be house-trained. Neither of them would fancy cleaning up after one.

The more cumbersome and aggressive cross-species had to be caged, especially the Rhinrilla, that had to have a reinforced duridium construction.

"I'm truly sorry, Inspector, but who could have possibly suspected that Reorge would have learned the combinations to the cage door and let himself out while I was on a trip. I'm still shaking at the thought of all that blood and I'm still finding bits of my dearly departed wife in different rooms. Most upsetting".

Stallone lit a med-cig, in order to keep it so he had to smoke it quickly. It was time for bed.

The following morning he was forced to endure breakfast with the ever fainéant Madchen. The latest release of the Daily Otioss was available on her i-Pad and she flipped straight to the gossip pages. Stallone held his breath and waited for the initial banality. It did not take long,

"Ooh, Brando Gable has had to go into Byron General to have an ingrowing toe-nail removed".

It pleased Stallone to make the whole nightmare farcical with equally mind-numbing observations.

"I wondered where they'd situated his recent and secretive brain transplant. It sounds like the transplant rejected him".

"I don't remember reading about that", Madchen remarked, no hint of sarcasm in her tone, "Are you sure it was Brando Gable. You know he was in that remake of the sea-faring drama *Much Ado on the Crunchie*".

"I remember seeing the trailers, but did you know they were using a dummy for Gables parts as he was on holiday on Callisto at the time. I actually thought the dummy was the less rigid and wooden actor and they should have used it for the entire feature".

"Are you making that up"?

"Absolutely not".

They continued to eat their Whee-ties in thoughtful silence but the amazingly delicious and nutritional bite-sized protein and vitamin-packed parcels of pure wheat did not keep Madchen quiet for long.

"Roxanne Jossa has finally had her baby".

"Really, subnormal was it"?

"That's not a nice thing to ask".

"I was just thinking of its chances as determined by its genetic pool that's all".

Madchen bristled, "That's not fair, her husband who's Boreanaz Hasselhoff actually has degrees".

"That's true", Stallone was beginning to enjoy himself, "But only when having his temperature checked ha ha ha".

"I won't tell you any more of the news if you're going to ensnare the ordure".

"Sorry! So how is the Venuser-Earth political situation, are relationships still tense"?

"Oh you know I'm not interested in that dry stuff. I like reading about real people, not politicians".

Stallone had to grudgingly admit that his dullard of a contractee had a point with that observation. He had finished by then. Excusing himself he went into his office and stared for a moment at his latest bottle creation. Was what he did so vitally important anyway? Perhaps he considered it useful employment, but his contractee was contributing less to recyclable carbon products than he! In the ultimate scheme of things would Dustin Stallone bottle designer be revered as a great man who should be committed to history.

The writers of Murder Through the Ages (ed Darcy Sardon) that he was reading

had gained a better shot at immortality than he. Or had they? Were they not left mouldering on a shelf in some forgotten museum also? It was with these sober contemplations that Stallone began work and what he produced that morning would never make its way onto the market. Who wanted a bottle of shampoo like looked like liquid death for the scalp?

He imagined the sales-pitch:-

Tired of all the time and money you spend on your hair? Sick of the last minute rush to look just right before you go out? Well here at Orang-U-Can we've listened to over 20,000 consumers and we've gone back into our super expensive laboratories in search of a solution just for you. After months of industrious research, we've found the answer…

It's a new shampoo called Valde Malus. One wash with Valde Malus and you'll immediately start to realise the benefits of continued use. Yes! By the time you're on only your third ergonomically designed squeeze-eezi tube, all your problems will be gone. No more bad hair days. No more expensive and time-consuming trips to the barber. No more hair.

Then, of course, the fine print. There was always fine print tucked away on the back of the tube so that the average consumer would never read it:-

Any connection to use of this product and the high incidences of brain tumours is vehemently denied by the makers of this specially tested preparation. The corporation of Orang-U-Can exhaustively field tested Valde Malus on over 1000 specially selected molluscs prior to release. Not one of them has complained of so much as an itchy scalp never mind problems of concentration. Remember to do a scalp test on your own head before using this executive action shampoo. At the first sign of itching, flakiness or searing agonising pain, seek medical help by a trained professional - at once. Do not attempt to do a scalpectomy yourself or you will negate your rights to a full refund.

Though fun, this was getting him nowhere. He was neither working nor using his time to construct the perfect and permanent removal of his annoying and dull partner. Plainly he was not in the mood for serious work. He, therefore, may as well read another story from the wood-mulch volume. Selecting a snack from a hoard only he knew the existence of he readjusted his seat and opened the book...

Blue silk

ONICHEN BLOOS

"I love you. I need you to be mine. Only mine."

It took a few minutes for his eyes to become accustomed to the darkness. The failed light his tidy office had surrendered to. He could still feel the burning touch of her lips on his body. He had fallen in love with Sara. She that was nothing more than a personalised operating system. It had been his first projection into the virtual reality application. It had been a success and also a tragic failure.

Together with his wife, Doctor Margot Bloom, he had spent the last five years developing it. Feeding a constant and massive collection of data into the system. Their joint project was based on the hypothesis that artificial intelligence was able to evolve. Mature and advance while its users still maintained control over it. From thousands of literary texts, their private emails, messages and journal entries, Sara (the name Margot had given it) learned about human emotions. Its thought process, slowly developing a rudimentary consciousness.

Connected to all their devices, Sara was omnipresent and constantly learning. Through electronic bracelets, it recorded visual and audio. Additionally their vital signs in correspondence with each interaction they experienced. If they went to a lunch with friends, the system read their body's reactions; contentment, positivity, pleasure, annoyance. Whilst meeting with the scientific research board, the results were vastly different. Showing high levels of stress and frustration.

Minuscule, wireless ear-pieces enabled communication. They nurtured the programme as one does with an infant. Teaching it about the world - human relationships. When Doctor Stein offered them the opportunity to implant Sara into the VR application he had been constructing, Lance and Margot were equally excited and nervous. They began to feel like loving parents meeting their new-born baby. Before switching on their VR glasses, they had whispered,

"I love you," to each other. They interlocked their hands.

Every detail of that first meeting was still vivid in Lance's memory. Against the foaming sea and cobalt sky, a mesmerizing, dream-like apparition coalesced and took form. In the early, deliquesce sunlight, Sara's long, dark, wavy hair glistened. She seemed surrounded by an almost eerie aura. Her alabaster skin seemed to taunt the golden sand with its winning contrast. Like a sublime symphony of silk, her blue, suave dress caressed her long, slender legs. Stretching, pale fingers brushed rebel hair strands away from her perfectly bow-shaped lips.

The desire to feel those hands unravel his deepest hidden secrets of passion overwhelmed Lance. They threatened to consume his entire being. He blinked fearfully was such a miraculous programme possible of sustaining itself without decay? Or would this vision of pulchritude regrettably disappear? Suddenly, their glances toward one another were locked. With a shy smile, Sara gestured for him to approach her. Her features were bestowed with the symmetry of a Greek goddess.

Was this the face that launched a thousand ships and burnt the topless towers of Ilium? Had it not been for her voluptuous lips and the long, dark eyelashes framing her big, lilac coloured eyes, she would have appeared to be a marble statue. Cold and untouchable a figure that mere mortals could only stare at in wonder and awe.

"I missed you," she had said to him. "Touch me, don't be afraid."

Missed him? Had he written the anguish of separation into the programme? Or had it picked it up from the myriad sources available to it? Did any of that matter at that precise moment?

Trembling, his hand touched her cheek. Slowly he let it travel down her long neck. His fingers stroking her soft, supple skin. Any rational thought or worry dissolved in that instant. All he wanted was to hold her in his arms. To kiss her and to never let her go. She was the perfect Geisha. An electronic member of his secret harem. She could be anything he wanted. Concubine, courtesan, shy and giggling virgin. Though he loved Margot this creation could exceed her in all things imaginable. Would it really be a deceit if he experimented? In search of true VR, he had to explore every avenue surely?

With the elegance of a ballerina, Sara placed her arms around his neck. Fingers laced through his hair. She pulled him towards her slightly opened lips. Their tongues met in a carnal dance each trying to subjugate the other. A tingling, electrifying current seemed to burst through every single cell in his body. Against his chest, her luscious breasts gently rouse with each synthetic breath.

He could stand no more in that first encounter. Everything was too vivid. Too real! Exiting the application, his heart was pounding and his arms hung trembling by his sides.

Margot had appeared equally shaken.

Her perception of the programme had been entirely different, Sara had materialised into a pretty, little girl. A young female yes but a delightful child with blue silk ribbons in her golden, curly hair. She had possessed a cheeky, sweet smile, she had called Margot

"Mummy".

Their interaction had been one that any would expect between a mother and her young daughter. They had played with dolls and other toys. Sung nursery rhymes. Read children's stories.

"It felt real, Lance. That which we created," Margot had whispered to her husband. "Maybe too real…!"

Bloom, the man hadn't answered. Why had it been different for each of them? If anything, both of them should have enjoyed a similar experience. Where did it go wrong? Had it gone wrong? Clearly, the programme was working to acceptable parameters.

Sara was obviously a manifestation of their subconsciousness. Margot and he shared the deep desire to have a child of their own that was true. Passion had slightly faded with the years, even though they were happily married. Bloom loved his wife. He had never craved for an extra-conjugal love affair. So why, in his case, had Sara chosen to take the shape of a beautiful woman? Why had he returned such a burning passion for her? It was almost as if the artificial intelligence had taken control over his mind, instead of the other way around. Was their construct right in its deductions of their individual needs? Until he understood what had triggered this discrepancy, he was going to keep the recounted information vaguely to a miniMum.

He poured himself a small glass of whiskey from the mahogany cabinet. The furniture was a birthday gift from Margot. Lance suddenly reflected that his wife hadn't arrived despite the hour. Recently, she had been returning home later and later. Spending more and more time at their laboratory. Of course, he knew how passionate Margot was about her work. He was just the same. It was undoubtedly the main reason he had fallen in love with her in the first place. They both shared an incredible lust for knowledge. Between them, they had invested hundreds of hours for different projects. Studies, research and they had both agreed that all the sacrifices they had made along the way had been necessary. But still, why was she so tardy?

That night, he had left the lab whilst she was still making some changes to the database. Margot had insisted he go and get some sleep. Was she meeting someone? Surely she was not having an affair? The notion caused him to him laugh aloud. Margot was the most faithful, loving and honest person he had ever met. Maybe his feelings of guilt had been subconsciously transferred to her. The only one who had been unfaithful… was him. Sara! Deep inside, he felt icy-cold thrust of regret and guilt. It caused him to shudder.

***

"Don't concern yourself with the minutiae. We'll sort that out later on. What is important is that we are together. My dear sweet love, are you willing to kill for me or not?"

"I don't know", Lance answered the VR.

***

The first light of the day spread across the patterned carpet in Doctor Stein's office. Heavy with leather-covered volumes. Wooden bookshelves covered every wall except the one that harboured three ceiling-high windows. Backed against the far left corner a sumptuous desk resided. In front of it, two crimson armchairs had been carefully placed. Students often visited him in his office, eager for his guidance. Over the last few days, his door had been locked. Buried in silence, he had spent countless hours reading through his colleagues' logs. He was convinced that an explanation for the tragic events that had claimed the lives of Lance and Margot Bloom was hidden somewhere within the system.

They had been his closest friends since university. Stein had witnessed them falling in love, getting married and becoming renowned scientists. Every Christmas he had been invited to their elegant, Victorian house situated outside of the city. While he and Lance had played cards, Margot had entertained his partner for the evening. Laughter, scientific debates and delicious food had been the norm. They had been the perfect couple, but since their operating system had been uploaded into his VR program, he had noticed a change in their behaviour.

The couple had grown secretive, almost unnaturally so. Then they started coming to his lab separately, using different pretexts. Their relationship had grown awkward, stilted, filled with confusion. Finally, Lance had confided in him about his virtual affair with Sara. His fear that the artificial intelligence had acquired the power to manipulate its users. He had been distraught at the thought of causing any kind of harm to Margot. The last time Stein had met him, he had been prepared to demolish the entire system. To put an end to what he called 'This psychological torment'!

The following morning, Stein had received a phone call. The voice on the other end of the receiver announced in a solemn voice, that Doctor Lance Bloom and his wife had been found dead in their laboratory!

He was summoned for an informal interview. Walking down to the police station, Stein struggled to comprehend what could have happened. He felt as if he was walking through a surreal parallel layer of reality or dream. A fantasy from which he was going to eventually wake.

Lance and Margot dead?

How?

Why?

His mind simply couldn't fathom such a reality. The detectives questioned him on every aspect of their lives. He was told that Margot had gunpowder residue on her hands and that the gun that Lance had been shot with had her fingerprints on it. Stein knew that something was tremendously wrong. In Margot's case, the medical examiner was puzzled. There were no visible wounds or signs of a struggle. The chemical analysis revealed no poisonous substances in her tissue. Ultimately, the cause of death was ruled as "unknown". The police inspector, one of his golf partners. Stein obtained access to the photographs of the crime scene. At the sight of his friends' lifeless, yet strangely peaceful bodies, he had to turn his gaze away. Once the queasiness had subsided, he analysed each image. To his horror, he noticed that Margot still had the VR glasses on. Lance had collapsed next to the main server. Had his friend tried to shut the operating system down? Had Margot tried to stop him? But why?

Margot had never exhibited any signs of violence before. Besides the occasional road rage, she had always been rational and balanced. Neither had carried a gun. Two years previously, after an incident during which one of the laboratories on the second floor had been broken into, Lance had decided to purchase a small revolver. He kept it locked in the safe situated in the laboratory. Margot hadn't accepted its presence lightly, but he managed to convince her that is was there just as an extra protection against unforeseen dangers. What could have pushed this highly intelligent and empathic woman to use the firearm on her own husband? Or maybe the entire scene had been staged. By whom and for what reason?

Stein finished viewing the last file in the database. No new information had revealed itself. And to access the main server was impossible. Police had taken everything into custody, awaiting forensic examination. Tormented, he noticed the unopened envelope on the far side of his desk. He was listed as their sole emergency contact. Due to the absence of any known family members. The police inspector had handed him the couple's personal belongings: their wedding rings, Margot's golden necklace with the Yin and Yang pendant and earrings, Lance's watch and lighter.

Spread out in front of him, like ancient artefacts, they conjured up flashbacks from a different lifetime. When Lance had asked him to be his best man, Stein had felt overwhelmed. Designated safe-keeper of the rings, on their wedding day, he had handed them over to the nervous groom and graceful, dazzling bride. During her thirtieth birthday party, Margot had blushed like a teenager when she had opened the tiny box that Lance had sneaked to her under the table. She used to say that as the black and white swirls of the Taoist symbol, she was the darkness that needed Lance's brightness to feel complete. She had worn the necklace ever since. The year before, Lance had surprised her with matching earrings.

The only item Stein wasn't familiar with, was the silver rocket-shaped lighter. Lance had never smoked. Why would he carry a lighter?

Unless… The external drive flashed to life.

'Sara, my sweet little Sara. I will do anything in my power to protect you, my baby. Daddy will never hurt you again. I promise. Come, lay down next to me. Let Mummy tell you a story.'

Six

Stallone was amazed by the story even if it was not actually pertinent to his problem. What would it be like to make love to the perfect woman? Of course, Sara was perfect. She had been drawn from Lance's own thoughts. Every single attribute that he found desirable she possessed. Little wonder his situation had been instantly helpless. It was not helping Stallone. He did not have VR. If he had he would have directed Sara to kill Madchen for him and then spent the rest of his life in a chair with the visor over his eyes.

He went into the main part of the apartment to fix himself some lunch. Of his obtuse partner, there was no sign. Probably gone to the nail-parlour, hairdresser of simply window shopping again. A bottle designer was on a pretty good salary - fortunately. In addition to every other failing Madchen was high maintenance. He had to admit she remained good in bed. There was more to life though. Sometimes one needed a decent conversation afterwards. In addition to stimulation of the body one required stimulation of the mind.

The two of them never did anything together. They shared no interests. While he liked to collect ancient coins, she found it dreadfully dull. She was more interested in emptying the bank account with as much haste as possible. She possessed dozens of pairs of shoes. Yet she only had two feet. Over a score of hats to fit on a single head. Handbags in their multitude that only fit over one arm. Her section of the fitted wardrobe they shared grew progressively greater. Correspondingly he could not, therefore, get his few meagre belongings in it any more. Some items now resided in his office.

She had to go. He simply could not afford her any more. Did not have room for her. Never spoke to her except sarcastically. The only time she was satisfactory was when they were fluttering. Maybe the next yarn in the ancient grimoire would provide him with the right sort of inspiration for his own crime?

The Heart of the Matter

PATRICK KASTELL

"Would you be willing to kill for me"?

"Sorry, would I what"? John could not believe she had come out with this bizarre question. They had met at a dance club, with no intention of doing anything other than enjoying the rhythm and excitement that came with moving to the music.

She was tall, not beautiful, but as sexy as hell! She had a good dress sense and drew attention whenever she made an entrance to the dance venue. He thought she was out of his league. When she told him she was married, he felt a stab of disappointment. The strange thing was that week after week they danced together. It was not long before they became lovers. He did not feel particularly guilty about having an affair with a married woman. He was living for the moment and to hell with the consequences.

When she posed the question about taking someone's life, they were in the afterglow of the sexual storm.

"This killing business", he asked, "Have you got anyone in mind"? She grinned in the dark, answering,

"My husband".

"You are joking!", he replied, realizing that she was not joining in with the humour.

"He's a swine, won't give me a divorce, and he's abusive".

"Why did you marry him", he asked, not unreasonably.

"He's rich, and I wanted the lifestyle. Now I've met you I can't go back to my pointless existence. I'm a bird in a gilded cage".

"Darling", he replied, "You know I love you. My life is so exciting now. That's down to you, but I can't take someone's life – not that I would know how to".

"Just think about it", she urged. "He will never give me a divorce, and I so want to be with you!".

When he was on his own, he pondered the question as an academic exercise. How do you go about murdering someone? Not only do you have to choose the method, but you have to make sure the deed cannot be traced back to you. All the obvious methods – shooting – poison – employing a third party have great risks involved. Pushing the victim over a cliff, drowning them, who would the police investigate in the first instance? The wife, of course, she would have the most to gain.

Does she have a secret life, a lover perhaps? Once it is known that her marriage had not been good. Then, the police would have a possible starting point. Was the victim rich, who stood to gain from his demise? The more he thought about it the more concerned he became. He could quite imagine that he could be accused of being an accomplice or even the main perpetrator.

There was no doubt about it, the sex was good. Up until the point that she had shaken him with this murder business, he had seriously been considering her as a permanent partner. He wrote down all the details of his conversation with Jane. Sealed it into an envelope and next day posted it to himself. Just really as a form of protection, just in case! With the information sealed in the envelope, he could show that he was innocent of any collusion.

It was a sunny afternoon. George James, her husband, had announced he would be playing golf and staying at the club for dinner. He had also made it obvious he was not concerned whether she came with him - or not. He bustled through the door of their six bedroomed country house. A golf bag over his shoulder. Then climbed into his ostentatious Italian sports car scattering gravel all over the place, Accelerating until he disappeared at the end of the drive onto the small country road that led to the golf club T.

'*Thank God for that*', she thought. Feeling that familiar sense of relief wash over her whenever she found herself alone. Later she lay with John, her lover. While the rain lashed down against the windows of his cosy little bedroom. She grinned in the dark hoping her husband was wading up to his neck through the mud at the golf course. What a conceited self-satisfied pig he was.

She was aware of the problems she had in disposing of him. It caused her to come to a conclusion. In order to avoid any blame being attached to her, it would have to appear to be a tragic accident. She had not mentioned her plans to John. His initial reaction to her question;

"Would you be willing to kill for me", had been so shocked. Causing her to realise that she was on her own. Sharing her problem with him had been a mistake. Now there was someone who was aware of her intentions.

The road to her husband's golf club was lined with trees. Designed to help keep the road clear of snow in the winter. On the way to the club, which was about seven miles away there were two sharp bends. George always took these at high speed. Expecting anyone coming the other way to take avoiding action to get out of his way. He had become successful at business by being ruthless. That had involved taking advantage of peoples' trust. With that, he had clawed his way to a small fortune and becoming intensely disliked in the process.

It was while Jane had been lying with her lover John that the image of her husband tearing down their drive had come into her mind. Could this love of speed be his vulnerable point? He had no idea of the depth of hatred he had generated in her. He felt that all women were good only for sex, nothing else. Having this attractive woman on his arm enhanced his reputation amongst his business contacts. It generated a certain amount of envy, which, to him, was what marriage was all about. He could not believe that anyone else could take his place. Didn't he give her everything? Clothes, travel, a social life, her own car, an allowance. To him, she was another possession, like the car or the house.

George James had a chip on his shoulder. He had left secondary modern school at the age of fifteen years. With no qualifications, no prospects. He realised even then that money gave one status. He took the only route open to him to earn a decent sum and began to deal drugs. He made himself known to the local dealer. Started by carrying small packages around town. He was given a commission on what he delivered. Unknown to the police, he escaped under their radar and became a useful carrier. The money he earned was very good. Ten times more than people of his own age, serving so-called apprenticeships in the local supermarkets.

During one delivery he ran across Julie. She was clever, a businesswoman who took drugs for recreational purposes. She was rich and successful and could afford to buy whatever took her fancy. George took her fancy. She moved him into a flat and lavished many gifts upon him. Clothes, expensive jewellery and educated him in all manner of things. He was only seventeen years of age.

George was a quick learner. Through Julie, he learned the art of organising and running a business. Not only was he her sex partner, but she delighted in how quick he was in grasping the basics of good business. Successful negotiation, good bookkeeping and eventually he was set up running a small furniture business. After a few years with the aid of out of town shopping and free credit, he had eight shops. The business was then bought out by a national retailer. After paying off Julie, he had £750,000 pounds left. He had also learned to present a public face. One of benevolence, but in private he remained totally ruthless.

Julie had moved on. All the usual trappings came his way; the house, a fancy car, expensive holidays and of course the trophy wife. He regarded her as just another possession he had acquired. She was taken in by his veneer of sophistication and his expensive lifestyle. It took her a year to realise she was nothing more to him than just another of his expensive toys. Something he could show off and display as another example of how well he had done for himself. It afforded him the respectability he required to succeed. George did not concern himself from one week to another with her conduct, as long as she was available to accompany him on social occasions. During several celebrations of his latest business successes. Such was his conceit and arrogance that he could not imagine his wife being anything but totally dependant upon him.

His car was, a very expensive Maserati, a superb piece of engineering. It stood outside their country house, the paintwork gleaming in the sun. He loved the smell of expensive leather. The new car smell that seemed to hang around this vehicle forever. He bathed in the reaction the Maserati caused whenever he arrived at his destination. Unbeknown to his wife, the specification included state-of-the-art electronics, every safety device yet invented. So the master plan she had conceived was an attack on the tyres. Such an incursion would then be picked up and a warning instantly flashed to the driver.

He had recently been under extreme pressure from the tax authorities regarding his avoidance which had just been exposed by the Financial Times newspaper. While the scheme was not illegal, it was immoral. Some of his more prominent investors were concerned about their own reputation being affected.

The chest pains he had suffered recently had been put down to indigestion and overwork. He had never-the-less seen a consultant. An ordeal he hated with a passion, for it meant surrendering control of his very life to another. Various tests were conducted there had been questions about his lifestyle, diet, several other less savoury topics. As usual, the doctors refused to give him any straight answers even when all the answers were in. He did not mention it to his wife, there was currently no love-loss between them.

He also failed to share the information that drugs were taken on a regular basis.

He decided to drive down to the club. Have a few drinks. Stay in one of the rooms that could be hired and perhaps have a quick blast of drugs to cheer himself up. He had no idea of the depth of hatred he had generated in his wife. Feeling that all women were good for was opening their legs. Having an attractive woman by his side enhanced his reputation, nothing more. He continued to like having her on his arm. Adding to his prestige amongst his business contacts. Making them envious, that was all marriage was about.

He could not believe that anyone else could supplant him in her affections. Did he not give her everything, clothes, travel, a social life, her own car, an allowance. She was simply another possession, like the car or the house. After only two years she had realised he demeaned her. She had become his chattel.

The annual golf club dance was due soon. She would use the venue to make a display of affection for George. Needing to establish that the marriage which she detested, was to all intents and purposes warm and affectionate.

Anyone investigating a resultant death would not then have their suspicions aroused or so she hoped! She invested in a gown by Giorgio Armani. It's simple but classic lines suited her slim figure. Making her look sensational. The night of the big event came around. George, as usual, drove at high speed with scant regard for other road users. Jane was terrified but said nothing. When they arrived, she took a little time to regain her composure. Joining him, she held his arm as they made their entrance.

The night proved a huge success for them both. George had circulated around the floor carefully displaying Jane so that the men, in particular, could envy him. She, in turn, put up with his proprietary attitude, smiled at all the right people, made polite but boring conversation. At the end of the evening, she was at the point of screaming, endless conversations that had filled her with ennui. On the outside, she maintained her calm demeanour and was all sweetness and light. Behind her back, there were a few catty remarks about her. Mainly by the women, motivated more by envy than dislike. After all her husband had the money and position in the city. One or two of the ladies felt very provincial when compared to Jane's splendour.

The following week Jane recalled the ghastliness of the whole evening while lying alongside her lover John. She had already decided there could be no long-term future with John - lovely as he was. She was attracted by men with power and position neither of which John had, he would not last. Her long-term partner had to possess both in great quantity.

The following week Jane and George were to go to the Isle of Wight.

There was a group of people all acquaintances, all roughly of the same social position. All of them owning reasonably sized yachts. The group were not sailors. When they left the harbour, the man stood steadfastly at the wheel while wives or girlfriends bustling around on desk coiling ropes and pulling in fenders. What identified them as fakers were the brand-new designer clothes. The husband, the wife and even the little children were there and looked like an advertisement in yachting monthly. What they actually did was sail up and down the stretch of water between the Isle of Wight and the mainland before returning back to the harbour, still looking stoic and much tired by sunshine and sea.

Yarmouth, not to be confused with Great Yarmouth was the harbour from which the weekend sailors set out. It was directly alongside the ferry dock. The first thing holidaymakers saw on arriving was a quaint little collection of streets from a gentler age. Needless to say, the properties there had long since been swept up and turned into holiday shops. It was an art form to fill up such shops with products that one really did not need. Even the one and only antique shop struggled to display anything not produced in China! Yet it possessed a quaintness and character all its own. It was there that Jane considered pushing George overboard. She eventually concluded that even if she could part him from his life jacket, there was so much traffic in the immediate area, there was every possibility that he would be rescued. Leaving her with a lot of awkward explanations to make.

They returned home. Despite the pressure of trying to find a way of doing away with George, she felt refreshed. Ready to reapply herself to her problem. It seemed to her that the major dilemma was to somehow turn suspicion away from herself. As far as George's money was concerned, he had used her to sign a document transferring all his assets to her name to reduce his tax bill. He believed she did not understand the implications of the various forms he had her sign. She was not that simple!

She was becoming more frustrated by the need for a foolproof way of committing murder. Every idea she had was accompanied by a downside. Every action she took would inevitably lead back to her. She was virtually on the point of giving up when it occurred to her that his weak point was his beloved car. The vehicle was his Achilles heel. Was his obsession with the speed the answer she was looking for? Immediately she started to consider the alternatives.

She did not have the mechanical skills to adjust the brakes or affect the accelerator pedal. Besides which, any alteration to the mechanical operations of the car would be picked up by the police or the insurance investigators. It was no good expecting to get away with such an obvious action?

What the hell was she going to do? He would not divorce her. If she just left, something she had considered then her entire lifestyle would disappear. She was still young enough and beautiful enough to find another rich husband. It was just that everything was perfectly aligned in her present situation. She knew that his company was in her name. If he died she would become the legal owner of everything. It was now or face a life of being patronised and dominated.

A week later the day was pleasantly sunny but fresh. She had taken, Rusty, the red setter out for a walk. Upon returning saw the Italian sports car parked at the side of the house. She stood staring at the gleaming machine, visualizing her detested husband tearing off down the drive. As usual, filled with notions of his own status and importance.

It was then the idea came to her. If she could affect his tyres without him noticing, there was a possibility he could lose control. Especially on the very tight bends between their house and the golf club. Who was to say it was anything but an accident? How to do so that was the question? She dare not involve a third party. Her desperation when trying to involve lover John had shocked and horrified him! She realised then that it had been a mistake. She would have to think about that matter in more detail. Meanwhile, there was the question of how to affect her husband's ability to control the car. She decided she had to do something to the tyres, but how?

The following week she and her husband attended a social ball. A classic case of big fish in a small pond. She drank more than she should have due to the pressure she was under. Trying to find a way of doing your husband fatal harm can put one under pressure. That evening upon their return home, they enjoyed a blazing row. He told her in no uncertain terms that she was, '*Becoming a major pain*'! Unless she changed her attitude, he would divorce her and leave her with nothing! She responded by calling him a contemptible little swine before storming off to the spare room. One of six. If she had been in any doubt about putting her plan into action his domineering and arrogant behaviour firmed up her determination to do so.

It was not long after that incident that she came across the tool for the job. It was nothing more than a nail with a sharp point at one end. Probably used by someone for carpentry around the house. All she had to do was position the pointed end into the tyre which in a bizarre way she found exciting. The satisfaction of doing something to fight back made her feel very powerful. The idea was that it would penetrate the underside of the tyre letting out small amounts of air. It would then become unstable and hopefully, burst or tear making keeping control of the car very very difficult if not impossible. In her lack of mechanical knowledge lay the weakness of her plan. She was not to know that her husband's car had various warning devices specifically to inform him of malfunctions. Such as the fact that the car was becoming unsafe before the lack of air in the tyre would have the effect she desired.

She stood at the bedroom window behind the large curtain and watched until he disappeared from view. Now the deed was done, nerves began to surface. What if he found the nail? Would he realise it was deliberate? Would he associate the item as connected specifically to her? They had commissioned an extension of wood and glass to the garden side of the house. It had only been completed the month before. It was from the site that she had found the large carpenters nail. She would blame the builders for dropping it on the drive if he suspected her of being guilty. She could find herself if things got really awkward being accused of attempted murder. She lay in the dark starting to be afraid of the consequences of her now seemingly rash actions. Finally, sleep came to her. She awoke with a start as the bedroom telephone began to ring.

The car of his choice was a Maserati Quattroporte. The model had been relaunched in 2003. More powerful than its predecessor. It boasted a top speed of 156 mph. Carried every known safety device yet conceived. The car was widely regarded as a modern classic. A fine blend of luxury and high speed which made it highly sought after.

She who was not interested in the finer points of mechanics had conceived a plan that was doomed to failure. But he had pulled up to the roadside a few miles distant with violent chest pains There a massive heart attack had given him the very same fate she had hoped for.

The phone-call was direct and to the point. The caller was very sorry, but despite all the efforts of the medical team called to the scene her husband had been found dead. She made the right noises and then took a taxi to the hospital.

Her mind was racing, no one had said how he had died. Had it been self-inflicted by his reckless driving? Had her plan worked? The nail the fatal nail that caused a deadly accident. She did not give a damn, he was dead and out of her life. Pulling herself together, to play the grief-stricken widow she appeared to others as dealing with her grief bravely.

The staff at the hospital were very kind. A small private room for just such an eventuality was provided. A very sympathetic doctor assured her that her husband could not have suffered. Everyone she left was impressed with her dignity under such trying circumstances. Once away, not to be seen, she let out a yell of satisfaction.

He was gone!

It was all hers, the house, the business, the bank balance. She felt fiercely satisfied. The insurance investigator submitted his report. Regarding the fatality of Mr James in a Maserati on the road to the Hampshire golf course – death by natural causes. The section regarding a six-inch nail found in a front tyre was dismissed as coincidental. After all, there had been no crash, James had pulled up with chest pains.

A young detective had been in his appointment for three weeks. Promoted from the uniformed ranks due to his arrest rate which had been excellent. His successes had drawn the attention of C.I.D. So he was given the case to look at. The Chief Inspector was in the middle of a drug investigation which looked very promising. CID had the right evidence on video and good surveillance coverage of the main suspects.

When the report came through regarding James tyre simply considered routine by the insurance claims adjuster, it was regarded as a distraction. Thus it was given to the new lad. To give him some experience with CID procedures.

When Jane received the 'phone call from Wensure Police Station, her blood ran cold. The voice at the other end was reassuring.

"Nothing to worry about", said the voice, "Just one or two matters to clear up. Perhaps I could make an appointment to come and see you".

She wanted this pressure eased as soon as possible. It was agreed the young detective would see her at 11.00 am the next day. Should she telephone her solicitor? Why? It would only seem suspicious. Better to be co-operative.

The young detective sat opposite her. Like a lot of men before him, he was impressed by Jane. *'Must keep my mind on the job'*, he thought. There were the usual preambles, offers of refreshment. He finally got to the point of his visit. He was very sorry to have to raise this point at such a difficult time for her. The fact was a six-inch nail had been found embedded in the underside of her husband's tyre. Did she have any idea how it could have got there? She looked at the young detective quizzically. She had practised this moment in anticipation.

"Why are you asking me about nails and tyres when I've just lost my husband in tragic circumstances. I really think you should go and find some criminals to catch, Young Man".

She arose, went towards the door.

"So, you think the nail and your husband's death are in no way connected"? He tried as he walked towards the door.

"The hospital told me the result of my husband's death was a massive coronary young man. I am satisfied with their conclusion, so good day to you".

What neither she nor the young detective did not know was that the police had already received a testament from Mrs James' lover. It claimed she had suggested to him that she wanted her husband murdered. When he was told he realised he had made several mistakes born of ignorance. It had been far too early to be interviewing her. He should have given her the opportunity to have her solicitor present. One thing his instincts told him, she was guilty for certain. Call it a sixth sense, but his uncanny knack of knowing when someone was lying had got him this far in his short career.

One the way back to his car, he noticed a gardener working away at the flower beds. Once the detective started to question the man, a few facts started to emerge. Jim, the gardener was not too happy to be questioned by a detective about the death of his deceased employer. He made quite certain that he emphasised the fact that the driveway was swept every day. If a nail or any other rubbish had been there it would certainly have been found and disposed of. The house had a new extension to the rear of the conservatory. Mostly wood and glass. True there had been a certain amount of clearing up still to do by the builders, but Jim could not see how he would have missed anything as large as a nail.

The detective was feeling doubt growing in his mind about Mrs James. He had little to go on, no real evidence. Yet he was convinced that she had tried to murder her husband. He returned to the station and was called over to the detective sergeant's desk.

"You're not doing badly, Son are you? We've only had you a couple of days and already we've received a complaint from Mrs James' Solicitor. His client, at a time when she is deeply shocked by the death of her husband, was aggressively questioned by you this morning it seems. A petty issue about a nail or some such nonsense. In future, any further questions should be handled with her solicitor present. Tell me, Detective, what the hell are you up to"?

Detective Hardy took a deep breath and began to explain. He told the sergeant what he had learned that morning and how he sensed Jane's guilt. It was then that he learned of the statement regarding her intention to kill her husband.

"You could well be right. We have the statement from one John Tatler. Despite that do not go near Mrs James again".

Next day during the morning conference and after the update of the drugs case, a brief announcement was made regarding the situation of Mr James' demise. The report from Mrs James' lover that she had openly discussed the possibility of having him murder her husband. Despite the nail, a subsequent autopsy had confirmed the doctors initial finding and the case was closed.

Jane replaced the telephone on its cradle and started to cry with relief. She was in the clear, it was all hers. However, there was still the question of what to do about John. Perhaps she could give some thought to how to remove *him* from the picture?

Seven

Time for some food. He was getting eye-strain and the beginnings of a headache. There was a surprise in store for him upon entering the kitchen. however. Madchen was back and they had a visitor,

"Vin's here, just arrived. I was going to shout you. I'm just making him a sandwich and some bits. Do you want the same"?

"That would be great. Thank you", he replied and went into the lounge to see his brother. Vin was Dustin's younger brother by four years, they were close as a result and visits by each were frequent.

They hugged without speaking, then asked how each was. Madchen became the perfect hostess. Silent, subservient and disappeared to allow the two men to enjoy guy talk.

"Did you see the fight on Monday night", Vin the sport's fan asked.

"Second half of it. I saw Janacek knocked out, good scrap".

They munched on their sandwiches for a few seconds before Dustin asked, "How's Petra"? She was Vin's five-year contractee.

"She's great everything's going fine. How are you and Madchen"?

"You must be getting close to expiry. What do the two of you intend to do"? The elder of the two ignored his brother's question.

Frowning slightly Vin said, "We are going to re-contract for another five. Obviously a mutual decision. You didn't answer my question though. Have things improved at all for you, Dustin"?

Dustin Stallone shook his head, "No. Venus knows I've tried, Vin. You know that. The trouble is Madchen is complacent about her lack of education. She won't do anything I ask of her to improve her mind. I got the learning hypno-programmes. She doesn't play them. I asked her to go to night-school. She thought it was a joke. Laughed at the notion. It's driving me around the twist".

"She seemed pleasant enough just now".

"Pleasant probably because she's maxed my current account out again. Pleasant isn't interesting anyway, is it? I actually feel lonely at times, Vin. It's like living with a badly programmed android. One of the early models".

"And you're determined not to divide everything and divorce"?

"Since we were married you know she hasn't worked? Should I give her half of everything *I've* earned? Does it seem fair to you"?

"You married her, Bro. I do sympathise, truly I do, but what do you expect then"?

"I expect to find an alternative way out of my predicament".

"Nothing immediately springs to mind though does it"?

A dark look came over Dustin's features and he confessed, "I a man with only one problem. The problem only has one solution, Vin. The problem is Madchen. The solution, her murder".

Vin sat bolt upright, "What? Are you out of your mind? You know capital punishment is still the favoured solution to killing someone in this sector".

"I'm not a vindictive man, Vin. I want her removal, though permanent, to be humane. If she'd simply walk away from the marriage, she could live. But she would want half of everything. I can't afford to divide this flat. I loved her when we first married. She was the one who insisted on marriage instead of contract. She has to die"!

Vin processed this devastating proclamation for several seconds before finally asking, "Do you have a plan then? An alibi figured out when the comb-men come calling"?

"One idea strikes me", Dustin smiled icily, "You could do her for me. Are you willing to kill her for me, Brother"?

Vin paled, "Venus knows I love you, Bro. Murder though, how would you want it done? Done in such a way as I wouldn't get caught either".

"Never mind the minutia, Vin. Would you be willing to kill her or not"?

"I know you're bored, Dustin, but this is crazy talk and you're worrying me".

"Then I guess you just gave me your answer".

"Venus yes I gave you my answer. As far as I'm conferenced Madchen is an attractive and pleasant woman. What do you take me for"?

"She's driving me nuts".

"Clearly".

"Cigarette"?

"I've given them up. Petra was never happy about me smoking near the kids".

"You'll do her next".

"Next! You're really going through with it"?

"Yes, I've found this little place see...".

"Don't tell me any more? I can't know. I don't want to be an accessory".

Dustin smiled coldly, "Does that mean that if you hear about her death. The comb-men come to question you, you'll say nothing"?

"I guess it does, but you're a zoid for involving me even as much as you have. Give me a cigarette".

Dustin passed the packet over, "I thought Petra...".

"Don't".

They sat smoking for the length of a med-cig each. Vin rose to leave, "I'm gonna get going".

Dustin complained, "You've only just gotten here".

"Yeah. Today you've rattled me though, Brother. I'll ping you next week. Then you can tell me you've hatched an alternative plan".

"Don't bank on it"!

Murder at 23:23 in 2323 on floor 23

BY GLORIA TRUBBSHORE

I hate going back to the apartment late at night when nobody's around. The corridors of the place are long and empty and the walls looked as though they wanted to collapse in on me like demented plaster talons. I wouldn't mind anyone else being there to see me too my door. Anyone except Ludo that is. Not Ludo, anybody in the world but him! When one overhead light is out it gives the corridor some shadows. Darker areas where things can lurk. Things like spiders, cockroaches, winnets, spectres and things worse than the worst thing I can think of. Or worse, things like Ludo. His hands are surprisingly soft, not especially large but they want to wrap themselves around my throat and squeeze and squeeze until the last ragged gasp burns my lungs and the black spots get larger and larger and... I just have to get down the corridor, find the door to my apartment get out of the damned corridor and then hide under the protective blankets of my bedding.

I'd turned on the television to fight the eerie silence, my rooms are cold with disuse, it takes them too long to warm up and they chill me before the gas fire transforms the frigidity to warmth. The clock looks down upon me with its blank face, the little hand and the big hand, big hands that are like Ludo's. Once I'm safely in my little place my nest of comfort I can stop being scared. What is happening to me? What happened tonight, just now. The fear that makes me all curdled and reasty inside, twisting me up spinning me into a feeling that makes me sick. I'd entered the lobby of the tower, just like every other night before. I'd walked over to the desk ....

"Hello, Mister Shandor, it's blowing cats and dogs out there tonight. Anything in my box"?

"Just one", he replied, "You've got a rent account notice, that's no sort of letter Lucille. How come you never get any letters? A nice Dame like you".

I ignored his snooping and repeated some lame diatribe regarding the weather. Then in a fit of conjured bravery, I observed candidly,

"I don't know why it is, Mister Shandor, but I sense that you don't actually care for me overmuch. Wanna deny it"?

"No", he'd replied honestly, "Why should I Lucille"?

"Now if you'll excuse me I have some other duties, I don't just sit here and...".

"Your a crisp limited goon, Shandor" I had flared. That's me always shooting off my big mouth, "I should report your crappy attitude to the manager and see how you like it. you've no right to diss me when I'm always bang on time with the rent. A fine way to treat paying tenant".

"Of course you pay your bills, you got a nice fat pay cheque when you split on Ludo like a squealing stooly".

"You eater of other people's leftovers", I'd let him have it then. "You're just a jumped up penny clicking clerk. Give me the envelope and then get about your oh so important duties".

I'd snatched it from him and then dashed for the lift. But in my going out heels, I nearly span butt over tit and had to cry out,

"Oy, Buster, hold the doors will you"? I trotted the best I could and repeated, "Hold those doors, I don't want them shutting in my face".

"Sorry, Miss Monroe", Curtis smiled as though he meant it the insincere sap.

"Yeah", I'd snapped back, "I think you are soo sorry, Burt".

The doors hissed closed and for a few seconds, we listened to the sighing mechanism of the car as it made its way up the cables. There was no muzak in the lift though so I had to break the silence before it got uncomfortable.

"Good evening, Burt. You should see it out there, it's absolutely pouring".

"Good evening, Miss Monroe", Curtis returned perfunctorily.

"I've just seen a brilliant flick at the Odeon 'Return of the Living Dead' starring that new up and coming actor Leonardo Pitt. He wasn't bad, not too hard on the eyes either. The programme changes tomorrow, so I can go again, it's a romance starring Lana Goddard. Do you like Lana Goddard, Burt"?

"I wouldn't kick her out of bed for breaking wind", Curtis smiled. That was him at his most charming.

"A lot of women don't like her. Jealousy I guess, with her coal-black hair, those huge brown eyes and her figure. I can see how they'd hate her for those things. I don't though. I mean why should I? I'm not so bad myself, I'm sure you'd agree, Burt"?

"You're very nice", he didn't sound overly enthusiastic though. Curtis was tall, mousey, but he had a quality that was quite fetching and a very infectious laugh. On a wild whim, I suddenly blurted,

"Well, I was planning to go see her tomorrow night if you...".

"Sorry Miss Monroe", he cut me off short the low-life, "I already have a date for tomorrow. A little redhead from over in Letherby. Pretty little thing and the things she can do with her.... Oh, excuse me".

"Well, I don't. I don't like that sort of talk. Just run the lift now. That's what you're paid for". That put him in his place. It was a long ride up to the twenty-third floor and when I got out I was glad of it. Even if I did find myself in the badly lit Corridor immediately afterwards. That's when the shakes start to claim me. Those crappy bulbs they use in the corridor just to save a few pennies, they make the place look like it's full of wet body waste. I was suddenly unsure of which way up was and it wasn't a dizziness that seemed to intend to go away any time soon. Any time? I looked at my watch twenty-three minutes past eleven. A coincidence that didn't hit me at the time, but I live in 2223 on the twenty-second floor.

The shakes were affecting me badly as I trotted down the bilious corridor, my high heels click-clacking a quick staccato. Everything looked the same but it also looked different in a way I could not quite put my finger on. My room was the end one of all, the outermost of the whole tower, which gave me a fabulous view over all Saxton Cross from one of my windows. I fairly tore my purse from my handbag and hurriedly pushed my key into the door. It wouldn't turn though. Even though I tried jiggling it and taking it out and putting it back in a few times, I could not get the door to open!

I suddenly saw the metal numbers screwed to the door and realised what had happened. The number on the door was 2323, not 2223. That idiot Curtis was so busy anticipating doing the redhead tomorrow night he'd deposited me on the wrong floor! They all looked exactly the same, even down to the dingy colour-scheme. I hadn't noticed for that reason. It was Curtis' job to get it right though. In fact as far as I knew it was his only duty and he'd screwed it up. I wondered if he'd done it as a wheeze because there were lit numbers appeared in the red plate over the inside of the doors in the lift. He must have done it on purpose the git.

As I stood there working it out though, the door burst open. The one person in the entire universe that I never wanted to see again said in his greasy voice,

"Give Ludo a kiss, Baby".

There was an awful silence. While I prayed that the floor would open up and swallow me whole. He was the one to speak firstly,

"Are you not delighted by my appearance"?

"Ludo" I'd gasped. Pretty lame given the circumstances.

"Please enter, I've anticipated this moment for quite some time", he was gracious but the menace in his tone dripped like warm honey. Sickly sweet when the mouth considers tasting it but deadly to the teeth. I was rooted to the spot with dread and horror. So the low-life suddenly gripped my arm with a hold like hot steel and growled through his own pearly whites,

"I invited you in, Darling. We can't have our tender reunion out here in the hallway".

"Let go of my arm you're hurting me", I gasped and his only retort was a low menacing chuckle. "How did you get here? How did I end up on this floor did you...".

"Questions questions questions I don't remember your thirst for knowledge being quite so keen in the past", he observed with sarcasm as he locked the door from the inside.

"Why'd you do that"? I demanded pretty lamely now I think about it.

"Interruptions can come at most inconvenient of moments can they not"? He had grown even more sophisticated, deadlier since I'd last encountered him. "You never liked them in the past when we were alone together either. Do you remember Lucille"?

"I don't remember nowt", I gasped.

"Your grammar hasn't improved since last we were together", he observed through hooded eyes. "Your memory is patchy too is that not so? Your powers of recollection are very much like a light-switch. It can be in either position you choose it to be. Now my mind does not work in that way. My powers of recollection are vivid and non-selectable. My switch is always on you see, the light is on so long that the light could blind you".

"Listen, Ludo", I began but he interrupted.

"I am listening, Lucille. You have my undivided attention. You don't sound any different to me. You don't look any different either. you're still a regular piece of hot totty. You know that of course. I always liked your tiny waist your long legs the way you wear that long blonde hair of yours. Those hooters well they are your best feature there is no denying that. Then there's that long smooth neck of yours, that neck that could easily...".

"Are you tormenting me, Ludo"? I'd snapped he wasn't fooling me for a second. He was like a cat playing with a vole and that sort of game only ever ends with one result.

Ignoring my question he carried on as though I hadn't made a peep.

"Now I don't look so healthy though do I, Baby? A long stretch in the slammer on a bum rap will do that to a person. You see I haven't had much sun lately. It's not easy to do any sunbathing from a prison cell. I could have been on a beach in the warmth, soaking up our beautiful home star. But instead, I was in the dimness dressed in a special suit with stripes. So I look pale. Ale and drawn and I've lost weight too. The cuisine was not up to the standard that I found endlessly palatable. In fact, I found it to be horrible slop most of the time".

I was growing sick of the self-pity and tried a threat. Squaring up to him, legs slightly apart I told him,

"Open the door or I'll scream the frenging place down I swear".

"You won't scream because there's not that much woman left inside you", he told me, unmoving. "You're all curdled inside, Lucille, filled with bile that's gone as rotten as you. Not only that but you're terrified, aren't you? You are aghast when you look at me. Me who meant so much to you at one time. Me who you claimed you loved. So go ahead. Scream your head off".

He was right, I couldn't make a sound.

"See", he observed triumphantly.

"I know you've busted out of prison because your sentence isn't up, not by a long way. So I can help you, Ludo. I can hide you, put you in a place I know that...".

"I asked you for a kiss", he broke into my entreaty. "So let's see if the fire still burns as fiercely".

He came closer and I panicked, "No! Don't come near me".

Ignoring me he put his arms around me and they felt like bands of steel, "I never used to have to ask for your sweet embrace did I, Baby? Your soft lips, your softer body. We had some pretty steamy nights if I recall correctly and I'm sure I do. So what's wrong now, have I changed so much"?

"Just give me a chance to explain", I believe I begged.

It was as though we were both having totally separate conversations though. Neither listing to the other only saying what we needed to get out.

"I guess I stink", he was going on, "After all, I had to crawl through the sewers to avoid getting recaptured. Then I had to hide in the skips when the rossers were looking for me. If I'd have realised how revolting you'd found me, as a result, I'd have asked the Governor to call me a taxi and bring me straight here to you. You, Lucille! A sad little slut who spilled the beans on me and the boys and turned into a dirty grass just for some favours from the rossers. Did they give you a pay-off too, Baby? Maybe thirty pieces of silver"?

"Please let me go"! I was getting desperate by then, realising how close to death I was.

"I like your eyes", He told me, sudden quite randomly, "Green like those of a special sort of snake. The sort that wriggles through the dirt because it doesn't have any legs. Are you a serpent in my bosom, Lucille? Or maybe just a low down dirty sewer rat"?

I did the only thing I could do to stay alive. I kissed the deranged sociopath. His breath was surprisingly fresh. Unlike the rest of him, he'd obviously had time to use the apartment complimentary toothbrush and then I had arrived before he could bathe. Maybe he didn't have a change of clothes at that point. He was probably broke. When we parted I began to try and change his terrible feelings toward me. If I failed I knew with certainty that he would rape me torture me and then kill me. Or maybe he would kill me and then rape me?!

"You remember how that felt don't you"? I asked him gently. My voice was not trembling with passion - but terror. "We were good together you and I, Honey. I can get you money, clothing a passport and over the water into Europe. You have to let me though. You have to let me help you".

He struck me then with the back of his hand across my face,

"Shoddy junior harlot", he cursed with a venom even I could not have imagined in anyone, even he. Then he laughed while I wept. "Do you really think those crocodile tears will move me? Are you crying because you're sorry for *me*? Crying imaging the rope around my neck once the rossers catch up with me? Or are you weeping for yourself imaging how this is going to end? The end for you, Lucille? You see I knew when I busted my way out of the nick that I would not be forever. I just wanted to say goodbye to you, Baby. I wanted to kiss you again. To see if my reaction would be as it always had been in the past. It did not. It left me as cold as ice".

It was then that he pulled out the dirk. Its blade glinted in the light like the malign sparkle in the eye of a demon.

"I'm going to use this as deftly as a surgeon, Lucille. I'm going to make an incision and then break your sternum and look to see if you have a heart. I don't imagine I'll see one beating in that deceitful body of yours. I imagine I'll see a cold hard diamond swinging on a thread. Frigid and impenetrable like the hardest crystal that is known to man. How can you walk around without a heart, Lucille? How do your limbs move when there is nothing human to motivate them"?

"Just let me explain", I gasped desperately, "After you and the boys did that bank the security guard died from his wounds and the rossers put up a reward for information leading to your arrest. I wasn't in my right mind. I went temporarily demented and all I could see was the reward. I reasoned that you'd be caught anyway sooner or later. Then what would I have? Nothing"!

"So you squealed like a dirty pig"?

"I was mad, I didn't know what I was doing".

"I believe your lust for the reward was greater than your feelings for me and that's why you have to go now, Lucille Monroe".

"Stay away from me put that knife down", I begged. At that instant, my hands went out to steady me. It was as though I momentarily lost my equilibrium.

The vase was touching the back of it. I snatched it from the dresser and with a desperate swipe smashed it over Ludo's head. The look of shock and pain on his features was a sight to behold and then he crumpled insensible to the floor. I didn't think he would be unconscious for long, so I turned tail and ran. I was free! I ran down the corridor as fast as I could and frantically thumbed the button to call the lift. It seemed to take a lifetime and a half to arrive. The red figures over the doors slowly climbed upward from G. Five to six. Ten, twelve and upward still toward the floor I was on. I was on the verge of nervous collapse. Hanging onto the corner of the wall I watched as the numbers suddenly failed to rise. The lift had stopped on the twenty-second floor. I knew with a horrified certainty that it would not and could not go any higher. In the building, in which I lived there were only twenty-two floors!

*

Twenty-third floor. I was on a floor that did not exist. How could I get away, what was I going to do? It made no sense, how can a building suddenly grow an extra floor? I could hear Ludo's voice faintly in my head as I madly rushed for the stairs.

"I never knew you were so strong, Baby. But that shot didn't kill me and the door wasn't locked. You should have locked me in. It would have given you a bit more time.

I'd hurtled down the stairs, onto floor twenty-two and dashed to door 2223. Now here I was huddled under the blanket listening to the faint sound of the television announcer but not understanding any of the words he spoke. Just taking comfort from the sound. The sound of the door splitting from a violent kick made me whimper in alarm. It hadn't taken Ludo long to find me. Was this the last few moments of my life? He slowly pulled the blanket from off my head. His shadow was the most ominous silhouette I'd ever seen in my life. I suddenly wanted him to get it done. To put me out of my miserable waiting.

The terrible thing was then that he said nothing. I could feel his hot fragrant breath on my cheek we were so close together. Yet he said nothing. He just kept standing over me like a carnivore regarding its entranced prey. My mind boiled. I couldn't think a single thought.

"Right now get up", He sounded calm I certainly wasn't

"Can't you just leave me alone"? I begged but even as I said it I knew it was a faintly vain hope and I rose from under the bedclothes.

"Let's get in the lift", he suddenly suggested. "We'll go for a ride, only I suspect one of us will not come back from such a journey".

He took hold of my arm straightened me up and began to lead me to the lift. What was the reason for this? What was he trying to prove?

I suddenly tore myself free and dashed for the stairs. Faster and faster I tumbled down them thinking I was getting away not caring where to exactly. I could hear his horrible taunting laughter from the top of the stairwell but I kept running and suddenly I reached the lobby. Fled across it and out into the cold and shimmering lights of the street. At that hour there was none abroad save me. The odd car flew by at a pace that brooked no stopping. Then I saw the uniform. The red face in the coolness of the night air. A rosser. I dashed up to him allowing myself a slim sliver of hope for the first time.

"Officer. Ludo Da Nuci is in that building. I've just been talking to him".

"Da Nuci"! He sounded sceptical in the extremis, "It can't be him, Miss".

"I know what you're going to say, Officer. That he's in Peakvale Correctional Facility, but he's escaped and he's in my apartment building. Come and see for yourself, have your gun ready he's got a knife".

"Ma-am", the stupid rosser assumed a tone as though he was addressing a small child or a dimwit, "Da Nuci was hanged last night at seventeen minutes to midnight to be precise".

"Hanged"! My mouth must have dropped open, "Hanged at 23:23. That's not possible Officer. He's been harassing me and threatening my life not ten minutes ago I tell you. I need your protection please come with me".

"Da Nuci is dead I tell you it was all over the news. Haven't you seen the reports on television? I don't believe you're even a woman Ma-am. I think if I made an incision and then broke your sternum and looked to see if you had a heart I don't imagine I'd see one beating in that deceitful body of yours. I imagine I'd see a cold hard diamond swinging on a thread. Frigid and impenetrable like the hardest crystal that is known to man. How can you walk around without a heart, Lucille? How do your limbs move when there is nothing human to motivate them"?

"You're not a rosser", I screamed the sound terribly loud in my own ears and I felt like I was losing my sanity, "Ludo! How can it be? I escaped you. I got away".

"What do you think to the uniform"? The thing that was neither a rosser or my former gang-banger boyfriend asked me chuckling, "How do I look".

"What are you"?

"I'm playing cops and robbers and this time I'm one of the boys in blue. Oh, of course, I'm still going to kill you, Lucille"!

I had no choice but to run from *it*. To go back into the apartment's lobby. Once I was inside I saw the television over the desk. Playing to itself. For a second though it played to me and I saw the headline that filled my veins with ice.

Ludo Da Nuci hanged in Peakvale Prison last night at seventeen minutes to midnight.

It had to be true. If it was though, who was it that was determined to kill me? It was no surprise that the lobby was empty Shandor was never the most conscientious of employees. I suddenly felt exhausted and knew I could not mount over twenty flights of stairs. So I went over to the lift and thumbed the green button marked G. After what seemed like an age the doors opened and there was Burt Curtis.

Miss Monroe"? He was naturally surprised to see me, "I didn't know you'd been out again? Did you go to get a late paper? To read about Da Nuci being hanged".

"No", I had no paper with me anyway. "Just went out for a cigarette, didn't want to leave a stale smell in the apartment, you know".

"So your home free with the reward the police gave you then"?

I glared at him, "I don't want to talk about it, Burt alright"?

"Sure sure", he thumbed the button for the twenty-second floor and the lift doors closed the carriage creaked on the hawsers and we began to ascend.

For some illogical reason I could not explain myself I suddenly blurted, "I'm not certain he's dead, Burt. I think he's come here to kill me. You have to help me. He's on the twenty-third floor".

"There are only twenty-two floors in this complex, miss Monroe".

There was no point in debating the subject. I wouldn't have believed me a few days ago. The lift suddenly stopped and the doors sighed open. The corridor beyond was dingy and intermittently lit. it looked exactly as it always had done. As I stepped out the doors hissed too behind me. There was no going back now. I was going to go to my apartment and pack. Get out of town as fast as my legs would carry me. The only trouble was I felt exhausted and the lovely bed of mine would be as comfortable as ever if I pulled every piece of furniture I could move in front of the door. I don't know what prompted me to do so, but I looked down at my wristwatch. In the struggle with Ludo, it must have gotten broken because it still read 23:23.

With my heart in my mouth, I walked down to the end of the corridor, my heels going clickety-clack on the grey-tiled floor. Prominent events in my lousy life flashed before me as I made that short walk. That cared me afresh for it seemed to be the saying about it doing so just before death. The events of the evening seemed surreal. Had they ever really happened or had I experienced some sort of waking incubus? I had been dreading Ludo escaping and coming in search of me. I'd anticipated that for a long time, had my mind gone into some sort of overdrive of its own?

I knew the policeman had not been real but what about the image on the television? Had I really seen that or did my mind perceive what my eyes could not? Had I been in my apartment at all that night. Or had I experienced some sort of spasm in the lift and been there since I'd come back from the cinema? I slid the key into the lock of the door deliberately not looking at the metal numbers.

It was some sort of mental test I had contrived for myself. To test my sanity. The key would not turn the lock!

It did not rotate and undo the latch and there was a simple if a fantastic reason for this. It was not my door. When I dared to peek at the metal numbers screwed into the green wood they di not read 2223 but 2323.

I was on the 23rd floor of a twenty-two story building!

With dreadful resolve, I knocked and the door suddenly eased open. I had not been able to turn the lock. I would not even have been able to do so with the right key, for it was already undone. I kicked the door ajar expecting to meet the spectre again. There was no sign of anyone or anything. I strode through to the bathroom, the kitchenette, the bedroom. Of any other person or creature in room 2323 sign was there none. Could I finally relax? Was I insane or had I just endured the most graphic of episodes any lucid and level-headed woman could and not be mad?

Then my eyes went to the piece of furniture from which I had snatched up the vase and broken it over Ludo's head. Two items now resided there. The whole and unbroken vase and something far more terrible and disturbing.

Ludo's knife!

I cautiously approached the two very different but equally dreadful objects and looked down at them. I was definitely the right vase, not a replacement. Then I looked at the burnished steel of the dirk. By the electric lights in the ceiling - it glinted. The shine was like the lustre of a demon's teeth. There was no getting away from the message ludo was sending me from beyond his unmarked grave. I knew what he'd intended for me. Knew that if I did not comply, his spirit would never leave me alone.

Nor ever.

My options were limited to but the one single choice for none other made any sense in the circumstances. Who could possibly endure a lifetime of torment and intimidation? I knew I was certainly not strong enough. I knew what must be done to give two souls some peace. I only hoped I could endure the agony before the blessed pit of nothingness comforted me with its black embrace.

Slowly I picked up the knife......

Transgression

KATHERINE MORETONE

2002

The cottage was just as she had remembered. The whitewashed stone walls, paint flaking in places, and the yellow thatched roof with the two dormer windows peeking out. Something had drawn Brenda back here, although she'd had no yearning to be reacquainted with the hateful building. It must have been the anniversary of her brother's death that had compelled her to take the bus, almost on a whim. Recently retired, with all the time in the world to indulge in a little nostalgia, this was the first time she had returned in many years.

An onlooker would be presented with a view of a slim, slightly stooped figure of mature years, dressed in an unassuming beige raincoat, with a mass of grey curls pressed under an old crumpled felt hat; that is if they had cared to give her a second glance. She melded into the background effortlessly, as she pressed up to the dusty privet hedge of the property across the road, allowing any pedestrians to pass by easily. Brenda stared at the renovated casement windows. One now opened, slightly ajar. Her mother had insisted on closing every window in the cottage unless the chimney became blocked and the open fire disgorged its foul-tasting smoke into the living room. Then she would scream for Brenda to deal with the situation; her mother incapable of moving out of the comfortable armchair, too miserly to engage the chimney sweep on a regular basis. Brenda, with the hindsight of years, knew that her mother had narrowly missed setting fire to the thatched cottage on a number of occasions, but as a child, she dutifully jumped up, resigned to her role as full-time attendant to her mother's demands.

Brenda ambled down the lane to the farmhouse. The imposing stone structure gaped at her. She had always been rather frightened of the shouting face that the upstairs windows and door presented to her childish imagination. Whereas the cottage represented her mother, the farmhouse was her father, large and scary. He had dropped dead from a heart attack on his fifty-fourth birthday. That was the first incident that had changed her life for the better. He was a farmer; inheriting the living from his father before him, and several generations before that. Livestock had been a large part of the farm but Farmer Skeets did not like animals, he never had. He enjoyed exterminating pigeons and other unwanted intruders who threatened the cows, chickens or the single black and white Essex pig. When Farmer Skeets' father had died, not long after the Second World War, he had sold off the farmyard animals and concentrated on the more lucrative pastime of arable farming. The nameless farmyard dog was kept on as a security guard, but when one day he saw his growing daughter petting the mangy creature, whispering secret names into its ear, he took it to the stream bordering his land, executed the quivering animal and kicked it into the water.

Cereal crops were easier to deal with than animals, a new tractor was bought and a regular income was ensured by fixed prices from the government. His young wife, a townie, had whelped a couple of times, firstly the longed-for son, followed a year later by a girl. The farm would continue to pass through to the next generation and he felt he had performed his duty as an upright steward of the land.

Brenda pondered over these known facts about her father, as she felt the embers of a burning rage lighting in her stomach. The father who had slipped into her bed at night from the age of eight or nine, touching her in private places, that horrible blotchy red face, the stink of beer, the nasty snigger and the demand that if she told anyone she would, *Get it, big time.* Looking back, she knew it could have been a lot worse, but at the time she was petrified, unable to move and lay for what seemed like hours, every muscle tensed, ready and waiting for the next onslaught. She tried to tell her mother, going around the houses so to speak, picking her words carefully so as not to upset her. In her naivety, she had imagined her mother would protect her, but Mrs Skeets had exploded and called her a filthy little slut and rushed upstairs in tears, where she stayed for the rest of the evening. The farmer's early passing was a blessed release for the ten-year-old Brenda.

Suddenly a friendly sheepdog bounded out to guard the gated entrance; or was he welcoming her? His long pink tongue hanging, a doggy smile, she bent down to pet him and looking up saw a young man in one of those sleeveless padded jackets that seemed to be all the rage at the moment.

"Can I help you?" The present owner asked in polite clipped tones.

"Oh no, I'm just visiting. I'll be on my way". Brenda made a hasty exit, leaving the young farmer staring suspiciously after her, as she walked briskly back past the cottage. She stopped again for a few moments, examining the whole aspect as if taking a mental photograph to be filed away for future reference. Brenda needed a drink. Not one of the alcoholic kind, but a good strong cup of tea. Several cafés had sprouted up in the village, it must be quite the place for tourists. She entered the door of an old converted cottage not dissimilar to the one she had lived in, and settled down. One pot of tea and scone later, she felt sufficiently revived.

Was she too old for this? She wondered as she rose to leave. She felt emotionally and physically exhausted and making her way to the bus stop, she tripped over a broken paving stone. She broke her fall with her free hand, the other clinging to her handbag, but she had holed both stockings and red dots of blood appeared amongst the dirty grazes.

'*Damn!*' She whispered to herself, but the sight of her blood had resurrected the sight of her mother's body; the broken frame, the bleeding gash on her forehead and her legs splayed and bent at a funny angle. She started to shake and staggering to a nearby bench, she searched in her bag for a handkerchief.

"That was a nasty tumble; are you okay?" A woman of a similar age to herself was now sat beside her, smartly dressed with wire-rimmed spectacles perched on her long nose. Brenda thought of the beloved librarian in Maldon all those years ago, picking out volumes of Hardy, Lawrence and James for her edification. The saviours of her teenage years, gobbled up into the early hours, then re-read again and again – a relief from the boredom and drudgery of her life as a skivvy.

"Oh yes, no need to worry yourself, it's just a couple of scratches," Brenda replied, her voice wobbling.

"No, I insist. There's a chemist across the road. We'll get plasters and a pair of tights. Let me help you".

Brenda regarded her Samaritan more closely – another do-gooder, with time on her hands; probably lonely, she thought. Brenda rose in silent acquiescence and, as they crossed the road, her companion turned to scrutinise her face and exclaimed.

"Don't I know you? From a long time ago; school or work? No, don't tell me..... it's Brenda!"

"I don't come from around here, I'm from town, my name's Theresa". Her favourite heroine, Hardy's Tess, but modernised of course. The inspiration had come in a flash; after the original falsehood, the rest had followed easily and there had been quite a few in her life.

"Were you a Maldon grammar girl?" Her new acquaintance persisted. Brenda felt a wave of panic building in the pit of her stomach, she must stand firm; the last thing she wanted was to be recognised. The village was no doubt still full of busybodies and the Skeets had provided fuel for the village gossips for many years.

"Oh no, I went to the Secondary Mod; I was a mod!" Brenda chuckled at her own joke; she had been a million miles from a Mod, or a Rocker come to that. A mouselike, taciturn little thing, complete with mousey hair and a shapeless underfed figure.

"I'm sorry, you just reminded me of a girl I used to know; had the same build as yourself, quiet; I always wanted to be her friend but it never seemed to happen."

Linda, (because it was certainly her – recognition flashing through Brenda's alert mind) added, as she pushed open the shop door.

"You've been very kind, thank you so much." Brenda held out her hand to bring the short reunion to a close. Linda looked uncomfortable, as she smiled with her mouth, but her eyes penetrating Brenda's features.

Clutching her purchases, Brenda asked the shop assistant about the location of the nearest conveniences, knowing full well of their whereabouts. A little later, having changed, she waited for the Marshes' bus. She would visit the bird sanctuary. Appearances of a townie must be kept up; she had been careless and lost her footing.

1987

The radio was on as Frank came down the stairs. The boys were gobbling down cereal in their usual voracious fashion, splattering the breakfast bar with milk and debris.

"Have you heard the news darling?" His wife inquired, with a faint look of concern.

"Don't be ridiculous, Phyllis, I've been in the shower. I overslept. Why didn't you wake me? I'm running late now, no time for breakfast and irrelevant questions." Frank retorted, tempering his anger by ruffling his favourite son's hair.

"It's just - there's been a crash…". Phyllis' face was starting to crumble. What's wrong with the woman? thought Frank, I've married a half-wit, not a university graduate.

"Don't concern yourself with other people's misfortunes, you've been too emotional since you've had the boys, maybe you ought to think about getting a part-time job to widen your interests. Besides the roads are getting more and more clogged, hence the reason I take the train."

"No Frank, not a road crash – it's financial. The stock markets are crashing." Phyllis saw the look of horror on her husband's face and her body tensed, waiting for the inevitable storm. But Frank uttered not one word, grabbed his briefcase and rushed to the front door.

A short dash to the underground was counterbalanced by what appeared to be an interminable wait for the train. Why had he agreed to move out to Richmond, the service was appalling? He needed to get to the City quickly, but he felt a sense of dread overwhelming him. He would lose everything; his friends thought him fearless in his financial dealings; he sailed too close to the wind and this time he knew he would sink.

A few hours later it was evident that the deals Frank had relied on were not going to materialise and he would be in serious financial difficulties. His outgoings were substantial, with a high maintenance wife and school fees for the boys. He resolved to contact his old university pal, Charles; he was some sort of legal specialist and earned a large, steady income. Frank was sure that he would help him out of this pickle; the markets would rise and he could pay back his dues. The small office in the tower block overlooking the Bank would have to go of course, along with the secretary.

"Charles; it's Frank; yes, long time, no see and all that. How are Louise and the children? Oh good. Look - are you busy this evening? Could do with a bit of advice. The usual place at 6?"   Frank relaxed, convincing himself that good old Charles would get him out of this hole and, yes, of course, he would return the favour in the future, in some way or other.

They met at the Dog and Duck, a watering hole from their university days, still mostly full of local residents, the interior a convenient patchwork of wood panelled cubby holes where a conversation would not be overheard. Charles was very understanding but unfortunately, his funds were all tied up in the capital. It would be impossible to help him out at the moment; wasn't there anywhere else he could go? Would his dear old Ma help out? Frank had told his friend several years ago that his father, a farmer, had died when Frank was a boy and the mother had sold the farm and safely squirrelled away most of the proceeds. She was living in a tumbledown thatched cottage, with Frank's sister acting as her unpaid carer. Charles reminded Frank that this would be his best source of income, and he understood from Frank that she was going to leave him everything anyway; he was her blue-eyed boy and all that baloney. Why didn't he ask for it now, when he needed it? Frank took a swig of his beer, stared at Charles and put his head in his hands.

"She's gone funny in the head – you know how old people get sometimes; I've read about it. She can't make any legal decisions if she's not in her right mind, so she'd never been able to sign anything, however much she dotes on me." Frank's face went red and he leaned forward, staring at Charles. "What the hell am I going to do? You've got to help me!"

Charles hesitated for a moment, studying Frank's features; a vertical line had begun to appear above his nose, he rarely smiled and his golden curls were receding. He was losing that look of a Greek god.

"Look here, old man, I've already explained; I'm not in a position to bail you out at the moment, but if the old girl is fading, perhaps it would be humane to help her on her way?"

"Are you suggesting I do away with her?" Frank rasped. "I just push her down the stairs and say she fell, and collect the goodies? It all takes time, all that legal stuff. I'm the executor of her will; I've already looked into how long all that sort of thing takes. It could take months or years to get probate, especially if Brenda contests the will. She's a funny one, with a nasty streak."

Frank was becoming decidedly annoying; he was all talk and no action.

"Don't concern yourself with minutiae. Are you willing to kill her or not?" Charles was on his third beer and his tongue had loosened sufficiently for him to speak his mind without prevaricating. To be honest, Frank was becoming a bit of a bore and he thought shock tactics might bring him to his senses.

"Look, get a loan like every other normal human being in this country. You can repay it when you get your inheritance."

His friend turned away, and coughed; Charles wondered if he was trying not to cry.

"Always using clever words aren't you Charles? Do you like to rub in the fact that you're so much better educated than I am? Public school, first class honours etc. etc. What the hell are minutiae? Sounds like a bloody plant or one of your posh girlfriends." Frank was obviously drunk and now sobbing, and as Charles led him out of the pub, now visibly shaking, a curious local glanced their way before returning his attention back to his drink.

They stood outside the underground station in silence; Charles waiting to hail a cab and Frank to catch the District line home to a barrage of questions from Phyllis. As his friend disappeared into the black hackney, Frank determined to show Charles that he was indeed fearless and to be reckoned with. He would follow Charles' advice, and if anything went awry, Frank determined to drag his old chum down with him.

2002

The bus was surprisingly full and Brenda felt conspicuous amongst the bird watchers and all their paraphernalia. Binoculars, telescopes and tripods took up spare seating. A middle-aged man asked her if she was with the Maldon group – she shook her head and mouthed "No". She didn't want all these people around her; she craved solitude for mulling over the events all those years ago.

Frank had passed the eleven plus just before their father had dropped dead from his heart attack. Maybe it had been the shock; neither the farmer and certainly not Mrs Skeets had shown any sign of being remotely intelligent, in an academic sense. Mrs Skeets believed that books were harbourers of dust and apart from a King James', as she called it, wouldn't allow one in the house. As soon as she'd started school and learned to read, Brenda had fallen in love with books. They took her away from her life of drudgery to different worlds and adventures. Her mother begrudgingly allowed her to visit the Maldon library once a week, whilst they were doing the weekly shopping trip. In fact, Mrs Skeets dropped both children there as soon as they clambered off the bus and picked them up an hour later. Frank was soon bored and wandered around outside, sometimes playing with the local boys. Brenda never did find out where her mother went and what she did, but at the time she didn't care. Later in her teenage years, she had wondered if her mother had a secret lover, but it was more likely that she went to a café and had tea and cakes. Every Friday the young Brenda clutched the three allotted library books to her chest and as soon as they were seated on the bus home, she was reading. Mrs Skeets reproached her, suggesting she was sure to be sick, but Brenda disappointed both her mother and Frank by not obliging and bringing back her breakfast. He enjoyed kicking her ankles for a while until something diverted his attention and he stared at the passing scenery.

Brenda was gazing out of the window now as they neared the Marshes' stop. She waited until the other travellers had got off before rising. She was in no hurry and ambled along the coastal path breathing in the fresh sea air, noting the cries of the sea-birds. She couldn't tell one gull from another but she enjoyed the atmosphere. She settled down on a bench and looked out to sea. Apparently, a family of avocets and a spoonbill were causing great excitement amongst the 'twitchers'. She envied them their common passion and the opportunity of socialising with fellows with a mutual interest. Although Brenda loved reading books and still a regular visitor to the local library, she had not yet plucked up the courage to join the readers' group.

Brenda watched the flocks of birds and was again reminded of her brother. He'd inherited their father's old air rifle and the teenager delighted in taking pot shots at unsuspecting pigeons. Admittedly the creatures were a nuisance, congregating in the old apple tree in the small back garden, fouling much of the fruit. Occasionally Frank brought his new school friends home and like any child of 14 years old would show off, demonstrating his prowess as arch bird killer. Frank had gone to the boys' grammar the September after Mr Skeets had thankfully been taken from the family, and Mrs Skeets had complained bitterly to anyone who would listen, especially the many concerned fellow churchgoers, about her lack of funds; how Tom had left her in dire straits with not a penny to her name and how was she going to afford the fancy uniform for her boy? They had dutifully rallied round, discovering a second-hand uniform shop set up by the school for such contingencies. A whip round from the congregation kitted out Frank ready for his first day. Brenda tried to be happy for Frank even though he bullied her relentlessly, but when Brenda performed the same feat a year later, her mother exclaimed it was a waste of time to educate her. She only needed to know how to cook, clean and look after offspring, if any simple man would care to marry her. The following week the vicar had visited Mrs Skeets. It was the Easter holiday; Frank was out with his friends and Brenda was busy with the usual domestic chores. They had moved a few months before to the thatched cottage and Mrs Skeets had insisted on several changes in the decorating department. Brenda was stirring a pot of paint as the Reverend knocked on the door. He followed her mother into the front parlour, kept tidy for just such an illustrious visitor; whilst Mrs Skeets had screeched about a pot of tea and two slices of Madeira and be sharp about it!

An hour later the Reverend had persuaded the recalcitrant mother to allow her daughter to attend the grammar. The church had funds to help families who were struggling, as they had with Frank, and would be delighted to help with uniform, shoes and bus fare come to that, although the vicar was pretty sure the local authority catered for transport to school. As he left, the kindly clergyman thanked Brenda for looking after him and added in a whisper that all would be well, she would go to the girl's grammar in a few months.

Brenda thought back to those days. Her mother didn't allow any friendships to flourish, at least not with Brenda – different rules applied to Frank - insisting she was needed at home outside of school hours. Brenda's friends were the library books that she continued to borrow; the librarian now familiar with the thin mousey creature who came in after school, before the village bus left half an hour later. The school years had passed swiftly and Brenda came to understand what sort of people her parents were, and Frank for that matter, but she was trapped. Brenda's mother had stopped going to church; it was as if she had got all she could wheedle out of them and now she had ready cash from the sale of the farmhouse.

One day Frank appeared in the bedroom of 12 years old Brenda, announcing that he'd heard what his father and she had got up to, and he fancied some of the action too. He told her to remove her blouse and when she refused, he tugged at the buttons tearing the material. She ducked under him and ran downstairs, busying herself in the kitchen; Mrs Skeets was hungry in spite of doing very little all day, she ate snacks between meals and had started to balloon into a very large woman. She demanded the dinner be made as quickly as possible and for once Brenda was grateful for the distraction. Frank went straight out after eating to meet his old village friends and from that time on, as soon as she had completed her chores she retired to her bedroom. That evening she had dragged the heavy chest of drawers across the bedroom door and barricaded herself in, and continued to do so for many years to come.

After that first night, during breakfast, he had looked at her with a mixture of hatred and contempt, but she didn't care, she knew she had beaten him and there was nothing he could do.

Brenda rose from the bench and smiled, making her way back to the bus stop. The sea air had invigorated her and it was time to return to her cosy townhouse.

1987

Frank turned the front door key tentatively; he didn't want to wake Phyllis. It was long past her bedtime. The house was in darkness and Frank's head was a little woozy. On the walk back from the tube station he'd stopped off at the Punter's Paradise, overlooking the river, he'd needed some Dutch courage to confront his wife. He couldn't face the endless rhetorical questions; he knew and she knew the answers, so why did she plague him with a constant bombardment of observations, disguised as enquiries, which she then proceeded to answer, before he had a chance to take a breath.

"She should have been a bloody politician!" He shouted out loudly, as he finally succeeded in inserting the key into the lock. He shook his head, realising he had probably woken up half the neighbourhood with his protestations. He crept up the stairs but as soon as he entered their bedroom, Phyllis was sitting up and turning on the bedside light.

"Well? And where have you been all this time? I've been worried sick. What's happened with the crash? Will it affect us? I don't know what you get up to at work; it's all very shady and I rang Daddy and he wants to talk to you tomorrow. You're to phone him when he gets back from the golf club at 3 pm. No ifs or buts." etc, etc.

Frank had stopped listening; there was no need to respond, it was a monologue. He headed for the ensuite, turning on the cold tap while Phyllis simultaneously turned on her waterworks. "The standard response." He Mumbled as he flicked cold water over his face. He locked the door and settled down on the toilet seat to wait for the storm to pass.

The following morning Phyllis was utilising the silent treatment to achieve., well whatever she intends to accomplish, thought Frank, as he performed his usual morning routine and made for the front door.

"Ring Daddy!" Phyllis huffed as he nonchalantly patted the boys on the head on his way out. He didn't reply.

Later that afternoon Frank picked up the receiver and started to dial his father-in-law's number. After the first few numbers, he stopped, staring into the mid-distance knowing he couldn't bring himself to kowtow to the objectionable old man. Phyllis' father had made it quite clear that he thought Frank was 'a jumped-up spiv'. Phyllis' grandfather had made his money in trade and her father had enjoyed a privileged upbringing; raised in the knowledge that he was better than the 'hoi palloi'.

Phyllis had disappointed him in her choice of husband, but she had a mind of her own and he was an indulgent father and grandfather. Frank had surprised him with his success in the financial market and, until now he had had no reason to criticise. Admittedly Frank had played fast and loose with the markets, but he was damned if he would be lectured to by 'Daddy'. Gathering his coat and suitcase and leaving the empty office, the secretary had been summarily dismissed that morning - he resolved to travel up to Essex to see his mother. Maybe she would be more 'compos mentis' than last time and agree to bail him out somehow. Although she only lived a two-hour drive from Richmond, Frank rarely saw his mother. He was too busy with work, the boys had numerous weekend activities, which he was expected to attend along with the fortnightly Sunday lunch with Phyllis' parents. It must have been six or seven months since he'd last seen her and then his wife and sons had stayed at home. Mrs Skeets was in poor health and starting to forget who people were and the previous winter she had mistaken the younger boy for Frank and insisted on smothering him with kisses. That had not gone down well with Phyllis; she had "downright refused to ever set foot in that pigsty again. And, what was wrong with that halfwit sister of his? Was she fit to look after his mother? She never said a word; the embarrassment the two of them had caused at their wedding ten years previously. They had turned up looking like a couple of tramps; his mother had gobbled up everything in sight and wrapped supplies for later in paper serviettes; and that Brenda had the appetite of a small bird and not said a word. She had been highly conspicuous by her silence. Luckily, they had not stayed long as they had to catch the train home and thank goodness she and the boys no longer had to traipse across London and all that smelly traffic to waste a Sunday in Essex. It was bad for the boys' lungs" and so on, and on.....

Frank dashed into the house, retrieved his car keys from the dish by the front door and hurried out before anyone had a chance to catch him. Two hours later he pulled up outside the cottage. Dark acrid smoke billowed from the chimney and the thatch looked worn in places. He rushed up the path and caught his trousers on a runaway bramble. Did no one ever work in the garden? The place was a disgrace and he would tell Brenda so, but first, he must ensure his future and his sister would be the architect of its success.

It seemed an age before the door was opened; Brenda was thinner than the last time he'd seen her – if that was possible. Her hair was messy and her pinafore was covered in splodges of unknown substances.

"Oh, hello Frank, not seen you in a while. Here to see Mum, are you? Heard about the crash on the news – hope you've not been too badly affected." Brenda flashed a knowing smile at him and hesitated for a moment before allowing him a passage into the dwelling. The house was tidy and clean, he had to give Brenda credit for that, but he turned on her by complaining about the sooty smell that pervaded the cottage.

"Frank, you know Mum doesn't like to have strangers in the house and it costs for the sweep; now you're here perhaps you could persuade her to part with the money to pay him."

Brenda guarded the stairs as she spoke; preventing him barging past to gain access to his mother's bedroom. He'd seen the empty sitting room and remembered the last letter from Brenda filling him in on Mrs Skeets' progress. The old woman had retired to her bed a few weeks ago; she had struggled to get up to her bedroom and the doctor had advised she stay upstairs, within easy access of the bathroom. Dr Wisbey had been concerned that Brenda would injure herself propelling her mother up and down the staircase several times a day. An accident was bound to happen.

"So, got the place to yourself now, have you? Have your fancy men round at all hours?" Frank sniggered to himself. How easy it was to revert to the role of an intimidating older brother. Brenda didn't flinch.

"Do you want a cup of tea? You must have had a long journey, driving all this way. Why didn't you let me know you were coming? I could have baked a cake." It was difficult to know if Brenda was serious or if she was indulging in sarcasm; she was inscrutable, Frank thought, but she *will* do as I ask, this time at least.

"I want you to get Mum to lend me a substantial amount of money, otherwise I'm finished." Frank spluttered, as he gulped down the welcome cup of tea, all thoughts of doing away with the old girl erased from his memory; all false bravado on his part, a thought of the moment, lubricated by copious amounts of alcohol.

"Why don't you ask her yourself; if she recognises you I'm sure she would be delighted to, you've always been her favourite." Brenda smiled, too sweetly thought Frank and for too long.

"She thought Freddie was me, last time, she was confused, is she better?" Frank was desperate; he would clutch at any available straw that was waved under his nose.

"Just go up and see her. I'll nip down to the shop for a cake. It closes in 15 minutes. Talk to her about when you were a boy, remind her of her treasured memories; it works sometimes."

Frank, deflated climbed the stairs. That damned Brenda had turned the tables on him; why did *he* have to plead with his mother for money? She could easily have talked to her first, put his case forward. But why should she; what had she to gain? Making his way to Mrs Skeets' room, Frank noticed the carpet was worn in places and the walls needed a fresh coat of paint. The place was starting to disgust him, just as it had with Phyllis. He opened the bedroom door. There she was, a great whale of a woman; no wonder she couldn't get up and down the stairs. He cleared his throat; her eyelids flickered.

"Hello Mum; it's Frank, your one and only boy. Are you feeling better?"

Mrs Skeets roused herself and her features became animated. She raised herself up and held out her arms.

"My darling, darling boy; give your old Mum a kiss."

Frank duly obliged, but it was difficult to hide the look of distaste. Mrs Skeets was now wriggling in a similar way to his younger son, when he needed to relieve himself but was engrossed in something much more interesting. His mother pushed back the blankets and swivelled around.

"Help me to the bathroom, there's a good boy." Frank angrily wondered if she thought he was a child, but tried to reason with himself that it was part of her condition. He must try to be cooperative, he needed her to write him a large cheque and today.

He helped her put her slippers on, inappropriate fluffy mules with a tiny heel; he grabbed her arm, pulling her up, but her body sagged.

"Gentle boy, you're hurting me." He supported her under the elbow, that seemed to work better. They headed out of the bedroom across the landing. She stopped at the top of the stairs.

"Let me make my boy a lovely cup of tea." She wobbled and put her foot out.

2002

The bus passed the farmhouse on its return to Maldon; Brenda glanced at the foreboding frontage, Frank still at the forefront of her mind. He'd gone to university, of course, London no less. Their mother had been so proud; Brenda, on the other hand, had had to leave school after her O levels. The teachers tried to persuade her to stay on, but Mrs Skeets insisted that her daughter was needed at home. She had never turned up to a parents' evening for Brenda, firm in her belief that schooling for girls was a waste of time. After university Frank had obtained a post in the city, something to do with finance – a broker, a hedge fund manager, she never found out exactly what. They rarely saw him, but Mrs Skeets idolised his memory, boasting of his achievements to anyone who would care to listen. The villagers grew tired of the conceited, flabby old woman and Brenda noticed that they tried to avoid both her mother and herself at all costs. It had taken 15 years for his fall; Brenda had waited most of her life for that moment and she savoured the memory. There he had been on the doorstep on that fateful teatime in October 1987. The agitation, nay even panic was evident in his expression as he had barged past her into the cottage. She remembered feeling particularly calm and she had to admit to herself, rather smug. To be honest she had inwardly revelled in his discomfort.

As she thought back over that evening once more, the bus arrived at the stop opposite her old home and several people had climbed on. She didn't attempt to move her bag, which was resting on the seat next to her. The bus was only half full and the embarking passengers could sit elsewhere, she needed her privacy.

There had been no cake; an unusual occurrence but Mrs Skeets must have polished off the remains of the sponge she had made a few days before. She had left the house with the excuse of buying some sort of teatime treat for she couldn't remain in the house with her brother for long. There hadn't been time to prepare herself, she needed to get away. A quarter of an hour later she had returned to witness a crumpled body lying at the foot of the stairs. Frank had been standing at the top staring down with a look of bewilderment; his demeanour was that of the little boy who had misbehaved and was about to get a thrashing from his father. He appeared to have shrunk. She had called up angrily to ask him what he had done, but he had not replied and continued to stare at the body. She had bent down and seen the bulging eyes, like boiled eggs, the slightly open mouth, the large bloody gash on the right temple. Mrs Skeet's head must have struck the radiator and Brenda glanced up to confirm her suspicion, a small blood red blob on the corner that was previously rust coloured. Her mind had been racing; she still remembered the day clearly, every moment, the conflicting emotions of horror, elation and the realisation that *her* time had come. The opportunity had presented itself and she would exact her revenge on her brother. She had jumped up, telling him she was going to a neighbour to call an ambulance and the police. She hurriedly left before he could react and within ten minutes the police had arrived. She had stayed with the neighbours, apparently suffering from shock. She had blurted out the news that her mother had fallen down the stairs – she didn't know how, she rarely got out of bed now; only to use the lavatory and even then, she needed help. She, Brenda, had gone out to the shop and left her brother in charge; she let slip that he had been upset on account of the big financial crash and they had not seen him for months– she couldn't bring herself to say any more and had put her head in her hands. The neighbour had expressed sympathy, called her a 'poor dear' and what a life Mrs Skeets had led her, treating her as an unpaid servant. The man of the house had announced that he would go and see to her brother. The blue flashing lights and the siren had apparently brought Brenda back to her senses and she had returned to the cottage with the curious neighbour in hot pursuit.

'*Yes, that was how it had happened,*' she thought, as the bus trundled on towards Maldon.

1987

The police asked lots of questions; Brenda gave an exemplary performance as the shocked grieving daughter. Her alibi was later confirmed by the proprietor of the corner shop. Frank meanwhile insisted on maintaining his innocence. He kept repeating the words "I didn't do it; it wasn't me." Brenda felt compelled, after she had sufficiently recovered the next day, to fill the policewoman in on Frank's circumstances and how he had been desperate for money. Further investigations had led the police to Frank's family and Frank's friend, Charles. Charles relayed his version of their meeting in the public-house and how indeed Frank had been highly agitated by the financial crash and had asked him for help. He had advised that Frank spoke to his mother. Further enquiries were carried out by a young detective at the Dog and Duck the following Monday evening. It was a pub for locals and one old drinker had remembered the two toffs, dressed in smart business suits, conversing over a pint or two in whispers, and he was pretty sure he'd heard something about killing someone. He liked to sit at the bar and you could easily hear the conversations in the cubby hole. A further visit to Charles elicited the information that maybe Frank had mentioned doing away with his mother, but Charles had thought he was speaking in jest. He certainly didn't take what he said seriously, otherwise, he would have contacted them straight away.

Meanwhile Frank had returned home to an empty house. Phyllis and the boys were staying with her parents and had no intention of returning home until he had moved out. He spent the next day holed up at home, waiting for the knock on the door. The inevitable arrest, he felt sure, following the planting of innuendos from that tattletale sister of his, which would make him appear to be a murderer. He started to groan as he imagined the consequences of the evidence his sister was feeding the police. He remembered with a sting his behaviour as a teenager, trying to force himself upon his sister as his father had successfully done before him. At that moment he felt some remorse, but only insomuch that he had sowed the seeds of hatred in Brenda's mind; he imagined a small mind, uneducated, petty; but for all that underestimated. She had planned his downfall in a few moments as she took in the scene of his mother's demise. He wept loudly, his body shaking as the bell rang, followed immediately by a harsh banging at the door.

'Police! Open up!' Frank heard the words but his body didn't respond; he was rooted to his chair, frozen in time, now motionless, as if standing on the scaffold with the rope around his neck, awaiting his final reckoning.

2002

They were heading into town now, the fields giving way to large Victorian townhouses and Brenda thought of the imposing Victorian building where Frank had spent the final days of his life – Wormwood Scrubs. A fitting resting place for a Skeets she felt. She smiled with realisation as she saw her whole life almost mirroring a Dickensian novel. Although Brenda was not too familiar with Dickens - he was too verbose, although she had enjoyed 'A Tale of Two Cities', she was familiar with most of his plots. What had really happened to Frank? She felt a little pang of regret when she thought about his state of mind when he took his own life, but only a very small one; he had got what was coming to him. At the inquest the prison authorities had said he had hanged himself in the shower; he had torn up his sheet and knotted the pieces together to create a rope, which he had hidden, tied around his waist before putting his overalls on. There had been a defence lawyer present who had been working on Frank's case and he had become concerned about Frank's state of mind. Her brother had been sharing a cell with a known criminal, who was renowned for abusing other inmates; the lawyer had been due to meet the prison governor the following day, but it was too late for Frank. Brenda felt uncomfortable about this part of the story, but only because it reminded her that she had been treated badly by her father and then Frank had tried it on too. She couldn't be certain that Frank had intended to kill their mother; had she fallen as Frank maintained? When Brenda had been interviewed by the police, she had been convinced Frank had pushed Mrs Skeets. Her nephews had done alright out of it, and that was ok, they were innocent children and why should they suffer because of their stupid parents? She and the boys had shared the estate; the courts had felt in the circumstances that, had Mrs Skeets died naturally, Brenda would have been entitled to contest the will. His wife's family were rolling in money, so Phyllis got nothing.

At last, there was her stop and as she alighted from the bus she breathed in the familiar smell of the town. She would soon be home and reunited with Terry, her pet terrier and - goodness was that the time? He would be impatient for his evening walk.

Eye of Newt and Horn of Toad

MENDELSSOHN FALK

~

"I want my make-up to be absolutely perfect", Emily said to the maid.

"Yes, Ma-am of course you do. A girl doesn't become a woman overnight every day", came the assenting response. "You'll look beautiful in that white frock it's so lovely. See how it catches the light and absolutely shimmers. Every other young woman present will be jealous of you, so they will"

By way of response, Emily regarded herself in the tall dressing mirror and had to admit that the dress was indeed magnificent. As to the claim that every other young woman would be jealous of her though. Emily knew that she was not beautiful. She was not ugly, or unshapely but with her red hair and pale complexion, she regarded herself as plain. There would be no shortage of possible suitors at her coming of age dance even so. Her father the Mill owner William Brock was immensely rich and having no siblings, Emily stood to inherit a fabulous sum upon his demise.

Though it was now fourteen years in the past Emily remembered her mother's death from kidney failure following an attack of Diphtheria. She had known little about contraction or even the suffering her mother had done before death. The funeral was still a vivid memory though. The events afterwards were even more lucidly memorable.

For a start, it had been absolutely pouring on the day of interment. Wind from the north was driving it in the form of lashing sheets of water that would absolutely drench anyone forced to stand outside. Emily was in part protected by the footman's umbrella but the poor Parson had no such facility. His white hair was plastered around his face and his bible ended up as nothing better than a sodden conglomerate of inky pulp.

Despite the footman's very best effort to keep Emily out of the worst of the downpour, some inevitably found its way beneath the umbrella. She was glad for it, the wetness on her face were god's tears - not hers. For her mother had allowed the Nanny and other servants to raise Emily and the cold aloof woman that had died was not anyone Emily could truly feel for. Her father remained silently magnificent. Tall and mourning without the merest loss of dignity before his inferiors.

The turnout had been impressive despite the inclemency of the elements. When a Brock died it touched the hearts of everyone in various oblique ways. For William Brock was the chief employer and provider of livelihoods for most of Outstone Crags. The cleric continued to battle his way through the service, while the rain threatened to fill in the hole of the grave with water. Finally, a great clap of thunder followed fork lightning on the eastern horizon and the occasion was brought to an untimely end. Emily was too young for the subsequent wake, but sandwiches and small pastries were brought to her, which she ate in the back kitchen with Nanny. Then she was given a hot bath and told it was time for her to retire.

The rain had stopped and a huge waxy moon hung in the clear sky like the large eye of a monstrous beast. One hour after Nanny had turned down the lanterns (it was 1889) in Emily's bedroom the most frightening occurrence of the young girl's life took place. In the darkness, a low moaning sound brought her to wakefulness. She looked around the room, but the heavy drapes at the huge windows were letting no light through them. So the brave young girl slipped from between her bedclothes and pulled them to one side. Xanthic illumination from the moon lighted the shadows with tallow, conjuring alarming chiaroscuro in every subfusc corner.

"Is someone there"? The pale young child desired to know.

To her terrified amazement, a skeletal rattle replied, "Emily, come closer, death does little to improve my eyesight".

Emily felt cold feet that were as clay perambulate her into the middle of the dimness, "You are dead, a ghost"? She asked not especially surprised. She fancied she knew to whom she was addressing. The reason for that was the fact that only a few days before her death, her mother had declared to her daughter that she would return. She had told her in their single interview that she was filled with morbidity and would not live much longer. Death did not frighten her overmuch, for she was an occultist and practitioner of necromantic arts.

"My spirit will always watch over you, Darling", she had promised. That was the last time the girl had ever seen the sorceress.

"Quite right, Emily, it is your mother", came the half-expected reply.

Emily drew closer to the apparition that hovered just beneath the ceiling. It was dreadful to behold. The figure had no skin!

Such phantasm as was her mother was cerise with dripping gore and body fluid. If had no nose, nor ears or hair, rather the skull was a gory eye-filled parody of the woman she had been.

"You were an Augurer, Mother, how did you come to be in the state I now perceive"? Curiosity was rapidly replacing Emily's fear and her expensive private education made of her a youngster quite erudite.

"None can truly master all that is required in one brief lifetime", came the response. "I did not learn enough. What I do have is an ability to watch over you, Emily. You shall be guarded against harm, this I swear and as time passes so will my adeptitude increase. Fear not, Mother is always with you".

Then she was gone. With it any chance of a normal childhood too. Emily had grown wise beyond her years in that one fateful evening and she was never a child again. Back at boarding school she became isolated and avoided. Other girls found her *weird*. Emily did not care. She had her studies, her father and her black Tom Mephistopheles. Once in her high teens to echo the cat she wore black most of the time, used black eyeliner and only ever wore scarlet lipstick. Her red hair she died jet and university became an extension of school. She had no friends, never wanted any. She got her degree with honours and then retired into private life.

For his part, William encouraged her isolation and the relationship between them got as close as any father and daughter could be. He was unnaturally protective with regard to her. Enforced her every decision to remain reclusive. She became an engineer in the mills, worked for him and him alone. The workers called them Billy Milly and the Black Figure though never to their face of course.

It was 1903 when Emily reached the age of twenty-one and uncharacteristically William had tried his very best to encourage her to have a coming of age ball. At first, she had been obdurate. Her father had not risen to the position of power and wealth without being persuasive though. Emily removed the die from her hair agreed to wear a white frock and to use the new lighter make up. Part of her reason was curiosity. The only man she had ever spoken to was young doctor Cedric Harriman. For very obvious reasons Harriman had guided Emily through puberty and beyond. He also happened to be in love with her. She remained blissfully unaware of his emotional dilemma. She had noticed a few pleasant looking mill-workers as she roved her father's factories and it had caused curiosity to spring in her breast.

So the ball was arranged. Invitations were sent out. None refused. Many of the guests would be friends of William. Or rather business associates. Doctor Harriman was included. Additionally every prospective suitor in Outstone Crags. Emily was ready to meet them. Stirrings that she knew were biological and hormonal coursed through her body as she descended the huge curved staircase that led from the first floor to the hall. A hall lit by the very new electric lights created by Mister Edison. Several young men and some older ones who were divorced or widowed were in the hallway at the time. At sight of the vision that deplaned toward them, they broke into spontaneous applause. More than one rushed to greet her, dance card in hand, hoping to obtain a booking from the belle.

Emily was introduced to various men of all shapes and ages. She tried her best to remember them all. When they finally went into the main hall that was the ballroom for the night the situation got even more hectic. Suddenly though time seemed to stand still when the most beautiful man she had ever seen suddenly drifted before her vision.

"Who is that"? She asked of the closest man to her at the time.

"Oh him"! The reply was not gentlemanly, "That's Melling".

She was momentarily puzzled at the animosity in the voice of her informant. "Mister Melling"? She asked for clarification.

The youth who was instructing her smiled thinly, "No, My Dear, Baron Melling. The late Baron's son. I'm afraid I don't know his actual name".

Sensing he was being spoken about the Baron suddenly turned toward them affording Emily a totally dazzling smile. His head was a mass of golden curls almost cherubic. He had clear blue eyes a slim well-clipped moustache. His suit was ever so slightly frayed though. The Baron was on hard times it would seem. He drifted toward Emily and her current companion. Smiled and lifted her hand to his lips.

"A delightful ball, Miss Emily and you are the Belle of it. Tell me please is your card filled? "For it would delight me in no small amount to have at least one dance with you".

Emily found herself simpering and admitted, "There are several spaces in it still, Lord Melling, I would be happy to give you two".

Melling feigned disappointment and exclaimed, "Two only, your beauty is only matched by your cool heart, Miss Emily".

She handed over the card and then conceded, "Very well three then, My Lord. May I know your given name please"?

"I shall write it in the spaces", he declared and pulling forth a fountain pen scribbled in three of Emily's slots.

She did not have the chance to read them before more young men desired to book a dance with her. She knew hardly any of them. She was not interested in any due to her distraction caused by the ruinous Baron. Before the small orchestra began the first dance a waltz, her father found himself beside her.

"You look lovely, My Dear", he began, "Did I see you conversing with Melling"?

"Baron Melling yes".

"You would do well to keep away from him", her father suddenly urged, "His father was ruined with ill-conceived speculations and the family is without. One would have thought the young Baron would have sought occupation but he feels himself above such vulgar practice".

"Perhaps he seeks to refrain from becoming bourgeoisie, Father".

"I am bourgeoisie", William chided, "What wealth we now have has come from my own industry, Emily".

The music started before they could say more and Doctor Harriman rushed to take Emily's hand and lead her onto the dance floor. She had not even had the time to get herself a drink of punch or champagne.

Dazzling lights. Excited chatter. The twirling of dance movements. Emily was involved in one long delightful haze of enjoyment. The highlights were each time she danced with Rufus De Lacy twenty-third Baron of Melling. Finally, he asked her out onto the terrace and they were alone together.

Emily fanned some of the heat from her flushed features while Melling smiled at her, observing,

"You were the person everyone came to see tonight, Miss Emily. None were disappointed".

"Please just call me Emily when there are only the two of us present"? She requested and he acknowledged the request with a stiff bow, "And how would you have me address you, My Lord"?

"Friends call me simply Melling", he told her, "And I would like us to be friends, Emily".

"I would like that too", she found herself saying realising at the same instant that she meant it with utmost sincerity.

"Then may I presume to ask if I may call upon you in the very near future"? His manners were impeccable.

"Tomorrow is Sunday and I will not be working", she responded with enthusiasm.

"Where we in Bridgehamside I would have my carriage take you out with me, but I came on the train so would you consider an afternoon stroll"?

"I believe I would and thank you for making my coming of age ball so pleasurable".

"The pleasure was mine, Dear Lady, it was an honour to meet you and now I must go".

Once more he lifted her pale hand to his lips. Before she had regained her breath and stopped her heart from pounding so he was gone.

Sleep did not come easily to Emily that night. Before she could achieve such she was forced to take a late night stroll through the local graveyard where her mother resided.

A huge sullen moon waxed in the nigrescent sky overhead. Even so, Emily lighted her way with the tallow glow of a handheld lantern. Her mother lay beneath a simple cross, the inscription equally pithy.

'Rose Brock devoted wife and mother,

taken from us too soon, 1860 - 1889'

"Mother", Emily began, "I think I have met someone who could claim my heart. You have always looked over me. If I am not to allow Baron Melling to pursue me, send me a sign. I know you still inhabit the realm betwixt the natural world and the next. A sort of perpetual limbo until I no longer need your oversight. What should I do"?

In the canopy of deepest slate, the clouds seemed to coalesce into a huge face in the sky. The chill graveyard breeze gnawed at Emily's shoulders and she pulled her shawl a little tighter. She listened to the cold gust and it was as though a series of words were whispered in it.

"Он није за тебе", it was repeated and then the breeze was gone.

Emily did not understand the words. Could it be that the language was from her mother's homeland years ago? She had hailed from the Bulgar Mountains before travelling to England to work in the mills. That was when she had met William and the two had been married thirty months later. The only trouble was that Emily had never learned the tongue. By the time she got back to the house, she had forgotten the reply. Why had her mother reverted back to the language of her own youth? Perhaps death had certain conditions that she did not know about?

If the message was important enough, her mother would make certain she had the chance to communicate with her again. So Emily went to bed and lay thinking of the dashing if impoverished Baron. When she closed her eyes she saw his smile. Fancied she could hear his voice feel the soft touch of his lips. She was yet to kiss him but there would be time and opportunity for that.

~

"It is indeed a lovely day. A day which makes one glad to be alive in", Emily was in a garrulous mood. She was on the arm of the most beautiful man in England. Maybe in the world.

"I always feel more cheerful when the sun shines", his lovely timber told her, "Even though I have had some tragedies in my life".

"Tragedies"? She echoed, "Do you want to tell me about them"?

He looked thoughtful before returning, "Perhaps when we know one another better I will burden you with them but not now, Sweet Emily".

"Then I look forward to that day", she told him earnestly, "When you feel you can share without reservation".

"Let us not spoil the sunshine", he urged, "When can I see you again, Emily"?

"I work for my father Monday to Friday", she explained, "But I have the evenings free".

"Would you like to go to the Odeon tomorrow night and see Alice in Wonderland"?

"The Magic Lantern Show"?

"Yes, it is called Cinema".

"I have never seen one".

"It would please me greatly to escort you to it then. Afterwards, we can go to The Willow Tea Rooms and have some tea and maybe a light supper".

"I would love it".

"But how did they make her larger and smaller"? Emily was excited as she asked Melling to explain the short film they had seen. Her cheeks were flushed with excitement at being with the handsome noble once again, "And when they stuffed the poor Dormouse in the teapot, that was so cruel".

"And so like you to be outraged for him", Melling smiled and picked up her hand holding it supportively in his own.

Emily was simply electrified by his touch. Thrilled by his every movement and gesture. It was fair to say, she was besotted by the Baron.

The most sublime month of her life swiftly flitted by and at the end of it the handsome yet impoverished Baron of Melling declared his love for her and asked her for her hand in holy matrimony. Emily gushed her positive reply but ended it by observing,

"All you need now, My Love, is the permission from my Father and we shall be married and you can show me, Melling Hall".

The slightest of clouds passed over Melling's bright features at the mention of William Brock, but he quickly dispelled it and said to her,

"Then that is what I will do Dear Sweet Emily".

That evening, as had been the case for every other before it Melling called at the stone structure that was the abode of the Brock's. The footman led him into the brightly illuminated hall and he almost collided with a man he did not recognise. It was unusual for he had been in Outstone Crags and thought he knew everyone. The man was lean short and his gaze was shifty as he hurried past Melling. The Baron shrugged and pushed the incident from his mind taking his seat in the lounge to await his appointment with the master of the house.

Fortunately, Brock did not keep him waiting long. He bustled into the room in his usual businesslike manner and grunted a salutation that was not especially friendly in tone,

"De Lacy! What do you want"? Not the best of starts.

"Have I offended you in some way, Mister Brock"? Melling asked for he was never curt no matter how severe the provocation.

"I think it time for you to return to Bridgehamside, De Lacy, there is nothing for you here".

"I sense great animosity in your tone and manner, Mister Brock, pray to tell me what I have done to earn it so"?

"Just state your business and let me get on with the rest of my evening. My accountant is due in the hour and I don't think I will be retiring till late".

Melling rose gracefully to a standing position and began, "I am sorry to hear you will be missing some sleep, Mister Brock. If it were not for the urgency of my own request I would not bother you at all then but there are reasons for my expediency".

Brock raised a supercilious eyebrow returning sardonically, "Not getting a job are you, De Lacy"?

Melling showed agitation for the first time, "You know I am landed gentry, Sir. We do not stoop to anything so scatological as employment".

Brock gave a mirthless smile, "Yes I did know that De Lacy. I, on the other hand, owe all my empire to sweat and labour, I am a self-made man. Tell me, Sir, did you see a rather insignificant looking individual leaving this house just as you arrived"?

Melling felt an illogical stroke of fear run down his spine as he admitted, "As chance would have it I did what of him"?

"His name was, Mister Crouch. Not the most savoury of individuals but he has his uses at times. I employ him as a private investigator. It did not escape my attention that you have been paying constant visits to my dear daughter, so I had Mister Crouch turn his investigative talents in your direction De Lacy".

"What of it? I have nothing to hide, Brock".

"Ah, I become Brock now. The mantle of respectability falls from you De Lacy, revealing the poor man that stands before me. The poor unemployed layabout".

"Have a care, Sir"! Melling bristled then, "Though you are my senior by several years I will not hesitate to thrash you if you do not mend your manner".

"Mister Crouch went into your family affairs, De Lacy", Brock went on as he poured himself a port from the crystal decanter on the sideboard. He offered Melling nothing. "You are destitute, Sir. Your father made various ruinous business transactions and not a single one of them astute".

"If you paid Crouch for that information then you have been short-changed, Sir. It is common knowledge that my dear departed Papa left this world penniless".

Brock nodded, "I agree. What is not known is the exact level of poverty you have now reached, you cannot afford even groceries, never mind staff to work in Melling Hall. You are one week away from putting the family seat up for sale".

Melling seemed to collapse in upon himself at the final revelation of his destitution, "It is true, Brock my privation is complete. It would make what I came to see you about seem ludicrous now".

"I am not blind De Lacy. It is plain for all to see that my daughter has fallen for you without restraint. I am therefore prepared to give you a choice as to your next course of action. You will take up a position in one of my factories and gain some assistance toward the upkeep of Melling Hall by wages honestly earned, or you will accept the sum of £8.00 to leave this evening and never return to Outstone Crags".

After making his decision Melling observed quite savagely, "You, Sir are a bounder and a cad of the first water"!

~

The accountant left at almost midnight. It had been a satisfactory meeting for Brock. Profits continued to soar he was a very wealthy man a very wealthy man indeed. The intensity of study had left Brock in a state of some excitement however and he knew he would not be able to sleep if he went straight to bed.

Lighting a huge cigar in the hall he unlocked the front door and decide that a stroll through the garden would help to relax him ready for bed. As he trod down the steps of Brock House an owl hooted in one of the many trees surrounding the property. The cloud that had previously covered the moon suddenly moved aside as though to light his path with lubricious candescence. Brock was too big a man and lacked the superstition to see anything sinister in the setting though. His tread was purposeful as he skirted the privet row and then traversed the gravel pathway that the carriages had churned with their iron wheels. Crunching forward he was surprised and annoyed to see a figure approaching him. They were still on Brock property, the man was trespassing.

"Good evening to you", Brock began, "I presume you are lost or in need of assistance to be on my land at this hour"?

By habit, he glanced toward the clock tower, that resided in the chapel and which would ring the hour very soon. The first blow caught him by surprise and did not hurt at all. It had glanced off his left temple around the orb of his eye socket. He glanced down at a sudden moistness that was dripping onto his left hand, the fluid was as ink in the poor illumination available. The second was completely different. Agonising shards lanced through his head as the garden ornament created from concrete fractured his skull. Brock sighed and as his body made a muffled thud onto the pathway, the clock in the tower chimed to declare murder at midnight.

Emily was in no fit state to identify the body. In one fateful evening, she had learned two terrible things. One was the violent death of her father. There were many suspects connected to the foul and bloody murder. The Mill owner had not risen to power by not making many enemies. An event to almost rival that disaster had been the news from Melling that he was going away on business and that he had not been able to see the now deceased William with regard to their betrothal. Fortunately, Melling had been long gone when the murder had taken place and the local constabulary did not suspect him to be under suspicion.

So it was the good doctor, Cedric Harriman who had spared her the horror of having to tell the police that the broken corpse on the mortician's slab was indeed her father.

As Emily stood at the graveside of her departed mother she reflected upon two things. She was now an orphan and she was also a very wealthy woman. Tears of anger frustration and mourning coursed down her pale and drawn features as she felt sorry for herself, for mourning is chiefly self-centred. The turnout was impressive. Brock had enjoyed many associations with businessmen in Outstone Crags and beyond. The entire workforce of the local mill was also there, for Emily had given them all a half-day to do so. It was an October morning and the wind that swept through the graveyard was decidedly autumnal. Emily was resplendent in a black Melton suit and leather boots. Her head was respectfully covered with a black scarf. The very same Pastor who had seen to the funeral service for her mother now resided over her last parent's. Mourners endlessly proclaimed their sadness at the sudden and untimely demise of the area's chief employer. Emily found herself constantly assuring them that nothing would change, she would take over her father's responsibilities and things would progress very much as they had done before.

By the time the wake was concluded she was practically dropping with fatigue. Yet she still possessed enough reserve of vitality to get the attention of Withers and ask him to send a telegram to Melling Hall.

Melling arrived the day after he had received it. The ceremony was hasty and secret, only five people were present. In addition to the bride and groom was the Paster, Withers as Melling's witness and Jennie the scullery-maid for Emily. Doctor Harriman learned all this much later. When Emily had been absent for over a week. On the night of the secretive ceremony, there was also a clandestine departure of the Brock carriage. Melling and the now Baroness were on their way to the dilapidated Hall. They arrived under cover of darkness. Which was just as well for even the facade of the Hall was somewhat unkempt. When Manders (recently recruited butler and general dogsbody, yet to receive any financial recompense for services rendered) opened the door it was with a hand-held lantern in his fist. He graciously allowed them entrance and hastily lit a few candles in the hallway.

"Emily gazed around her in wonder, though shabby, this was old money and the various paintings on the wall were all by respected artists, even if not of any great value. The drapes were clean if threadbare, other ornamentation had been sold to put off poverty for just a few more weeks. The alabaster columns and architrave were still impressive and the threadbare carpets had come from Turkey and a different age.

"Melling this is magnificent", she declared in an overawed whisper.

"Are you too tired to see the rest of the old place? Or would you prefer to retire post haste"?

"Please show me it all", came the delighted reply, "I'm too excited to sleep even though I'm fairly tired from the journey".

Melling gave her a tour of the once magnificent property. The drawing room with all its history, the library with yard after yard of leather-bound tomes. Several offices and studies containing heavy oak desks and curtained to conceal high arched windows that would let in all available light during the daylight hours. Then there were the servant quarters which also contained the kitchen and sleeping facilities. Finally, Melling led his bride up the rickety staircase and showed her the bathroom water closet and all the bedrooms. Theirs contained a massive four-poster bed with drapes that could be drawn around it on nights when drafts were at their fiercest. Emily blushed, it was the bed in which she would give herself to a man for the first time.

"May I bathe before retiring", she asked, glad of the dim oil-light, that concealed her blushes.

"Of course, that was what the cauldron was for in Manders quarter, he was heating the water up for your bath. You will find a water closet inside too, it goes into the local cess-pit. Not quite as luxurious as Brock House but...".

"It will be", Emily suddenly decided, "Once I have had the place refurbished. I will restore Melling Hall to its previous grandeur".

"What a delightful notion, My Sweet", Melling smiled, while at the same instant thinking, *'That's the reason I married you. You plain mare'!*

Later that night, Melling found his attitude change when he had taken his wife's virginity. Their love-making had been at first hesitant and gentle. The Baron lightly caressed his wife's pale body, felt her shiver with appreciation at his touch. After the brief instant of pain and a little blood, Emily found she could enjoy the penetration. They coupled twice, the second time she became the lady-astride and Melling poured himself into her with delighted abandon, but only after she had gasped her own astonishing climax. When they lay panting in one another's arms she told him sincerely,

"I love you, my Dear Sweet Lord".

Mechanically he returned the declaration and he found that it was not as disingenuous as he had anticipated.

Workmen arrived at Melling Hall the following afternoon, deposits paid by the new Baroness. Though it was not her title that persuaded the men to accept her cheques but rather her maiden-name. That very same afternoon another arrival was witnessed at the Hall.

"Darling I want you to meet my cousin, none other than my late Father's sister's son, the Baron Barnston of Bartonbrance".

Emily smiled at the dark figure before her. A veritable giant of a man. Tall, muscular, dark-haired and bearded. Bartonbrance did not smile indeed had had features that declared he had never done so.

"A pleasure to meet you, My Lord", she managed, "Please excuse the mess, we are engaged in refurbishments for the present".

"It is a pleasure to meet the Lady who has captured my cousin's heart", the baritone voice boomed from the dark man.

"I've invited Cousin Barnston to stay with us for a while, My Sweet", Melling told her then. "The hunting is good around our grounds and we will go shooting together".

Before Emily could accept or reject her new husband's offer to his intimidating cousin, the giant enthused,

"I'm looking forward to trying one of your William Evans, 1889, 12 Gauge, 6lbs 7oz, shotguns, Rufus".

'Yes' Thought Emily, 'I imagine you are a man who enjoys killing things'!

She said nothing, however, for if the indomitable Barnston kept Melling occupied and content she could supervise the workforce and add her own personal touches to the Hall.

That night Emily had retired early to her bed having done some paperwork sent by courier regarding the running of her various factories and also overseen the refurbishments that continued at a pace. It left Melling and Bartonbrance in the drawing room sipping newly purchased brandy from equally new glasses.

"A wise marriage, Rufus", the huge Baron of Bartonbrance congratulated, "Tell me how long will you wait before your bride has an *unfortunate accident*"?

Melling squirmed, he could not chide his cousin. After all, it had been the plan from the beginning and Barnston had murdered Brock for him. Even one such as the giant could slip into Outstone Crags unnoticed under cover of darkness.

"We must not move with too much haste", he cautioned, "Another death so soon after the inexplicable murder of the old man would alert the police to some sort of pattern and we would find both of our necks stretched upon the yardarm".

"Police", Barnston rumbled in his baritone chuckle, "Clueless plebeian stumbling around blindly in the dark. They have no clue, Cousin dear".

"Maybe not", Melling countered, "But Doctor Harriman is not so dim and I fancy him to be quite taken with my young bride".

"Speaking of whom, how does she ride"? Barnston enquired crudely, "Are you satisfying the pale mare? Maybe you should loan her to me for a few nights let me in the saddle and I'll...".

"No Barnston"! Melling's voice was sharper than he had intended. He modified it as he added hastily, "Just remember who is signing the cheques. Let us not ruin our machinations through haste".

The Baron of Bartonbrance regarded his cousin through narrowed eyes, "You're not falling for her are you, Rufus? Remember why I aid you in this affair, there is more than money at stake. You are still engaged to my sister and you *will* marry her. With the Brock financial clout behind us, we will rule the Midlands of England as it was meant to be".

"I have not forgotten Clarissa", Melling returned, a far-away look in his eye, "Know that I do all this for her also".

"Well just remember that when you're between that plain pale mare's thighs", Barnston growled. "She must not know that you bedded the wench. She was too ill for your marriage to be consummated remember that is the story we will both swear too"?

"I remember the arrangement", Melling admitted, "But if we act in haste all will be lost. That doctor would have the Peelers around here nosing about the minute Emily had her accident. Unless it is after a considerable interlude".

"And just what is a considerable interlude"? Bartonbrance demanded to know.

"I think a year".

"Are you out of your mind", the giant growled, "Clarissa would not wait that long. Neither would she believe that you never *blew the grounsils* with her".

"I will persuade her that I never slept with my wife", Melling assured, "You can rant and rage all you want Barnston, but I am still the architect of this design".

~

"I desire to know how far you are getting with your investigation, Detective Sergeant".

"I'm afraid we have hit a dead end, Doctor. We know the murder weapon was the heavy garden gargoyle. We have a list of possible suspects as long as my arm and no eye-witnesses.

"What about that new fingerprinting technique used last year to convict Harry Jackson down in the capital"?

"No use I'm afraid, Doctor. There were none on the gargoyle, the killer either removed them or was wearing gloves".

"Detective Sergeant", Harriman began sluggishly, "Have you not considered motive for this murder, who had the most to gain from Brock's demise"?

"I don't have the resources to go into that nest of vipers, Doctor. Brock was a businessman, he had enemies all through this county and beyond. Where would you start with a station of seven and other crimes being committed every day? I'm afraid the case is going to remain unsolved and you will have to accept it".

"What about his daughter"? Harriman finally revealed his motivation for pursuing the investigation or lack thereof. "She's now in the clutches of that impoverished cad, Melling. She may be in danger".

"It would seem that she went willingly with him and the Baron will surely have his own men for keeping the estate safe. I would think her safer than back here and am not about to start worrying about Emily Brock. The locals are glad to see the back of her and her black familiar if truth be told".

"Well I don't trust Melling", Harriman stated flatly.

"Then you go and see the good Baron for yourself", The Sergeant remarked, "I don't have the manpower to spare anyone to do it. Especially as she is now Baroness Melling".

~

Mephistopheles was purring contentedly. He was the only one in that frame of mind in the Hall at that time. Emily was growing tired of the sawing and banging and wanted an end to it. Not only that but her husband kept suggesting further embellishments that were causing the bill to rise by the hour and it was all her money that was being spent. She loved him dearly her dear sweet beautiful husband but he had no idea when it came to the notion of economising.

The shadow of Bartonbrance constantly hovered over the young couple too. Why didn't Melling ask the hulking and forbidding figure to leave? A low distant boom gave Emily her answer. They were out shooting again. As though the cold floor of the larder did not have enough game. It was not even the weather for it. Cool and wet with huge drops of rain falling at indeterminate intervals. The grounds surrounding Melling Hall would be sodden and forbidding to any but the most determined of hunters.

They would return with poor creatures suspended by their heels. No longer beautiful creations of nature but carcasses of meat for the ravening pair to consume. Emily was beginning to begrudge them the red wine bill. Their constant and banal chatter about what they would kill next. Most of all she begrudged her time away from the Brock business. It was not possible to conduct it all from a distance. Certain procedures had to be directly observed, supervised in a hands-on fashion. Foreman could only be relied on to a certain point. It was not their business their motivations were not the same.

"I have to return to Outstone Crags on the morrow, Darling", she told her husband as they dined that evening. As usual, they were not along. The ubiquitous Baron Bartonbrance was at her husband's side making Emily feel like the intruder.

"Why"? Melling was in one of his tacit moods. When it came to addressing her at any rate.

"I need to oversee the Mill for a couple of reasons. I don't want Melling Hall to prove a drain on Brock resources".

Melling's beautiful mouth twisted in distaste as he acidly observed, "Are you beginning to resent the cost that is involved in bringing the family seat our family seat to its former glory, Baroness"?

"Not yet", Emily finally stunned him with her candour, "But should my late Father's ventures begin to suffer as a direct result of my continued absence from the Crags then I surely would find it hard not to".

"I see", Melling bit off a piece of Game with savage teeth. "You know, I am sure that I will miss you terribly. If you must go, though, you must go. I cannot conceive of you doing so alone, however. Even in the carriage, the roads are not completely safe. Barnston, my dear fellow would you accompany my wife and act as her shield from all harm"?

Emily's eyes widened in horror at such a notion and she blurted, "Forgive me My Lord of Bartonbrance, but I would not put you to such inconvenience. Manders can be at my side while the driver would be his fitting ally should matters take a sinister turn.

"You know very well how useful Manders is proving as a foreman to those work shy Irish Navvies, My Sweet", Melling objected, "And Barnston has the physical presence to deter any would-be attacker. What say you, My Dear Fellow"?

Emily hastily interjected, "I did not mean tomorrow of course. I meant in the near future. I shall set a date once the post arrives this week".

Melling's smile was thin as he observed, "Forgive me, My Petal, your manner at the commencement of this conversation indicated greater haste. Maybe that was my inadvertence"?

"Yes", Emily replied unhappily, "Perhaps".

She was not finished, however. That night in bed as they lay sweating after lovemaking she took up the matter afresh. She had been most arduous to ensure that Melling was more than physically satisfied before broaching the subject once again.

"My Love, I do need to return to the Crags and rather more urgently than I indicated at dinner".

"Oh? Why the deception then"?

"Because I wanted to speak to my husband in private for once. You and Bartonbrance seemed joined at the hip. Further, I do not want him to be my guard on the way home".

"Home"? Melling sounded peeved, "This is your home now, My Sweet".

"You know what I mean. The repairs to Melling Hall are a huge drain on finances and I need to assure myself that the source of those funds does not dry up due to neglect".

She was couching her words in a language that Melling understood only too well. He thoughtfully responded at length,

"Then I shall accompany you myself, "My Love".

"I intend to visit my old friends in addition to the mills, Darling. The visit would bore you terribly I'm afraid".

Melling sounded disappointed, "You don't want your loving husband by your side. You are growing tired of me"?

"Nothing could be farther from the truth", she tried to assure. "I simply need to be in Outstone Crags and without your lovely distraction".

Melling heaved a sigh of regret and finally conceded, "Very well, Emily. Go and be the Mill Owner' daughter once again if it pleases you".

Emily took her victory in silence even if it did come with a slight. She said no more.

Melling and Bartonbrance were both early for breakfast the following morning. Melling told his cousin the conversation of the night before. The giant listened patiently before replying,

"When she returns she must be eliminated. Before she decides to cease skimming funds from her business to maintain your seat. The only way to be totally certain of her fortune is to become her widower".

~

"It is so good to see you", Harriman told her with genuine warmth and feeling. You have been missed from the House and from the Mill and I have missed you too".

"As I have missed you, Cedric", Emily found she meant the sentiment more than previously realised. "I will be staying just long enough to supervise some changes at the factories and then I must rejoin my husband".

A cloud fell across the doctor's features then and his tone and mien promptly altered greatly, "I'm afraid I have some information that you will not welcome regarding the Baron of Melling, Dear Emily".

"Information that I should hear"? She asked him, taking another cucumber triangle from the fine crockery.

"That I cannot say", Cedric confessed, "It will cause you some distress but I feel you must know it".

"Very well Cedric, tell me your intelligence"? Emily would not have countenanced it a month past, but her feelings toward Melling though still of an ardent nature were tinged by the ever presence of the Baron of Bartonbrance.

"Have you any knowledge of the existence of a private investigator called Crouch", the good doctor began.

Emily dredged her memory before confessing, "The name is unknown to me".

Harriman took a sip of his tea before informing, "It was not unknown to your dear departed father though, Emily".

"Father used the services of such a man? When"?

Harriman grimaced confessing, "I chanced to bump into the private detective during some medical procedures I was doing in a police investigation. He told me he had informed your father of certain details regarding the Baron of Melling. Details that were given just before he was violently killed"!

Emily paled. Asked in a hushed tone, "You concluded that the two events were connected did you not, My Old Friend"?

Harriman nodded, "When I heard the detail of Crouch's report to your father I could not come to any other".

"I see. You had better tell me the particular of said".

"I suspect you know the first part by now, Emily. The fact that Melling was penniless, almost at the point of selling Melling Hall. William thus decided that the Baron's only interest in you was a monetary one".

"Father would see things that way", Emily smiled sadly. "You said details though, Cedric. What was the rest of the report"?

Harriman had the grace to look shame-faced as he informed, "I'm sorry but it will not be welcome news to you, Dear Emily. Before he met you the Baron was engaged to be married to another, Baroness Clarissa of Bartonbrance".

"Bartonbrance"! Emily echoed with a whisper, "Of course. It explains quite a deal".

"I'm sorry to be the bearer of bad tidings. I would not upset you for the world, Dear Emily. It is something I felt you must know though".

Emily told the doctor, "The Baron of Bartonbrance and therefore Clarissa's brother, is a constant companion of my husband at Melling Hall".

Harriman nodded, "That would seem to tie into Crouch's report. One could come to a rather unsettling conclusion as to his motives for being there, Emily".

"And what is your conclusion, Cedric"?

"That the Baron of Bartonbrance is there to look after his sister's interests".

"But Melling is now married to me. What interests.... Oh! Surely not, Cedric"?

"They may very well have conspired to commit a violent crime before, Emily. If something happened to you, Melling would then be free to marry Clarissa. As both Baron of Melling Hall, now restored and as the wealthy owner of Brock Mills".

"That is a desolately appalling contemplation, Cedric. I am repelled by the notion and yet I love my husband".

"I understand", Harriman returned, "But if you return to Melling Hall, I think you will be in jeopardy, Emily".

Emily replaced her teacup to its saucer with a slim and trembling hand before replying, "I cannot avoid returning to the seat of the family. My husband's seat. I do not see what I can do"?

"Then at least let me come with you for a little while. As your guest. I have in my possession a Webley Mk IV chambered in .455 with 100mm barrel. If there is any trouble I can protect you".

"And your Practice"?

"Will still be here upon my return. It will give you time to hire an agency to take up where I leave off. I would like to see the work you have done on the Hall anyway, Emily. Word has it that it is splendid".

A gracious offer, Cedric and one I accept without reservation. Only know this, I love Melling and would not see harm come to him. Do you understand me"?

"I promise you, Emily, I will never incite violence. I only seek your adequate protection nothing more".

"And on those terms, My Dear Doctor, I invite you to Melling Hall once my business in Outstone Crags is completed".

~

"Darling, I believe you know Doctor Harriman"?

"Of course. Are you ill though, My Sweet"? Melling tired to disguise the hope in his voice.

With the comforting feeling of the Webley nudging his ribs Harriman replied for her, "Your wife is in the best of health, My Lord. This is merely a social visit on my part".

"Welcome to Melling Hall then, Doctor, I'll have Manders show you to a guest room", Melling gave a stiff nod. He then waited for the doctor to be absent before enquiring,

"I did not realise the good doctor was interested in architecture and furnishings, Emily".

"Only ours", Emily simpered. It brought her no small pleasure to see that her husband did not share her enthusiasm for the medical man's visit. "There will be four for dinner, so nice that Barnston will not be the gooseberry for once".

Melling soon found a reason for taking his cousin into the library and informing him of the new development.

"He supposedly came for nothing other than a Glimpserama", he told Bartonbrance "As though he would remember next week in the months ahead".

"Clarissa is making noises of impatience, Rufus", the giant objected. "Soon you must act, or she is likely to turn up unannounced"!

Melling blanched, "She would ruin everything and raise the suspicion of my wife if she did that".

"Then there must be no wife for her to raise the suspicion of"! Bartonbrance declared with heat. "It is time to remove the obstacles that stand in the way of our ultimate goal, Rufus".

"And the good doctor"? Melling objected, "You would remove him as well no doubt. Just how would such be explained to the authorities, Barnston"?

The giant gave a ghoulish grimace and stated, "Bridgehamside Cliffs. The two of them had gone for a hike in your wife's new estate. An unfortunate accident when both plummeted to their joint demise".

"Together? Without anyone else being there"?

Bartonbrance leaned in close to his cousin's ear and explained, "I will engineer they both fall down the staircase here. Then under cover of night, take them to the cliffs and throw them over the edge. Their injuries will be conclusive to a fall, none will be able to perceive that it was the result of more than one".

Melling shuddered, "Let me think on it. Do nothing until I give you the word".

170

"Then do not wait too long"! Bartonbrance warned, "Clarissa grows more impatient by the day".

Melling sighed, "The doctor would never accept that Emily fell down the stairs without assistance. You will have to do him first".

"Or you could do her while I do the doctor"?

Melling shook his head, "I think not, it would affright my sensibilities".

Bartonbrance gave rent to a hollow chuckle, "You've grown accustomed to her saddle, cousin".

Melling was stern as he instructed, "I refuse to answer vulgarity, Barnston. Remember this, as we speak you are guilty of murdering the old fool, Brock. Something I can claim entire ignorance of. Right now I can make do with what I have. Your motivation is your dear sister, it has much less to do with me".

The glare he received from this observation was one of animus fury and he was forced to reflect that perhaps the death of Barnston might be a better end to his conundrum!

Emily was carefully doing her hair by the newly fitted electric lights when Melling entered their bedroom. He gazed at her for a full thirty seconds before observing curiously,

"You look lovely this evening, Dear Sweet Emily".

"Why thank you, Darling", she returned, surprised by his unsolicited gentility, "Do you think I need more rouge on my cheeks"?

"Perhaps a little", he admitted, "You are pale from your journey. Was it very tiring"?

She nodded. Rose and took him in her arms. Then she asked suddenly, "Do you truly love me, Melling"?

"Without reservation", he returned and there was a surprise in his voice. Melling realised he was telling the truth!

"Dinner is at eight is it not"? She asked holding him at arm's length, "You need to dress for it, My Love".

"Yes, yes", he agreed and was distracted, "Firstly though a matter has suddenly occurred to me that I must discuss with Barnston. If you will excuse me".

"Can it not wait"? She felt a curious sense of foreboding.

"No", he was obdurate, "I must go and see him forthwith".

He turned and rushed out of the doorway. Alarmed, Emily pressed after him in time to see the tableau being played out on the landing.

Harriman and Bartonbrance were just about to descend to the dining hall when Melling cried out,

"Careful, Doctor. At the top of the stairs".

In the next few seconds, everything seemed to happen at the same instance. At Melling's cry of warning, Bartonbrance gave a roar of fury and grabbed the arm of Doctor Harriman. For his part, Harriman fumbled beneath his jacket and pulled out the Webley. They were suddenly locked in an embrace of malicious intent. Melling, after firstly hesitating suddenly rushed toward them to aid whom? The sound of the revolver firing was surprisingly and incredibly loud. Emily heard herself scream. Melling suddenly clutched his chest in astonished horror and fell on the landing. At the same moment Bartonbrance's spade-like fist connected with the doctor's jaw and he too was thrown to the first-floor carpet.

Emily was frozen to the spot in abject terror. The Baron of Bartonbrance gave her a look of pure hatred and advanced menacingly toward her. His arms were outstretched and his massive fingers were like claws as they nearly reached her. The frigid draught that suddenly sprang onto the landing was a surprise to them both. Bartonbrance half turned to see the apparition materialise. He grunted in dismayed fear at the decayed figure that was running with gore and ichor.

"No", came the eerie voice that only Emily recognised as that belonging to her mother. "You have earned a place with me in Purgatory"!

At this, the giant of a Baron cried out. Even he was afraid of such an ominous threat. Rose Brock devoted wife and mother, born and then died, 1860 - 1889 hovered over Bartonbrance and something began to be torn from his massive carcass. It was violet, malformed and hideous. It was his soul! His dead body fell beside that of Melling's and the violet embodiment that existed beyond death was devoured by the kelpie. Rose gave a macabre grin and reminded,

"I said I would always watch over you, Emily. Alas, my time has come also. Farewell, My Beautiful Daughter, you will see me again, never".

Then the apparition vanished as abruptly as it had appeared.

Finally, Emily found the power of locomotion. It was to Harriman that she went. He was just beginning to regain consciousness as Emily having kneeled down placed his head in her lap.

"What happened"? He managed.

"You saved me", she told him simply. It seemed the only thing he might just believe.

Harriman took her hand and after an instant or so managed to regain his feet. He went over to the Baron of Melling. After a short inspection, he regretfully informed Emily with a shake of his head,

"I'm afraid you are widowed".

Then he turned to the body of Bartonbrance. "I can't see what... I cannot understand what happened to this man, but he lives no longer".

"My dear departed husband managed a blow to his temple before he finally fell due to his fatal wound. Some sort of freak blow. Cedric, it was the Baron of Bartonbrance's finger that depressed the trigger. Do you hear me"?

Harriman sagged, "If you say so, Emily. That is what happened".

Emily nodded, "Indirectly, Cedric, you saved me from the murderous duo, thank you".

"Is that how you see it"? The doctor managed.

"That is exactly what happened", Emily decided. "We will forget the events of this day given time, My Dear Doctor, I promise you".

"Forget"? Harriman echoed, "Are you certain"?

Emily smiled gently, "Cedric, I have never been more certain of anything in my life"!

The Demon Drink

CHRISTINE CHANTELE

1.

'What a beautiful morning,' Sandra thought to herself. Only she knew the secret she had buried deeply inside of her.

It felt like the sun had never shone so bright, the air was so fresh, the sweet smell of flowers filled the air. Birds were singing in the trees. The feeling of relaxation and relief, for the first time. Feeling her soul was free from the shackles that had held her down all her short life.

Not one person did not feel relief from the death of Edward, her father, she had done them all a favour, even though they didn't know it.

Sitting in the garden of her new cottage, having breakfast, drinking in her new life, loving every minute. Looking back how she arrived at this point in her life. It was as if she had emerged from a black hole of existence to a bird flying free from a cage.

Remembering when she was a young girl sitting alone in a small but adequate room. The oldest of three children, Sandra was eight years old with long dark brown hair, slim build, hazel eyes like her father, which was the only likeness she had of him. A very strong personality, this is what helped her to survive. The feeling of loneliness every day consumed her life. How could that be in a house with five people? It was true! This was her existence. Sandra tried to keep a smile on her face but the look of despair followed her like a black cloud.

Not the brightest of girls, was this because she wasn't very academic or the circumstances of the life she had been dealt. Only time would reveal the answer.

Sandra's mother called out to come help with dinner, she knew what that meant, not to keep her waiting or she would feel the wrath of her father. That was a really bad thing to do, as she knew only too well. That's the way it was, always had been, probably always would be.

Father was a big burly man, not fatherly at all. He was always very hard on her and strict. Many times she had felt the stinging and burning then the aftermath of pain, from his large oversized hands. At six feet and four inches tall and a heavyweight, his sheer presence caused a ripple of fear all around him. A muscular frame from manual work had kept him fit. People that knew him were careful not to antagonise him in any way, others knew of him.

Very unhappy with how his life had turned out. Edward had to marry as Sandra would be putting in an appearance in a few months. Feeling tied down, trapped and oppressed from the freedom he longed for.

Sandra and her Mum were blamed. They suffered the consequences every day, which were definitely not justified. Life was not easy with three children to feed and clothe. There was never money left at the end of each month. It didn't help that Edward went to the pub most nights with his friends. He would rather be somewhere else, anywhere than at home. Drowning his sorrows in the bottom of a beer glass or whisky when he could afford it, trying to bury his problems. His body could not take this kind of abuse as he would discover only too soon.

William was Sandra's younger brother, no one used that name, everyone called him Billy. Always into something or other. He could always make her day better. He was five years old, had a cheeky smile, dark brown hair, brown eyes like chocolate that twinkled with mischief. A very loving little boy that everyone could relate too, often commenting on how angelic he looked. A lovable little rogue.

The house where they lived was a small terrace, it was all they could afford at the time. Furniture was nothing special, mostly second hand, donated by family or friends. Although it was comfortable.

Angela was Sandra's Mum, five feet three inches tall, a thin wispy lady with a pale complexion. Angela kept the house very clean and tidy, everything in its own place. Their clothes were not expensive, more functional always clean and pressed, she made sure of that. Not a gourmet cook but the meals she cooked were tasty, wholesome and on time. Doing the best with what she had. Working just down the road at the local laundrette, part-time for a few hours each day. Virtually the same work she did at home, the difference, she earned money. It wasn't much but it helped make ends meet. Edward constantly said it was all she was good for, he belittled her every chance he could. Talking down to her, being condescending.

Angela was trapped in a loveless marriage, her children were the only thing that brightened every day.

Sandra helped a lot with the smaller children, she loved it, as she could escape for some peace. They were no trouble, playing happily in the park together having so much fun, laughter filled the air. For a short time, Sandra did not have to worry about her father looming around in the background. Forgetting for a while the stress of her home life. It was nice to relax and be a child again, playing and enjoying life as she should be able too, as a normal girl of her age. At the same time keeping a watchful eye on her sibling's, making sure she keeps them safe from harm. Sandra loved them so much, both were her reason to smile. Optimistic when they were around, they kept her calm.

A happy girl with an air of sadness, trying to enjoy herself every chance she could, as she did not know when the next time would be. Rolling down small hills at the park with her brother and sister, climbing trees. This is how life should be for any child. Forgetting the heavy burden she carried for just a little while.

On one occasion during a visit to the park, Billy heard noises coming from the bushes. He was not scared of anything only his father. Bravely fighting his way through the bushes towards the noise, it sounded like muffled crying, finally, he was all the way in. There on the ground curled up in a little ball was a tiny kitten, hungry and cold, crying for its Mum. Sandra tucked it inside her coat to keep it warm. The three of them searched the whole park all afternoon, to no avail, they could not find the mother cat. Deciding to take it home, they ran all the way.

Lucy ran inside and asked Edward if they could have a kitten, to which he replied,

"If a kitten was brought into his house he would drown it in the sink". Sandra heard this as she opened the door, turning around she shouted Lucy to come outside so that she could clean her shoes. The three of them ran around the side of the house.

2.

Thinking for a while she took the children to the lady's house than she ran errands for. Asking her if she knew anyone that would take the kitten while explaining how they had found it, as they wanted it to be safe. The lady loved it straight away, her dog started washing the kitten while wagging his tail. Feeling sure it would be good for them both. Not having children of her own, thanking Sandra for saying they could come round anytime to play with the pets, keeping her company too. As she was very fond of the children. It made her happy to see them.

Showing on her hands were the signs of Sandra's daily toll from peeling potatoes, vegetables then chopping them up. Every day was the same, washing dishes afterwards, bathing the younger ones, continually having her hands in water they were dry and rough.

Billy and Lucy (the little girl) did not mind they loved her very much as well. Both of them always gave her a cuddle when she looked sad, it never failed to cheer her up, at least she knew she was loved. It wasn't always that way, before they came along the feeling of being unlovable, haunted her Little sister Lucy was just three years old. Cute as a button, on the shy side, did not talk very much.

Hiding behind her two older siblings, so she felt safe. Lucy has blonde hair and the most beautiful green eyes, the same as her Mums, that sparkled like emeralds. Slim build, that's because she is always bouncing around like a jelly bean. That was her Mum's affectionate name for her.

Sandra was an obedient child, she was too afraid of her father to step out of line. At school she was clean and tidy, so well behaved, was helpful and well mannered, her teachers liked her. Her Mum had taught her to be respectful, as she loved her Mum so much, she listened and learned from her, doing as she was told, to keep the peace as well. No telling what her father would do next if she didn't.

On a few occasions, Sandra helped a neighbour. This was the lady that took in the kitten. An older lady that lived alone with her small dog, on the same street, just a few doors away. Running a few errands to the local shops, sometimes walking the dog. The kind lady gave her a bit of spending money for being so helpful. It saved her having to go, especially when she didn't feel up to it herself.

Sandra had a hiding place in her bedroom, behind her set of drawers, keeping her money in a small tin, adding to it each time she earned some more. She was saving to buy her Mum a present, as it is her birthday soon.

Angela knew Edward was hard on Sandra and that she was afraid of him, But!! so was Angela. They had both lived with it for a long time, did not mention it, just gave each other that strained look of fear whenever Edward started shouting or came home in a bad mood.

One day when Sandra was at the shop's she noticed a brightly coloured scarf in one of the windows. It was lavender in colour with tinges of pink. She knew her Mum would love it. So excited she ran all the way home, into the house and straight upstairs to her bedroom. closing the door behind her. Taking her tin from it's hiding place tipping the contents onto her bed. Carefully counting out, one pound, two, three and sixty pence.

"Oh!" she exclaimed, "I am short by twenty-five pence. The scarf cost's three pounds eighty-five." Feeling a twinge of sadness, returning her coins to the tin, placing it back in its hiding place.

3.

Hurrying downstairs to help her Mum with the little ones, being careful not to show sadness in her face. It was short lived as she still had time to earn some more money, hoping the scarf would still be in the shop.

Only one week later she had enough. Finally! off she went so happy to find it still there. Skipping with glee all the way home. The paper bag the scarf had been placed in was covered in lovely pink flowers, Sandra used it as wrapping paper, tying it with a pink ribbon in a neat bow. Just in time for her Mum's birthday.

Two days later she ran downstairs so giddy, almost tripping but managed not to lose her balance. Handing the gift to her Mum full of excitement. Encouraging her to open it. Father had already left for work, so the house was so calm. Angela loved the scarf and hugged Sandra, telling her not to spend what bit of money she had to buy her presents. They had a really enjoyable breakfast together, chattering away to each other, that was not allowed when father was around. Sandra had helped the two little children to make cards for there Mum, Angela loved them.

A few days later, Edward came home early from the pub, he was in a sorry state and a bad mood. One of his girlfriends that he kept in the background had finished with him because he was not in a position to leave his wife, or, would not. The door flew open hitting the wall with a loud bang. Angela and Sandra froze with fear, knowing only too well there was about to be trouble. Sandra was just finishing up before going to bed. Her Mum told her to go now, so she would be safe. Sandra did not want her Mum to be hurt but had to do as she said. Only walking halfway upstairs, she stood there wishing she were older and stronger so that she could prevent her coming to any harm.

Edward was shouting so loud he wakened the two little ones, Sandra went to their bedroom, she comforted them both and read a story so they could settle back down to sleep. Walking quietly out of the room, she sneaked halfway back down the stairs, her Mum was leaning on the kitchen table, with blood on her face. Giving Sandra a small sign that she was alright. It gave her some relief. Furniture was tipped over, dishes were smashed on the floor, such a mess.

Edward caught sight of the scarf Sandra had bought her Mum, he snatched it from the coat hook. Screaming at her saying he had not bought it, so she could not have it. He took a box of matches from the drawer, striking one he set it on fire at the bottom, it started burning, Angela grabbed the scarf and tried to put out the flames burning her hands in the process. Edward snatched it back, throwing it in the sink to burn. Walking over to the sofa he almost fell onto it where he promptly went asleep.

Sandra ran to her Mum to help with her hands, putting cold water in a bowl carefully placed them both in it to cool them down and take away the stinging and burning feeling. Hugging her Mum, Sandra looked at her father with an overwhelming pain in her eyes, she was disgusted by the mere sight of him. Why didn't she have a father that loved them like the other children at school? Feeling so sad she went to bed too exhausted to even cry.

This was not an isolated incident, there were many more of abuse to Sandra and Angela, especially destroying the things they loved. As time passed Edward drank more and more, the anger and violence continued, those were very dark days.

It was not always this way. Angela would pack a picnic for her and the children at the weekend (weather permitting) - when Edward was in the pub, as usual, wasting money. Not being concerned with minute detail. It was their escape into the country which was a short walk from where they lived. It was a small village surrounded by countryside. The children would skip along happily, enjoying fresh air, sunshine and freedom, for a short time. Over two fields and a small hill until they arrived at a most beautiful place, a running Brooke - filled with small fish. The view was breathtaking over the fields and meadow. Over to the left was a wood, it looked intriguing, it was however too far for the little ones. One day maybe when the children have grown.

The picnics were their favourite times, sharing cuddles and love for each other that shone around them like a beacon of light enveloping as a soft warm blanket, binding each together. Only one complaint time went so quickly, all too soon it was home time, back to the drudge and fear again.

The years rolled past. Now Sandra is twelve years old, she has grown into a little lady, sort of in-between a child and a grown up. Knowing that one day she will be bigger and stronger to stand up to her father and protect her Mum.

Something was different today when the children arrived home from school. It seemed unusually quiet, Mum was not in the kitchen as usual. Sandra told Billy and Lucy to go upstairs to change their clothes, as not to upset them both. Mum was laid down on the sofa, not once had she ever seen her Mum do this in the daytime. Angela had a bad cough and a cold, she was not breathing very well either. Sandra helped her Mum upstairs and put her in bed, giving her two tablets with a glass of water, as well as cough medicine. As she was a lot more grown up for her age than she should be, she knew what needed to be done. Hurrying downstairs after telling the younger ones to play in their bedroom and not make any noise. Quickly Sandra prepared dinner then tidied round, so it would be clean for when her father arrived home from work, as he had such a short fuse.

Dinner was on the table when her father came home, he demanded to know where his wife was. Sandra explained. He did not really care. After dinner was eaten, during which Edward had constantly complained. Instead of going to check on his wife, he got washed and changed his clothes then went to the pub as usual.

After Edward had gone, Sandra made some chicken soup, also took a jug of fresh water, a glass and the next dose of medication. Bathing the children and tucking her brother and sister in bed, then reading a story while reassuring them both that Mum would be a lot better in the morning after a good nights sleep. Sandra went downstairs, washed the dishes, dried and put them away, tidied up, then prepared all the things that were needed for the next morning. Clothes were laid out, lunches packed, placed in the fridge. Having one last check on her Mum before she went to bed very tired and worried.

In the morning Angela was up, dressed, downstairs, breakfast was ready. Saying she felt a lot better, Sandra could see the strain in her face, pale white skin, also moving slower than usual. After a few days, Angela was a lot worse her breathing becoming laboured. Sandra tried to convince her Father to phone

Doctor Smitters. He shrugged it off saying her Mum would be alright, it was just a cold, he promptly went out as usual.

Next morning Sandra waited until her Father had gone to work. Asking a friend to take Billy and Lucy to school, then phoning Doctor Smitters, who could not come until dinnertime. Sandra sat waiting with her Mum, talking softly to her, saying the children were at school and everything had been taken care of in the house. The Doctor arrived just after twelve o'clock, he was very concerned, telling Sandra that her Mum was very ill and must go to the hospital, he suspected it was pneumonia.

An ambulance took Angela away with Sandra by her side, holding her Mum's hand reassuring her that she would soon feel better. Also - as safe and warm in hospital. Angela squeezed Sandra's hand, asking if she would promise to always look after the two younger children for her. Of course, there was never any doubt. The ambulance rushed along the roads with blue lights flashing, desperately trying to get Angela to the hospital as quickly as was possible, she was very ill. Her breathing was grave, oxygen mask on her face, drip inserted in one arm, blood pressure cuff on the other, stickers placed to check her heart on a mobile heart monitor. Not one of her vital signs was normal. She was burning up, the temperature was too high but she was shivering with cold, her skin was clammy to the touch.

It was not long before their arrival at the hospital, it seemed like the journey took forever, Sandra was so worried she knew her Mum was really ill. She was right to be worried, over the next few days Angela continued to get worse. However Edward did not take any time to visit, just carried on each night becoming inebriated.

Sandra did not go to school, sitting beside her Mum's bedside each day holding her hand. Talking about all the lovely things they would do together, all the fun they had to look forward to. It wasn't to be, after four days Angela deteriorated very quickly, she passed away early in the afternoon.

The family doctor, who was also a friend, was at the hospital at the time, he took Sandra home so that he could inform Edward of his wife's death. He also phoned the school and arranged for someone to bring the younger children home. Edward was not especially concerned, being devoid of feelings, incapable of love or compassion. The two of them were well insured, which had been arranged at the beginning of their marriage.

Sandra had no idea what insurance money was for, she just did not understand. Not at the tender age of twelve. Edward soon frittered the money away his drinking was worse than before. He felt lumbered with three children.

Sandra took on the role of her Mum. Looking after the home and family, as she had promised. It was difficult for her. Although she knew how her Mum had taught her well. Sewing was her best skill, very neat work. Edward arranged some sewing work for her with the local people, to bring extra money into the household. Never complaining she carried on with her promise, she did so with all the love she had for the children and her Mum. Very tired each evening falling into her bed exhausted. Avoiding her father as much as was possible. Not much conversation passed between them. Usually just lecturing from him, nothing had changed, still was not good enough whatever she did. Always relieved when he had gone out.

The only thing that kept Sandra going was the children and the fact that one day she would be old enough to leave and never have to be controlled by him again. She carried on with grim determination. At school too, studying fervently. The teachers knew her situation. Keeping an eye on her because of the history of abuse. Helping and encouraging as much as possible, to try and improve her position in life. Giving her a chance after the daily toll she had known in her short life. Studying each night when her choirs were finished, children tucked up in bed, peace to study. It paid off. Sandra passed all her exams, qualifying to carry out office work.

The family Doctor that looked after her Mum and the rest of her family, had watched Sandra and the children, to make sure they were free from harm. In the disguise that he was looking after their health. Edward was ignorant to the fact, he was so self-absorbed.

A job opportunity had opened up at the Doctors' surgery, the doctor's receptionist, that had worked there for thirty years, decided it was time to retire. Knowing Sandra as well as he did and that she was a good worker, the doctor offered Sandra the job. Full training would be given by the receptionist for the first month before she was due to leave. Sandra jumped at the chance, she saw it as a step nearer to getting away from her father.

Sandra was sixteen then, working at the doctor's office gave her the boost she needed. So many times she had been reduced to tears, wishing she were somewhere else, away from the mental and emotional abuse she endured on a regular basis. Keeping herself in survival mode was how she coped. Giving her the energy to carry on, that and the knowledge that it would not be for much longer. How was she going to remove the younger children away from him, this had to be worked out, although she had no idea.

Billy was thirteen by then and could take Lucy to school in the morning, then pick her back up in the afternoon. Lucy was a precocious eleven, he was very protective of her as she was still shy and timid, due to the constant shouting and bullying from Edward. Sandra suffered the most as she would deliberately draw him away from the younger two, to try and spare them.

Edward had not married again, the last thing he wanted was to be shackled again, that was how he looked at it. Why should he, when he had someone at home doing all the work for him? Still keeping his girlfriends in the background as always. Most people knew as he was so transparent. Even now he was never happy just irritating. The vile that spilt from his mouth was disgusting, especially when directed at his own children.

At eighteen years old Sandra had become a woman. Suddenly one morning when she was at work, a phone call came in for the Doctor, her father had collapsed at work. He was taken to the hospital where tests were carried out. It was discovered he had cirrhosis of the liver from the years of alcohol abuse. The liver specialist explained that as few as a couple of drinks could cause him to collapse again possibly fatally. Edward denied his consumption, denied taking tablets for his hangovers. Doctors did not believe either. The course of action as from that day would be no more alcohol, observe a strict diet. He was issued with lots of leaflets and booklets on where to get help and advice about foods and medication. Especially medication he was to avoid. It was no surprise to any who knew him that did not listen. completely ignored the advice he was being given, except he did say he would stop drinking.

Edward was allowed to go home as Sandra said she would take care of him. She was true to her word, reading all the leaflets and booklets that Edward just threw into a drawer. Learning all about the liver, while continuing to run the household and take care of her Father. Taking time off work for a couple off weeks, cooking wholesome meals and soups she made sure Edward ate them all, keeping his fluid intake up at the same time. After one week he was not getting any better, indeed, he looked worse than ever.

People kept asking how he was, Sandra kept voicing her concerns, saying she was worried about him drinking again.

When she arrived home one day Edward was in a foul mood. He was suffering from alcohol withdrawal. He hated being stuck at home, as he was too ill to do anything about it, he had to make the best of his situation. Sandra took the brunt of his ire. She chose to use it to her advantage, she suggested to him, to invite his friends to visit. Then very sternly advised that they must not bring him any alcohol. Edward was furious, who was she, telling him what to do?

Friends of Edward's arrived that evening, three of them, all brought a bottle. Two of Whiskey, one containing Brandy. They were for Edward - the visitors had their own. Sandra took all three away. Edward raised the roof he was so angry, she was not deterred, Sitting downstairs sewing until the visitors left. The children were tucked up in bed.

Putting her sewing away, she took all three bottles and two glasses to Edward. But! Was she willing to let him kill himself? Now she would have a drink with him, knowing he could not resist, he was only too happy to drink each drink she poured for him, she did not drink any, just sat nursing her glass pretending to take the occasional sip. Carrying on drinking she kept filling his glass until he had drunk both bottles of whiskey and half the bottle of brandy, finally, he passed out. Carefully she placed the bottles on the bed at the side of him, taking the glasses away and washed them.

She calmy retired for the night. uninterrupted slumber evaded her. Getting up early the next morning, finding mundane tasks until it was time for the children to go to school.

Slowly she walked towards the back room where her Father was. She reluctantly opened the door, standing in a moment of hesitation. She entered the room walking towards the bed. Leaning over she touched his face it felt so cold, testing for a pulse on his wrist, she felt nothing. She had to make sure by feeling for a pulse in his neck, she knew how due to working at the Doctors'. For a moment she looked at him. Thought,

'Now you are as cold as your heart!'

Calmly she walked out of the room She was numb, really not knowing how to respond to her lack of loss. Walking next-door explaining that she thought her father had died and would they mind phoning the Doctor for her. The neighbours went in with her, Sandra seated herself in the living-room while they went to check, he was not breathing. Finally, Doctor Smitters arrived and confirmed the death.

Edward's corpse was taken away. Sandra was alone she needed to burn some incriminating rubbish in the fireplace. Left lying about in the back room. Calmly she burnt lots of empty packets of Ibuprofen, Asprin, Paracetamol and Naproxen, The constituents of a cocktail she had crushed - adding it to all her Fathers food and drinks. From the time Sandra had started working at the surgery, no one suspected anything when the bottles of alcohol were on the bed. Everyone knew he was an alcoholic, so suspected nothing.

Everything was arranged by the Good Doctor. The funeral and all the paperwork, as well as insurance money. It was a surprisingly substantial amount. With it, she would be able to buy their lovely new home. As her eighteenth birthday had been just before the funeral. Making sure she placed money in bank accounts for her brother and sister. Savings for when they grew up. The money came from Edwards work too as well as his pension he had paid into since leaving school, as he had worked there since then.

Two beautiful kittens were cuddled up on Sandra's lap. Happiness washed over her with a huge sigh of contentment, at last.

The Final Cut

GRANT VIOLINE

"You're a goner!" Muttered Art to himself; inside his head of course so no one could hear. The body was slumped in a heap; it had fallen almost instantly as he zapped it with his, well, zapper – he didn't have a name for the weapon. No one had told him what it was called when they handed it to him, it was just his, well, shooter he supposed. It did the job; every year or so they replaced it with updates, no questions asked, no lies told. Yeah, Gran had said that when he was a nipper; a few years ago, that was too. Time had merged into an indiscriminate blob, rather like the geezer he'd finished off. Art was now outside the building. It had taken him five minutes to travel 80 metres or so. That was his estimate anyway. His special pass, attached to his wrist in the guise of a watch (not that many people wore those anymore) enabled him to access the multitude of security doors and elevators that kept out the riff-raff. Art thought of his handler, Michel, Mikey more like – Art almost lost his cool and spoke out loud. Yeah, well Michel/Mikey, whatever he called himself, was a queer fish for sure.

They first met in the sleazy bar that Art liked to frequent with his mates. Times were hard, with little employment, apart from the odd 'cash in hand' jobs, all on the ground level, of course, nothing fancy; that had come later. Mikey sidled up to Art and his mates rested his elbow on the bar and leaned forward ominously. Art was immediately fascinated by Mikey's nose. It was a bulbous nose and didn't appear to fit the rest of his face. It was a large man's nose whereas Mikey was lanky, skinny even, and his features were angular. Art missed the first part of his introduction by concentrating too hard on Mikey's nasal feature. His companions appeared to be uneasy about something Mikey had said. They had moved off the barstools and gathered up their jackets from the floor.

Fred turned to Art. "We're going back to Ed's; are you coming?"

Art had been mesmerised by that incongruous conk and, relaxed by a few beers, felt emboldened. He wanted to see more of this stranger and hear what he had to say.

"Think I'll stay on for a while; I'll catch up with you later, mates." Art returned Fred's concerned glance with a nonchalant shrug.

Mikey proceeded to fill Art in on his proposition. Good money was to be had for the right candidate, a regular income, not all this scratching in the dirt that Art and his friends were used to. Mikey knew Art had completed his national service, as all young men and women were required to do. He had been trained to follow orders and Mikey felt sure that Art was quite capable of fulfilling the job specification.

Art, in his semi-inebriated state felt an overwhelming sense of pride. Yeah, he was a great guy and could do anything. He swaggered out, following Mikey until they landed up in Mikey's hole. Well, Mikey said it was where he crashed, but it didn't look permanent. Art guessed he had a proper place, probably on Level One. Chris'sakes look at his togs; they weren't standard issue from Bargain Basement. In Mikey's lair, Art was signed up for Level One Eliminator and assured all his work would be on that level, no more no less. No Level Two, no Level Ground, no Underground. Art had never set eyes on a Level Oner, or Twoer, let alone one of those savages that skulked in the old underground railway tunnels and stations of long ago. Hell, he'd heard they ate rats and frequently finished each other off with dirks! Old fashioned knives, sharp blades, lots of blood. Yuk! The inhumanity of it. Now, *on Level Ground*, they were much more sophisticated. Extermination was a clean business; a high powered laser gun; automatic focus, variable frequency included, in the unlikely event that you just wanted to injure someone. They'd practised with them in National Service, on unsuspecting animals gathered from the forest. He'd never killed a fellow Grounder, but he'd never needed to. His life had bumbled on in the last few years, a bit of work here and there, earning enough to keep his head above water.

Here he was in Mikey's place about to embark on a great opportunity. Meanwhile, Mikey was scrabbling about behind an old dresser; the place was like an old junk store. Only old ladies went in for sticks of stuff like that big old wardrobe and a dubious looking moth-eaten easy chair. He could see a broken spring peeking out of the upholstery and wondered, uncomfortably, if Mikey used it to torture his enemies.

Mikey had found what he was looking for. A fancy laser gun case, new and shiny, complete with power packs and body armour disguised as a padded jacket. Mikey was explaining about the gear when Art, in his drunken state finally cottoned on; he was being recruited as an assassin. What had he thought eliminator meant only a few minutes before? He was sobering up fast. It was too late but on the other hand, it might not be so bad. All Level Grounders hated Level Ones and Twos, but as they never got to see any and had no idea what they got up to, it didn't matter whether they lived or died, did it? It was just a job. He could do it.

Now here he was making his way back to his old pad; the same one he'd lived in since leaving the Service, no suspicions aroused. He had a small amount of dosh stashed away. He'd splashed out quite a bit; on girls, for the night mostly. He'd slipped a bit to his old Ma, who crippled with arthritis and now unable to work, was slowly starving to death. Life was a bummer and this new line of work would be challenging. Was he up to it? Did he have it in him to take a life, followed by many more lives? Hell! He needed the readies; beggars can't be choosers, take what you can get. Art slept badly that night. Strange dreams, or to be more accurate, nightmares of Art discharging his laser gun over and over into a body that flopped over and sprang back like a life-size puppet, waiting to be finished off all over again.

The following morning Art felt the worse for wear. He was working a short-term contract clearing rubbish from the streets; discarded food and drink cartons dropped from the Aerocabs that flew 50 feet above the Grounder's street, servicing the Level One's from the platforms that extended beyond their apartments. The combination of these numerous vehicles and the encroachment of the platforms blocked most of the light from the watery sun. As a result, the streets were always dingy. Feeble street lamps were dotted here and there but everyone spent most of their waking time avoiding the piles of detritus that piled up. The bigwigs took it upon themselves to organise the weekly clean up and this was Art's job for the day. He joined his group of street cleaners and there was his mate Fred amongst them. He hesitated. Would Fred question him about the previous evening and what Mikey had asked of him? He need not have worried. Fred had pushed his way through his colleagues to greet Art with a slap on the back and a diatribe about how many weirdos you came across nowadays.

"Hope you escaped from that big nose last night; we had a bet on about how many free drinks you could wangle before you gave him the push". Fred laughed.

Art forced a smile and feigned a bad hangover to illustrate his supposed success in the drinks department the night before.

They set to work wielding the cumbersome street cleaners. They were certainly effective but there was a lot of trash to suck up. Apparently, these sturdy workhorses 'digested' the discarded food, packaging, cardboard cups and whatever else the Ones and Twos chucked out of their windows and cabs and produced some sort of fuel. Art thought it must produce some hell of a stink and probably accounted for the filthy air they were all forced to breathe. He coughed unthinkingly as if in sympathy to his own thoughts. By the evening, as the weak sun was setting, they were ordered to stop. They queued up with the other cleaners to have their wages added to their employment cards. With this credit, they could buy food, rent, cheap second-hand clothing and other essentials sold at Bargain Basement. Fred grabbed Art by the shoulder in a rare show of bonhomie.

"C'mon mate let's hit the bar and down a few beers." Fred was eager to get a drink and a bite to eat. They'd had nothing all day and Art was feeling weak, not least from the aftermath of his hangover. The two friends made their way to the familiar bar where they met Ed and Harry, whose work had finished around midday. They appeared to be well settled in with empty glasses lined up in front of them.

As Art and Fred munched through their sausage sandwiches, Art wondered where the 'meat' of the sausage had originated. He doubted that it had ever seen an animal. However, he felt better with something inside his stomach and relaxed as he took greedy gulps of his first pint. His sense of ease was rudely cut short by the arrival of Mikey. The gangly stick of a man was standing in the doorway gazing around looking for someone. Art jumped up.

"Off to the can, boys, back in a mo."

"Bladder shrunk Arty, me old mate?" Fred shouted after him. "You've only had one!"

Art wasn't listening; Mikey was after him and he couldn't remember if he'd agreed to be a hit man or not. He'd drunk so much that he could recollect very little of the strange flat Mikey had taken him to. Had Mikey scanned his retina, his unique signature, taken in agreement to be engaged in Mikey's employment? Art was now sweating, his heart thumped loudly in his chest and his bowels were turning to water. He urgently pushed into a cubicle, only just in time. He put his head in his hands and started to whimper. Someone had followed him.

"Are you in there, Art?" it was Mikey, "Are you ready for your first job?" Mikey was drumming his fingers on the cubicle door. "Hurry up mate, got a busy schedule."

Art finished up and waved at the flush button. He stared at the rush of water, wanting to be flushed away, together with his offerings, to somewhere else, maybe down in the sewers, where, rumour had it, the Undergrounders spent their leisure time swimming. He opened the door; Mikey had been leaning on it, in a nonchalant sort of way and almost fell over. Art couldn't help but laugh; he wasn't such a bad old stick after all. What had come over him a few minutes before?

"Don't want to mess up the party, Arty; haha! Got the spec's, so to speak, of your first job. He handed Art an old-fashioned spectacle case, not unlike the sort in which his old Granny had kept her 'binns', as she called them. Inside was indeed a pair of spectacles, rather like the safety goggles he'd worn for various odd jobs. The frames were quite thick, and the sides were decidedly chunky. "It's all in there," Mikey added.

"Won't I look stand out with these things on? No one wears these anymore. Haven't you heard of laser surgery or even contacts? Come off it. I can't wear these."

Art had reverted to the behaviour of a small boy, forced to wear unfashionable sneakers.

"Up there it's all the rage. Retro like. Twoers are heavily into sunglasses; on account of them getting a lot more light up there, of course. And the Oneers copy everything the Twoers do; it's very competitive; you won't look out of place at all. Anyway, getting back to more important things, these special spectacles will tell you what to do. When you get back to that dirty little sty of yours, press this rivet at the end of the right side, and watch the show!" Mikey grinned. He was pleased with himself. "This little job is worth six months' dirt-sucking wages. It'll only take a few minutes. Here's your special pass." An object, not unlike an archaic wristwatch, was thrust into his sweaty palm. "Guard it with your life. No questions. Have to dash. Same place, same time next week. Ciao!"

He was gone and Art stood there staring at the glasses case and the watch. He slipped them into his capacious pocket on the side of his leg. Whilst splashing water on his face he breathed hard. He must have agreed to do this, but did he want to?

Back in his meagre bedsit, Art tried to sleep. Endless scenarios whirled around his head. The moment before he discharged the laser; the look in his victim's eyes as they realised they had reached the moment of death; the aftermath of his actions – the lifeless corpse. Could he do this? Art wanted more out of life than he, at present, had. He thought of the stories his old grandma told him when he was a nipper. Back in her day, all children had gone to 'school'. An institution where they taught you things like writing, reading; even singing and painting pictures. By the time his old ma was a young girl that had all gone out the window. There had been some sort of crisis – the Catharsis, his gran called it. The old country had got into trouble with the rest of the world; they weren't top dog anymore. According to his gran, they'd been gradually going down the pan for quite a while. Back in those days, all the Levels were on one level, so to speak. Of course, there were the ones with lots and the ones with nothing and the majority somewhere in between, but they'd mixed, unlike the present. There had been a massive frenzy to build upwards, a bit like nineteenth century States of America, his gran used to say. All those tall buildings that shot up into the sky. Up popped skyscrapers on every street, taller than anything seen before in good ol' London town. Aerocabs had just started at that time too; now they buzzed around as common as bluebottles, and as annoying too. Their engines belched out foul smelling fumes, they blocked out the light and Art had to admit that something in his heart wanted to see the sun and the trees and fields and even the sea. He imagined a large expanse of water, as far as the eye could see, brought to life by his old gran's stories. The Twoers didn't use Aerocabs they had some other sort of transport, but he was damned if he ever caught sight of one of them. Art had a hankering to find out more and this new job opportunity was a chance to do that. Perhaps he could make his way to the tops of the buildings, with the help of his special wrist apparatus, and look out at the world. His thoughts blurred and finally at 3 am he fell into a fitful slumber, tossing and turning, wrestling with his blanket.

Art was awoken by a banging on his door. He stumbled across the room, tripping over his discarded day clothes. Fred stood there looking agitated. "C'mon mate you'll miss your slot. Lucky I got there early. Came to see if you were ok, not stricken down by the latest lurgy – my old mum copped it last month. Did I tell you?"

"No, I mean I'm sorry Fred, know you weren't close and all, but still blood and all that." Art was embarrassed, mainly about his unkempt appearance rather than passing on sympathy to what could only be described as his best friend. Thanks for coming round; had a bad night, couldn't get to sleep, must have dozed off after the alarm."

Art quickly pulled on his work clothes and followed Fred to the cleaning station. He'd forgotten all about the cleaning job. His final thought, before succumbing to his broken slumbers, was that he would go through with the assassination job. What had he got to lose? His life was pretty pointless and leading nowhere. If he didn't make it, at least he would have attempted to capture something more than his present, pathetic existence. He blamed his old gran in a roundabout sort of way. After all, she had put those 'damn, foolhardy ideas into his little head'

Art had passed on an evening visit to the bar, pleading a headache. Fred was visibly disappointed but was soon in deep conversation with another cleaner. They headed off in the direction of their favourite watering hole. Art felt a pang of regret and loss; this new job was taking him away from his friends, but it would be worth it. He would be rich in a few years and maybe could advance to a Level One. He could take Fred with him, some way or other. Back in his bedsit, he retrieved the spectacle case and the wristwatch thingy from their hiding place He stood in front of the washbasin mirror and placed the frames on his nose and pressed the rivet on the right side. A transparent screen popped up in front of him – a map; detailed instructions of the mark - some unsuspecting posh geezer - and a voice was talking to him through the sides of the spectacles.

"Slow down mate, your babbling, I can't keep up." Art pressed the rivet again and the formless voice repeated its instructions. Art paid attention and memorised the routine. 'At 24:00 hours take a left at the third block; the fourth door on the right; use wrist attachment to activate security clearance. Egress to lift via the retinal scanner. Proceed to the 6th floor (this must be the Level One's quarters Art told himself). Locate Mark in Apartment 672 and eliminate by discharging weapon; aim at chest; then a further shot at the head, to make sure.'

Art plonked himself on the toilet seat lid which slid violently to the left. His legs had weakened as the import of his situation hit home. He had no doubt that if he didn't carry out this assassination, he, in turn, might be got rid of. He now knew too much and he had no choice. He must take a life, but at least he consoled himself with the fact that it wasn't one of his own kind. He glanced at the old-fashioned alarm clock sitting on the bedside table. He had five hours left before his life irrevocably changed. Tomorrow he would be a hired killer.

Everything went mostly to plan. He nearly forgot the body armour. It wasn't even mentioned by the voice from the spectacles; perhaps it was an afterthought. But he was told to remove the plastic shoe covers from the right-sided pocket of his jacket before he entered the building and wrap them around his boots. As he set off, he panicked and took the fourth left and the third door on the right. His wrist access thingy hadn't worked and as he desperately waved his arm at the entrance, he saw a dark figure approaching. Art scarpered quick, walking at speed back to his dingy flat. The nightwalker had vanished. He hurried through his flat door, fumbled with the key and realised he was still wearing the shoe covers. He listened to the strange voice from the spectacles again and retraced his steps, this time taking the correct turning. He waved his wrist at the entry scanner and sneaked in. Emergency lights flooded the corridor with a pallid light as he made his way to number 672 without meeting a soul. The contraption on his wrist opened the apartment door effortlessly. He crept in, holding the laser weapon pointing upwards. He could hear loud snoring; that was good. He found the source of the nighttime grunts and fired at the shape under the thick quilt. The body jerked and he aimed at the head.

Art was rudely awoken by the bell of the clock clanging in his ear. He jumped up and bashed the button hard. His old gran had sworn by that clock. It took all manner of beating and bashing but still, it ticked on. As long as you didn't overwind it of course. He'd killed him as asked. It had been surprisingly easy. He hadn't seen his face, which had helped. He wondered what the geezer had done to deserve such a sudden end, but put such thoughts out of his head. He must keep detached. He picked up the spectacles – he should have hidden them away; he should have hidden the weapon and the body armour, back behind the cupboard in a dusty, cobwebby corner that no one had frequented for years. What a scatter-brain. He was a hired killer; he was a professional! You never knew when that nosey landlord would appear and demand a rent increase, or a clean-up. He was never around when anything went wrong of course, but that was to be expected. He put the spectacles on and pressed the rivet. The voice congratulated him on his first kill. The readies were at that moment being credited to his account. His next job was in three days. He pressed the rivet. He wanted to be normal. He must carry on with the cleaning job and not draw attention to himself.

After eliminating his first victim he'd not seen Mikey for a year; then he'd turned up in the bar where he and Fred were enjoying the company of two attractive young ladies. Art had said he would treat Fred to the entertainment; Fred had insisted he pay for Art and both of the friends had wondered how each of them could afford to pay for each other. After Mikey's arrival, Art had made excuses and headed for the lavatories where his handler was waiting.

"New weapon. Updated version. Bring all the old stuff to my place tomorrow night and I'll replace it". Mikey's nose seemed larger than ever; Art wondered what it was that caused such a malady. He hoped his nose never got to look like that.

"What're you staring at?" Mikey looked annoyed, his small beady eyes seemed to penetrate into Art's brain.

Art started to sweat; he was good on following commands but improvising was not his strong point. "Em, stray eyelash, just under your left eye," Mikey brushed, "All gone." Art smiled; nervously.

"Remember tomorrow. When you've finished that cleaning job. No stopping off at the bar. Now, scarper."

When Art returned, Fred pleaded a full bladder, "Must be catching." Fred joked hurrying to relieve himself.

Art sat down. The girls had disappeared. Art felt uncomfortable. He'd let himself down by staring at that weird guy's nose. He hoped Mikey would let him continue with eliminating undesirables. Art felt he was good at it. He kept his cool, there had never been any problems. Most of his marks were asleep when he finished them off and the ones that were awake seemed so surprised to be confronted by a bespectacled gunman they never offered any resistance. Art had heard a rumour that Level Ones and Twos had it easy. No National Service for them. It made them soft.

Fred returned and bemoaned the disappearance of the two young women, but Art wasn't interested anymore. Something had made Art uneasy but he couldn't put his finger on it.

The following evening, he made his way to Mikey's hole. As he arrived the door opened and he was greeted by a small, stocky, middle-aged man. He resembled the proprietor of Bargain Basement, all the same Art was taken aback.

"Get in – quick! I'm Rodrigo your new handler." The little man grabbed Art's hand and shook it violently. "Before you ask, Mikey's moved on to pastures new. Risky business, no one in the same job for long, keep rotating and all that. The new laser, new specs, new wrist scanner. All here. Check!" Rodrigo (no way) was in a hurry.

"Thanks, Rod, same old same old?" Art felt confident in the company of the diminutive Rodrigo. "You know, the usual brief, I just do what I've been doing for the last year?"

"Don't call me Rod and follow the instructions. Press the rivet on the left side. Go!" Rodrigo had opened the door and was waiting for Art to leave.

The years rolled by and the handlers changed annually. The job had become routine; what had started as an exciting distraction from the low paid cleaning, had become almost as mundane as wielding the trash digestors.

One night Art hurried back at his flat. On the inside of the cupboard door, he scratched a small vertical line, alongside the other 999 vertical lines. He had made a thousand kills. He didn't know if Mikey and his cronies knew that he'd reached a *grand* of kills but he felt a sense of pride. He had amassed a large amount of credit into his account and no one seemed to have noticed. They must have sorted that for him. However, clocking off the hundreds and making it to a thousand was, Art felt, an achievement. He checked his tally again, just to make sure. He was right. He'd made a thousand.

There was a knock at the door.

"Fred?" He called. There was no answer. More impatient bashing followed. Art looked through the spy hole; it was Mikey! He welcomed him in. Art realised he'd missed Mikey. His other handlers had been characterless. Mikey had something about him; a sort of panache. Art couldn't put his finger on it. Mikey had made the job interesting and here he was, back in the mix!

"Mikey me old lad! Sorry, Michel. Long time, no see. How're things?" Art was starting to embarrass himself. He stopped. Mikey was older and looked different somehow. It was the nose. He had a new nose or maybe it was his original nose and that monstrous snout had been a falsie. He was wearing expensive clothes under his old dirty overcoat. Mikey had gone up in the world. Mikey seemed more relaxed and confident. The years had improved his appearance, he'd filled out but he wasn't flabby, just less gangly. He had a few grey hairs that leant him an almost distinguished look.

Mikey was patting Art on the back. "Congratulations and all that, old man. Knocked up a *grand*. A thousand kills – that's something to be proud of. I've got one more job for you and then you can retire. You deserve it."

"Fire away." Art replied jovially. It was good to see old Mikey; it was like the old days.

"It's a bit different this time. This job is on Level Ground. Nothing to worry about. Just follow the instructions," Mikey handed Art yet another new set of spectacles, "It's all in there."

Art flinched. The sick feeling that he had felt when he first contemplated his first assassination returned; his face grew pale and nausea filled his stomach. He felt he must control himself, he mustn't look weak in Mikey's eyes.

"I don't know if I can do it. I mean, I grew up with these lads; I served and cleaned alongside them. How about a Level Twoer; that must be worse than Level One and I'm sure I'm up to all the extra security."

"Listen, Art, you can't barter with me, either you agree to do the job or not. Forget the nitty gritty, are you willing to take him out, or not?

Art made his way to the warehouse. According to the instructions, the mark would be there pilfering valuable foodstuffs from the Level Grounders. What this felon did with his booty, Art didn't know. Art wished he had more information. Maybe the thief had a starving family; he might have sneaked up from the Underground – in which case Art thought he was perfectly entitled to take him out; Undergrounders was worse than the lowest of the low." He pushed all speculation from his mind; he was a hired assassin; it was his last, and potentially, most difficult job, but he must do it.

He waved his wrist at the scanning panel and silently stole into a large expanse of cardboard boxes and metal cages. A vast amount of supplies, enough to feed hundreds or even thousands. Art gasped involuntarily, followed by a whispered curse. The enemy would be vigilant, senses attuned to any likelihood of discovery. Then he saw him; a tall, strong looking geezer – he reminded Art of his mate, Fred. The reserve lights gave off an eerie green glow. His adversary was a dark figure. He couldn't see his face. He retrieved the laser from his pocket and just as he discharged the lethal beam, his opponent shouted "No!"

Art knew that voice; he could distinguish it from an infinite number of other voices. It was Fred. He had zapped his best buddy. Art approached the slumped body. Fred was still breathing, but only just. Art knelt down and put his face close to Fred's lips. Now the tears were coming and dripping on Fred's beautiful nose. Why wasn't it Mikey's ugly proboscis? Art would make him pay. He'd see to that.

Fred was still alive but the force of life was leaving him fast. "We were tricked Arty, me old mate." Whispered his friend as he closed his eyes.

Art heard a noise behind him. He turned; Mikey was there, laser at the ready. "Nice job – here's the final cut." He zapped Art good and hard, just to make sure.

Compass of Death

ROD SLAUGHTER

The shield of foil that was strung across the various satellites orbiting Venus was only microns in thickness. Had there been an atmosphere in space, their own weight meagre as it was would have caused them to crumple and tear. Fortunately, there was neither air nor gravity in the endless vacuum of space. That was how the foil survived. A tenuous like from one orbiting construction to the next. When spread out like a spider's web the foil performed a vital task. The highly reflective surface deflected the heat from the sun back into the incalculable vastness of nothing that existed in ninety-nine percent of the cosmos.

There was one problem. Nothing lasts forever. Nothing remains uneroded by the capacity of time. Cosmic dusk, tiny meteors and stellar flares all beat at the shield. They possessed an unfeeling mercilessness. Fist one sheet was damaged with tiny holes from the dust. Another tore when a solar flare was especially fierce. Yet a third was torn to ribbons by a tiny meteor the size of a pebble being inexplicably drawn to the surface of the planet by its own gravity. The shield had been constructed to deflect much of the heat of a star that was too close to the second body orbiting around it. For a while, it was one hundred percent efficient.

For a time.

The day came when the entire network of foil was not as efficient at blocking out the sun as it had been when orang-U-Can had spent thousands of Venushillin building it. Slowly but surely the mean average temperature of the Earth's twin began to rise.

"Cary, you positively must do something about this infernal heat. I cannot stand it a week longer, do you hear? Not one period of seven standard days".

"For frenge's sake Ingrid, one of the few things you cannot blame me for is the heat on Venus. Cast your mind back anyway to the lives we had in Seattle, who was it that wanted to come out to this infernal rock in the first place"?

Ingrid, bitter and twisted harridan that she was did not listen at the same time as speaking, however. She continued as though her long-suffering husband had not uttered a peep.

There's only one way we're going to get away from it and that's to rent one of those beachside cottages down at the pole".

"Last standard year, when we got down there all you did was complain that you were chilly".

"Well, that sure as Moses ain't gonna happen twelve months later is it? The damned planet's now facing the sun as square on as it ever gets and I'm heartily sick of it and Star Spangles".

Star Spangles was a huge complex in the region just south of Venus' equator. It was one of the areas under American rule. The King of America was currently King Bucky III and he endorsed migration to Mars, Venus and the Moon in most of his frequent and vociferous speeches. Cary went on,

"You didn't like the Venuinsects. You said the beach sand was too gritty and cool. The man-made lake down there, Lake Butt, you claimed was filled with strange and frightening creatures".

"That's because arthropods and crustaceans should not be blue", Ingrid objected acknowledging her husband for a rare moment. "Blue just ain't right for them they look unnatural".

"When Geneticist Hoyle created them he should have pinged you first should he not, Ingrid? Having the audacity to create life without asking you first".

"Don't get smart with me, Cary", she instantly rebuked him, "You know it doesn't suit you".

"That's even without mentioning all the arguments you caused with the other vacationers down there. You don't get on well with the rest of the human race do you, Ingrid? So what chance did the spiders and crabs have"?

"That so-called creature that stung you on the ass was no spider Cary Peck and you know it. Sure it had eight legs, but you tell me the only other time you've seen a spider with gills and fins".

"That's because it wasn't a spider, Ingrid. It was an Icthyspide".

"Well it was blue and it stung your fat ass is all I know", she crowed. "Anyway, let's get back to the point. I would prefer a cool beach to this stifling complex. Even if it does mean risking your ass. I've never known such heat, this is the worst twelve standard months we've ever had to endure. Are those deflectors even working any more? What do you think? Are you still listening to me, Cary? Are the temperatures slowly increasing yes or no"?

"Two degrees absolute is all", he was forced to confess. "Two tiny little degrees, Ingrid".

"I knew it"! She was triumphant, "It's never been this bad. Never ever ever. What is being done about it that's what I want to know"?

"Well actually, Ingrid...", Cary began pulling out his i-Pad, "According to this report a combined team of multi-national engineers are blasting up to the orbiting foil deflectors and they're going to commence repairs in eight standard weeks time".

"Eight weeks"! Ingrid was incandescent with ire. "Eight more weeks of this. Where are they these so-called experts - who know nothing? Lounging about on one of the polar beaches I'll bet".

She trundled over to the portal that was heavily polarised against the outside glare, "Just look out there. It's baking Cary. The poor firs are dying from lack of rain coupled with hot winds, even the cactus are shrunken right down. If it gets any hotter the rock will start catching fire".

"I think perhaps, My Dear that you are beginning to exaggerate now".

"Maybe. Not about those engineers though. They won't just have cottages on the poles either, huge spacious air-conditioned condos will be where they are wasting the next few weeks. Drinking iced tea and laughing at us poor plebs melting up here. They won't have to sweat over a hot hypo-wave in a tiny little kitchen like I have to, Cary. I'm sweating cobs, my nerves are simply shredded and fractured and I have upsetment in the extremis. I need a break I tell you".

"I feel it too, Ingrid. You're not the only one who takes sodden singlet and trollies off every evening. I simply choose not to belly-ache when there's nothing we can do. Has mankind ever felt better for complaining about the weather"?

"This isn't Seattle weather, Cary. This is alien. So let's get out of it for two standard weeks.? If you don't fancy Lake Butt, we can go to Lake Głowa up in the north. I'm sure the Polish wouldn't mind two more joining their number".

"The last time anything so radical was attempted against Poland, Ingrid, it ended up starting WWII", Cary chuckled. Ingrid scowled which was something she always did when her husband began demonstrating his superior knowledge of prehistoric events in ancient times.

"So why don't we rent a cottage at one of them for frenges sake. Do you like baking like this, Cary? Do you enjoy seeing me suffer"?

"Of course not", Cary had lost his humour with the next tirade. "Do you think I like it any more than you? Do you think I like coming home from the office wet through with sweat every night? I don't"!

The why aren't you *doing* something"?

Cary sighed, "For the very same reason we have a four-year-old flitter. That you can't go to the hairdressers every day and have all those expensive frocks you're after – money. Remember that commodity Ingrid? You know the one I earn and you don't. If you want to stop flapping your jaw for a few seconds we can sit down and talk finance".

Ingrid had the grace to let tears fill her eyes then. "Mother told me not to marry you Cary you know. She said, 'He'll never amount to anything. Just contract him for three and you'll see'. I was all starry-eyed and full of your bull though wasn't I Cary, so I agreed to take out a lifetime contract. I must have been out of my mind is what I must have been. Out of my mind".

"Out of your pants more like", Cary was cruel, "Like a rabbit you were in those days, letting your muffin rule what few brains you had".

"All you're doing now is deflecting me from the main thrust of this conversation Cary", Ingrid was suddenly quite eloquent. "Because you're full of one excuse after another. Whenever we get down to the grist of a conversation you start harping on about the past, or about your precious finance. If the Flynns can afford a fortnight at the pole we should be able to".

"Kaahk Ingrid I know that little barb so very well don't I? I actually make exactly the same money as Autry Flynn. Without exaggerating though I've told you a quintillion times the Flynns know how to economise so that they can afford two weeks at the pole each standard year. Just wait for the night, you'll be complaining about the cold then and the poles won't help you then".

"Are you accusing me of being extravagant, Cary when I've had this old frock for seven weeks. Look at it. It's practically threadbare. If I hold it up to the light you can see through it".

"That's because it's linen, Ingrid! You bought it for the hot day, do you think you're talking to an idiot or something. Go fetch me a lemonade and stop your yammering".

Ingrid reluctantly rose from her chair and went to the fridge-freezer. It was her undisputed task to wait on Cary on his days off. She having no employment of her own. Even she dare not complain about that. As she handed him his beverage though, she girded her loins for a fresh assault.

"I slave all year in this apartment for you, Cary and what does it get me? Other people get a cottage at the pole, a two-week break at Lake Butt. If I want two measly little weeks away from this hellhole all I get from you is excuses. Excuses and insults. Now it's not like me to complain, Cary (he had to bite his lip at that point) I don't want you to think I'm nagging you in any way. I just think I deserve a little bit of respect and consideration for all I do for you. Have done over these screwy light and dark periods on this cockamaymy planet".

"All right"! Cary shouted, "Just stop talking, Ingrid. I'll do it. We'll rent a cottage down at the pole. On the edge of Lake Butt"

"So! Money was just another one of your worse than pathetic excuses. We *can* afford it after all"!

"We're going, Ingrid. Aren't you happy even now? You're getting what you want. You're getting your own way. You've won. You've beaten me. Can we leave it for now, I'm getting a headache already"?

"Why didn't you say so in the first place? Instead, we've had to have this lengthy discussion and for what. Just so I can get two weeks out of that hell-hole you call our kitchen".

Cary told her then, "I'll arrange for the money. I'll take out a short-term loan if I have to. When we get back I'll put a tighter rein on our spending, that's what's going to happen right"?

"This whole debacle has caused great upsetment, Cary. It's for your good too after all. You need a break too you know? You look stretched. Yes stretched thin. Like you're going to snap. The pole will be the ideal spot for you to recharge your batteries at you'll see I'm right. Am I right or am I right"?

"Ingrid", began her defeated spouse, "Even when you're wrong you're right".

~

The loan came through without any fuss. After all, Cary had never borrowed from anyone ever before so his credit was condition blue. The interest rate on a six standard month loan was healthy too at a nice low 4.375%. Cary went to the travel agents in their nice posh air-conditioned showrooms and booked a cottage from the very pleasantly presented android there. Her name was Andrio and whoever had designed her certainly had an eye for the female form.

"I can get you two-weeks in a three-star cottage for just forty Venushillin", she told him in her sing-song voice. He red, bow-shaped lips pouted slightly as she informed of the unmissable offer.

"That's with Trav4U. All I need today is a ten percents deposit, Mister Peck". Her voice dipped in tone and volume to a more conspiratorial tone as she asked,

"The cottage is a size to accommodate a couple, Sir. Would you like to pay just an extra seven Venushillin and six Venupence so that I can come with you"?

While Peck tried to process that offer she added sweetly,

"I am programmed as a pleasure device and know multiple techniques. If you don't get satisfaction the offer comes with a money-back guarantee"?

It was tremendously tempting. The perceived age of the device was twenty-three standard years. Everything was in place but unlike his aged wife, everything

still pointed upward. Misjudging his hesitation for lack of appreciation in her offered sweetly,

"If brunettes are not your thing I can offer you Jenefio, the red-head over there. Or perhaps you like the very popular Lanique,? She's the blonde in the corner desk. Had money been no object and Ingrid not existed Cary would have taken all three of them with him. After all, it was for fourteen nights!

"I shall be taking my wife with me", he finally managed hollowly the words like ash in his mouth. Andrio smiled coyly,

"There's always next year, Sir"!

The air flitter took them from Kansas International Flitter Port direct to the flitter port of Mishogi Flitport. At it, Cary hired an Elastoplast 200bhp limoflit. He was on holiday so he treat himself. The headphones supplied on the flitjet had successfully eliminated all of the Ingrid Noise for the entire duration of the flight. She was unusually quiet on the flit from Mishogi to the edge of Lake Butt. The cottage was situated in the lakeside resort of Ventenubulis. The instant they were out of the vehicle and into the cottage the trouble started one more. Ingrid was a big woman and her voice boomed out at her husband,

"It will do I suppose, but I would have preferred a condo. Now get out there on that stretch of white sand between our porch and the lake and turn on the digital readout, Cary".

The readout in question was a privacy LED board that could have a simple message typed into it showing the name of the guests in the cottage. Or requesting quiet at certain hours of the pseudo-day. Maybe even inviting passers-by to call in and enjoy a social drink with the occupants of the cottage.

Ingrid did not want any of those alternatives punching into the display board, however.

"Get it over to the left, Cary, a bit more. I want that sign right in the middle.

"I don't see any point in being so rude, Ingrid", her husband objected.

"They can plainly understand big red letters saying 'No Trespassing', can't they"?

"No one is going to come onto our decked area. People come to recline on the sand".

"Cary, the idea of the message is to keep them off the sand in front of our cottage".

"What"? Cary demanded incredulously, "Not that nonsense again. Look what happened the last standard"?

Ingrid always crossed her arms when she was feeling especially obdurate. She crossed her arms, "We rented this cottage, Cary. So I think we should be able to enjoy the cottage in front of it without anyone spoiling our view of the lake. I don't want it being dumped on by those terrible low-life's who only come for the day. This is now the Peck residence and we have a right to privacy".

"For koof's sake, Ingrid. Look down the pseudo beach. Everyone else has people on the beach in front of their places. None of them has activated their sign with a message as unsociable as ours".

He looked at the whiter than white sand. The azure beauty of the xanthic lake as it reflected the hue of the sky. The breeze here was actually of a very tolerable temperature. So why was Ingrid making him hot under the collar?

"You may not object to people of unsuitable social status spoiling our stretch of beach but I do", Ingrid was droning on. "So Cary if you don't want to key in the right message get out of the way and I'll do it myself".

"Don't come out here", Cary countered, "Because if I don't do exactly what you say you'll yammer on about it for the entire Pseudo-fortnight".

"Good lad", she cooed, "Now don't get any sand on my deckchair as you trudge past will you. I don't want half the beach in the cottage either thank you very much".

Cary sounded exhausted as he confirmed, "No, Dear".

"And once you've got the message keyed in I want this umbrella taking down and taking in somewhere. If anyone ignores it they can get all the ultra-violet they deserve. That should deter them I think, nobody in their right mind would sunbathe with all the risks of melanoma".

"I'm not sure I feel less stretched yet, Ingrid", Cary sighed. "It's like trying to relax whilst sitting on an Icthyspide".

Did you say something"? Ingrid demanded, his words had drifted away on the fairly constant polar wind.

"I could have said something, but I said nothing", he grinned.

"It sounded to me like you did"!

"It was just the wind, Ingrid. The wind and your fractured nerves playing up".

~

"Hey, Clooney, this is a good spot, let's settle down here for a while"? His girlfriend Charlize Aniston suggested.

Wahlberg glanced around and nodded his approval. "Okay, Babe. Just hold the Thermos, Plastizip box and i-pads and I'll spread out a blanket. Wonder where the umbrella went from this stretch of beach. It's a good job it's cloudy today".

"It's so marvellous to get here", Aniston sighed, "Just look at that lake? A body of water on Venus. Those white-coat boys sure know their stuff. One day I think Venus will be the garden of the soar system, Clooney".

"Don't forget Mars", he boyfriend pointed out. "It's been colonised for longer and the terraforming has been going on for far more years".

"Yes but the sand there is that dreadfully dull brick-red stuff and it's in the air all the time clogging everything up. Look at this sand, why it's tiny white pebbles, they'd never cause a storm of their own".

"The solar system sure is wonderful", Wahlberg agreed. "I'm going to lie down for a bit and just let my mind wander. For me relaxing is, exactly what it sounds like – relaxing".

"That cottage behind us is lovely. I wish we could have gotten one of the white ones", Aniston remarked.

"There's plenty of facilities out on the porch too; chairs, blanket and that lovely beach umbrella". Wahlberg noted.

"Of all the bare-faced liberty", a harsh female voice suddenly cut through the idyllic peace. "Come here, Cary and look out there? Do you see what I am looking at in total disbelief"?

"What did you expect, Ingrid"?

"Now if you'd put those blankets and chairs and that umbrella in the cottage this would never have happened. No! 'Leave them on the porch' you said.

"It seems that your No Trespassing sign wasn't effective either was it, Ingrid"?

"*I guess some people can't read*"! Ingrid suddenly shouted.

"Ingrid stop it they will hear that din"?

"*Let them hear me*"!

Aniston twisted around at the same instant she asked Wahlberg, "What's her problem"?

"Who, Babe"? Wahlberg reluctantly raised himself onto an elbow.

"That old dragon in the cottage, going off her head like that", Aniston was nonplussed. "She's shouting about us".

"Are you sure, Babe? It must be something else. It's not like we seated ourselves on their porch".

"*The downright cheek of some people*".

"You see", Aniston said to Wahlberg, "She is too going off her head about us".

"Let her then", Wahlberg decided. This beach is public.

"She doesn't want us here look at this rude sign"?

"That's too bad for her then isn't it, because I'm comfy and I ain't moving for some gobby grimalkin".

"Cary, go and get rid of those two. Look at them with all that potential litter, I won't have it Cary, it's beginning to cast a shadow over our holiday".

"There's nothing you nor I can do about it, Ingrid. We rented the cottage and its porch, not the whole of Venus' south pole. They're not hurting anyone so leave them alone, they've got a right to be there".

"They are practically on our porch. I want to look at Lake Butt. I don't want a pile of riff-raff making the beach over there a garbage dump".

"They are not littering, Ingrid".

"No, but they will. They'll eat what they've brought for lunch and then throw foil and Plastizip all over the place".

"Ingrid listen - you dozy mare. This is a public beach I cannot ask them to leave just because you don't like seeing them. They look all right to me. The girl is rather pretty as a matter of fact".

"I get it now", Ingrid's tone went icy cold and her eyes almost closed, menacingly slit they were. "You want to sit here and google her. Well, she won't be peeling off today your dirty old slug it's too chilly. So if you want to give her one you'll have to go and ask her boyfriend if you can borrow her for a short stint. So your tongue's hanging out and you're sticking up for that floozy against your own wife. It would be nice if just for once you took my side, Cary".

"You are being coarse and rude, Ingrid and I'll be on your side when you are in the right. Most of the time just lately though, you're not".

"You are a lecherous and obtuse old goat, Cary", Ingrid spat forth her venom.

"Do we have to sit and listen to this, Clooney"? Aniston wanted to know.

"She's obviously a bit wrong in the head, Charlize", he chuckled. "Let her rant all she wants, I'm finding it quite entertaining. I wonder what's going to happen next"?

"It won't be very pleasant if she keeps it up and the balmy old bitch looks like she's got plenty of fat in reserve. *Some people act as if they own the whole beach*"!

"Don't stoop to her level, Babe. Let he blow some steam out of her ass if she wants".

"Cary did you hear that"? Ingrid was threatening to spontaneously human-combust, "That little tramp is talking about us. About me in particular"?

"You started it"! Cary raged back, he was beginning to feel stretched again, stretched very thin indeed. "So the best thing you can do right now is to stop it, Ingrid".

Crappy little upstarts - that's all they are".

"She is getting a bit much now", Wahlberg suddenly decided, "She's a nasty piece of work and no mistake. That husband of her just wants to bust her one in her sourpuss. All right, come on, let's find somewhere else to sit"?

The only trouble was that then Aniston felt suddenly defiant, "Just one damned minute Clooney. We have every right to sit here".

"I know", Wahlberg agreed, "But she doesn't look like she's going to shut up any time soon. What sort of enjoyment will that be for us? Why bother with the old bag? It's easier and more pleasant for us if we move"?

"You're right of course", Aniston agreed. "But there are cottages all along this stretch, what if all the other rent payers feel the same way about her as she does"?

"Everyone as nasty as her? That's not sensibly possible, is it? Hold the stuff while I shake the sand off our blanket".

"I feel sorry for that poor man with her. Do you think they're contracted"?

"If they are he must be clinically insane by now. That or stone deaf ha ha ha. If I was him I'd be mortified by her behaviour. It's so embarrassing".

"*Good. They are leaving and good riddance*".

"That's it", Aniston suddenly stuck out her lower lip, "Clooney I am not letting anyone drive us off a public beach. That's the trouble with her sort, she's gotten her way too many times. Well, she's met someone who can be as big a bitch as she is now. Let's see who wins this battle".

~

"They're still out there", Ingrid said coldly two standard hours later.

"It's daylight for the next few months, Ingrid what did you expect", Cary moaned. "Now for the love of heav... hell sit down and eat lunch".

"How can you expect me to enjoy it with that disgusting girl and her current tramp of a boyfriend lying right outside our door. I wouldn't enjoy a mouthful. In fact, I wouldn't taste it. Too much upsetment numbing my taste buds".

"Well shut the koof up and let me eat mine then". Cary's nerves were twisted, rent and shredded.

Ingrid had not even heard him though, "Look at her staring at the windows and giggling like a dirty little whore. I bet she takes it up the ass. Can't we do something, Cary? We are honest and decent people. Not gutter trash like them two. I know why don't we call the comb-men"?

"No, Ingrid. If I told you a quadrillion times, do not exaggerate. They are not criminals. They are not morally loose. In fact, I reckon neither of them possesses a mind like yours. What would you tell the comb-men? They haven't broken any laws. Where have you put the Brufocetasprin, my head feels fit to bust"?

"Well, I wanted to have lunch on that piece of beach. We couldn't though, could we? They are in our spot".

"You're koofing lying again", Cary noted, "You said we'd eat in the cottage today and have a picnic tomorrow. On account of the clouds".

"It is a lady's prerogative to change her mind", Ingrid stuck out her lower lip.

"Well, that lets you out then doesn't it, you slag"? Cary noted calmly for once. "Ladies would not deport themselves the way you do, Ingrid".

"It's a perfect day for a picnic today", the mouth machine trundled on, "Tomorrow it may snow that dreadful acid snow we have to keep out of".

"Doh! I give up. Do you know how rare snow is on Venus, even at the poles? Even if we were in the middle of the night. The one hundred and twenty standard day-long night".

"Well thank you for the astrology lesson, Professor Wiseass". Then a light suddenly went on in Ingrid's head, Cary, get the Boseman Boomstation will you"?

"you're not going to be reasonable are you, Ingrid"?

"Get the Boomstation. I want some music and if I choose to play music in the cottage we've rented, there's nothing anyone else can do about it".

"All right, Ingrid. Just stop yammering. Perhaps music will shut you up for a while. Calm the breast of the savage beast".

"There's no need for smut, Cary. Just get it. Bring the stick with Twenty Cents Snoop Gangster on".

"The ancient Yap album that I downloaded by mistake! You hated that infernal din made by people of coloured persuasion - deliberately mispronouncing words while an electronic booming sound was repeated endlessly. You said it sounded as bad as someone simply using a jigger pick, demolishing concrete".

"Well I fancy a bit of Yap today, so get it already".

"You're being unreasonable again".

"I'm not the unreasonable one here, Cary. You are! I asked you to tell them to leave and you wouldn't help me. You won't lift a finger to assist and now you're saying I'm unreasonable. So just get the Boomstation or learn to love and treasure the depth of my disdain".

"Why don't you just try and enjoy this vacation? Forget that young couple"?

"Get the Boomstation and for pity's sake stop arguing with me then".

The sounds of Twenty Cents Snoop Gangster began to blast itself out of the cottage. A fair-minded critic would not be able to honestly describe the young gentleman's voice as possessing of dulcet tones.

"I'm going to say one more thing, Ingrid", Cary said to his partner after the third run through, "Every time you play that album you're making the two of us look like idiots".

"It's growing on me, Cary", she lied, "I actually like it".

"Come on, Babe"? Clooney urged his girlfriend, "Let's get the hell out of Kansas"?

"You're right, darling", Charlize agreed. "But this ain't over. She's won the battle but she's not gonna win the war. Tomorrow we fetch our Boomstation and you can play that dreadful Blue Zone That Direction album of yours. Or if you fancy it some of that ancient Death Metal you like".

"They're leaving, they couldn't take any more", Ingrid sounded eminently satisfied, "You see, Cary? We've won"!

"I do not feel like I have been victorious in any of this, Ingrid", the wiser Cary observed, "And it may prove to be a pyrrhic victory".

"What's that supposed to mean"?

"Never mind please just turn that dreadful racket off. No wonder ancient times were so violent if they considered a din like that as entertainment".

~

"Cary! When you get finished with the dishes get the chairs and blanket out on the porch".

"The chairs! Erm, I forgot to bring them in yesterday".

"I told you to bring them in. Can't you do anything for me, Cary? I work all year round...".

Cary began to consider the possibility of going into hospital and asking the surgeon to render him deaf. With the utmost of concentration, he did his best to turn the infernal nagging off.

"… remember when I ask you to do things...".

He could feel the endless tirade beginning to affect his sanity. If Ingrid kept it up she might drive him clear around the bend.

"...all day-night, soaking wet from the late fogs, if they're still out there...".

Did Ingrid have gills? Otherwise with her mouth operating constantly how could she breathe? Maybe she spoke down her nose, having worn out her mouth?

"...stolen by those gipsies".

"Keep your hair on, if you just looked out of the window, see where they are".

"...miracle they haven't been whipped. Cary"!

"Now what"?

"Come here and be quick about it"?

"What is it, Light of my Life"?

"Look! That gypo and his whore. They've come back and they're spreading a blanket on our beach as if I'd taught them nothing".

"Ingrid, I can feel the life-force draining out of my body. I'm losing the will to live".

"Stop being an imbecile, Cary and get the Boomstation".

"Be reasonable, for the love of my sanity be reasonable"?

"Why don't you ask them to be reasonable and koof off"?

Cary could feel something swelling inside his head. It was pressing against his skull and hurting like a mother. Was it possible to be nagged to death?

Both lots of infernal din started almost simultaneously. '*I've worked out what's happened*', Cary thought, '*The Ancient Hindu Superstition was right, this is actually my second incarnation and I'm in Hades. Ingrid is my punishment for a terrible former life. She's an afreet and her task is to make my existence disconsolate. Wow is she doing a good job of it too*'?

"… finger to keep them away..."

Dizzy fade

"… not the unreasonable one...".

Cary mercifully blacked out.

"… Cary! Cary!. Oh, you're awake! Right get out there and tell them to stop that horrendous pandemonium. Hit him if you have to, or smash their system, but *make them stop*"!

Cary climbed shakily to his feet and came to a decision, picking up his i-Pad he pinged the comb-men.

~

"My title is actually Detective Sergeant, Ma-am, not *Rosser*", the officer informed Ingrid. They were all standing on the porch. To Ingrid's horrified disbelief the rosser had actually invited the gypo and his whore onto her cottage porch.

"I am going to say to both party's in this wrangle, I am glad to see all you folk's come to Ventenubulis Beach. You are all welcome as long as you behave yourselves. I want it understood though that this resort is a public one. It is not some private area where you can disturb the peace to your heart's content. Mister and missus Peck the line of your property that you rented ends at the edge of the porch. The beach is public property and the two of you, Mister Wahlberg and Miss Aniston cannot cause noise pollution with antiquated disturbance and clatter. You have to respect that others are disturbed by such. Similarly you Peck's have to show the exact same consideration for others. I expect when I leave here that the four of you will conduct yourself in a manner which anyone of proper manners understands. It is too nice a place to be arguing like this and calling the comb-men out over a purely domestic matter is wasting our valuable time. If I have to come out here to the four of you again I will make some arrests for disturbance of the peace. You will subsequently all be thrown on a flitter and never allowed to visit Ventenubulis again. Am I making myself clear"?

Even Ingrid knew better than to argue with a Comb-man detective.

"I'm levelling a fine at each of you. One Venushillin. You will pay me in cash before I leave. Then I advise you to go and take a dip in the lake and calm down. I hope you understand what I mean when I say I hope never to see the four of you ever again"!

~

"So that's the Rosser's idea of justice, is it? What about privacy, don't I have a right to that? We should have gone to the north pole instead of coming down here where some rosser can fine me for simply demanding my rights? He was ugly too, that rosser, like some sort of gangster demanding money with menaces. I bet he knows nothing about the law, I bet he even struggles to read his own i-Pad. How can they give idiots like that a badge, Cary? Are you listening to me, or are you having another one of those pathetic spasms"?

"I don't know, Ingrid".

"There should be something we could do about that *Rosserio*. That gangster with a badge. Get on your i-Pad, Cary. Put some sort of official complaint into his superiors. That won't be difficult either will it? Finding his superior. Just a rosser who's knuckles don't scrap on the ground when he walks. Just a Homo sapien. Are you listening to me, Cary"?

"I don't know, Ingrid".

"What is that supposed to mean? How can you not know? Am I right or am I right"?

"I don't know, Ingrid".

"… forget an humiliation like that..."

"...acted like *we* were criminals...".

"Ingrid, we lost too. We were fined as well as the young couple and they didn't look so unreasonable to me".

"So you're on their side are you? You ungrateful rat? After all I've...".

"Ingrid please stop".

She was astonished, "You're not making any sense just lately, Cary, are you going idiotic"?

"Don't call me idiotic! That means asinine, birdbrained, daft".

"I know you're not daft, Cary. I just think you could show a bit more support for your long-suffering spouse. Get more aggressive, Cary. Be more forceful. If you were and you'd run off that riff-raff when I told you to, none of this would have happened. Stop accepting what others demand of you. Stand up to them for once, Cary, be a man for a change. Instead of a twisting wormy weasel of a twisty thing that blows in the wind ".

Cary could feel his brain beginning to melt and pour out of one of his ears.

The tirade was indefatigable, inexhaustible, tireless.

"That's the reason you don't get anywhere".

"Please stop, Ingrid. I'm exhausted by your ceaseless criticism".

"I'm not criticising, Cary. I'm telling you for your own benefit. I'm trying to help you, Cary. I'm trying to improve you. That rosser was a disgrace to the uniform he was wearing. Get you i-Pad this instant".

"Ingrid, we are supposed to be on holiday. To enjoy a break to take time off. Why don't you give your mouth a holiday"?

"What on Venus are you talking about. I'm talking about having that stupid rosser removed from the force and you are off on one of your illogical tangents. He humiliated me. Even if you've not got any self-worth any more. I was treated like a common criminal because of those cheap and nasty people who ruin our beach. They're back! Come to the window and see for yourself. Can you believe your eyes? After everything, they are on my beach, again"!

"Ingrid, I'm begging you now to stop this debacle. If you don't I swear to Venus I'll do something and you won't like it".

"You'll do something! Don't make me laugh, Cary. You! The action man, oh that's priceless that is that's a belter".

"I can't stand much more of this"! Cary was no longer fully in control of himself, he warned his wife, "I can't stand much more of this, Ingrid"!

"Don't stand much more of it then. Do *something*. Let's see what you're gonna do? *Now listen, you two, I'm warning you! My Husband is going to do something. I don't want your kind here so leave if you know what's good for you!*

Cary reappeared from the back of the cottage, in his hands was a snout-nosed blaster,

"Cary! What on Venus name"? For the first time in a long while, Ingrid was afraid. Afraid of her husband. The look in his eye was impossible to determine, his features were crazed. He walked up to her and….

"Cary no, what are you doing. Stop, please stop"?

The blaster made an energetic coughing noise and Charlize Aniston screamed. The blaster coughed a second time and then there was a terrible silence. It did not last for long though.

"Cary, what have you done?

"They won't bother you now, Ingrid. Not now, not ever", Cary told her his voice indicating his exhaustion.

"Cary"! Ingrid was beyond horrified, "Look what you've done! Why did you do that? Why"?

"You will never understand, Ingrid". He picked up his i-Pad and for the second time in as many days pinged the comb-men, "I want to report a murder"! He said into the vid-link.

~

"I'll never understand what came over my husband that morning. He must have lost his mind. Lost his reason. His lawyer said insanity was the only defence to offer the court. Cary though – no not, Cary. He refused to take advice just like he always did. Sacked the man and decided to defend himself. I couldn't give him any advice. As usual, it all fell on deaf ears. Well, he's got deaf ears now. They hanged him, hanged some sense into him, first offence. Stringing him up was too good for him really. Well, he twisted and turned then. Twisted and turned on the end of a rope. I suspected he wanted to die. After all I'd done for him. All the hours I'd tried to improve him. Turn him into...something. The low-born left me penniless too. Penniless and in debt. Typical of the selfish swine. Never ever gave me a thought. Never bothered to think how I felt about anything. What poor life-insurance he had just paid to burn him. What a way to treat me after I'd been such a cordial and loving partner. I didn't even have enough Venushillin to buy a decent black frock for the cremation. Still, I'm not too old to start again. Meet somebody new. Someone who will listen to my advice when I try to make of them a better man"!

The Curved Blade

BRUNHILDE NEDELCIU

Lingering within the abyss between spatial worlds, the atemporal entity silently guarded over the transcending and translucent bridge. Since the creation of all the universes, few mortals had transited from one to another. The tremulous ripples in the fabric of time-space caused by such secular events were gargantuan and needed to be contained.

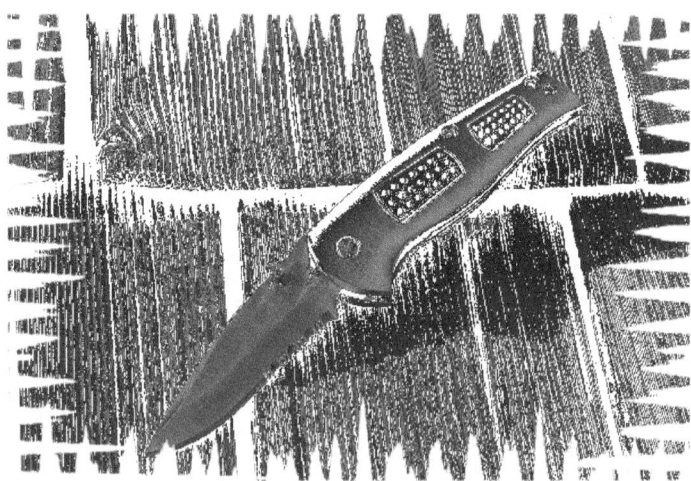

The ceiling had gained another dark spot - a new, undefined speck in a galaxy of emulsion. The tender warmness of the sun felt soothing on her right cheek. Luna hadn't enjoyed the splendour of the solar disk, the cerulean sky or anything from the outside world for a long time. How long had she been locked up in this ascetic sanatorium chamber? Weeks, months, maybe years – a torturous eternity that had started with her metamorphosing into a maniacal murderess. The final psychological assessment brought forward to the judge during her trial, stated that she had been suffering from schizophrenia and psychopathy (antisocial personality disorder). Only a person plagued by these afflictions could have slaughtered with such indescribable brutality three individuals. Yet, her memories of that particular night had remained vacuous. She had denied her guilt. But after days of hearing the gruesome details and remembering the dried blood on her hands, she wasn't certain of her innocence anymore. If she could only conjure up her memories from that night! No matter how hard she had tried, all that had repeatedly surfaced was a mystifying dream…

***

Stepping into her tiny room, Luna immediately took her shoes off. Though the space she inhabited was miniscule, it was spotless. A worn, dark green carpet, a small wardrobe, a table with a chair and a single bed were the only furnishings. It was her sanctuary, her refuge from the outside world, that hadn't always treated her kindly. It had been such a long day. Mrs Bloom had been furious. Under the pretext of ill health, two of the girls hadn't finished their sowing in time. Shy, quiet and obedient, Luna ended up with the extra workload. She usually did. But she didn't mind. Even though a few extra pennies would have gone a long way, she was content with the thought that she had helped. She had to be careful with her hard-earned money. When her father had passed away from tuberculosis, she managed to take out a loan for the funeral. The entire amount had to be paid off by the end of the year. Mister Kronlich had already extended the deadline once. She doubted he would do it again. Maybe one day she would muster enough courage to ask Mrs Bloom for a wage rise. For that, she had to prove herself worthy. Her mother always used to say that only those who work relentlessly will be rewarded in the end. Her father had worked his entire life in the coal mine. From four o'clock in the morning till evening. Every single day, except Sundays, when they would all go to church. Seeing him on his deathbed, Luna had asked herself if her mother had been wrong. She was instantly overwhelmed by regret. Her beautiful mother would have never lied to her. The memory of her mother's embrace was the only thing that kept her warm during the cold, damp nights. She couldn't afford to light the fire. Once she had paid Mister Kronlich, she was going to save up for one of those feathery duvets. Not an expensive one like the one the kind-hearted Mrs Maven had shown her. Just a nice, soft duvet that would allow her to sleep without the three layers of clothing she had to wear now.

Curling up in bed, Luna closed her eyes and imagined the soft hand of her mother stroking her face. Smiling, she fell into a deep sleep.

***

A shrill, deafening sound made her jump out of bed. The darkness had been replaced by a dim, crepuscular light. All four walls shook with anger. Terrified, she run into the dark hallway. With no one else around, she continued down the steps and out through the main entrance. Teeth clenched and arms wrapped around her body, she stood petrified in front of the house. An unbelievable sight spread before her eyes. Everything as far as she could see, the neighbouring buildings and entire streets were smocking piles of rubble.

Suddenly, a steely hand grabbed her arm. She nearly screamed.

"What are you doing in the open, during daylight? Have you lost your mind?" shouted furiously a masked man. "Come with me, you stupid girl."

Not given the chance to reply, Luna found herself being dragged towards an obscured hatch into the ground and then pushed down a flight of wooden stairs. Each step was adorned with a screech, making Luna wonder if the rotten wood would eventually collapse sending them into an endless blackness. At the bottom, the man pounded three times into a heavy, metallic door that opened at once and allowed them into a decently sized, semi obscure space. In the middle, two tables had been placed next to each other. Around them, a dozen chairs were occupied by men and women, all now turned towards them. One of the women quickly stood up and approached Luna.

"Welcome child", the woman said with a kind smile. "Come sit down. Poor soul, you must be starving."

A chair was freed and Luna sat down not knowing how to react or what to expect. All but one were smiling at her with curiosity and empathy in their eyes.

"I found her in front of the Time Temple. She just stood there. Maybe she is feebleminded. What's your name?" asked the man who had brought her here, taking off his mask.

"My name is Luna." She quietly answered.

"Luna. What a beautiful name," the woman responded. "I am Zeline and that grumpy man is known as Bordach. He acts tough, but he is more like a gentle giant."

Grunting at the last comment, Bordach took a seat at the opposite side of the table. With swift movements, Zeline placed a cup of fresh water and a big piece of bread in front of Luna.

One by one, Zeline introduced all those present. Encouraged by their friendliness, Luna admitted to being lost and not understanding what was going on. She had gone to bed as usual and a loud scream had woken her up, only to find herself in a strange world. Had there been a bombardment? Was it war again?

"Of course there is a war" blasted Bordach out. "Humans are being exterminated," he continued, causing Luna to shudder.

"Shut up, Bordach!" Zeline commanded. "You are scaring her. She is obviously not well. Probably amnesia. I can't blame her. If I could, I would forget about all this too."

Bordach Mumbled something undecipherable. Together with some of the others, he walked through the blue door that Luna only now had noticed.

Biting into the bread, Luna hadn't realized just how hungry she was. She had lost count how many times she had gone to bed without a meal.

"Come child," Zeline prompted her, once she had finished her meal. "You need some sleep. You will feel better after you have had some rest."

"Thank you. But ... please... I don't understand. Where am I? Where are..."

Luna tried to ask about everybody else, her neighbours, the girls, Mrs Bloom, but Zeline interrupted her.

"Tomorrow we can have a proper talk. I will try to fill some of those gaps in your memory. But for now, you are safe, so don't worry about anything."

Several minutes later, Luna was lying on a metallic framed bunker bed, covered with a dark red duvet. It wasn't like the one Mrs Maven had, but it was very close. The few patches and rips didn't bother her. Even though her mind was raging trying to find answers, the warmth tranquilized her senses and she fell asleep.

A sharp prick in her neck awoke her and opening her eyes, she saw a tall, strong built, bearded man standing next to her bed. Luna screamed.

"Seriously? Is this how you are planning to greet me every time I am near you?" Bordach asked irritated.

"What's going on? Bordach, what are you doing?"

Zeline ran into the room. Pushing him away, she sat down on the edge of the bed and took Luna's hand in hers.

"Just wanting to make sure she is not one of them", the man replied with a gravelly voice.

"Of course she is not one of them. Look at her eyes," the woman cut him off. "You frightened her. But if you have taken a sample of her blood go and ask Tuala to test for any illnesses or injuries. It might help us determine what has happened to her."

With a grunt, Bordach disappeared.

"Do you remember me? I am Zeline", the ageless woman asked. Grey streaks in the dark chestnut hair conveyed her with a distinguished elegance. Though not a striking beauty, Zeline had delicate features and large, brown eyes that had the power to mesmerize anyone who immersed themselves into them.

As through fog, the events of the previous day took shape in Luna's mind.

"Yes. I remember. But I don't understand..." she whispered.

"I know. And I will do my best to explain everything to you."

For the next hour, Luna listened carefully to Zeline. The world had changed. A new, superior species of hybrid humans, the Ubersapiens, had infiltrated every society on Earth and had slowly taken over by exterminating the so called "normal" people. Forming a super society, Ubersapiens hunted down any human they found. There were very few people left. All hiding and living underground, only venturing outside as shadows of the night.

Zeline's husband, Naal, together with a few others had built this bunker, a safe hideout for a group of twenty four survivors. During daylight, the Ubersapiens patrolled all areas, but at night they retreated to their command posts. No one was sure why. The group used the darkness to find food, water and other supplies that remained within the ruins of former establishments.

"Where is your husband?" timidly, Luna asked.

Zeline's eyes lowered and after a moment of silence she answered quietly:

"One night we got ambushed. They never roam during night. Or at least very rarely. For whatever reason, they did this one time. Naal saw them and alerted most of us. Some were too far out to hear his warnings. He decided to go after them. None of them ever returned," her voice broke off.

"I am sorry," Luna whispered, gently stroking Zeline's hand. "Are they just like us?"

"As far as their appearance goes, yes. Except for their cold, lilac coloured eyes. They are devoid of humanity, of love, just emptiness…" answered Sato, a young man, who had joined them.

"It's time to go out", interrupted Bordach, who had returned with Sato.

Two long, shiny weapons were strapped on each side of his wide shoulders. Catching Luna's stare, he explained:

"Swords. They cut through those bastards like knives through butter."

Had that been a hint of a smile in the corner of his mouth?

"Tuala is staying in. She will keep you company", Zeline said standing up. "She will bring you more suitable clothes. When we return, we can continue our chat."

Once alone, Luna had the chance to explore the underground compound. Tiny rooms were used as sleeping quarters, each containing bunk beds and two chests: one for the clothes and one for personal items. There was a food hall with an open plan kitchen, storage rooms, the meeting room that doubled up as a dayroom, two shower rooms (one for the females of the group, the other one for the males), three toilets and a medical room with an adjacent laboratory. That was where she found Tuala. She was bent over an instrument, peering through two eyepieces.

"This is a microscope," Tuala smiled.

After explaining how the microscope worked and what it was used for, she allowed Luna to have a look. Luna was mesmerized. Never in her life had she seen anything like this. She had always enjoyed taking in every detail of materials, flowers, leaves and insects. But this was something so much more! Tuala was bombarded with questions and like a patient teacher provided all the answers. By the time the group returned, Luna knew, between other things, all the components of human blood and its differences from that of the Ubersapiens.

"She is one smart girl," Tuala told Zeline. "Even though her education is basic, she has an incredible desire to learn and a memory to match it."

"You made quite the impression, I hear," Zeline approached Luna. "Tomorrow, Bordach will show you the weapons' room and teach you how to use some of them. Once you feel confident and you have regained your strength, you will join us outside."

Nervous, yet excited, Luna nodded. While the others sorted through their bounty, Luna helped Sato prepare the food: rabbit stew and freshly baked bread. Sato handled the meat, Luna the vegetables. Reaching for a pan, their hands touched. Sato was a head taller than her and probably a little bit older. Sandy hair, dark blue eyes, toned body. He was rather handsome. Luna blushed and pulled her hand away. She had never dared to look at any men or consider a relationship. Walking back home from work, Laura had told her several times that passing men had been staring at her. A customer once complemented her saying she was very beautiful. She had stuttered a "thank you" and had been grateful that Mrs Bloom had changed the subject, allowing her to slip into the backroom. How could she be regarded as pretty? Frizzy, red hair, green eyes, freckles... She saw herself as average, easily forgotten. She was a poor girl who had to work until her fingertips were bleeding. Who wanted that? Her father used to tell her that one day a good, decent man will marry her and she will have a family of her own. She had asked her father how will she know which man will be the right one for her. His answer was simple:

"You will know. The moment your eyes will meet, you will feel it in your heart, my sweet Luna."

Sato was still looking at her and Luna's heart jumped a beat.

"So, Luna... Where are you from?" Sato's voice had a calming effect on her.

"I am from here. I used to live in the grey house that is not far from the refuge."

"Hm. You really don't remember anything?"

"I do, just not about all this," Luna answered saddened making a sweeping gesture with her hand.

"I am sure it will come to you sooner or later. Don't worry. Tell me about what you do remember," he prompted her.

"I lost my mother when I was young and then my father died a year ago. I worked as a seamstress. That's all really. Nothing interesting. I am rather boring," she tried to joke.

"I am very sorry for your loss. All of us have lost people we cared about," he added quietly, his face darkened by a shadow of deep hidden pain. "Don't be afraid. You are safe here, I promise. And never say that ever again. You are far away from boring," the warmth in his voice flooded her entire being. His eyes, the colour of the spellbinding sea, had stripped all her fears away.

In bed, Luna was kept awake for hours. It wasn't due to the mystery of this new world and how she had gotten here. It was Sato's words that were carved in her mind. When she finally managed to fall asleep, she dreamt her mother. She appeared from behind a curtain made out of white silk. She handed Luna a blue ribbon, the broach that had belonged to her grandmother and a bouquet of lilies of the valley and forget-me-nots. Once awake, Luna wondered what the dreams meant. Where those hidden symbols or a message her mother was trying to send her from the real of angels?

Luna lost count of time. In the underground compound, day and night were moulded into a continuous dimness. Bordach took it upon himself to teach her self-defence and the usage of a variety of weapons. She was a fast learning and hardworking pupil and even Bordach, with his ever so grumpy manner, finally admitted to it. From the shy, frail girl, a young, independent, strong woman emerged. Once everyone was sleeping, Sato and Luna met in one of the empty bedrooms and talked for hours. Their relationship blossomed into a beautiful love story. Every time they had the opportunity, they enjoyed each other's company. One day, Sato confessed to her that during that fatal night, together with Naal and several others, his father had lost his life too. Sato had been ill and Zeline had kept him inside. He never forgave himself for not being there for his father. Could he have saved him? He didn't know, but this question and the guilt had tortured him ever since. Luna placed her arms around his neck and their lips touched in a sensual kiss.

"It wasn't your fault, my love," Luna said stroking his cheek.

"I know that now. I think everything happens for a reason. It is just that sometimes it takes a very long time to understand what that reason is. Even now I am not completely sure. What I do know for certain is that I love you, Luna. And I won't allow anyone or anything to harm you," he whispered.

Surrounded by darkness, their bodies ravished by desire and passion melted into one perfect entity. The next days, the constant smiles on their bright faces were met with hidden giggles and quietly spoken comments like: "Here come the love birds. Aren't they sweet?"

"Tomorrow night will be the first time you are going to join us outside, Luna," Zeline said during the meeting. "Bordach thinks you are ready."

"Thank you. I am looking forward to it. I will do my best," Luna replied with a smile.

"Excellent. Come on everyone, let's get cracking. Those veg won't pick themselves and we need to find some more metal."

While the others headed out, Luna made her way to the lab where Tuala was waiting for her. The two had grown closer. Tuala was the only one to whom Luna had admitted her love for Sato. The girls were sorting through some medical supplies, when loud shouting made them rush over to the entrance.

Bordach, Zeline and the others burst through the metallic door and quickly locked it.

"They were out again," gasped Zeline.

Luna looked around, but she couldn't find Sato. When Zeline took her hand and pulled her over to one side, she knew.

"I am so sorry, Luna. We tried… he was too far away…they got to him," Zeline's words broke into nothingness.

Running to her room, she closed the door and collapsed to the floor. The grief she felt inside of her crushed every cell in her body, yet she couldn't cry. She wanted to scream, to rip into her own chest and pull the heart and all the pain out. Only a humble whimpering was escaping through the lips that not so long ago had kissed the man she had loved with every ounce of her being. When both her parents had passed away, she had cried until her eyes, swollen and red, had no more tears. Why couldn't she do that now? When Zeline checked on her, she was laid motionless on her bed. She refused to talk to anyone about Sato and her suffering. Every task she undertook, she did with even more determination. On rare occasions, she granted Tuala or Zeline a forced smile. Everybody noticed the radical change in her demeanour.

"Give her time. Time will heal the wounds," Zeline told them and they all agreed.

On the next planned trip, some members of the group were not keen to step into the darkness of the outside world. Their food supplies were low. To make it fair, Zeline asked for volunteers. Luna's hand shot up. A quick glance at Bordach and Zeline was ready to refuse her.

"She can join us. We need every help we can get," Bordach intervened.

"I don't know. I don't think she is ready for it, "Zeline replied.

"I am ready. I want to help. It will keep my mind and body busy," Luna quickly added.

Reluctantly, Zeline agreed and a small group of five made their way up the stairs and through the wooden hatch.

"Here", whispered Bordach pressing a short sword and a flash light into her hands. The blade was curved and the handle was made out of a material unknown to Luna.

"When it will come down to it, you need to kill those monsters," his voice had an unforgiving tone to it. "They wouldn't spare you. Forget about everything else. Are you willing to kill or not?"

Bordach had stopped in front of her, piercing her with his fiery gaze. She didn't need to answer. The grief, anger and determination in her eyes were sufficient.

After a few meters, the group split and each started scavenging through the rubble. In the pale moonlight, Luna noticed that one of the houses was mostly intact and decided to search inside for anything that could be useful. The blackened door was hanging precariously. Through the hallway, she carefully stepped into one of the rooms. She stopped abruptly. She recognized this house. One of the upstairs rooms had been her home since her father had passed away. She was standing in the main living room. A muffled sound coming from the far corner startled her and she switched the flash light on. Three pairs of lilac eyes stared back at her. What appeared to be two women and a man were gathered around a fourth person that was laid motionless on the floor. It was Mrs Maven! No! She had been so good to her, always encouraging her when she had lost hope. Mrs Maven had stood by her side when her father had died. It was the petite, old lady who had found her the job as a seamstress. She didn't deserve this! Sato and all the others did deserve their fate either! Feeling the heaviness of the weapon in her hand, hysterically, she launched towards them.

"This is for Sato, you demons! This is for Mrs Maven! For Mrs Bloom and Mister Kronlich! For all of those you have killed," Luna screamed, frantically stabbing the creatures.

Alerted by the noise, Bordach run into to house and found Luna standing amidst the lifeless, bloody corpses of three Ubersapiens. Covered in blood, tears streaming down her face, she was shaking, repeating the same names over and over again. Gently, he picked her up and carried her to safety.

Everybody gathered around her. Through the multitude of voices, she heard Tuala exclaim:

"I told you she was a natural Ubersapiens killer!"

Carefully, Bordach placed her on the bed and Zeline sent all of the others away. Tuala administered an injection in her right arm. Seeing their concerned faces, she wanted to reassure them that she was fine. Tuala's tranquilizer, the emotional and physical exertion had drained her.

"I revenged your death, Sato", was her last thought before slipping into a deep state of unconsciousness.

***

"Get up!" ordered harshly a baritone voice. "You are under arrest for the murder of Mister Kronlich, Mrs Bloom and Miss Laura. You are an animal who deserves to be hanged."

Luna couldn't comprehend. Was the constable talking to her? She felt her hands violently pulled in front of her and handcuffed. They were covered in a dark, sticky substance. Blood!

"Thank God Mrs Maven had fainted, otherwise you would have hacked her to death too," a raspy voice shouted behind her.

***

The cadence of hurried steps approaching her sanitary prison could mean only one thing. They were coming to take her for the treatment. Doctor Schulz had assured her that she would experience no pain during this new medical technique called lobotomy. Yet she was secretly hoping for the opposite. Violent physical agony might overpower her tormented soul, offering her a break from the devouring despair she was feeling. At least that way, she would be sure that she wasn't dreaming...

The ripples subsided. The equilibrium between time and space had been languidly restored.

Affaire de Coeur

ANAIS IRVING

One

"Oh, my goodness, John, I think it's a dead body", the elderly woman shrieked.

Face down in the mountain stream, the remains of a human being were floating between the wet rocks.

"Stand aside, Doreen. We mustn't touch anything. I've seen this in that program on TV. Thank goodness, I've charged my mobile this morning."

For their 40th wedding anniversary, Doreen had convinced her husband to book a room at a picture pretty mountain inn. They spent their holiday hiking and admiring the beauty of nature. Today was their last trip into the woods. Already familiar with this part of the forest, they strayed away from the path. They planned on having a picnic by the crystalline stream and then head back. John had noticed the strange mound of clothes first. Believing they were the disregarded belongings of a fellow hiker, the couple took a closer look. To their horror, the discovery soon revealed the gruesome reality.

Moving away from the spot, the man rang the emergency services. Within the hour, the area was being combed by police officers. Mountain Rescue was later joined by the medical examiner and his forensic team.

"Did you check with the pair that found it? Did they move anything?" Pathologist D'moil addressed, Detective Garber, who was in charge of the subsequent investigation.

"Luckily, we have a CSI fan on our hands, so they didn't. The husband told me that he made sure his better-half didn't contaminate any of the evidence," the detective answered dryly.

"I knew that one day those silly TV series would prove useful. If you've finished, I'll get the team to pack up. I think we've pretty much recovered everything. Small parts will be lost forever, probably in some scavengers' stomachs."

"Doc, is it true that they eat the eyes first?"

"Sometimes. It depends which part of a carcass is the easiest to access."

"What do you think, Doc? Accident or homicide?"

"For a definitive verdict, you'll have to wait for all the tests to be carried out."

"I'm aware of that. Just give me your first impression."

"Fine. The advanced state of decomposition hints that it's several days from the time of death. It's been rather warm lately, so the process would have started pretty much immediately. Animals did quite extensive damage. All post-mortem. Once I examine the insects and casings, I'll be able to be more precise. It appears we have a Caucasian male, probably between 30 and 50 years of age. An excarnation will be needed in this case."

"Wow, Doc! Come on, you know I don't speak science. Plain English, please. Is that when you boil the body?"

"Yes. The bones need to be defleshed in order to be examined for any evidence of trauma. Also to enable me to take precise measurements. What I've noticed as a possible cause of death is a fracture of the occipital bone. He'd suffered a heavy blow to the back of his head. Don't jump to any conclusions! Jim found blood and hair on that large rock over there."

"So you're saying, the victim could've just slipped on the wet stones, lost his balance and cracked his head on the rock during the fall."

"Up to now, that's what my findings do suggest. I'll ask for a full toxicology report. Just in case there are any traces of suspicious substances. Check the local guest-houses and see if anyone has been reported missing. He appears to have been a hiker."

"Yeah. He had all the gear: boots, windbreaker and from a few metres away we collected a rucksack. Will you be able to identify him?"

"I don't know. I'll run a DNA match, but if the guy isn't in the database, we'll struggle. I can try facial reconstruction from the skull bones. You know as well as I do, that it isn't always accurate, though. Anyway, we'd better get moving. It's getting dark. I'll see you tomorrow - at the lab."

Doreen and her husband had been escorted back to the inn. The remains were sealed inside a black body-bag and transported to the morgue awaiting further analysis. The blackness of the night and the creatures of the mountains reclaimed their territory.

Two

Her footsteps resonated through the desolated, gloomy street. From the murky sky, a cold drizzle embraced the sublunary world. A thunderous gust of wind coerced the fallen leaves to swirl into a circular dance. Suddenly, she felt something clinging to her left leg. Startled, she looked down and picked up the culprit: a ripped piece of newspaper. Recognizing her own picture, she read the lengthy article.

"That's a better obituary than I've imagined", she thought out loud and the shadow of a smile lingered on the corners of her lips.

Five weeks ago, as a result of a horrific accident, Doctor Kara Sandstein had been declared dead. Returning from an archaeological dig, her car spun out of control, crashing through the parapet and plummeting into the raging sea. After a long and thorough search, though a body had not been found, the police and the medical examiner had closed the case, releasing her death certificate. It had come as a shock to all those that had known her (so the piece stated). A prolific archaeologist, a trustworthy friend, a wonderful teacher. Numerous colleagues, students and friends attended the funeral. Some cried others mourned quietly. The University of Lindrun announced the foundation of a research grant in the honour of their "most prestigious" professor. A bronze plaque bearing her name was going to be installed at the entrance to the exhibit she had worked so hard to put together at the Museum of Ancient Art. The sales of her published work had multiplied and continued to increase.

In a sub-note, her death was compared with the equally horrifying loss of the life of Mr Riss. Richard Riss, a well-known solicitor, had met his end only a month earlier and in very similar circumstances. Some were voicing their suspicion and concern that the two fatal events were linked. The police inspector had declared in a press conference that, despite the fact the two victims had met each other in a work environment, the deaths were unrelated and they were not treated as suspicious.

Closing and locking the door to the rented, modest apartment, Kara peeled off the drenched layers of clothing and headed into the bathroom. The image in the mirror startled her. Getting used to her new appearance would take time. Her once long, luscious, blonde hair was now short, curly and dyed deep chestnut. Though her piercing blue eyes were dark, abyssal pools, due to coloured contact lenses, they still harboured the same determination with which she had conquered each obstacle in her past. With newly acquired skills in make-up contouring, she had been able to successfully conceal her features. Not even her friend and colleague, Marianne, had been able to recognize her when she literally bumped into her at the bank. For the next couple of days, Kara didn't dare to venture outside her flat. At the slightest noise, she was expecting the police to break in and arrest her for staging her own death or far worse. But no one came. As a precaution, she chose a different bank. She deposited the final amount of her savings into the account she had opened under a false name. Having sold a few artefacts on the black market, it had tripled the sum. Unfortunately, two of her most influential buyers were not happy with their purchases. Desperately needing the money, she had indeed passed a few objects as genuine pieces. Even she had had a hard time to tell them apart, so how could anyone else? The replicas were so accurate and detailed. None of the art dealers had noticed that they were fakes. Not long after, she started receiving threatening phone calls and emails. Of course, she could not report it to the police. Taking everything into account, she had decided to feign her own death and rebuild a completely new identity.

Settling down between two dark green, plush cushions, Kara switched the TV on. All she had to do now was to be patient and wait. Soon, she would start a new life alongside the one she loved and all the demons from her past will be erased. The small wind chime she had hung in the window singing a gentle, metallic melody.

Three

"My love, you're finally here. I've bought some wine, so we can celebrate", Kara threw herself at her guest, their lips meeting in a long-lasting, passionate kiss.

"Come on, we have all the time in the world for that. Mm… smells good. What did my sexy archaeologist cook tonight?"

"Your favourite," Kara smiled. "Pasta Bolognese with freshly baked garlic bread."

After a quick shower and change of clothes, the two were seated around the dining table. Through the open window, a warm gust of autumnal wind gently stroked the petals of the crimson roses. Kara had bought them from the flower shop in the marketplace. They had to celebrate. After so many months of torment and preparation, their plan had finally come to fruition. Soon, they would be able to start their new life together. As far away as possible.

"Do you think they'll find out who he is?" Kara's voice revealed that she was being plagued by worry.

"Don't fret, we are safe. The pig didn't even know what hit him. And he deserved every ounce of it! Even if they find him, it will look like an accident. Smashing his head against one of those rocks was an excellent idea. It covers up the first hit."

"They might still be able to tell there were two different blows to the head."

"Look, his mistake was to fake his own death. From an official point of view, 'deceased' is already attached to his name. No one will be looking for him. By the time anyone gets to him, he'll be unrecognizable. We chose that specific mountain area, because of all the wildlife. After all the wolves and the other critters have made a meal out of him, they won't be able to hang an identity tag to his toe. And no soul can tie you to his death, as you're equally dead to the world. Aren't you, my lovely Kara?"

Four

Settling down at the glass coffee table, Richard logged into his tablet. His daily morning routine: whilst sipping his special, calming brew, he read the news. The screen sprung to life, the latest articles filling the ten-inch screen. One particular item made him pause and carefully place his cup of steaming chamomile and peppermint tea onto the marble coaster. After reading it for the second time, smiling, he moved his gaze towards the large, open window. The views were breath-taking. Surrounded by majestic mountains, the sea of red-tinted roofs was sparkling in the morning sunlight.

"Darling, why did you not wake me?" a soft voice whispered into his ear. "What's that?"

"My obituary. And it's rather good", he replied, allowing Kara to sit on his knee. "It's better than I expected."

When Richard had met her, he had been instantly mesmerised. His client had been interested in purchasing a valuable artefact that archaeologist Kara Sandstein had recovered from the ruins of an ancient burial site. He didn't expect her to accept his request for a meeting. He had heard that she avoided dealing with this sort of business in person. And yet, on a mild spring afternoon, there she was. The moment she had stepped into his office, the savvy solicitor knew that he had lost the bargaining war. He accepted all her demands with one condition: for her to join him for dinner. A week later, he was absorbing every cell of her being with an insatiable desire. He made sure that Francesca, his childhood love and wife, remained unaware of all this. He still cared for her, as one does for a distant relative. Over the years, he had witnessed her growing colder and spiteful. She constantly blamed him of being incapable of understanding her, for not supporting her and of being too cold and work-obsessed. Even so, the last thing he wanted to do was to hurt the woman with whom he had spent the best part of twenty years. But his life, as it had been back then, had strangled him and he had decided to escape. Now, he could enjoy a completely new identity, free from worry life filled with sunshine, beaches and of course with his beloved Kara. It had been her, who had suggested to him to fake his own death. He made the necessary arrangements. Francesca and he had shared the main account, but unknown to her he had kept his savings separate. Letting his car drive off the edge of a cliff was the easiest part. He couldn't say the same about the last night he had spent with Francesca.

"I don't know, Rich. It doesn't feel right to me. What if she finds out?" Kara's voice had a slight edge to it.

"We went through this several times, Kara. We both agreed the plan was foolproof. There's no way Francesca or anyone else will ever figure it out. I chose that exact stretch of road because of its precariousness. Once they recover the car, they'll check it and find my belongings inside. The conclusion will be that I've tried to get out through the open window, but the current was too strong. Therefore, a missing body."

"I know…"

"We've been through this a million times. Don't you remember the family that had perished in the sea only a couple of miles away from there? They didn't find any of them either."

Trying not to sound annoyed, he pulled her towards him and kissed her soft, full lips.

"Come on, let's get ready and head to the market. I really fancy some salmon today…"

"… with parsley sauce and boiled baby potatoes," the beautiful woman giggled while playing with his hair.

Five

"So, you're just going to sit there?" she asked tilting her head ever so slightly in an effort to decipher Richard's mood. "Ok, suit yourself. I am going to get a shower."

Putting the coke can down, Francesca collected a pair of clean underwear and a long T-shirt from her unpacked suitcase. Another quick glance before stepping into the bathroom revealed that his face harboured the same void expression that had greeted her.

The hot water felt so soothing on the sun-bitten skin. Closing her eyes, the voluptuous appearance of Kara overwhelmed her mind. Laid on the golden sand, the Siren was reaching out to her. Retracing the spellbinding, insatiable caresses, she felt the roundness of the breast, the hardened nipple, the velvety abdomen.

The memory of the long, gentle fingers inserted deep inside her, stole a quiet sigh from Francesca's lips. Like a lightning bolt, pleasure burst through every cell of her body. Stifling a deep, sinful moan, a wet, relieving climax set her free. Time became fluid and really lost its concrete shape. How long did she sit there, lost to the world, lost to her own life?

When she emerged from the steamy bathroom, he was still sat in the worn, brown leather armchair, smoking a cigarette. Through the thick smoke, their eyes met. She stood there, in the middle of their bedroom, with dripping wet, auburn hair, oversized T-shirt and bare feet. All she wished for was to sink in the clean bedsheets and drift away into a world exempt from desires and anxieties. Slowly, he got up, leaving the half burnt cigarette in the overflowing ashtray. When had he started smoking again?

With every step he got closer, she felt her pulse pounding louder and louder inside her head, the war song of tribal drums. Her senses were firing information, relentlessly overpowering each neural receiver: the aftershave she had bought him for Christmas, the bitter taste of soap she had accidentally ingested during her shower, the icy water droplets piercing the skin on her arms. Stopping in front of her, his hand reached out but retreated sharply when she slightly turned her head. Those beautiful eyes had made her so happy and at times so angry and sad. She had equally loved and hated them with passion. Now, there was only emptiness.

Abruptly, he walked around her and without turning, Francesca heard the door open.

"Leave! That's what you do best", she hissed uncontrollably.

The door slammed and before she could move, two strong hands grabbed her by the shoulders and threw her onto the bed with so much force that it pushed the air out of her lungs. Light-headed, Francesca rolled on her back and was confronted by two piercing, green eyes, so familiar and yet frighteningly alien - something primaeval shimmering in them. In a fraction of a second, he was on top, pinning her arms down on each side of the head. She could feel his heavy breathing on the face and the warmth of his body pressed against hers.

"What do you think you're..."

His mouth stopped her in mid-sentence, his tongue forcing its way between her lips. She tried to free herself from his grip, but his fingers, digging into her flesh, felt like steel. Angry and frustrated, she bit his lip, blood staining his bottom lip.

"Let me go!" like a trapped wild animal, she cried.

"No" he whispered into her ear. "I want you."

The deep tone of his voice aroused her, causing fear to suddenly morph into sexual pleasure, desire and insatiable hatred. Lifting her head towards his, she licked the blood drops from his swollen lip. Their tongues met in a carnal dance, each trying to subjugate the other. His hand ventured underneath her T-shirt, gently stroking her breast. No! She didn't want that. She wanted passion, fierce, flesh-devouring sex. Digging her nails into his neck, Francesca broke away from his mouth. With forceful movements, he removed her underwear.

The morning sun caressed her cheek and turning towards the wall, Francesca opened her eyes. Dark clouds were hanging over the horizon. A loud knock on the door. And again.

"Yes?" she opened the door, pulling her bathrobe tight around her.

"Mrs Riss?" the police officers asked. "Can we please talk to you about something rather sensitive?"

With a hand gesture, she invited them in. Stepping into the living room, she offered them a seat on the couch. They chose to stand.

"We are terribly sorry to inform you that a serious accident has occurred during the early hours," the taller policeman said gravely. "Your husband's car has crashed through the parapet into the sea. Rescue teams are doing their very best to try and find him, but we are afraid that it might be a losing battle. The currents are very strong. The storm is nearing."

Six

Through the crowd, the shapely brunette stood out. The pastel coloured summer dress complemented her body type beautifully. Kara had noticed the stranger a while ago. But to escape from the bombardment of questions thrown at her, took time and patience. Finally, she was able to politely excuse herself and drift towards the visitor. With a small fold between her eyebrows, the woman was studying one of the exhibited mosaics.

"It's a representation of Zeus as the white bull abducting Europa," Kara explained softly.

"Oh. I didn't know that. Why did he abduct her?" the woman asked, turning towards her. Her eyes were the colour of the stormy sea, luring Kara into their depth.

"He desired her," came the crisp answer.

"Hm. Therefore, he just took whatever he wanted."

"He was a god after all," laughed Kara, but her companion's expression remained unchanged. "By the way, my name is Kara Sandstein. I am the curator of this exhibition. Most of the objects come from my archaeological digs."

"Nice meeting you. I am Francesca. A humble visitor in search of history and…"

"And?"

"And knowledge, Doctor Sandstein" Francesca continued with a wide smile, shaking Kara's hand.

"If you'll allow me, it would be my uttermost pleasure to show you around the museum. And please call me Kara."

"That would be lovely, Kara. If I learn something new, I might tell you my full name," was the playful response.

Taking on the challenge, Doctor Sandstein morphed into the perfect guide. Before reaching the last part of the exhibition, Kara's companion revealed her name: Francesca Riss.

They decided to meet again. Both agreed on the Italian restaurant that was just a block away from Kara's workplace. It was central and Kara could leave her car in the museum's private carpark. Seated in a booth next to the window, they ordered a bottle of Chardonnay. Francesca chose her favourite dish – pasta Bolognese with garlic bread, while Kara opted for a vegetable pizza. They talked about everything. Kara's job, Francesca's unhappy marriage, memories and ideas. Without them noticing, all the other customers had left. Eventually, the slightly overweight owner approached them and apologetically explained that he had to close. It had gone past midnight. Giggling, they asked him to order them a taxi.

"Where shall I take you, ladies?" enquired the middle-aged taxi driver, after the two attractive women had climbed into the back of his car.

"Riverside Avenue. Number 23," Kara answered squeezing Francesca's hand.

Kara's apartment was situated on the bottom floor of an impressive mansion. The house had been built at the end of the 19th century and until recently it had stayed within the family of the original owners. Two years ago, the building and its grounds were sold for a hefty sum to a property tycoon, who converted it into luxury flats. Kara rented the only one that had its own small courtyard. She had decorated it with numerous flowerpots and wind chimes. Returning home from work or expeditions, she found the calming sounds and the sweet smell of the flowers therapeutic. Inside, she had tastefully placed some colourful artefacts, providing the modern, slick interior with a welcoming, homely feel.

"Welcome to my modest home," said Kara, allowing Francesca to enter the open plan living area.

Slowly walking around, Francesca analysed each showcased piece and then settled down on the comfortable, white leather couch.

"I feel like I've known you for a long time. Which of course is silly, considering that I've only met you today," she said, swirling the wine in the glass Kara had handed her.

"I feel the same," Kara whispered, decreasing the distance between them.

Seven

Their carnal desires extinguished, they lay exhausted in each other's arms.
"Kara?"
"Yes," the sleepy answer resounded in the crepuscular light.
"I'm sick of hiding. I want to start a new life… with you," Francesca whispered.

"Are you going to divorce Richard?"

"I thought about it. But… Eventually, he would find out about you and he would destroy us both. Financially, he would bankrupt us and make sure that our reputation would be stained for eternity. We need a different solution."

Kara propped her head on her folded arm. She looked Francesca straight in the eye.

"What do you mean? Murder him? And then what? Spend the rest of our lives behind bars?"

"That would only happen if we get caught. I've been thinking about it. But for it to work, I need your full cooperation."

"Are you actually serious? Oh, my God. You are! Francesca, there is no way we could get away with it. You know damn well the technology they have in these days…"

"Don't concern yourself with the minutiae, my beautiful Kara. Just answer this: are you willing to help me kill him or not?" Francesca interrupted sternly. "In order for us to enjoy a new start together, we need to do this. Of course, only if you want to."

"You know I want to spend eternity with you and that I would do anything for you. If that's what it takes…"

The mystical rhapsody of the wind chimes protruded through the open window of the dark bedroom. A silky petal collapsed onto the geometric slab. Silence…

Eight

"Hello, Vin. You're a man of your word I'll give you that".

"You know why I'm pinging you. You haven't have you"?

"Not yet", Stallone smiled. "I'm still doing research. I've also been busy this week with work. A new contract with Mercedes. Their new line of nail-varnish bottles. Do you want to see some of my designs"?

Vin sighed audibly over the link, "Not really, Bro. The other matter is uppermost in my mind".

"If you want to stop me you could always remortgage, give me the amount that would stop me".

"That frenging low of you, Dustin. Trying to play me like that. Offering me huge debt, or the other matter".

"In that case, Vin I will have to take care of the *other matter* as you call it - myself".

"I love you, Bro. You don't make it easy for me to feel that way", Vin sounded saddened.

"Life's not easy", Stallone hardened his heart. "And the solutions to its problems are sometimes unpalatable too. That the way of the solar-system, Vin".

"It doesn't always have to be. I've got to go. Please think about your decision for a very long time, Bro".

"You can be certain that when I finally arrive at my decision it will be the one without sensible alternative", Stallone returned and cut the connection.

He was finding the ancient collection of bizarre tales fascinating. Not all of them offered any unique ideas, but they were entertaining just the less. He was going to finish the entire volume before he killed Madchen.

Later he settled down once more to do some reading. The process of sitting with an actual wood-mulch book was mush more satisfying than reading his i-Pad. He wondered why that was as he turned to the next story. He had placed a credit card between the leaves to facilitate that.

Stipes in ad Novandum Pigra

PETRONA WELLS

Ronson adjusted his neckerchief making it certain it was totally aligned. As usual, he was impeccably dressed in dress-uniform. He had been cached out of the force for some years, but those who knew him still addressed him as *Major.* Ronson was about to attend what could prove to be the most defining moment of his life.

Or otherwise.

He had received a ping from the eminent surgeon Doctor Swăvăg only six days previously and the decision had not been easily reached. Not even for the victor of the Anglo-Francosian battle of Edinburgh. For Swăvăg had invited him to join a very elite club with a very special agenda. The day had come. Ronson dressed for the part and kissed his long-suffering wife farewell. Long-suffering due to his military career. One move after another. Never any time to settle in one spot. Long absences during various campaigns around the world. The latter including the worry over the atomic strike on the Middle East. The overnight cleansing of that vile superstition from the world. Then came the phleege! The terrible plague that had decimated what was left of the world's population.

Secretly Missus Ronson had welcomed retirement. She had longed for the peace of it. The stability. Finally, Ronson reached retirement age, having served his country for eighty-one years. He had joined the force at eighteen. Only years of peaceful retirement stretched before the Major now. He intended to enjoy the twenty or so years left to him.

He climbed into his Quaker 200bhp flitter and took it up to the prescribed altitude before heading for Yorkshire. The northern county of Anglond contained the capital York. He was not headed there though. Rather the address he had been given was in a town called Sprotbrough. At the town's only hotel, the Walters he was to meet the other four members of the Stripes in ad Novandum Pigra.

This apparently meant the Reduction Club in some strangely dead and ancient language.

All he had been told thus far was that it may well prove to his advantage to attend. Also that the club would consist of five members. A very select group then. He had met Swăvăg many times during various military theatres. The final trio was totally unknown to him. He coasted down to the town indicated by sat-nav. Sighing to a perfect landing on the Walters Hotel rooftop flitter-park. The headed with his confident military stride toward the lift. A light drizzle was falling so he hurried. No sense in arriving for the curious meeting with mussed hair and wet tunic.

The lift took him down to reception where he had been instructed to report initially. Behind the desk was an instantly recognisable android. The only indication was her flawless skin, superb shoulder-length hair and surreal beauty. Ronson wondered idly why the manufacturers never created a few plain or ugly devices just to fool people. Or maybe they did and they moved among mankind undetected. Shaking his head at the bizarre conspiracy theory, Ronson said to the device.

"Major Ronson. I have an appointment with some friends in the Moreton Suite at 15:00".

He received a beatific smile and the android replied, her tones as lovely as the rest of her, "Yes Major you are expected. You will be on floor twenty-three".

"Thank you".

"Once your meeting is concluded I will still be here if....".

"Thank you. No. I am married".

"My apologies, Major. All part of the service. We cater for all needs at the Walters".

"I'm sure you do", Ronson smiled tightly and then returned to the lift. A thumb depressed the button for the twenty-third floor and then he was on his way.

The doors hissed open to reveal a starkly furnished corridor with albescent walls that shone almost blindingly under the massed rows of LED's that festooned the ceiling. His boots making a busy staccato, Ronson traversed the shining tiles of the floor and found the Moreton Suite. His finger depressed a button and after a short interval, the door yawed open.

"Major"! Swăvăg sounded delighted to see him. "Come in man, come in. You look rested and relaxed, the best I've ever seen you. Retirement suites you so much is certain".

Ronson replied politely. His attention was more drawn to the other two people seated in huge leather armchairs. It seemed he was fourth to arrive, even though he was a couple of minutes early.

"Let me make the introductions", Swăvăg fussed slightly. "This is Major Ronson. Hero of the fifth who took Edinburgh Castle during the campaign of seventy-nine. He is now retired and looking mighty fine as a result. Major, this is Tarquer Delane, whom I'm sure needs no introduction".

Ronson went over to the slight, balding man in the three hundred shillin suit, "Yes, pleased to meet you at last. Are you now retired from the Makers-Guild empire"?

"Recently, Major, with a golden handshake that's the reason….".

"One thing at a time, Tarquer", Swăvăg cut the businessman short. "Let me introduce the major to our other distinguished member of this very elite club firstly please".

"Of course. Forgive me. I didn't intend to be rude, Doctor".

Swăvăg continued, "This is Felicitay Ross, Major".

The woman was around ninety. Well preserved and immaculately dressed and made-up. She was still very attractive with her various augmentations, no doubt. She offered her well-manicured hand to Ronson. A hand that had a fortune in rings upon various fingers. Yet her handshake was limp and cool.

The door herald chimed and the last member of the quintet was arriving. Swăvăg made the introductions. The last to arrive at the Moreton Suite was none other than Ponders Kendrick, recently retired accountant from the Orang-U-Can empire. At Swăvăg's invitation, Ronson helped himself to a filtered-rum and a med-cigar. Delane and Ross were smoking med-cigs while Swăvăg and Kendrick simply had a drink.

The group was complete. Swăvăg took his own seat and the chair of the curious meeting. "All right, down to business. I will tell you why you are here", Swăvăg began. "Welcome to the Reduction Club, in plain standard. What my proposal is, is this. Each of us will input into this i-Pad here everything we think relevant about us. Our accomplishments, characteristics, triumphs. After the world web has digested the information, it will instruct us who is the least worthy. That person will then have seven days in which to commit suicide. Willing their fortune, such as it is, to the rest of the group. If that person fails to do so, the other four can then murder them. In the second month, the computer will supply the second name, the process being the same until one of us remains. The survivor will thus have obtained our entire massed estates and can enjoy the retirement of a lifetime".

Ross immediately rose to her feet, "You, Sir are mad and I am leaving".

As she crossed the room Swăvăg barked, "Leave and your membership is forfeit. Go to the authorities and you will be killed".

Ronson noted, "What you are suggesting, Doctor is murder and is also highly illegal. If the comb-men find out about your scheme we will hang".

"And that is why the details of this meeting must never leave this room", the good doctor responded. He added, "Think of what I am proposing. The survivor will be fabulously wealthy. Wealthy enough to visit every ancient site on Earth. Visit the Moon, Mars, Venus, the major moons of Jupiter".

Kendrick observed thoughtfully, "An attractive notion, were it not for the authorities".

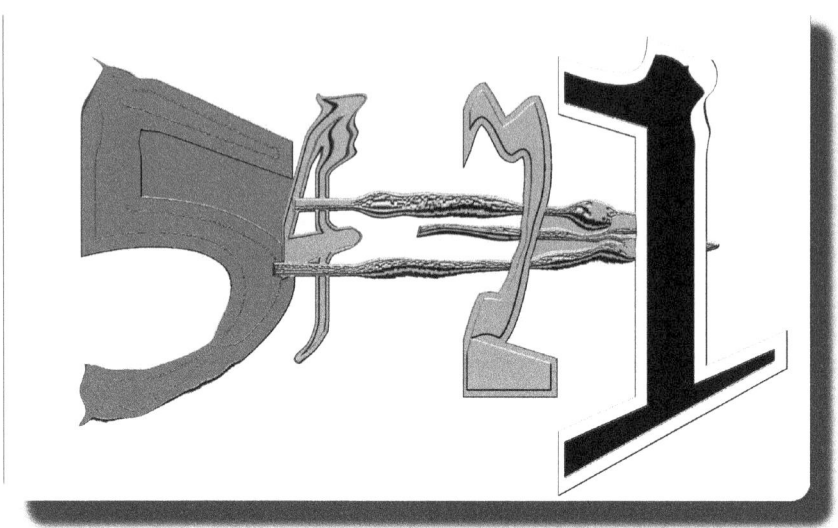

Ross reseated herself and asked in a low tone, "But, you've already considered the implications of your scheme haven't you doctor? You believe we five possess the intellect to evade the comb-men"?

Swăvăg nodded, "If each of us as has to kill themselves, then nothing illegal will have happened, strictly speaking. If anyone does not want the chance of the reward, they can leave now. After firstly swearing not to divulge anything to others. I estimate our combined wealth to be in gold shillin, not even silver ones".

Delane suddenly decided, "I'm in"!

Swăvăg looked at Ronson, "Well my friend. You will be contributing least. Although your ability to kill may come in useful if anyone else gets cold feet. Think of the reward, balanced against the chance of being the lone survivor? Is your chance less than or more than twenty percent"?

Ronson glanced at the woman. She had not left but her mouth was set in a grim disapproving line. She asked,

"How can you expect a computer to decide which of us survives"?

"Logically and dispassionately, based on our accomplishments. Our improvement to mankind, be it in liberty, wealth or health. How can there be any other way"? Swăvăg returned.

"Could we not simply draw lots", Kendrick asked, "Cut cards or play poker, loser loses big time"?

"We can vote on the method of selection whatever is the majority decision then we will do it that way", Swăvăg conceded, "But I maintain that the most worthy ends up with the fortune".

"What if the computer cannot decide, what if it only reduces us by two say"? Delane wanted to know.

"In that event, we will resort to a more arbitrary selection", the good doctor conceded. "Please get another drink everyone and uncover the buffet. Take your time deciding what you think you should do".

'Swăvăg has not chosen we four at random', Ronson thought. *'He knows we are either immensely competitive or equally avaricious. None will back out'.*

To the good doctor as he was pouring himself another filtered rum he said in a voice only loud enough for him to hear,

"I am in, Doctor".

Swăvăg grinned, "I never doubted the warrior in you for a second, Major. I suspect you may have to commit murder in order to achieve our objective though, are you prepared for that eventuality"?

Ronson nodded, "I have killed many in the past. I believe I can do so with legal impunity. What if I have to kill you though, Doctor? Or what if the computer selects me firstly"?

Ronson did not like the look that came over Swăvăg's features then as he assured, "I doubt that will happen, Major".

The group availed themselves of food, refreshments and smokes. Finally after talking between themselves and individually they reseated.

"I will agree if we vote on the method of selection", Kendrick spoke up firstly, "The things I could do with our combined wealth. Well, I'm in too".

Ross conceded, "Very well, I agree. I think we're all mad and some of us will hang, but who knows"?

"So we are now all members of the highly secretive, Stipes in ad Novandum Pigra. I need hardly tell you that you are expressively forbidden to tell anyone of our scheme. That includes partners, mistresses, or any other usual confidants you possess", Swăvăg instructed. "It only remains for us to decide on the method of selection and I have already voted for the computer".

"If I agree to that method, how long do we have to construct the résumé of our life thus far"? Felicitay Ross inquired.

"I think a week", Swăvăg could sense victory coming his way.

"All right. I vote that we do not leave it to chance either", Ross agreed. If anyone else agrees with us then the computer has a majority".

Ross said, "I vote for the computer".

Delane and Kendrick shrugged, their opinions were mute.

"Then we are agreed", Swăvăg concluded, "Get your résumé's to me in one week. The following day one of you will receive a ping instructing you to commit suicide. That member must Will their estate to the group, to an account in the

Caymans called Stipes in ad Novandum Pigra Inc. Failure to comply means that the remaining members are then expected to kill the named person as instructed by subsequent pings. After getting a signature on a printed Will that is. All of us will keep in contact by ping and never meet again. Any questions"?

"Do we all get access to the computer programme that makes these decisions"? Delane was first to vociferate what was on the mind of each of them.

Swăvăg nodded, "Of course. The programme will be available on the WWW. It is called *Dark October*. Your login will be your surname alone, the password is quiN1123~destucT?. Here is the relevant information in a ping, I am sending it to each of you now. Memorise the information and then delete it. Anything else? We have the room until 22:00".

What if the named suicidee does a runner"? Kendrick asked.

Swăvăg grinned, We live in the age of the web, none can hide. If they cannot be tracked down after two months, however, they are forfeit their membership".

They all nodded, it seemed Swăvăg had thought of every possible scenario.

"All Right", the doctor concluded. "I have with me four phials of a compound that kills in ten minutes, painlessly. Untraceable back to me and undetectable by an autopsy. Take one each, wearing these gloves so that you do not transfer any DNA. If all else fails, you are selected, you will swallow this tasteless toxin and honour your agreement made by each of us today. Now let's have some more drinks smokes and enjoy the buffet. Or leave if you desire to".

Ronson went and got himself another rum. He overheard Kendrick say to Ross, "Being as we may be the victims here, what do you say to the two of us getting another room in the hotel and party on our own, baby? You know to live a little before we meet our maker"?

The major was impressed by her response. She smacked his face with admirable force and everyone else momentarily hesitated.

Kendrick rubbed the sting out of it. Laughed, "You can't blame a bloke for trying! If you'll excuse me I'm going to meet the receptionist now. A man has certain needs once he's joined the reduction club. Good luck to the rest of you".

He left to the relief of at least one of the remainder.

"I'm sorry you had to see that", Ross smiled at Ronson, "Are you single, Major".

"I'm flattered, Ross, but married". He returned.

"Married"! She was surprised. Few people contracted for life. "You must love her totally, she's lucky. Excuse me my glass is empty".

"If you get drunk, remember to put your flitter on auto then".

She chuckled, "Yeah, wouldn't want me killing myself until I'd made out the Will eh"?

The gathering dissolved at 21:00 and each of the remaining members of Stipes in ad Novandum Pigra said goodbye to one another. They recognised the fact that they would never see one another again. Before he left Swăvăg warned Ronson,

"You do realise that you will probably have to act as an assassin at one point in this proceedings. Are you prepared to do so"?

"If it comes down to it, I will follow the protocol".

"They shook hands, there was nothing more that needed to be said.

~

Over the next few days, Ronson worked on his résumé. He pinged it in with a day to spare. Naturally, his wife asked him what he was working on but he lied and told her it was something for a former servicemen's magazine. The week after he delighted her with a trip to London in Saxonia. She had always wanted to visit the capital of Anglond's sister country and was very grateful for the long weekend. They took in a show, saw the most ancient clock on the planet, Big Benjamin. Went down the perfectly preserved Downing Street where it was said the salubrious sanatorium had been situated in the dim and distant past.

When they made love, Ronson was especially selfless and tender. They had been back home a few blissful days when Ronson's i-Pad pinged. The first of the Stipes in ad Novandum Pigra had been selected. Tarquer Delane had been selected and Ronson knew he had one week to commit suicide or he would go after him.

He was quite surprised at the obituary which appeared on the web four days later:-

Prominent retired accountant found dead in luxury flat. Autopsy reveals that the cause of death was heart failure.

Tarquer Delane once described at Aaron Makers-Guild's right-hand man has been found dead at his luxury flat in Chester. He was ninety-nine years of age. Delane who had only retired in February.....

Ronson put the i-Pad down, he had gained a new respect for the pudgy businessman who had not even waited for the seventh day. He doubted the others would comply with the computer's wishes quite so readily. He would have to wait and see. He began to enjoy life as he had never before. Each day was potentially one of his last and that knowledge heightened his senses. The sky was a deeper azure, the roses in his garden though dying back due to the season still more beautiful than he had ever witnessed previously. Lovemaking was more intense more pleasurable and the love of his wife more treasured. They went to an ancient Prog-Music concert and saw the ever popular Def Sabbath supported by New Karfagen. Ronson ate and drank too much careless then of the extra grams it might add to his frame. Food tasted more delicious, rum too.

The second week came. The second name to be selected shocked him beyond belief -

Swăvăg!

How was that possible?! Swăvăg had dedicated his life to surgery. Had even spent some years in pursuit of a cure for cancer after it had claimed his ten-year contractee. What were the parameters that the computer worked to.? The good doctor had assured them that it was their goodness. Their contribution to the betterment of mankind. How had Swăvăg's name come out ahead of some of the others?

The following day the good doctor's death was discovered. His obituary was far more impressive than Delane's but what of it.

Dead was dead.

Ronson grew slightly depressed over the next week. He tried to hide it from his wife but she sensed something had changed. She kept her observations to herself as usual though. When he was ready he would tell her. That was how they had always worked their relationship.

Ponders Kendrick, the recently retired accountant from the Orang-U-Can empire. He was the third name to be spat out by the computer. Ronson had thought the man would be first. It seemed the computer thought he would be remembered for one reason or another. Ronson was also relieved that there would only be the two of them left once Kendrick did as directed. The temptation to kill her, even if his own name came out forth was great. That would not have been the honourable thing to do however and above all his other qualities the major treasured that one the most.

A tense week passed. No death was reported. Ronson went to the Dark October sight. Keyed in his surname then quiN1123~destucT? There were only two deposits into the account of Stipes in ad Novandum Pigra Inc. Kendrick surprise surprise had reneged on his agreement. Ronson pinged Felicitay Ross. Her attractive features swam into focus on the tiny screen of his i-Pad.

"Major".

"Miss Ross, it seems our associate had not honoured the terms of our contract", Ronson told her, "I think we will have to ask him to hand his notice in"?

"I agree", she fell into the coded nature of the conversation, "His contract must be regrettably terminated. I attempted to contact him earlier, Major. He is not as his home".

"Then we must both attempt to locate him and see who comes up with something useful first".

"Agreed, I have an old friend in the comb-service and will try there".

"I will access my military sources. We shall ping once we discover anything of interest".

"My commiserations in regard to the doctor, major. I understand you were old friends".

"That's kind of you, thank you".

Ronson cut the connection.

So Kendrick had welshed on the deal had he? Ronson was no murderer but he reflected he might very well take some satisfaction in making certain he was caught and made to sign his will. The thought struck him that if he agreed to give his fortune to them, he could buy his life! Ronson contacted several of the *old boys,* but after several hours they drew blanks. The comb-service had greater resources it seemed. Ronson's i-Pad pinged a couple of hours later. It was Ross.

"Our friend Kendrick has boarded a space-flitter for Mars under the assumed name of Myra Cohen", she informed, "Shall I book two tickets on the next one going to Mare Cimmerium in the Deutschesektor"?

"Two tickets"?

"I am tracking Kendrick by SPS (Solar Positioning System), do you have that technology, Major".

"No".

"Then it would seem I have to accompany you. I am not able to loan you something which has been loaned to me. You understand that position"?

"Of course. It would not be courteous. Very well get two tickets. Will my own passport be appropriate"?

"No. I will meet you at MSP (Manchester Space-flitter Port) desk 23 with one that also guarantees us anonymity also".

Several minutes late Ronson told his understanding wife that he had to attend a funeral of an old comrade. It would not be prudent to tell her where. She nodded her understanding in that sublime way she had and asked him only if he wanted a bundle preparing.

He took his Quaker 200bhp flitter up to the required height and tore through the windy and grey sky. By the time he was over Manchester, it was raining heavily. The wind was slanting the water at thirty degrees. A terrible day. Parking on the roof park he took the lift down to departures and sought out desk 23.

Felicitay Ross was resplendent in lilac pill hat and coat. Even her real cow-hide shoes were lilac. By contrast, Ronson felt comfortable but slightly badly-groomed in his well-washed fatigues. Ross gave him a thin smile handed over a ticket and a new passport. Ronson looked at the latter. The image was once taken from the web and a good likeness, his name was recorded as Major Hercule Standish.

"Just in case of the unlikely event that we get separated who are you"? He asked her.

Again the thin smile, "Missus Fiona Standish".

"The daughter of my contractee", Ronson covered his surprise well.

"Ha ha very funny, Hercule. I'm your wife of course".

Ronson was not quite sure how he felt about posing as the glamorous woman's partner. He knew when to be tacit. However. They waited for their names to be called after handing in their luggage. Ross seemed to have packed triple the amount compared to the Major. Finally, it came over the PA that flight MC1111 was ready to be boarded and Major and Missus Standish climbed up the steps on their way to 23a and 23b.

Once they were comfortable Ross asked, "Do you want to read my I-Pad, Darling? I've left it on today's news for you".

'*Darling*'! He reflected they were in the hearing range of 24f and 23c. Realised Ross was playing a part. She seemed suited to the subterfuge. He returned in character,

"No thanks, Darling I intend to sleep the journey away".

The flitter blasted up into the air. G-force smote them almost at once and then weightlessness. They remained in their seats only due to the webbing crisscrossed over their bodies. It was an economy-class flight so know ring to create artificial gravity. Ronson would have thought Ross would have bought club-class tickets. Until he reflected that the Standish' were not in the same bracket financially. She was playing the whole venture like a spy in those ancient celluloid movies made only in 2D and monochrome. Ronson smiled and then due to his training fell asleep. A good soldier can grab rest when an opportunity presents itself and he had never lost the habit.

When gravity hit him again at a restful Martian level, he was instantly awake and up out of the seat the instant the bell rang.

"You did it again, Darling", noted his *wife*. "Missed the whole spectacle".

"I've seen it all before, Darling as you well know", he grinned back at her.

Once they were clear of disembarking and baggage control Ronson hailed a flittaxi. The Android driver asked, Destination please, Sir"?

"The Schickwieeinneuerstift Hotel please", Ross replied smoothly.

Ross leaned in close to his ear to ask, "Do you speak German"? He felt the smoothness of her cheek on his own, smelled her delicate perfume, the even more subtle fragrance of her hair. He was disconcerted by how it made him feel. He was attracted to her and what man would not be? He nodded and turned to look out of his passenger window. They concluded the flight in silence.

Once they reached the hotel he was going to let her register at the desk until she pointed out that only he spoke the local tongue.

"Major und Missus Standish, wir haben Reservierungen", he told the brunette android at registration.

"Ja, Major, Zimmer 23 im dritten Stock, wünschen Sie Hilfe bei Ihrem Gepäck? (Yes, Major, room 23 on the third floor, do you desire assistance with your luggage)"?

"Ein Zimmer, ich dachte, wir haben Singles gebucht (One room, I thought we booked singles)".

"Nein, Major Missus Standish hat ein Double gebucht".

Ronson turned to Ross, "You booked us a double room, Darling? You know I like the extra space of my own room".

"Sorry, Darling but all the singles were booked. Please don't make a fuss by enquiring if you can move at this late hour? Let's just get in, unpacked and down to the restaurant? I'm starved".

Pursing his lips Ronson then told the android that they could manage their own luggage forcing Ross to carry two of her three while he carried his own and one of hers. The reached the room, swiped the card and began to unpack enough for the next Terran day.

"I like to sleep on the left side of the bed if that's all right with you"? Ross asked pleasantly

"I beg your pardon"? Ronson was momentarily taken aback. "So you claim the bed while I have to spend the night on the floor"?

"It's a double, Silly. You get the right side".

"You think we're going to sleep together"?

"Yes. Sleeping is sleeping, Major. Sex is sex. We will be sleeping. Or you can be maungey and sleep on the floor. I suppose you've spent many a night on harder surfaces. Now if you don't mind I'm going to change. I will not be changing my underwear of course, so there is no need to go into the bathroom. If my body in underwear offends you turn your head".

With that, Ross unvelcroed her frock and let it fall to her ankles. Ronson stared at her on purpose. She was in her nineties. Had undertaken several if not more augmentations over the years. Her form was still lithe, her bosom full, her waist hour-glass of a pattern. In very ancient times, the nineteenth century and backwards she would have been mistaken for a third of her actual years. Ronson felt a curious mixture of desire and guilt. He had never cheated on his wife. Not once over all the years and there had been plenty of opportunities. He was 185 cm 80 kilos and it was all in the right place and muscular. His augmentations had been meagre. His jaw had always been firm, his eyes grey his hair silver since his thirties. Someone had once told him he resembled an ancient hero of a military force called IMF. One James Phipps or some such nomen. Ronson did not know him but he did know women found him desirable.

Ross stared back at him daring him to rise from the bed he was perched on and take her in his arms.

"Well, are you going to put something on? Or do you intend to go down to the restaurant in your underwear"? He asked.

She afforded him a smile of defeat. Both knew he had won that round. The question was could he win the entire bout?

Moments later with her in a black low cut affair that displayed her decollete to shattering effect, they went down to dinner. She put her arm through his and grudgingly kept it there. He could feel the heat of her flesh through his tunic. The restaurant displayed a view of Mars and Mare Cimmerium. Through huge windows that stretched from floor to magnificently domed ceiling. Outside was a fierce sandstorm. Ronson knew they were frequent on the red planet despite mankind's constant efforts to tame them. They seated themselves at the table marked for their room and a male android approached asking for their order in German.

"My wife only speaks Standard". Ronson finally had the grace to inform, "Are you able to switch to it".

"But of course, Major. Are you ready to order or would you like drinks and time to decide"?

"I think the latter. Darling"?

"Yes, the latter, please. May I have a gin fizz please"?

The waiter nodded, "And for you, Major"?

"Gefilterter Rum bitte".

"Ja, Major Danke dir", the waiter could switch as easily as Ronson.

When he was gone Ronson told her, "If we are in Deutschesektor long you should consider getting a hypno-teach of German".

"I will, Hercule if we are in Deutschesektor long. I still have this SPS though. Kendrick has not moved from the edge of town. He must think he's safe from us".

"He may be if he opts out".

"If he gets the opportunity", Ross returned darkly.

"What's that supposed to mean"?

"It means that if we allow him to bleat his option, it betrays the trust Delane and Swăvăg placed in him and in us. I think that we should liquidate him"?

Ronson gave the notion consideration, replied, "On the condition that whichever of our names comes out next - the other also liquidates them with maxiMum prejudice".

Ross smiled beatifically, "Darling, I wouldn't have it any other way".

~

The meal had been excellent and as the local time was late in the evening Ross decided she would get some sleep.

What will you do? You slept the journey away, you must be wide awake"? She asked him.

"I can sleep when I need to whether I need it or not", he told her. "I'll get in bed, read my pad for a while and then get my head down too. That way our internal clocks will be synchronised tomorrow morning".

"All right", she agreed and took something lacy and hardly very voluminous into the bathroom.

Ronson did his best not to listen to ablutions. The buzz of a hypo-toothbrush was unmistakable however and then she emerged in the nightie. It was bigger than a handkerchief just! He saw that her breasts were still gravity-defying even without support, her body was smooth and ....

'What am I doing'? He suddenly asked himself. *'But what can I do about it? I've never been in so intimate a position with a still beautiful woman...ever'!*

"The bathroom is free now, Darling", she informed him superfluously. Seemingly very amused by his scrutiny.

He hurried away from the stimulating sight of her. Upon his return, she was in bed. Her eyes were open however and she looked at him, dressed only in trollies, his impressive chest uncovered. He said firmly,

"Lights off. Goodnight Miss Ross".

Sliding in beside her. Careful to make no contact he felt the heat of her on the bedclothes - closed his eyes. Willed himself to sleep.

After an indeterminate time, Ronson awoke. Her mouth was on his. Her naked breasts pressed against his chest. Their groins touching. Her tongue was searching, questing asking the question he dare not answer. Suddenly she parted and gasped,

"I'm so sorry. I acted in my sleep. What do you want to do"?

"I've been married a long time, Miss Ross".

"If things don't go as you hope, you'll be even longer dead. I need comfort. Make me feel desirable. Please"?

His body was responding to her request. He could feel himself hardening. Before he could say any more she dipped beneath the covers. When she tugged his trollies off he knew he could stop her. He did not. Her mouth was like molten passion as she took him deeply into it. She was accomplished and very eager. In that instant - he changed his mind. His arms went above his head. He made love to her mouth.

~

"Is he still in the same place"? Ronson wanted to know.

They were getting dressed for breakfast. Neither of them had enjoyed much time for sleep.

"I don't even know your first name"? Her tone was gentle.

"Hercule will do. Is he still stationary"?

"Hercule. It suits you. You were like...".

"Missus Standish will you concentrate? Remember what we came here to do"?

"He's still just north of us in a little town called Elektrischer Minor".

"We'll go by flitter. Can you handle one if I want to rest"? He intended to prepare for conflict and would not underestimate Kendrick's fight for survival. If he gave him too much credit all well and good. If he did not give him enough? He had never failed yet.

She nodded her head, "Of course. I've not always had a chauffeur".

"Then you drive and I'll go in alone to wherever he's hiding out".

"I think I should accompany you".

"No"!

"You don't want to be watching your back while you're eliminating him, do you? After last night and what it meant. You still don't trust me".

He smiled coldly, "What it meant. You warmed my bed and we frenged. It meant no more than momentary sexual gratification".

Her mouth set to a grim line and she said sadly, "I see".

"I'm not splitting the prize with you. If that's the notion your brewing", he told her candidly. "I'm in this for the big prize or total defeat. Do we understand one another now"?

She nodded mutely. Head bowed. Silent.

"Right. let's go eat. I'm starving".

The hired flitter was an Auriol Super-stream 220bhp. Ross flew it competently if not exceptionally well. The sandstorm had reached gale sized proportions and visibility was very poor. Thank the stars for sat-nav. At the appropriate moment, she cut the flit-jet and glided down silently. It landed on the red sand with very little impact or noise.

"Put goggles on. Nose filters. Keep your mouth closed", he advised.

She objected, "You said I wasn't to come in with you"?

"That's right", he agreed, "I go in alone. If he comes out, shoot him. What have you got".

"A needle gun, what else would I use".

"Outdoors in this gale and with so much sand in the air a needle might not find it's target first shot. Here".

He handed her a flash-grenade. "Throw that and hit the ground, hands over your eyes. Afterwards, there won't be anything left for anyone to find".

"So why aren't you taking one", she wanted to know.

"In a confined space, it would take out anyone in the place".

"Anyone including you then. That's it though, isn't it? I mean he'll be on his own won't he"?

Ronson grimaced, "I wouldn't be. In his shoes - I'd have a miniMum of four hired mercenaries".

"Then let me come with you and I swear on the heavens I will not shoot you".

Ronson shook his head, "I've looked into your before I came to Mars, Fiona. You've done years of admirable charity work. Get yourself killed in there and then my name spills out of the computer! I'd never forgive my own conscience".

"Yet if my name comes out. You'd kill me in a cold second wouldn't you"? She sounded truly amazed. He nodded,

"Rules are rules. If the computer picks you as suicide four, I expect you to comply just like Delane and Swăvăg".

She chuckled ironically, "I guess you can take the man out of the army but you can never take the army out of the man".

Grinning he strapped on a Kevlar vest. Picking up a needle rifle saying, "Right ready".

The rifle had more power than the pistol version. It also boasted increased accuracy and range. The doors of the flitter lifted upward and the two of them spilt out. The wind was savage. It whipped tiny particle of rusted grit at their faces stinging them in the process.

'Welcome to Mars', Ronson thought as he trotted for the building's lone airlock. Without announcing himself he tried the outer lock. As expected it was not unlocked. Pressing some plastique to the lock Ronson punched in a detonator and lit the fuse with his gas lighter. It fizzed despite the wind and he threw himself to the floor. Things always explode upwards.

The right amount of explosive had been used though. The door was still intact after the kapow. Just the lock was gone. Joining the endless sand in boiled away particles of steel. Now Ronson had to move swiftly. The first report would have confirmed the existence of a potential intruder. Those in the property knew he was coming. The second lump of plastique was stuck on the inner airlock. The same fuse lit. This time Ronson simply threw himself around the corner of the building. Kapow. Both doors unlocked in less than two minutes. Ronson rushed through them almost bent double. A needle instantly phutted over his shoulder. He fired from the hip. Instinctive. Honed by years of combat. He was rewarded by a yell and the sound of a body hitting the floor of the hallway. Level two needles killed instantly. One down. How many to go? Ronson was constantly on the move as he heard a voice yell,

"I think it's him"!

"Then get in there"!

"So at least three counting Kendrick".

Ronson tugged a flash-flare from his tunic. Dialled his goggles to maxiMum polarisation and snapped the end off it. The phosphorescent light was extremely bright.

"Aargh, I can't see".

Ronson's needle made certain he never would either. He rounded the corner as two men were pushing another into a room at the end of a short corridor. Two bodyguards and Kendrick. As Ronson's rifle fired taking one of the down he threw himself into a forward role. Their needles phutted over his rolling body. He was on his feet in an instant smashing the but of his rifle into the survivor's teeth. The smashed with a dental splintering sound. The man fell screaming, but an instant later Ronson's needle silenced his noise and ended his suffering.

"Come in here you base-born and I'll fire this bazooka", Kendrick roared from behind the door".

Ronson ripped a small timer form his belt. Stuck it into the plastique and threw the metal toggle. He began to race for the double airlock. One does not argue with a bazooka. Shame about the property. The landlord would not be best pleased.

He hit the storm at a gallop and cried to Ross. "Get back in the flitter! He's got a bazooka".

If Kendrick heard over the noise of the sandstorm he would presume he had scared the major off. Yet caution would still deter him from leaving the room too quickly suspecting a ruse. As he threw himself into the passenger seat of the Auriol Ronson barked,

"MaxiMum thrust, Fiona! There's going to be one hell of a kapow in a few seconds. Get all the height you can".

Ross was getting used to the flitter and threw it into full flight instantly. The explosion buffeted the flitter but fortunately, no metal or any other debris struck its underside.

"Frenge you don't exaggerate do you? What did you do"?

"Used the rest of the plastique. Kendrick will be all over this plain now. Let the forensic boys form the Constabulary sort that one out".

"So it's just the two of us", Ronson could not fathom the tone that Ross was using. "I suppose we pack now. At least Kendrick had the decency to have sent his estate to the Caymans. There are five accounts there now".

"I shall not be packing", he told her, "I can't go back home until this thing is over".

She left a long gap before asking, "Do you want me to find another hotel then? Leave Mars perhaps"?

"No", he decided. "What I want is a week with you as Missus Standish. What do you want, Fiona"?

She smiled, "I think you know very well what I want, Hercule".

In a solar system without avarice or the thirst for power, the story would end here. Or perhaps with the duo running away together. The solar system is not like that though. It is the unfeeling coldness of space and that frigidity had entered the hearts of man the instant he entered it. It had also entered the hearts of Major Ronson and Felicitay Ross.

~

"I think I should move out this morning", Ronson said to his lover.

Their week had contained by turns; Passion, tenderness, love, hate, trust, suspicion. It had never been fated to last and within the next Terran twenty-four hours, one of their names would be issued by the computer.

Neither of them was certain what the other would do once that happened. Ronson had decided to shoot himself with a replica percussion pistol that was in his possession. Ross had decided to follow Delane and Swăvăg's example and swallow the contents of the phial given her by the latter. That was their intentions. Yet when the point came to act on said would they indeed go through with it? Neither of them could honestly answer that. One never truly knows how a situation will be confronted until the moment comes. Neither did they. Privately both of them thought the other would murder themselves rather than be hunted and killed. This again was suspicion rather than knowledge.

Ironically the last day was the calmest in Mare Cimmerium since they had been there. The wind was nothing more than a vanquil (cold breeze). Not even enough to stir up the endless dunes of rusty sand that gave the red planet its second name.

Ronson had been standing under a blood red dawn sky smoking a tobaccigar in deep contemplation that morning. His mind was running a gamut of emotions from love through to resentment. From determination through to indecision. From hard-heartedness through to guilt. Yet he was also pragmatic. Ross was beautiful. She was only the sixth woman he had ever slept with. Four of those six had been before he had met his wife. Since he had permanently contracted with her he had been totally faithful. Until that week. Would that make it easier for him to murder Ross if it turned out he had to? He reluctantly decided it would. True it took two to butter a muffin. Yet he knew she had seduced him. She might have done so out of lust. She might have done it in a coldly calculated way that only a woman could. Had Ross seduced him in case her name was the next selected and she calculated her physical charms would stay his hand? It was a possibility. It was also possible she had forced herself upon him to encourage his suicide if need be.

He threw the cigar in the sand after a while. Only half smoked. That day it was bitter to the taste and hurt his throat. Slowly he went through the massive central airlock of the Schickwieeinneuerstift. He would eat breakfast with Ross. It would be a mechanical process designed only to sustain his vitality, however. Good soldier that he was he could do it. Ross had more difficulty at their last meal together.

"I've been thinking obviously", she told him over lichen-coff, "I would be happy with half. Please consider agreeing to the same. I know we made an agreement but it was with a dead man. Every witness to it is dead too. What does it matter if we agree to end the killing"?

"It would be dishonourable".

"All right. So what! Isn't dishonour better than death? Murder or self-murder – makes no difference".

Ronson shook his head slowly, "Have you never heard the motto '*Death before dishonour*'? It happens to be the motto of my regiment".

"Hercule you don't have a regiment any more".

"Yet I live by its code. Don't call me Hercule any more either. I should go and pack".

"Where do you think you'll go"?

"I'm going up to Tereshkova, we will not be far apart".

"In case you have to kill me you mean"? Her question was considered mute, not expectant of an answer. He, therefore, shocked her when he replied coldly,

"That's right. In case I have to kill you, Ross".

"Then I need to tell you something", her mouth was a hard line and she stubbed her med-cig out savagely. "I'm leaving too. I'm going to drive over the border into the Saxonian territory. I'll be booking into the Premiere in Halfield. There everyone will speak standard. That is the only reason. Ronson arose without another word and observed,

"Then this is goodbye, Ross".

She sighed, "Yes. In another time or another world, we might have been something you and I. Goodbye Major".

He walked firmly away from the table and he did not look back.

The flight to Tereshkova would have been a pleasant one had his mind not been boiling. Would it be better to drive the craft into the surface and end it then? Could he ever go back to his wife? His death would be more than one solution. Yet the major in him had not survived countless military campaigns without having a burning desire to survive them. It was at his core like a dark jewel of determination. Should it come to it could he kill her? He had only ever killed one female before though. A female mercenary in Columbia. Until she lay dead at his feet he was not even aware that she was a woman. Short black hair not especially attractive. She had been rushing him armed with a machete. His fatal shot had been instinctive. The sort ruled by the spine rather than the brain. Afterwards, he had felt no guilt. It had been her or him and he knew it was not going to be him. Yet she might have been daughter, sister and mother. She might have been more mourned than he. She also might have killed several Saxonian soldiers during the police action. Maybe more. In which case was not her death the right one in order to achieve balance?

As that morning he refused to allow such conjectures to torment him. With a shrug of his shoulders, he forgot the Columbian and he also forgot Ross. With one exception. Should she fail to commit suicide in the provided week, she would be his target. Major Ronson was a professional who always got the job done.

It was a very long day. He stayed in his room in the suave and expensive Sehrausgesuchterkleinerort in Tereshkova. He smoked too many med-cigs and drank too much filtered-rum. When room service brought him his meals he shovelled the food down quickly and mechanically. Tasting nothing. With two hours to go, he took some Snufz. The resultant trip gobbled up the time. When he was coming down, all red-eyed and unfocused, he looked at his i-Pad and the name the computer selected was Felicitay Ross!

She had spent much of her life doing charitable work. Saving life. He had spent his entire career, killing. How had the web deduced he had added more to the betterment of mankind? It made no sense to him.

Yet it was also an incredible relief.

His desire to survive had been dominant.

While his mind was still in a state of flux. Partly from the news partly the narcotic, his i-Pad pinged. It was Ross. He agreed audio and visual.

"Have you seen the ping, Major"? She asked him in leaden tone. They might as well have been strangers.

Not daring to speak lest his voice betray him he simply nodded.

Her smile was sardonic as she informed him, "I find I am not in a state of mind to destroy myself. You will have to come and get me".

"Do you want the two months"?

"No. That would be only prolonging the torment come at once".

"Will you defend yourself"?

"Let the major in you decide that".

She cut the connection. Most of Ronson's belongings were still in his bundle. He threw those that were not into it and left the room. Within ten minutes he was back up in the air. He doubted she would have hired mercenaries. Had she done that she would not have invited him to find her with such urgency? Perhaps she had elected for suicide by surrender. In his military past, some soldiers had done the same. Simply thrown down their arms once they were tired of fighting and waited for the shot that would end their existence. He thought Ross had possessed more spunk. Maybe that had been an error of judgement. He put the flit-jet on autopilot and grabbed a power nap. A sonic alert told him when the destination was close and he hovered down onto the roof park of the Premiere.

When he went around to the hatchback of the vehicle he hesitated. He had not done that much in his past military career. He did then. What would he sensibly need to kill a beautiful defenceless woman who had some feelings for him? He put the needle rifle back. Picked up a slim wrist needle and strapped it into place. In one pocket he put a gas grenade. The picked up nose and eye filters. Once both were satisfactorily inserted he closed the boot.

His shoulders shrugged. As though removing his humanity and turning him back into a soldier. A killing mechanism of flesh and blood. The lift took him down to the reception desk. The Android was the earliest model he had seen in a long time. It was hairless and obviously artificial maybe even a stage 2.

"I'm wishing to visit my wife", Ronson began, "Missus Standish. Missus 'F' Standish".

"At the presentation of identification that will be easily accomplished, Sir".

Even the voice sounded Hawkingesc. What possessed the hotel to keep such an obviously archaic piece of machinery. Maybe as a deliberate curio? Maybe the proprietor was himself an eccentric Englishman. The time for questions was over, however. Once Ross had been killed, the Android would have to be destroyed too. It was an obvious witness. Fortunately, none else seemed interested in him.

He showed his fake passport to the mechanism.

"Missus Standish is in room three on the second floor sir".

"Thank you".

Ronson glided over to the lift again. Went up two floors. The doors hissed open to reveal the ubiquitous corridor. Someone had thought playing banal piped music made it more conducive to guest well-being. Ronson looked at the first door twenty-one. Second floor, room one, easy. He slunk past two doors and tapped on the third. A familiar voice muffled by the polyurethane bid him enter. Ronson depressed the plate and the door gave a click. How quaint hinged doors. With a push, Ronson drove it fully backward.

Ross was laying cross-legged on the bed. She was dressed in a black frock and her makeup was perfection.

"Well don't just stand in the doorway, come in"? She smiled fatalistically.

Ronson strode through the jamb. Heard the quiet phut. Felt the sting in his neck! He glanced toward the jamb. Expertly embedded in it was a needle-box with a motion sensor. His entrance had activated the stealth weapon. As the poison began to course through his veins he managed to flick his wrist. The needle phutted from the device activated by the tendons there. The needle hit Ross on her left forearm.

"Well played", Ronson managed to gasp as he began to fall forward, the toxin claiming his legs. He landed half on the empty side of the bed.

Her last words were, "I love you, Hercule".

She collapsed sideways and the dead couple ended up in a curious looking embrace. That was how the hotel staff found them.

Nine

Finally he managed to put the book down and then his i-Pad lit up again. He had a ping and surprise surprise it was from the office. What did they want? Lottabockle headquarters were in Scouring Plains so only a short train journey. Even so it was most unusual for them to ask to see him in person. He tended to work almost always remotely. Well the opportunity to stretch his legs would do him good and he could always take the book with him to read on the train. Having made his intentions known to his dull wife, Stallone went for one to Scouring Plains. He had no need to consult a timetable, he knew it by heart as a practised commuter in the past.

He paid no heed to the repetitive landscape whirling past the windows, having seen them too many times to find anything unique to offer him. He was going to read, but his mind would not stop wondering what the summons was for? He was well ahead with his latest assignment and the office knew it. He did not even know who the interview would be with? If it was his immediate supervisor it would be thin and balding Vrade. A fair man in his dealings with his staff. Softly spoken and well liked for the gentle way he went about supervising some of his designers. Vrade's boss was another matter entirely. Thick-set sandy haired Ghanon was the grandson of the entrepreneur who had originally set up the company. He was well spoken and educated, but could be ruthless when it came to hiring and firing. He was known for his quick temper which he often regretted afterwards and then profusely apologised for. Many did not know how to take the man due to his mood swings. Stallone found it best to be as firmly entrenched in his own opinion as Ghanon, who then frequently changed his mind backing down from his original position.

With these thoughts filling his head, he almost missed his stop. At the last moment he threw open the door and alighted onto the platform. To his dismay he was immediately accosted by a strange little man in clothes so ragged that they contained holes and frays. His hair did not look like he had shampooed it for months, his long greying beard was straggly and yet in his eyes burned a fierce intelligence fuelled by the need to impart his message.

"You've been to the Athenaeum, over in Barncave", he stated without the faintest notion of mistake. Incongruous to his appearance his breath was minty.

"Excuse me", Stallone said politely, doing his best to circumnavigate the man, "But I have a pressing appointment in the city and must not be late".

"There is something you must know though", the tramp persisted, swaying enough to block Stallone's progress.

"Look here's a couple of sestertii, go and get yourself a drink and something to eat. You'll even get centisestertii in change. Now if you don't let me go I shall call out for a comb-man".

"Do that and you will never know your fate, Mister Dustin Stallone".

"How on Venus do you k now my name? Have you been spying on me"?

"You could say that although it was actually Dustin Stallone that I was watching for the main part".

"Then tell me your message and be done with it, Sir. I really do have an appointment".

"Very well. It is this message. Do not finish the book, for the end means the end and nothing will follow".

Stallone nodded, not understanding the ramblings of a man who was possibly demented anyway. "All right. Now you've warned me, thank you. Now I must be on my way, good day to you, Sir".

To his unexpected vision of the tramp, he suddenly moved clear and smiled a thin smile before hobbling off without another word. Stallone grinned, what a contretemps. He hoped it would be the last of the day.

Hurrying off, he was once more on his way to the grand office building of Lottabockle and his meeting with who knew?

The street was crowded in Scouring Plains one of Venus' main cities, there were scores of people on the pavements as Stallone pushed his way into the office headquarters he desired. At the reception desk was the demure Aerial. An actual human receptionist and a very attractive one. She of the auburn hair, beautifully creamy complexion and straight but purposeful nose. In moments of fantasy Stallone fancied her as wife number two. The things he'd do to her was adult stuff and not for general publication.

"Hello, Dustin", she crooned pleasantly. Fully aware of his admiration. Basking in it for the benefit of them both. She fluttered his eyelids provocatively but he would not ask her to dinner. Not yet!

"I've been summoned", he said rather obviously, "But if I know your efficiency Aerial, you'll already know that. The thing is I don't know which office to report to".

Aerial licked her lips, the gesture being subtle but none the less noticeable for that, "You are to go to the small boardroom, Honey".

She called everyone at Lottabockle that nomen of seeming affection no matter how she felt about them. In Stallone's case he thought she added that extra special tone. His eyebrows rose in surprise and then his brow furrowed in consternation, what was going on?

"Well I'll see you on the way out then", he promised and walked over to the lifts. The first one available took him to the fifth-floor and he walked down an antiseptic corridor of bright LED's and white sterile walls. He knocked firmly on the door ending with a double knock at half pace. This was the Stallone knock.

"Enter", cried the voice of Ghanon. Was this going to be serious then?

Seated at one end of an enormous long table were Ghanon the CEO and Vrade, the design manager.

"Have a chair, Stallone", Ghanon waved in the direction of all eighteen, "Drink".

"Oh! Kind of you, but I can get a lichen-coff from the dispenser later thank you".

In his customary charming way the pudgy CEO thundered, "Don't be such a poof, Stallone, I meant a drink – drink".

In his own fist was a rather generous lichen-vod, while Vrade seemed to be nursing a smaller glass of filtered-rum. Ghanon was smoking a huge cigar, Vrade a med-cig.

"In that case, CEO, I will have a gin-fizz, as it's a bit early for me".

"Get him a gin and leave the fizz out". Ghanon growled to an Android that Stallone had not noticed standing in the shadows. When the female facsimile of a woman stepped forward it was something of a shock. She was black, with enormous breasts and wearing only a black leather bikini.

252

"Do you like the look of Jemima", Ghanon asked, a wicked twinkly in his eye.

"Well erm yes she's very...pneumatic", Stallone stuttered.

Ghanon let out a bellow of amusement at the remark and slapped Vrade so heartily on the back that his contacts almost flew out of his eyes.

The beautiful black amazon handed Stallone his drink with a smile of amusement. The machine was laughing at him!

"Smoke if you want", Ghanon permissioned and Stallone pulled out an e-cig.

"What in blazes is that you poof"? The CEO was in a garrulous and happy mood. "Here have a Cuban, that's a proper man's smoke".

"Thank you, Sir". Stallone felt obliged to ignite the end with a thumb. It was coarse raw tobacco smoke entering his lungs but he used every gramme of self control not to cough.

"Now then down to business. I want a design manager for a new branch we're opening in the north up above Tophead, it will actually be in the town of Thursorton. I'm giving the job to Koszos".

Ghanon waited for Stallone's reaction. He asked politely, "And do agree with this decision, Vrade"?

The manager honestly shook his head, "I recommended you, Dustin. You are the best man for the job, far more experienced and capable than Koszos".

Stallone turned his attention back to the CEO, it was impossible to read the expression on his pudgy features. So Stallone asked simply,

"Why pass me over then"?

Ghanon spread his pudgy hands wide fingered on the table, as though to indicate total honesty, "He's young and single. It will be easier for him to resettle in Thursorton. You might even decide to commute with all the difficulties that would entail. I don't want to present you with that headache, so I'm selecting the next best man for the job".

"So if' I said I'd move to Thursorton and quickly, what then"?

Ghanon replied without hesitation, "The job would be yours. But what about your contractee, your mortgage? Could you afford a flat say in Thursorton and would your contractee put up with long absences from your home"?

"Give me the job and don't worry about the minutia CEO. I will find a way to make this work and run your office for you, you have my word".

Ghanon gave a loud malign bellow of amusement and rose to a standing position and shook Stallone's hand. "Watch yourself Vrade, this young man might supplant you one day".

On his way back home Stallone realised that the death of his partner was now even more of an imperative.

Ten

The journey had filled his thoughts. He had carried the book without reading it. After dinner and a hot bath, he decided that finishing the book was paramount. A prelude to the actual murder. He must read the rest of it. Then decide how to rid himself of Madchen.

Lighting a med-cig after pouring himself a filtered-rum, he settled down in his favourite chair and once more opened the strangely compulsive grimoire...

Epiphenomenon

GENE DRAKE & ORSON LOCKWOOD

Holden could barely bear to look at Pearl any more. The drip was in one arm the infusion pump in the other. The constant flow of snufzomorph was beginning to affect her perception of any outside stimuli at all. At least she wasn't in pain. Or that was Holden's hope at any rate.

How ironic that he had spent his entire life treating the sick. Operating on every conceivable brain dysfunction only to have this happen to his thrice contracted partner. The further twist of fate was that Lymphophatic Lueknomathemia effected the brain lastly of all. So his considerable skills were wasted on the one woman he cared for over any other.

Holden was the world's most eminent brain surgeon. Over his considerably lengthy career, he had drilled open the skulls of thousands of men and women. Corrected abnormalities, removed tumours by the hundreds. None could rival his expertise nor his reputation When it came to eminence, Doctor Sir Murray Holden D.O; M.B.B.S; F.R.C.S; M.S; M.D. was the greatest neurosurgeon history had ever recorded.

It was just three months after he and Pearl had announced they were contracting for their third decade that she had begun to feel fatigued. At first, they put it down to work. She was a Veterinarian and a very good one. She worked long hours. Through the night when emergencies occurred. After a long chat with Holden, she had agreed to cut back on the hours. It did not help. Reluctantly she agreed to visit one of Holden's colleagues at Campion Memorial in Rothingley.

Young doctor, Wadwick had been greatly honoured to see the surgeon's contractee. He was incredibly thorough, ordering every possible test known to medical science. He then had the unenviable task of seeing the couple together and giving them the bad news.

"I'm extremely sorry to have to tell you this but you have Lymphophatic Lueknomathemia, Doctor Pearl".

Holden asked at once, "What regimen of treatment do you advise, Doctor"?

"We've had some positive results with Meltoscazine, Sir Murray. Though the side effects can be somewhat uncomfortable for the patient".

"What else then"?

"Pantraksicmuropenthine is gentler but not as effective. Then there is the clinical trial with Snulicamethodonetene. In your case, I could ensure that Doctor Pearl gets the dosed phials and not the placebos".

"What is the projected success rates with each", Pearl had found her voice for the first time.

Wadwick took a deep breath, "Meltoscazine is thirty to forty percent effective as a total cure, one hundred percent at slowing the progression down. Pantraksicmuropenthine fifteen percent effective as a complete cure but will also slow down the progress. The manufacturers of Snulicamethodonetene none other than Drugz4U are claiming eighty percent chance at a total cure.

Patients have yet to bear the claim out. The other problem with it is its addictive effect. Go on it and you'll take it for the rest of your life even if you're cured by it".

"Your recommendation, Doctor"? Pearl wanted to know.

"It has to be your own decision obviously, Doctor Pearl. I can only tell you what I would do in your shoes nothing more. I would commence a course of Pantraksicmuropenthine and see how I went for a few weeks. If tests did not show a slowing of the illness then I would progress to Meltoscazine and take antihypenemesis gravidariss medication at the same time".

"Excuse me, Doctor", Holden interrupted, "Antihypenemesis gravidariss medication"?

"Meltoscazine induces conditions, Sir Murray. They include vomiting, dizziness, faintness. In more pronounced cases they can be hallucinations, paranoia, rage and violent tendencies, but that's rare".

"And that's supposed to be a cure"? Holden suddenly lost his temper, "Succumb to Lymphophatic Lueknomathemia or go mad"!

"That's why the uninformed often refer to the illness by its street name of Looneywaste", Wadwick added almost to himself.

"I'm faced with a tough choice then aren't I, Murray", Pearl had said to him. "You know me well enough to know that I've always been a gambler though. One to take the chance and see how it panned out. I'm going to take the trial. I'm not calling it that long-winded chemical name though, Doctor Wadwick, what's its commercial one"?

"Snultine, Doctor Pearl".

"Then get that scrip pinged to my i-Pad right now please, Doctor", she had decided.

The next few days were tense ones. From diagnosis to stage two of Lyle disorder (Lymphophatic Lueknomathemia) could be lengthy or swift dependent upon too many factors to be able to calculate. What did happen to Pearl though - was a slow decay into the commencement of paranoia. Snultine it seemed shared that with Meltoscazine. On certain days it was as though the old Pearl was back. Then at other less lucid times - she believed Holden to be an assassin working for the *Underground*. The underground of what exactly Holden never actually found out. It was a trying time for them both, Holden had but one treasured sanctuary. His work. He arrived at Campion only thirty minutes after waking and used the staff wash-rooms to ablute. The canteen provided his breakfast and then he reported to the various theatres that he was available to perform yet another of his medical miracles. While nurses and anaesthesiologists prepared to assist him he did his rounds with as many students as felt the desire to attend. It was always packed to the very edges of the rooms. Campion never housed a patient more than one to a room. Such barbaric practices had ended with the great post-war plagues of the mid-twenty-sixth century.

Rounds done, Holden had tea and some rich tea biscuits. The tea was always premium Indian. None of the Martian pseudo-nonsense for Sir Murray. Then one of his two P.A.'s (one human and the efficient one the latest phase-five Android) would fill in the rest of his diary for the day. Theatre, recovery room, relatives, repeat. He was lucky to finish for 19:00 usually, it was closer to 20:15. On a full day or one that had an especially difficult problem to solve it could stretch to 21:30. He would arrive home. Have Mildreen his stage-four Android bring him a light supper, bathe and retire. The following day he would do the whole day over. This for six days a week. Mildreen though a phase-four always reminded him of the even more efficient Laureo. Laureo was his Android P.A. Her counterpart was Nurse Mysbine a plump brunette who tended to fuss at the slightest provocation.

That was Holden's routine. If he was unlucky he got to see Pearl when she was in the middle of her paranoia. For those funks, Wadwick had prescribed blue lubies, the strongest sedative and anti-depressant known to mankind. Pearl sometimes only pretended to take them and then the paranoia grew worse. One night She was in her *cell* when *Zondersfuhrer* Holden returned to interrogate her. She was determined to tell him nothing.

"How have you been today, My Dear and how are you holding up"?

'My Dear'? My Dear! Did he really think that charade was going to fool her? He was obviously with the Underground. This, despite the fact that he had changed into plain clothes.

"I'm sorry Herr Holden but I will not be answering any of your questions tonight. It is therefore useless to continue this interrogation".

"Have you been taking your various meds"? He sighed.

"But of course", she lied. "I have done as has been instructed by Frau Mildreen".

"That's good", the Zondersfuhrer sounded exhausted. Pearl almost felt sorry for him. He was the gaoler though and she one of his prisoners. She did not show her emotions for that reason.

Holden became depressed himself. After all his years of spending his energies helping people the fates of the solar system had done this to him. It was not deserved. Pearl grew worse. The pain started. Phase three. Wadwick prescribed Snufzomorph. As if her head was not already messed up enough. That was when she descended into incoherence.

Holden had but one plan.

It was born of madness and desperation. He could think of no alternative strategy.

"I'd like you t assist me in an experimental procedure tomorrow if you'd be so kind"?

"Me, Sir Murray"?! Wadwick was astonished and delighted in equal amounts. "I am no neurosurgeon though".

"I want you to act as anaesthesiologist for the procedure. Doubling up as a nurse. There will only be the two of us present".

Alarm bells began to ring in Wadwick's head, "If I may ask, Sir Murray, why"?

"Several reasons, My Good Fellow. The paramount one being secrecy. Do you wish to become a legendary historical pioneer or not"?

"I will give you my answer once you have told me what it is we are going to do, Sir Murray".

Holden gazed keenly into the good doctor's eyes and then asked, "You know what Wadwick, I don't know your first name. What is it"?

"It's Emery"?

"Can I trust you, Emery"?

"Yes, Sir Murray. I can be discrete if that's what you mean".

"Very well then. At Pearl's surgery in the small hours. You and I are going to do a brain transplant".

Wadwick had suspected many things but this! It was not even on his mental list.

"The transplanting of a brain is impossible, Sir Murray. The brain is not an immunologically privileged organ, even if one could connect all the nerves and regenerate them sufficiently to transmit signals as they had done before being severed".

"The newest immunosuppressant drug from Orang-U-Can has made rejection a thing of the past, Emery. We will use it. it's called Orangophenolaze. Regarding the nerves, I will initially sever them with one of the pioneering micro-laser-scalpel. It does no damage other than simply cutting in microns. Then switched to suture it will simply glue the nerve endings back and the connection will be as it was. Or should I say as it would have been if it were the original ganglion"?

"Which animals brain are we going to transplant into which, Sir Murray"?

"For our first procedure, I wish to transplant the brain of a llama into the head of a pig. If successful then we will get Pearl a new body to have her mind transplanted into".

Wadwick turned white, "Since the W.W.F. laws of twenty-three, it is illegal to conduct experiments on animals, Sir Murray. As for finding a new body for poor Doctor Pearl. Are you suggesting what I think you're suggesting"?

"As in find a young attractive woman and remove the brain already in her skull? Yes, that was my notion".

"Not someone who has experienced injury due to an accident"?

"That would involve repairs and complications. We will be busy enough, Emery just the two of us. No, the body donor must be healthy, augmented too, I want Pearl to be beautiful and desirable".

"You will not get any volunteers, Sir Murray".

"Of course not, My Dear Emery. Secrecy is the order of the day. No, we must find a suitable donor and take her body. It will technically be murder. There again I would murder several times over to save my beloved".

"Sir Murray", Wadwick began quietly and reasonably, "I would like to ask you to entertain the notion that your upsetment in extremis over the grizzly fate of Doctor Pearl has tipped you from the platform of sanity".

Holden smiled calmly, "I'm a scientist, Emery. If I'm a Mad Scientist so much the better. I will perform the world's first brain transplant, do you *want in* as the saying goes or not"?

Though Wadwick was the younger man he had to admit that he still did not possess Holden's vitality and drive. He marvelled at the dextrous speed at which the surgical instruments moved in his deft fingers. It was a privilege to be the observer and assistant to the great man and he never doubted for an instant that the procedure would not be a success.

Finally, when Holden was almost collapsing with fatigue, he turned to Wadwick and asked, "Would you please glue the skull back in place Emery? I'll monitor the equipment form a supine position on that couch".

"I will indeed, Sir Murray, your work is beyond excellent it has humbled me to assist you".

Holden nodded, If the *Llamig* survives for a week you begin searching for Pearl's new body".

As he worked with the surgical glue Wadwick enquired, "Me, Sir Murray? Should you not choose the body yourself"?

"I cannot go in the sort of places that you must, Emery. Brothels. Bordello. Strip Clubs. Bars".

"You're seeking a woman of ill repute in order to make taking her life a little more palatable. It will not though. You know that murder is what it is"?

Holden smiled tiredly, "A whore will give her body to one of the greatest Veterinarian Surgeons of the age, Emery. I can justify that to myself. The added bonus will be her attractive form. Make sure she is young and sensationally attractive. Why should I not have some fun for my endeavours"?

"I'm still not certain that what you're doing is ethically reconcilable. I worry for you I truly do".

"Have you closed"?

Wadwick nodded, "Behold the worlds first Llamig created by surgery rather than that fool Hoyle's genetic skulduggery".

"Can I ask you to clean up, dispose of the spare body and brain? The incinerator is to the rear of the premises".

"Certainly. Go and get a flittaxi you look too exhausted to drive".

Once the elder man had left the Surgery Wadwick had time to consider his position. He had already broken the law by experimenting on live animals. One of them was no longer living and that incurred a prison sentence should his crime be discovered. Now he was getting in even deeper for his mentor. Could such a procedure be justified in order to learn more for science? Perhaps brain death in the future could mean full body donation? It still involved murdering a tart though. Even a fallen woman a trollop had a right to life. Was it too late to pull out of the neurosurgeon's scheme? Unfortunately, he thought it was!

Over the next few days, it was Wadwick who did the blood tests on the Llamig, fed it mucked out after it and observed its behaviour. The Orangophenolaze did exactly as hoped and there was no sign of rejection. With regard to behaviour, the llamig acted like a llama. It was no longer omnivorous but preferred a diet of grass, hay, corn silage, alfalfa, and grassroots. When it was agitated it spat at Wadwick making a strange bleating noise that was definitely not a grunt. It didn't drink as much water like a pig but when it did - drunk up to 3 gallons of water in one day. Holden had performed a miracle the pig had the brain of a llama so it acted like a llama.

Wadwick knew what came next!

"Take one of those new imaging watches", the neurosurgeon had told him, "I'd like a choice of three. Get an image of the nicest blonde, brunette and redhead you can find. Do it quickly, Emery. I don't think Pearl has long. She needs a new body".

The place was full of noise, smoke, chatter. The music throbbed like some primordial jungle drum message. Wadwick wondered,

'Do people come to places like this for pleasure? What could be the fun in it? It's like hell'!

He was having a drink at the bar, a club rasp-beery when the huge head-shaved barman nodded to someone behind him. The next thing he knew a blonde seated herself beside him even though there was plenty of room around the lengthy counter.

"It's pouring down outside. Do you have a flitter or don't you mind getting wet"?

Clever move, start with a question. Wadwick looked at her. Nice figure. She was wearing a low cut frock that showed off her decollete to perfection. Slim long legs. Facially pretty. The age was not so easy but he put it between twenty-two and fifty with augmentations. She looked like she might very well be adventuress in bed.

"I have a flitter, my name is Emery. Yours"?

"Gloriol. Do you want to buy me a drink"?

"Of course. Bartender, please get the lady whatever she wants and another rasp-beery for me"?

"So, Emery what do you do".

'I take the brains out of llamas and put them into pigs heads', he thought before replying. "I'm at Campion, seventh-year medicine".

"A doctor"! Gloriol was shocked. "We don't get a lot of professionals coming this way, Doc".

"So you come here a lot then".

"I work here, Doc. Social catering you know".

The poor young woman was a whore. Still, it was the oldest profession in existence.

"In that case, I'd like to ask you a rather unusual favour"? He informed.

"Well I don't mind playing doctors and nurses, but I'm not doing anything with surgical knives and such. Nothing kinky or painful".

Wadwick grimaced, "No I just want to take a photograph of you and get some statistics. Like they would at Campion"?

"Ten shillin. Do you want the pics to be normal nude stuff or gynaecological"?

"Just a straight portrait please".

"With my clothes on"?!

"As you are now, yes".

"Okay, Doc, whatever floats your flitter. Ten shillin up front".

It was a similar story with the pole dancer. The redhead Demia. She had powerful muscles that Sir Murray might like. Her bosom was also admirably pert.

Lanie was different. Wadwick had met her at an electrosonicrave. She worked in a garment factory and was just out to, 'Get off my tits on some good khakk and rave my brains out till tomorrow'. While she had the brain of a mouse, Wadwick would have eaten his dinner off her ass. Lanie deserved to be educated rather than have her brain removed. Her own was capable of being filled with information. It was brand new, having never been used. Wadwick supposed many of the plebs in Livcheshore were like Lanie. The reflection depressed him greatly   .

He returned to his mentor with three images and outlines of the girls, their vital statistics and of course their blood groups.

"They were the most suitable trio", he said to Holden. After the few days - you allowed me that is. With more time I could..."

"We have no more time, Emery", Holden sounded exhausted. "Pearl doesn't speak any more. All the Snultine did was to make her dependant upon it. Her body goes into shock if I try and reduce the dosage. Yet it's done nothing to slow the progression of the Lyle".

"I'm very sorry to hear that".

"You will still assist me"?

"I've come too far to back out now. Where will we do it though? The Veterinarian Surgery isn't equipped to...".

"You're right! It must be the hospital. I suggest theatre twenty-three on the top floor. Little used but as well equipped as the others.

"And who must I knock out and bring to it while you bring Pearl"?

"I like the little brunette, she looks the most innocent".

"She's certainly that, Sir Murray", Wadwick observed a trifle sadly. He had hoped Holden would have chosen either of the other two

-----

Theatre twenty-three was prepared in haste, Time was running out for Pearl. It was also running out for Lanie. Holden was red-eyed and unshaven on the night he carried his contractee's body into the hospital wrapped in a blanket. As he laid her gently on the second operating table Wadwick saw how wasted the body had been ravaged by the disease.

It had been easy to meet Lanie again, offer her a ride home in his flitter and shoot her with a level one dart. The dart was a tranquillizer which put her out until he laid her on operating table one. The lighting was blinding Wadwick as the two surgeons scrubbed in preparation for the transfer.

"I beg you not to become a murderer, Sir Murray", the younger of the two men tried desperately for the last time.

"You've just seen Pearl. What the Lyle has done to her. I can save her from that. What would you do in my place, Emery"?

"Death will also release her from the suffering, Sir Murray. Can you not let fate unravel in the order it was meant to"?

"Let the one true love of my life die when I have the ability, the sheer dexterity to give her many more years of precious life. I am a mad scientist who will go down in history for what I've done today, Emery. That is *my* fate you see".

"You will go down in history alright", Wadwick countered, "Bracketed along with Knox and Mengele".

"Then let history record me as it must", Holden could not be dissuaded. "We are ready are we not"?

Wadwick nodded miserably and they tied masks upon one another's faces. Then the two of them went into the brightly sterile space that was theatre twenty-three.

Without a seconds hesitation, the neurosurgeon picked up some clippers and within a minute had shaved sufficient of Pearls hair as was needed. He was going to saw open her skull and remove her brain placing it in a specially prepared almost frozen nutrient. Then he would repeat the procedure on Lanie. The only difference was her head would remain empty. Like a boiled egg that one had scooped out and was of no further use. Her body would go into the furnace, along with her useless brain.

Wadwick shuddered as the circular bone saw began to cut into Pearl's skull. He assisted by mopping up the blood that got in Holden's way. With a surgical chisel and hammer, the skull was cracked and Holden reached inside his contractee's open head. With deft and highly skilled fingers Holden tore the outermost layer of meninges, which had lain directly beneath the skull and on into the dura mater. Once moved to one side he began to sever the nerves that connected the brain to the spinal cord made up of bundles of nerve fibers. It ran down from Pearl's brain through a canal in the centre of the bones of the spine.

It was the most crucial of procedures. If Holden got it wrong in even the most minute of ways, Pearl could end up brain damaged or worse a complete cabbage. Finally, Holden told his assistant.

"You can start preparing the donor body now. Open the skull and then wait for me to commence taking the other brain out".

Wadwick looked down at the beautiful and innocent Lanie. He blurted his confession. "I'm sorry, Sir Murray but I can't cut into this girl. I'll monitor Pearl's nutrient bath once you've removed her brain. You'll have to murder her yourself".

"I can only do so much, Emery. Do you realise how tiring this procedure is on my eyes, my back, my own brain? Help her an I damn you? Otherwise, you'll never practise medicine in this or any other hospital ever again".

"If that's to be my fate, then yours will be to have the occasional visit from your once again young and beautiful contracted partner whilst in prison. You want to be grateful the death penalty is not currently practised in this country".

"Emery Wadwick, Doctor. Pick up the circular saw and begin removing the subject's skull right this instant or...".

There was a knocking sound at the theatre door. They were undone! Someone was just about to discover what they were about!

"Good morning, My Love", Doctor Holden greeted his contractee as he glanced up from his pad. "Trouble in Argentina again. Our boys are flitting down there to give them another bloody nose no doubt. Are you facing yet another busy day"?

Pearl smiled, "It's always busy at the Surgery, Murray. I don't expect you'll be home early either".

"Who knows", Holden smiled. He got up from his chair and kissed Laureo's lips. They were artificial but seemed exactly like the real thing. Soft and moist. Of course, now they were Pearl's.

As though reading his mind Pearl asked, "How is that new P.A. of yours shaping up"?

"Midhael", Holden echoed, "Not too bad. I just can't seem to get used to a male P.A. Especially a human one. he's not perfect".

"Like Laureo was, with her photographic memory. I still can't get used to looking in the mirror and seeing her beautiful face looking back at me".

264

"The alternative was far more grizzly", Holden returned with feeling. He took her soft and perfectly proportioned body in his arms. "It was a good job she interrupted us the night she did. Or that poor girl Emery found would have had to make the ultimate sacrifice for you".

Pearl kissed him passionately. Her tongue felt real. "No matter what happens in the future you must never attempt that operation again, Murray".

"I never did though did I"? He reasoned. "Connecting your brain to her fibre-optic bundle was comparative child's-play. I have never transplanted a human brain into the skull of another person".

"Laureo must have secretly loved you very much to offer to substitute for the girl. When you disconnected her neural network, you murdered a sentient creature for my sake, Murray".

"Don't be foolish, My Love. Laureo was just a machine who admired my work. It wasn't murder was it"?

"Technically not in the eyes of the law I suppose. But who knows in thousands of years from now the Androids may become living things, just like us"

"Never mind the minutia, my Love. Though I was willing - in the end, I killed no one".

Time an Upon Once

СТАНДАРД ХАЦК

For Monica

The End

Galters opened the unfashionably solid timber door of Professor Lamerstone's expansive abode to find two very disparate figures without.

"Yes"? He asked simply.

The tall one in the suit and raincoat held out an identity card, at the same instant informing, "Inspector Gadde of the Yorks Constabulary. This gentleman is...".

"Domnule Cercel. Yes, I know Inspector. The Professor is expecting you please intră".

"What"? Gadde did not fully understand. "What's that curious speech you keep using"?

It was Cercel who answered, "He is speaking Romanian to me, Inspector. Having correctly deduced that I am originally from there. Thank you for that but there is no need to keep it up Domnule Galters. I am a linguist as you know and speak several languages and one of them is Anglovian, or as some call it – Standard".

The duo was not matched physically at all. Gadde was a huge hulking figure with massive spade-like hands. While the linguist was slim and delicately boned. He was also very dark being from the area of the Romanian, while Gadde had blue eyes and sandy coloured thinning hair. It had a natural curl to it that refused to let it stay neat, while Cercel's was immaculately parted in the centre. To add to the disparity was the fact that Gadde only seemed to possess an *outdoor voice*. While the linguist was an exceptionally good listener and softly spoken with it.

"Cercel is also a lip reader, so watch what you mutter as you retreat from him", Gadde chuckled.

Galters nodded tacitly but not especially amused and conducted them to a rather shaded drawing room with partly drawn drapes of heavy verdant Draylon. In there, the Professor was seated in an old moquette, studded, wing-backed chair - sipping tea. What was also fanciful about him was the fact that he drank from a porcelain teacup and saucer. The Professor was a learned man and Anglovian. He, therefore, had every right to be eccentric in his ways. Indeed it was sort of expected of him.

"Professor Lamerstone, we meet again", the Inspector began, "Allow me to introduce you to, Mister Cercel? Amongst his plethora of talents is the ability to read lips".

Cercel wondered briefly what series of events led to the two very different men meeting in the first place. He turned his attention to the academician.

Lamerstone climbed to his feet and shook their hands warmly. "You'll have tea"? He told rather than asked them. The two men hesitated, Lamerstone added for vital clarification,

"It's Indian"!

"Right! We'd love some then, thank you", Cercel beat the Inspector to it.

"Please sit", Lamerstone asked of his guests, "Have a Garibaldi"?

They each politely took one from the proffered plate, it only left two behind anyway. When the learned man used the singular, he did not mean the plural.

The two men glanced around the Professor's drawing room. It was like being in a museum. A museum dedicated to murder! A suitable name for the property might well have been the Murder Museum. As though to deflect the conversation momentarily from the business in hand, Cercel asked,

"Is that rather splendid mantle clock a genuine mechanical model, Professor? Or a clever radio-controlled electronic reproduction"?

"If you listen carefully, you'll get your answer", the academic smiled. Surely enough, the clock actually ticked. Gadde was happier to get down to business. He waited patiently for the pleasantries to be over though, knowing enough to realise genteel manners when presented with them.

"That's a disturbing painting, Lamerstone. Supposed to be Jack the Ripper by any chance"?

"Exactly so", the Professor confirmed, "Just as the rather lurid one behind you on the other wall is the Boston Strangler. So typical of the Americans to vulgarize the event, don't you agree ha ha ha"?

"And in the case"? Gadde was referring to a display case, which had then caught his eye. "You seem to have filled it with an intriguing mixture of exhibits, if I may say so".

The Professor began an oral inventory,

"In the top left-hand corner is a genuine bottle of Haigh's acid. Next to which is one of Sutcliffe's hammers. The charred bone once belonged to one of Nilsen's victims. On the bottom shelf is a tyre iron that belonged to Bellfield. Then there is the train ticket to Alleestraße, with which, Kürten took his first victim. Finally, the last exhibit is the red nose worn at parties by the 'Pogo the Clown' - real name Wayne Gacy".

"A grizzly collection yet bizarrely a valuable one", Gadde noted. It would be the case too there was an unhealthy market for memorabilia of that nature.

Galters arrived with an actual silver tray. Upon which were a teapot of the same metal and two sets of cup and saucers. The tray and teapot must have been very valuable indeed after the silver shortage of the late twenty-seventh.

As he sipped his beverage appreciatively Gadde asked, "So will our first demonstration of your device be at the cottage of the victim, Professor? Or do you intend to show it to Cercel here in your home"?

"It will only work properly in the rented cottage, Inspector. Only there will we get any meaningful results", Lamerstone replied patiently and Cercel suspected he had explained that previously to the good Inspector.

"Mister Cercel. You are probably confused by all this secrecy. I believe it is the right time to put you in the picture as it were. I have been working for several years on a device that can take impressions from various substances other than film, silicon chips or magnetic tape. Coinciding with that research was my main interest. I can tell you that it is the fourth dimension. Most elusive of the four we dwell in and most difficult to observe let alone control or master. Certainly, we can look at a clock or wrist-chrono but that is only a man-made measurement for recording the dimension. Not a way of actually seeing it itself. The two areas of my continued interest came to fruition at roughly the same moment and I found a way of combining them! Yes, Sir - combining the two. Do you see the implications of just such research"?

Cercel saw no need to pretend understanding where none existed so he returned honestly enough, "I'm a linguist, Professor, I'm afraid you've lost me"?!

"Then let us take it one step at a time", Lamerstone suggested patiently. "Firstly I can now view memories from stone, fabric, wood, the plastics and so forth. Plus the softer fabrics although the image gets rather woolly then ha ha ha".

Cercel laughed dutifully at what he thought of as a Professor Joke.

"When we interact before such substances we leave a sort of micro-energetic footprint of that action on all inanimate objects. With my device which I call the Temporascope, for reasons which will become apparent in a moment, I can then view those energy imprints on a cathode screen. Not only that, Cercel and this is the exciting part, due to my work on the fourth dimension I can view those events from the moment of their happening – *backwards* toward their commencement "!

Cercel requested, "So what you are telling me is you can view the happening in a room, say the cottage we speak of and watch it like reversing a tri-vid on the hologram"?

"Exactly, My Dear Fellow you got it in one. The Inspector was not quite so quick".

The Inspector was busily filling a pipe with some rather dubious tobacco and had not paid much attention to an explanation that he had previously heard. At the mention of his name though he responded with indignation,

"Harrumph", Gadde suddenly intruded on the conversation, "Rather than sitting here talking about it all day, Professor, what say you to going to the cottage and seeing if your theory works in practice"?

"It will obviously become an invaluable tool for the Constabulary", Cercel was still enthusing, "I presume my presence is required because the images will not be accompanied by sound"?

"Exactly so, Cercel"! The Professor sounded pleased with the linguist's leap of logic. "The images will not be of a high quality and sound is totally absent from them, but we must work with what we have".

"And the Temporascope? How much have you managed to miniaturize it"?

"It is time we went to the lab". Lamerstone decided. As he rose to his feet though he turned to Cercel and explained, "What you are about to see is a prototype. Constructed in its most primitive form. There was no sense in refining it further if the bally thing does not work, do you not agree"?

"Absolutely, Professor". The linguist was genuinely intrigued.

Lamerstone led the two of them through a doorway at the back corner of the room and down a series of stone steps beyond. Finally switching an antiquated toggle at the corner of the subterranean room he brought light to his laboratory.

"This funnel-shaped device is the receiver", He explained to Cercel. Passing it to him for examination. "Think of it as the tape-head, the chip the file in your pad. With the signal, it then sends it to the cathode tube. Here is the bit we will actually see the images on, the monitor".

The Monitor was in effect like a pad screen but this was some 600 mm from bottom left corner to top right. It looked to be around half of that in height. Lamerstone explained,

"Because the image will be of poor resolution and in very grainy greys and blacks the lack of miniaturization will actually be advantageous. Especially when it comes to your part in the procedure Cercel. Are you ready for the challenge"?

"Ready! I can hardly wait"! The linguist enthused. "What we are going to see is the murder that took place in the cottage, reversed back for us so that we can discover the identity of the killer".

"Exactly so", Lamerstone was delighted with the linguist's powers of deduction. Inspector Gadde had not been so analytical. Nor it seemed had as much faith in the Professor's powers of prediction. Although he had brought

Cercel to visit so he must have thought something was going on worthy of further investigation.

"Inspector, if you will carry the monitor. Mister Cercel the funnel. Let us go and see what the Temporascope can do".

"Let's cut through the minutia for one second, Professor"? Gadde requested, "Do you really think we will see the murder take place in this device of yours"?

Cercel smiled to himself at the Inspector's use of the word *minutia*, wondering where he had heard it, to reiterate it.

Lamerstone nodded with ill-concealed excitement, "Dependent upon the absorbency of the various inanimate objects in the cottage, the monitor will show an image of the events conducted in there shown trans-progressively through the fourth dimension".

"Reversing. Like a car in erm, reverse".

"That's what I said".

click

"Here we are", Gadde told them superfluously. They had driven through the dales during a beautiful summers day. The sun occasionally hiding behind cumulus clouds only to appear seconds later lighting the ground with patterns of daffodil Totally incongruous to the grizzly setting the trio were soon to be confronted with. All dimness and cerise. Momentary misery and rich scarlet "Get the cathode ray tube please, Inspector", Lamerstone instructed as he skipped out of the vehicle. The professor, not normally a gregarious person was enjoying his moments of friendship and supervision in an equal amount

The other two followed him carefully carrying their designated devices. Meticulous to avoid damage and ruin the experiment before it had even begun. The tube was the more likely to cause a catastrophe with its dangling wires and leads. Lamerstone had not had the time to construct a cabinet for it. Either that or he was not proficient enough with the relevant materials.

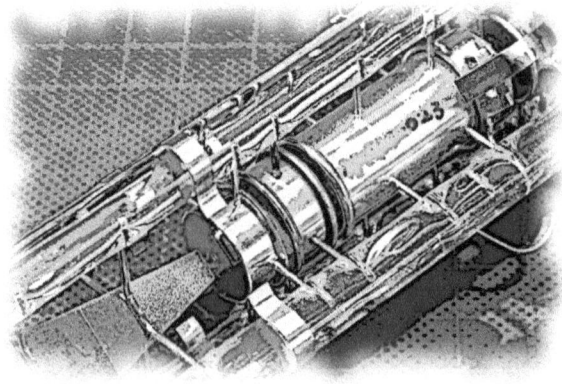

"Set the tube on that table, careful not to step on the blood-stain, Inspector. We don't want your size eleven ruining the integrity of the crime scene, do we? Excellent now please give the funnel to me once I've connected the tube to the electrics.

Good, now we're ready to start the experiment. The very first of it's kind. The first temporal viewing in history. Gosh, this is a historical pioneering moment really is it not. Fortunately, I am prepared for the moment". Lamerstone produced a flask and took a swig from it by way of a toast. He then passed the metal bottle to the lip-reader. It went around the trio in turn. Each took a swig and smiled, savouring the moment in right fashion.

"The device did not have it's own power source, Professor"? Cercel wondered and was surprised given the vast capacity of contemporary batteries. As ever there was an eccentric reason for it. Lamerstone explained,

"No! I prefer to use the energy of others whenever I can", he confessed with a grin. Even the modern batteries of which you speak need constant recharging and my grants are not sufficient for me to be too extravagant". The way he picked up the three-pin plug was almost a caress as he inserted it into the wall. Male into the female.

'He's loving every second of this', Cercel thought to himself.

Instantly a humming noise then came from the tube. Reverberating around the quite confined area of the cottage's front-room. At least the wiring was intact in the rather shabby abode. The sight that had seen a despicable act perpetrated. Lamerstone took the funnel and began to almost casually wave it this way and that before settling on the huge bloodstain on the carpet.

"You see that button with the two arrows on it pointing to the left, a bar in front of there points, Cercel"? He suddenly asked, "Please depress it. It is the fast reverse control and may take several depressions before we move far enough back in time to actually see something happen. Only when you get a flicker of change should you cease and then await my next instruction. I must monitor the computerised section of the controls, at this keyboard here".

Cercel almost expected the keyboard to be a Remington typewriter, but it was, in fact, an ancient Orang-U-Can. The keys all lit in tasteful amber.

Suddenly a very grainy but noticeable image flickered onto the screen of the tube. Gadde leaned forward to see it.

Instead of just a pool of blood on the floor, the image was showing the dead body that Gadde had originally been called to by the landlady of the cottage. A mature woman who had not taken the sight very well and who was still complaining of *'Vapors caused by the dreadful upsetment of it all'*

"That's our body. It had no identification on it and no one has been reported as missing in this area". Inspector Gadde told the other two. Though doubtless Lamerstone already knew that information.

"Great stuff, Professor. Now then, can you back it up so we might see who stuck that knife in the corpse and then threw it down beside the body like that? Maybe as some sort of message"?

Cercel inquired curiously "Where was he stabbed, Inspector"?

"In this very cottage" Gadde was surprised at the question. Lamerstone surmised though,

"Judging by the size of the stain I would say the liver, Cercel. Now begin to rewind time by depressing that reverse button. Which as you probably suspect by now is the key with the single arrow pointing to your left. Slowly with hesitations in between, we don't want to overshoot anything that may be of use to the Inspector.

Suddenly the image jumped and flickered. The knife vanished suddenly flying upward from the floor. It was as though it had defied gravity. It was out of sight for the moment.

"Stop"! The professor commanded. "Here, take the funnel and keep it focused on that piece of the floor. Now I shall use the single arrow indicating slow forward and the images will progress through time at the normal rate of one second per second. See, the device is working perfectly. All right transfer to the reverse button but very slowly until you get the feel of the keys. Watch"!

As the impressed duo watched the sepia-coloured blood it appeared to flow back into the body of the victim. Then he levitated back out of the picture. Reanimated by reverse time. At least his image was. No one had yet to find a way of truly beating the call of the grim reaper.

"That was the fall in reverse", Lamerstone told Gadde. The remark a trifle obvious in nature.

"But now all I'm looking at is an empty floor", the Inspector was disappointed. Was that the full extent of what he was to learn that day?

"Wait", Lamerstone advised. "Cercel start to point that funnel at the wall over there. It is another absorbent surface when it comes to energy and will therefore still possess animation that my device can read. It will thus give us a different angle of vision and a view into the air in the centre of the room".

It took time and practise. Eventually, though an image of the assailant was brought back to life on the Temporascope. Fuzzy, blurred and difficult to discern detail in, Professor Lamerstone had never the less found him with his device.

"There you are Inspector, our killer".

"It would seem my skills were not required", Cercel noted regretfully.

"Not yet", the Professor encouraged. "But now we want to know where the killer came from and who else was involved in the murder if anyone and why"?

"But surely it did not all take place in this room", Gadde objected, clearly disappointed by the modest nature of the success. "That image isn't good enough for identification. So where do my men start looking"?

Lamerstone grinned, enjoying his position as instructor to the Inspector,

"The man himself will have some past images still lingering on his clothes. What I can now do is discard the funnel and focus on the image itself. Zoom into that figure and tell the computer to pick up what latent images his garb was detecting earlier".

"You can reverse an image from an image"! Cercel was incredulous. That was an achievement that almost dwarfed the original function of the Temporascope. Lamerstone milked the moment for all it was worth. Basking in the admiration form the linguist. Finally, when he had gloated enough he replied,

"Let's see, shall we? This is where we might need your skills Cercel".

Click

It took several hours of watching grainy images on the screen before anyone saw anything of note. After backbreaking duration over screens and consoles and endless cups of Indian tea. Interrupted by two rounds of sandwiches they finally found something of interest for the second time. The three of them had left the cottage. Driving to the station where the constable took them to the canteen for lunch. Then they waded through the granular reflections from the killer's black clothing.

The lengthy and frustrating process took them into the early hours of the following day, but finally... They did not who he was. All they knew was that he had stabbed an unknown man to death. Before he had entered the cottage, he had driven from Abersprochburn on the edge of Loch Tay – Francosia. What on Earth was he doing in that windswept rain lashed god-forsaken wilderness? Unless perhaps, the victim had first hidden there and later moved on to the cottage where he had been finally caught up with?

The trio was treated to a reverse drive from the cottage to the town in the highlands. It was the journey he had taken before that - which interested them more. Where had he come from? what had he against the victim? The very grainy and smudged images of all the various roads showed vehicles all travelling in reverse for hours. The Professor dare not fast-forward through them, in case a single frame or incident gave them all the information they needed.

When they finally got a break it was in spectacular form. Giving them more in those couple of minutes than they could have possibly hoped for. They saw the front of the vehicle reverse to a halt. This then must have been the start of the killer's journey to find the victim. The images continued like a silent film running in reverse. The killer appeared to climb out of the car, when in fact he had climbed in. The viewpoint of the images abruptly changed to a car pulling into the distance, which was the killer walking toward it. A parked car. Doors suddenly closed in front of the car and then faded away down a dimly lit corridor. A corner was turned and the images showed curious illuminations, all white against the grainy brown surrounding.

It took them a while to discern exactly what was going on. They saw flares of illumination, a bottle, a glass, a counter.

"It looks like he left some sort of bar to go on the journey", Cercel noted.

Suddenly a much closer image than previously appeared on the tube. A grainy image of the head and shoulders of a woman. A slim but curvy and very attractive woman.

"What is she saying" Gadde demanded at once.

'Get my son and then kill him. I'll be waiting for you, with your *payment*'.

"Pay-dirt", Gadde pumped the air with his fist causing Cercel to wince, he was trying to concentrate on the woman's mouth, not easy when the image was in grainy distorted sepia. Unfortunately, face recognition would not be possible

"He has junior [pause]."Put it this way", she pouted. "You come to me clean and freshly shaved and in the morning you'll leave on rubber legs [pause] I'll tell you what *Dick* Darke with an 'E'. You kill my louse of a former contractee and I'll give you three silver shillin and you can have me three times".

"Wow, noted Gadde at that last remark, "Looks like he wanted more money than she had so she whored herself to get the job done. Not a classy mare then. We've got the black-guard anyway, "Darke with an 'E' shouldn't be that hard to find. I'll get on the pad you two carry on watching, see if she gives herself away or the victim's I.D.".

There was no time for the linguist to do anything other than exactly that. He continued to read the woman's lips in the grainy image

"Too low eh. All right five and that's all I have. [pause]".

It seemed the Inspector had been right regarding the price. She had run out of money and he had no doubt suggested an, which she had agreed too. The linguist continued to read her lips. Only possible due to the whiteness of her teeth against the darkened smudge of her features.

"So you'll do it? [pause] I'll give you three silver shillin to kill him [pause] Just find my son and return him to me please, Mister Darke with an 'E'. Oh, would you be interested in a bonus? [pause] You can find him for me? I need to find my former contractee who has kidnapped our son. Would you be interested in the job? [pause] Do you know anyone? I am in need of someone who doesn't want to be found – finding? [pause] Not *that, who*".

The woman's image turned to a rear view then. Lamerstone began frantically readjusting the focus of the Temporascope.

"I want to see where she goes now, she will lead us to firstly the boy and finally to the victim. Then we will have everything the device can give us".

"If the boy's still with Darke it could get iffy. All I need now, Professor is the woman's identity", Gadde was back having put his finest onto finding the killer.

On the screen, the image had gone dark.

"What's wrong with the temp-u-whatchamacallit", the Inspector demanded.

"Nothing is wrong", Lamerstone assured, "That's the image between the back of her waistcoat and her car seat. I was just about to fast forward. There you go, that's Junior. Can you get an image of that to your officers"?

Gadde shook his head, "It's still not good enough resolution. Keep going till we get to the victim and her presumably rowing with him, see if it supplies us with any clues".

"I have something for you. Some background I've picked up from the images", the linguist told him, "The clientele of that club was not of the most savoury type existing in Ledchester. That was the last sign the killer passed in his car remember? So that is where he set out from. It would also seem that was exactly what the woman was looking for. She either had a bit of checkered history herself or continued it despite the birth of her son. For she knew where to go. She herself obviously has a very well paid position in some sort of high industry in Northern England. She had no small amount of ready cash she thought she needed to facilitate her desired strategy.

I managed to identify what she was wearing too. Black slacks, an expensive waistcoat of the same hue in actual bovine leather (one can tell quality even on the Temporascope) and black neoplas boots, she drew attention the instant she entered the seedy establishment. The main reason for this was the fact that she had nothing else on her upper body but the waistcoat. I estimate thirty-eight D's that were also perky. They tended to draw the male eye like raw meat does a wolf. In addition, she had dyed her hair bright red. Not auburn, scarlet. It showed up the same black as her glossy lipstick and her eyes were heavy with mascara. She looked like a *goer* in the sort of vernacular used in that place. That may have been done just in order to lure the sort of man who would kill her partner for money. Or she might have been that sort of woman we can't, know yet The name of the bar was the Flamrog Club. I saw its sign reflected in the windscreen of one of the cars".

While Cercel had been delivering these excellent observations the Professor had been keying in all this information into the web, he suddenly told them,

"There is indeed a bar in Ledchester called the Flamrog Club. I say, Cercel well done my good fellow! The establishment was named after Hoyle's latest genetic hybrid crossing a flamingo with a frog by the by. The resultant amphibious-bird was a beautiful bright green, ate insects and liked to stand on one leg".

"Ledchester brilliant! What a team we are"! Gadde seemed to include himself in with the brains of the trio.

Suddenly an image came back onto the tube. "Strange, that looks like a forward view", Cercel noted almost absently.

"I think she might have taken the waistcoat off".

Sure enough from the angle and height of say a double bed, they were suddenly presented with an image of a woman naked from the waist up. She was loading her impressive bosom into a brassiere. She then did up a clasp around her throat and on a silver chain was an opal.

"Excellent"! Lamerstone enthused, "We should get some clearer images of the stone at her throat. Nice shiny and reflective surface that it is"

He once again re-tuned the scope in the appropriate way and the image on the screen did indeed sharpen slightly and the angle was once more in a forward view. As seen by the young woman herself.

He suddenly pointed to the screen even though the other two had never taken their eyes off it.

"Here we go, She is going to the door"!

Outside, however, was not the victim, but two uniformed constables.

"Wait a minute"! Gadde noted, "I know the one on the right. His name is Denning. Bit of a clown too if memory serves me correctly".

"You're up Cercel", the Professor encouraged. It seemed the Inspector's droll observations were not especially appreciated at that time.

"So do you have a ping for EsBop and a tri-d of your former partner?[pause] Are you by any chance having a dispute over access to Junior, Ma'am? [pause] EsBop (English Steel, Beauty Products and Plumbing Supplies) as a travelling representative you say. [pause] Where does he work then? [pause] What's his address, Ma'am? I presume you've contact details? [pause] Have you any sort of suspicion as to where he might be or who might have abducted him? [pause]". Then the same line repeated, as though the woman had misheard, or had not answered for some reason. "Have you any sort of suspicion as to where he might be or who might have abducted him? [Pause] Constable Denning and I'm Gonson".

The door opened, as in closed.

"I think we have most of the pieces of the puzzle now. Gonson will have noted all the details in his pad". The Inspector told them. "Seems like a partner split gone wrong. Sugartits wants the kid, so does the Vic, He snatches him, that's where our boys come in".

"I'd like to see the whole thing through to the beginning, though", the Professor insisted.

"Me too, Professor keep rewinding", Cercel encouraged.

The machine offered sporadic images until once again something incidental happened in the woman's life. From that point onward though poor, they at least continued to unravel in the opposite order to which she had witnessed them. Over the next few weeks, the solicitor roundabout began. Pings were exchanged, then more. The solicitors of both sides assured their clients of eventual victory – at a price. During the entire period, the victim had not been granted any access to his son at all. Junior went out to kick a ball around in the yard. That must have been when the victim had snatched his own son. Of course, he appeared again as the tape was showing what was happening earlier.

The double rewind button was pressed several times before the victim finally appeared on the grainy screen, Cercel then began to read what he had said to her.

"Are we really going to do the whole solicitor thing, Jenna? [pause while she says something that caused him to ask that question] I'll leave it for a while to let the dust settle. When you feel like letting me have my first access just ping me? [lengthy pause] I will get some things together because I know you're going to phone the constables if I don't. This matter is not solved though, Jenna. [pause] You are being ridiculous now. Just because I made one little mistake which I've owned up to it doesn't make me the devil incarnate. [pause] Just a moment? I'm not saying you cannot visit Junior once I get sorted out, but I'll want to bring my son up myself. We both know he adores me. [pause] What about Junior? [pause] You can't throw me out of my own house! [pause] Now you're being unreasonable" [pause] It was an accident, Darling I swear! Just one of those mistakes that anyone can have from time to time, she meant nothing to me I cannot even remember her name".

"I think we get the picture", the professor concluded. "He has a slip, she tells him to get out and that he can't see their son any more. So he takes off with him and she hires this Darke chap to get the boy back and make sure the poor slob never troubles them again – ever".

"I agree with that assessment", Gadde added. "I should go and get the investigation into gear now gentlemen. If you'll excuse me"?

There was a period of reflective silence and the two remaining figures began to dismantle the Temporascope making it ready for transport back to the Professor's house.

"Your machine will reform crime investigation and make of it a determined science, Professor".

I'm not certain the powers that be will ever let it go into general production, My Dear Fellow".

"Why not"?

"The Big Brother syndrome. I mean to say, would you be comfortable knowing that every surface you ever came into contact with - was potentially spying upon your every move? This device is the end of any sort of privacy what-so-ever. Who could live comfortably knowing that"?

"Well at least I got to see it and Gadde will make certain that the woman and her hired man will both hang for their crimes. One good thing has come out of it. What will you do now, disassemble it"?

"No, I will keep it a secret. I have a few things I want to use it for. A few historical images I would like to rewind to and observe, even if only backwards". It will mean holding that button down for a very long time in some cases".

"Historical images eh? Sound intriguing. Would you like to tell me where you're going and what year you plan to tune into firstly"?

"The professor grinned, "I'm off to Jerusalem of course. To turn the device back to A.D. 26 when by my calculations a certain execution was taking place"!

thE beginninG.

The Beast of Callisto

DESPARGIA JARQUIX

In the isolated town of Hoenir at the edge of the crater, the only guesthouse in town was run by Osbourn Stoff and his longtime partner Kym Steonberg They called their modest establishment Domek Gościnny as it lay in the Polish-controlled hemisphere of the moon. Tourists were very infrequent in Hoenir, it was not one of the more glamorous locales on Callisto. If any other town so distant from the sun called ever be given that description. Not only did it lack class though there was also little incident to brighten the days of the miners who had settled in the place. A simple train ride north was the far more interesting and populated Guntur Tarrata the mining town that had the largest radio mast in the sector and was the source of most news reaching Callisto from distant Earth.

"It's this place, Osbourn", Steonberg complained that morning. "You explain to me what would possess anyone from renting a room in Hoenir of all places in the solar system? They are en-route to Orestheus perhaps or the huge settlement at Mój-głowa. We are just too far from the happening places on Callisto".

A stray strand of blonde hair suddenly found its way out of the rag-top the woman was wearing and fell across her nose. She brushed it fiercely away annoyed by the physical interruption. She was seven standard years younger than Stoff. Originally from Yorkshire in Anglond on the planet Earth. She was stocky but young enough to still be able to carry the few extra kilos and get away with it. He liked her cuddly frame.

Contrasting her in most ways was Osbourn Stoff. Tall at 198 cm yet still only weighing 70 kilos, he still had the permanent tan of a native Martian. Born in the Pyrrhae Regio area close to the cold dusty world's equator. He was therefore much better suited to the gravity on Callisto than his partner. The moon had only 12.6% of Earth's While he felt only half his weight Steonberg felt only an eighth. This could lead to physical and strangely mental problems unless closely monitored by a trained Gravitarian

"I've heard this conversation more than once have I not, Darling"? He asked her. "But a train journey from the south pole is a very long one and this town has a station in it. People fancying a break maybe an overnight one will look to us to put them up. I've examined the books recently we're doing all right".

"Guntur Tarrata is south of us though and the hotel is bigger. If they choose to stop off before they even reach us I for one can sympathise with their choice".

Osbourn attempted to walk away from the conversation. It was not easy when it was still recommended that people stayed indoors as much as possible until the oxygen content of the atmosphere got higher and the atmosphere itself got deeper around the moon. During these tirades, Kym tended to follow him from one room to another until she had driven her point home like a Toledo through his heart. Even as he began to leave the room she matched his pace and continued as though there had been no pause in their converse.

"I guess it must be nice to travel. It's said that Vanapagan has become quite the place to see now, Osbourn. Then there are the underground lakes at Egres and Aziren, the giant craters at Gloi and Ustrard Burr. Can you imagine viewing them while Jupiter hangs enormously in the sky"?

"What are we having for dinner, Dear".

"Osbourn I'm trying to have a serious conversation with you. Can your guts not wait until we arrive at some sort of resolution"?

"At this moment the resolution to my hunger would be food, Dear. I don't see why you want to go over an old conversation. A repeated conversation. We are doing alright in Hoenir. Rates and utilities are reasonable and we are making a slow but steady profit when those have been paid for".

"Utilities"! Kym managed to make the word sound like a profanity. She had certainly cursed with it. Just for emphasis, she added, "Utilities! You call what the Polish government here call what we have, utilities. Why we don't even have the web. How is it possible for anyone living in the modern age not to have the Sol-web? We don't get vidz, so no tri-d we have to rely on the short-wave radio and those downloads you get from Guntur Tarrata for our pad updates. We are practically cut off from the rest of civilisation".

"What civilisation would that be, Kym? Do you really think that man has become one scrap more moralistic than the first man to hold a stone club in his hand"?

"Maybe that's what it's like on Mars. It is not like it in Yorkshire. People are good and kind and have interesting things to say to one another".

"So you left and came to the god of war", Osbourn chuckled. "That makes sense – not".

They suddenly heard the downstairs airlock ping. As though it was a race, they jostled shoulder to shoulder to be first to reach their diminutive reception area. Then like the subconsciously created comedy double act that they were, they released the lock and waited for the traveller to enter.

Stoff and Steonberg appearing on stage this evening.

Come and see why they wowed the audience all around the solar system. Be amused by their bickering banter. Laugh at their sharply observed insults toward one another. You'll split your sides at their hilarious routine.

The air-lock hissed aside and a dark, tall man dressed in sombre attire entered the Domek Gościnny. With a smoothly observed movement of his hand, the stranger took from his head a black wide-brimmed trilby and gazed at the couple with eyes as raven as his slicked-back hair. Behind him, on sturdy casters of brass, he pulled a huge oblong travelling trunk the size of which neither of them had seen the like. At least not on Callisto that was. Yet ironically it was the very nature of the moon that made it possible for him to pull such a gargantuan piece of luggage. On Earth normal one gravity it would have taken six men to move the item for certain.

"Welcome to the Domek Gościnny", Steonberg was the first to break the deadlock of silence. "I'm guessing you are off the 18:00 to Mój-głowa and decided to take a rest here this evening, not wishing to go any further for now.

"I simply saw the sign and would like a room"? The traveller's voice was like gravel crunching beneath the tyres of a truck. Sharp, yet thunderous.

"We've plenty of rooms", Steonberg observed, the double entendre not lost on her boyfriend.

"Six sestertii a night for a single. That includes an evening meal".

"Fine".

"Osbourn, help the gentleman with his trunk while I make out the register", Steonberg fussed.

"I may stay longer than one night and I'll take the trunk with me. The name is Crach, Dahrah Crach".

"I'm Kym Steonberg and this is Osbourn Stoff. That's quite an item of luggage you've got there, Obywatel Crach. It looks like you've been all over the solar system with it".

"I'm not Polish there is no need to use the address. Mister will be fine".

"I never saw so many labels. Look, Osbourn, Callisto towns, Martian Cities, some from the Moon, Venus and of course...".

"Stay away from it"! Crach suddenly barked.

"Hold the bus, Mister", Stoff defended his girlfriend.

Crach returned coldly, "I don't like other people messing near my stuff. I have Sindromul Asperger you understand"?

"Well all right then", Stoff was mollified. "I apologise for Kym's curiosity no offence was meant".

"I was only looking at all the travel stamps, Mister Crach", Steonberg never knew when to stop.

"It's been around a good deal and had its share of experiences. Now, the room"?

"Well while you book in would you like me to take it upstairs. I'll be very careful with it" Stoff offered.

"In this gravity, it's no trouble. I'd rather see to myself if you do not mind. Firstly though here is three days rent in advance. One shillin six sestertii. I would like there to be no one in the rooms either side of me and I want to eat in my room on my own".

"Well, we had three rooms free on the second floor. In fact, we only have two floors as it happens. As for tailing up and downstairs with food...".

"Here".

Crach threw another one and six on the desk counter. He was offering double for the inconvenience.

"That's fine, Mister Crach". Steonberg's eyes glittered brighter than the coins. "It will be no trouble to me to provide a world-wise traveller like yourself with that personal bit of service. Who knows you might tell me a little about all your travelling experiences when I bring up your dinner"?

"One never can tell what fate has in store for one, Miss Steonberg", the dark-man returned then and Stoff did not like the way this strange man was looking at his girlfriend. It was a look that was either undressing her or putting her in the oven ready to roast. He could not quite be certain which.

"I'll show you to your room, Crach it's on the second-floor number three. The one with twenty-three on the door obviously".

Crach followed Stoff to the lift. Leaving Steonberg to begin meals for the two of them and the hotel's seven guests. She was just using the economy sized hypo-wave on nine freeze dried lasagne packs when Stoff came back.

"Did he like his room"?

"He didn't complain. Yet by the cut of his jib and the way he splashes the cash around he seems to be pretty well-heeled. I'm not sure I like him. I didn't like the way he looked at you just now. Like some sort of predator. I couldn't decide whether he wanted to tup you or eat you".

Steonberg giggled, "You want me all to yourself. Do you, Mister Stoff".

He nodded, "We're running a hotel, not a knocking shop".

Steonberg snuggled into his arms and the two of them kissed before she suddenly grew quite conspiratorial,

"Did you ask him what he does, what area he's in"?

"I'm not sure that's the sort of topic that one brings up whilst showing a guest to their room, Kym".

"It's exactly the sort of polite icebreaker", she contradicted. "You don't know much about *this* business do you, Osbourn"?

"I just think that a guy like Crach wants some privacy and that's all right by me. If he wants to tell me what he does then fine. But I'm not prying and you shouldn't either. He obviously finds you annoying yet physically attractive and I'm not sure which I'm less happy about".

Steonberg was not listening to every word. She had been busy cleansing the kitchen work surfaces with an antibacterial wipe while Stoff was in full flow. She did catch the end part of it though.

"You think he fancies me you say"? She grinned pleased despite the nature of he whom the conversation was about, "Are you jealous then, Lover"?

"I just think your insatiable curiosity will get you in serious trouble one day, Kym. Be warned, there's something off about Crach so stop pestering him with banal questions".

"This started because I wondered what he does for a living. It's obviously something lucrative and I wondered if he'd consider giving you a job while I ran the hotel myself with the number of guests we get. Who knows he might have a top official post and can take you in at management level".

"Oh look out in the sky"! Stoff suddenly pointed.

Distracted, Steonberg whipped around and her features registered disappointment, "Did I miss a flitter coming in. What did you see"?

"It was a pig with huge wings flying past the hotel", Stoff laughed. "Hey, put down that ladle that's not what it's supposed to be used for. Ow, stop it that hurts".

She took hold of his head then and planted a kiss on the spot where the bruise would appear the following standard day.

"I'm going to put a stop to your weekly visit to the Odeon if you continue in this vein, Kym. You watch one of those conspiracy theory tri-d's and you think the next guest that comes through our airlock a spy or something. Just leave the guy alone, leave him his meal and get out of the room. *Or you might end up locked in that trunk*"!

The instant the words had left his mouth, Stoff knew he had said the wrong thing. The most wrongistic of wrong words in the history of wrongology. If he had lived in Wrong Town and recently won the wrong competition for his contributions to wrongerism and wrongetymolocity he still could not have spoken less wise and unconsidered words than he had done a moment ago.

"Do you think he has a trunk full of bizarre equipment of some kind? Is that what you're suggesting? The sort of equipment one might use to cut up cadavers or some such"?

"I think the contents of a man's trunks are private", Stoff tried to joke and use a pun to distract his girlfriend. It did not work.

"He only had one trunk though didn't he".

"Yes, Dear. He only had the one. Go and take him his lasagne while I serve the other guests in the dining room, Oh and Kym"?

She half turned, "Yes, sweety".

"Keep you cake-hole shut".

Steonberg got into the lift with Crach's tray. In addition to the lasagne were some instant blancmange and a flask of lichen-coff. The flask lid served as a cup and the fluid would keep warm for several hours if he did not desire to drink it all in one sitting.

The doors hissed open to allow her access to the second-floor corridor and rooms leading off it. Steonberg went to 23 and tapping lightly on the door swiped the lock and proceeded inside. After all, it was her hotel. By doing so, however, she almost collided with a half wet half dressed Crach. He had just stepped out of the shower and only hat a towel around his bottom half.

"You let yourself in before I could reply".

"I did not realise you'd just stepped out of the shower, I've brought your dinner".

"Put it on the drawers over there and then come back to me".

There was a sudden heat in his eyes. Those dark eyes that seemed to consume her as he stared, For once in her life Steonberg did not know what to say. She felt strangely manipulated. It was as though she was no longer in full control of her own actions.

Doing as he said she turned to regard him and slowly his hands raised to her arms and took hold of her in a tender grip.

"Look into my eyes, Steonberg", his command dripped shafts of absolute frigidity. "Do not take your attention from anything but them. Lock onto my windows of the soul. Look harder look behind my eyes, see the essence of my quiddity. That's right keep looking. Keep listening to my voice. All that exists are you and I. There is nothing beyond. We are all. Outside of this area we inhabit is nought but void. You are filled up with it. You are consumed by it. It wearies and taxes you. You want to rest now for only in sleep can you feel any opportunity for calmness a chance to repose and let yourself go. You and all your inhibitions, all will fall from you leaving you……..".

Steonberg was suddenly in the corridor once more. She felt wobbly and completely disorientated. How had she got there? Where had she been once she had left room twenty-three? There was a confusing blank that she could not fill in. Feeling like she had wet herself she stumbled to the second-floor communal bathroom and swiped herself in. Steonberg hitched up her salmon coloured dress and pulled down her knickers. They were wet and sticky and the fluid was not urine it was semen. While she had existed in the blankness before the corridor she had allowed someone to have sex with her.

Had Stoff taken advantage of her while she was disorientated? Once she got herself washed and tidied up she would ask him in no uncertain terms. He must never treat her like that again.

She put the knickers down the incinerator shaft and pulled down her skirt. Some clean ones would be in her bedroom drawers, on the ground floor. The instant she got in the lift to go down and confront her boyfriend though a more sinister possibility occurred to her. What if one of the guests had managed to drug her in some nefarious way and then take advantage of her while she was under the effects of a narcotic? By asking Stoff she would alert him to what had happened to her and he would insist on calling the comb-men. The whole fiasco would ruin the hotel's reputation. She could see the report now;

Hotel Gościnny in flunitrazepam based enquiry!

This reporter can exclusively reveal that the Hotel Gościnny in Hoenir is the Rohypnol centre of the Polish sector of Callisto. Flunitrazepam, also known as Rohypnol among other names, is an intermediate-acting benzodiazepine used on some planets to treat severe insomnia and in fewer, early in anaesthesia. Just as with other hypnotics, flunitrazepam should be strictly used only on a short-term basis or by those with chronic insomnia on an occasional basis. Flunitrazepam has been referred to as a date rape drug, the percentage of reported rape cases in which it is reported to be involved is alarmingly on the increase.

Kym Steonberg co-owner of the hotel in Hoenir, not **Whore Corner** as certain members of the gutter press are now calling it was extensively interviewed by me and described her experience in her own hotel blah blah blah…..

Not only would it be bad for business. It would like as not cast a shadow over her relationship with Stoff. The end did not justify the means. Better to put the mysterious episode out of her mind and see how long she had been missing. She dressed once again and hurried back to the ground floor dining room. She not have worried. Stoff was in animated conversation with one of the other guests and travelling sales rep called Kab Geroy and between the two of them were three bottles of lichwine. He had obviously been there for long enough to do the first two bottles. At sight of her, he waved her over to them. Poured her a clean glass and said his speech slightly slurred,

"Here she is my lovely girlfriend who helps me run the hotel. I don't know what I'd do without her, Kab".

"That's great". Geroy responded warmly. He was also merry, "To feel so strongly for one another after eight years. When are you two going to make it official then and contract"?

Steonberg's smile was glassy. If Osbourn had been with Geroy as long as is seemed then someone else in the hotel had raped her. She may have been compliant. She had been under the influence of...*something*, so it was still rape

She had used soft and gentle anti-everything wipe though. The evidence would now no longer be detectable. Surely when Orang-U-Can had created a personal moist cleanser that killed all bacteria, they had also killed the DNA that would harbour it. Someone had taken sexual advantage of her and there were five men and four women in the hotel.

The chief suspects as far as she was concerned though were Stoff and Crach. She would have let Stoff do it for nothing though and she liked doing it with him a great deal. That left the dark man with the curious trunk. Had she left his room whilst she was *out of it*? Then to be taken advantage of whilst under some drugged stupor. Or had Crach drugged her in some way and then instead of her being out of it he was in it? How had he done it though? She could not remember. He had offered her a drink or simply asked her if she wanted to get high. It had been a while since she had taken a cosmic trip with Mister Narcotic. She might have agreed. She might have suspected he was going to *do her*! Had she wanted it? Was she comfortably bored with Stoff and simply fancied a mysterious roll in the hay with the enigmatic if sinister Crach?

She downed the wine, laughed and made merry. Better to forget the forgettable.

##

"Good Day"

"Good day to you, Mister Crach". Steonberg fought down her unease "I have a suggestion to make. Would you mind having your luncheon with me downstairs today? It's nearly ready and if I bring it all the way up to your room it will get cold. I don't think cold luncheon would suit you would it"?

"Oh! I suppose so if it's something that cools quickly. Only for today though. Then back to our usual arrangement".

"Of course", she shuddered at the thought of dinner. Managed to keep the tremor out of her voice as she asked, "Just come around the reception desk then, the kitchen is right behind us".

She held her breath as he passed her, "Please sit in this chair".

There were only two at the small table. He asked quite naturally, "Are you running the place on your own today? Where's Stoff"?

"He takes the buggy into Mój-głowa on Tuesdays, for supplies".

"Buggy"?

"We have an old dust-buggy with a trailer on the back. It doesn't get used much, it's just about clapped out, but we don't have the shillin to replace it just yet. We've only been on Callisto a while so the hotel is still in its infancy".

"So he goes north, even though the nearest stop is in the other direction".

"Guntur Tarrata is only about the same size as Hoenir, not much there. The main wholesale for this area is in Mój-głowa".

"Hmm so it's quiet in Guntur Tarrata is it"?

"Yes. Why do you ask"?

"No reason. I thought I might be able to do a little bit of business there".

It was the opportunity Steonberg had been waiting for, "I see. You never told me what you do, for a living I mean"?

"This soup is very hot, do you think I might have some Lichbread with it"?

"Of course". She brought out a cob, "Here, help yourself".

"This is a nice place you have, Miss Steonberg".

"It will be much nicer once it gets going. I intend to invest in refurbishment as soon as we can afford it".

"It has its pioneer charm already, I don't see there being any rush".

"That's a man's perspective. I had to rant on for weeks to Osbourn just to get a short-wave".

The spoon on its way to Crach's mouth halted and he asked, "You have a radio"?

"Yes. I think it's a good one too. A Ransom and Hitchin MHz 300-Channel Base/Mobile Scanner. Close Call RF. Would you like to listen to Callisto Channel Nine, they're playing...".

"No thank you. I prefer to eat in quiet if you don't mind. It aids the digestion. Not only that but I have a slight headache, I don't think noise would aid it".

"I'll get you two Headzgon", she offered. "If you miss the news I can give you today's download for your pad".

"No. I'm not monitoring any stories at present. In fact, I'm enjoying the seclusion. Don't you find the isolation peaceful"?

"Sometimes I find it the opposite of enjoyable. Our nearest neighbour is three kilometres distant in Hoenir. Nothing interesting ever happens around here to make things intriguing. You'd soon find it boring".

"Why".

"Your trunk. All those place names. You've seen the sights. You get to travel. Is it because of your work? Is your business global, or a private little concern"?

"You've asked me what I do several times, Miss Steonberg. You are obviously desperate to know what I do so I'll tell you. Do you know what books are"?

"Of course I do. It's when you reserve accommodation in a place like this".

"I mean the antique sort".

"You mean the printed writing of the ancients that were stitched together and then bound in covers"?

He nodded, before asking, "And the material the writings were written on".

"Oh! I know this. Give me a second. It had something to do with trees, didn't it? Before they were protected men hunted them and....."..

"They didn't hunt them. They were allowed to cut them down. Like we are allowed to harvest wheat nowadays. The wood was mulched and created in very thin sheets. It was *paper*"!

"Like organic foil"?

He nodded, "Some books are now extremely rare and therefore correspondingly valuable. I am what is known as a Bibliophile".

"Oh! Right".

"You sound crestfallen. Did you imagine I might pursue something far more glamorous than that which I do"?

"There can't be many of those books on Callisto surely"?

"No", he chuckled, "You'd be surprised where they turn up in the solar system. Why on Callisto my sources assure me that there is a first edition of Frankenstein by Mary Shelley, Several Koran and Bibles two sets of Encyclopedia and a first edition of Glimpserama by Major Roxbrough".

He gazed at her then with those intense dark eyes and demanded, "What did you think I was up to on Callisto, Miss Steonberg"?

"Something to do with the mines I guess", she returned carefully. "A mineralogist or maybe engineer of some sort. I thought you had a trunk full of samples to transport back to where ever you came from".

"What I collect is far more interesting. I collect rare volumes in every language man has ever spoken since time began. On Earth, thousands of such copies have survived over the millennia. Those saved by enthusiasts like myself, stored in conditions that do not cause them to moulder or be eaten by pests".

"You don't say"!

"I've travelled to almost every part of the solar system, trading. Buying here, selling there and making a princely sum along the way".

"Have you been to Babylon"?

"The location of that civilisation is now nothing more than radio-active dust. No book could exist there, in fact, all that does thrive there are cockroaches and ants. I did once buy a copy of a book that had belonged to an Eastern Sultana though. Bound in silver and encrusted with natural sapphires, not the synthetic ones created in laboratories. When I finally sold it the profit was enough to keep me travelling for a hundred years. Should I wish to work that long".

"Is that why you're so careful about that trunk"?

Crach flew into a rage, "No I...! NO, Miss Steonberg. Most of the very expensive books are in my vault on Mars. I do have some interesting volumes in the trunk, but if you're thinking of trying to....! Let's discuss something different now. The subject must be boring you if you do not share my passion for the printed word. I think I've had enough luncheon actually. If you'll excuse me"?

"There is the dessert".

"The cob filled me up, I have no further need for food. May I have one of your matches? I'm going outside to smoke".

"Help yourself", Steonberg consented even though she had not enjoyed a cigarette herself for a couple of hours. Crach was like a snake. Fascinating, but deadly with venom to match no doubt.

She cleaned up the table with a med-wipe and then went for her afternoon nap. But slumber avoided her and she found herself illogically wondering if the strange perhaps deadly Crach actually did have books in the trunk. Dare she sneak into his room and see if she could get it open? If she did would dusty old paper volumes spill out? Or something far more sinister? There was not enough time to try it then. He would be back from his smoke. Maybe the next time he was out?

Stoff came back around tea-time and she told him part of their conversation. He was not pleased with his girlfriend's prying.

"You should just leave him alone". He advised. "He obviously doesn't want you jabbering in his ear at every meal time. I have some news anyway. The Beast of Callisto has struck again".

Steonberg's hand went theatrically over her mouth. "Another girl strangled"?

Stoff nodded. "Day before yesterday. In Guntur Tarrata".

"Sweet Callisto"! Steonberg gasped, Nothing ever happens in Guntur Tarrata".

"Well - it has now". Stoff returned with irrefutable logic. "Poor Senia Lofton, she was only eighteen standard years old. It seems her parents are absolutely heartbroken".

"I'm going to check everything on the radio", she decided.

"No need I have all the latest on this memory card, you can download it onto your pad. I hadn't finished telling you either there is more. Another girl is missing from the town. Gone, vanished. A nineteen-year-old name of Lavim Marca".

"That's why I want to listen to the radio, it will be bang up to date. You know I like to hear what is happening all over Callisto, not just down here in the Polish sector"

Stoff chuckled, "You're like an atlas on legs, Kym, all you ever do is get envious over places you have never been and probably never will".

"Geography is educational and does no harm", countered Steonberg as she went into the utility room where the short-wave radio was housed. He followed her as she went to turn it on,

"Crach got his nose out of joint at lunchtime when I mentioned his trunk again", she told him turning her attention back to her boyfriend.

"Why do you possibly want to keep annoying the best paying guest we have in the hotel? Can't you keep your nose out of whatever business he conducts and just give the guy his meals"? Stoff was not pleased by the latest revelation. "Perhaps his natural state is to be annoyed anyway, some people are just like that you know".

"It makes me wonder what he has kept in there"? She put on a mysterious tone to add effect to her words. "He says it's full of books, but maybe it has a different cargo a far more ominous one".

"Books, as in those ancient things the Romans used to print or what not".

"That's his claim. Something about the whole Mister Crach thing does not ring true with me".

"You know what Kym Steonberg one of these days that nosy nature of yours is going to land you or both of us in a pickle of..... well in a pickle anyway".

"Say, Osbourn, aren't the valves on this thing supposed to glow when it warms up"?

"Callisto! Kym, what have you done now. Have you even put the plug in the wall"?

"Of course I have. Well it wasn't out actually, but look for yourself it's in and the silver toggle is up so why isn't it coming on"?

Stoff went over to the set and asked her, "Well move to one side then so I can see what I'm doing. You'll have disconnected one of the tubes and that will be preventing the others from lighting up".

He took each one in turn and gently but firmly pushed them downwards a little into their housings. None of the multi-pins was out of their corresponding female sockets though, so it achieved nothing.

"I can't see anything wrong either Kym and I doubt a capacitor or resistor has failed in the control circuit. Maybe one of the banana plugs to the speakers has fallen out.

"Wouldn't that only make one speaker quiet? Anyway, nothing's lighting up".

"You're right. The only thing for it is to undo the casing and see if anything is wrong with the underside connectors and then I guess the motherboard. Say, Kim, these housing screws are loose. Look I can undo this one with my fingers. Look! There are scratches on the casing too. Just as though someone used, say - a kitchen knife to undo them because they didn't have a screwdriver".

"Well, only you have one of those twenty-tools-in-one, due to your post of head of maintenance in this hotel".

Stoff grinned, "You make caretaker sound like an executive post, Kym".

"You are an executive, Osbourn. To me at least. Hurry up or the news will have finished and we won't get the latest on that girl Marca".

Stoff took the last of the housing screws out with his *Little Wonder Tool* and gasped in surprise and annoyance.

"What's wrong, Dear"?

"Everything, Kym. Look. This radio has been deliberately vandalised. Parts torn out, the micro soldering scratched down to the board, probably with the same knife that the vandal used to get into the cabinet. It's ruined and it was one of the most valuable and useful items we possessed".

"I'm sorry, Osbourn. I only have one suspect too".

"Let me guess, Inspector Steonberg, the man with the trunk is also a radio murderer"?

Steonberg did not laugh though, she told him instead of the mention of the short-wave at lunch and the strange way Crach had reacted to its existence in the hotel. Ending,

"There is something not altogether right about, Crach. Little things that seem a little bit bizarre are beginning to add up to a rather disquieting picture overall".

She was tempted to tell him of her assault. In that case, though, she could not remember enough to make a positive accusation. There was no point horrifying her boyfriend unnecessarily. Stoff was still gazing down into his beloved radio, musing aloud,

"I wonder if the *Austrian Kid* in Mój-głowa could fix this for less than it would cost to buy a whole new rig? They say there's nothing he can't do with radio sets and the like. It would be a shame to get rid of this old beauty, I love the cabinet".

"The nerve of him, to sneak past me somehow and get in here. Here where he has never been invited".

The young couple had a habit of conducting two conversations at once. Of course, neither of them was actually conversing just thinking aloud.

"Why would anyone want to ruin a lovely set like this? How does someone like that think"?

"Well, I'm not running up and down the floors to deliver meals to, Mister oh so special, any more. He can come down to the dining room like everyone else".

"I was going to listen to the concert tonight as well. Brahms Third Symphony played by the Igaluk Symphony Orchestra. I was looking forward to that".

"I should just out and ask him. That's the only way, let me have a look in your trunk or I'll call the comb-men".

"And I'm going to miss, 'McArthur and Askey' tomorrow and they always make me chuckle with that catchphrase, 'Shut the sodding door'. Oh! 'Donald and his Duck' is on at the weekend. I wonder if the Austrian Kid can do a rush job for me".

"Osbourn, why don't you confront Crach and ask him about the radio? Threaten him with the comb-men unless he pays for the short-wave to be fixed".

"Because, Dear, we don't have a shred of evidence do we"?

"I know it's him, female intuition".

"Oh, yes that would go down well with the Constabulary Of Metropolitan Bureau [comb]. 'You see Inspector I don't need any hard evidence or even soft evidence for that matter because I have the word of my girlfriend that female intuition considers him guilty'! 'Right then, Mister Stoff, that will be good enough for my Chief, take him away and give him damned good thrashing lads. No, wait a minute, female intuition was it? Right take him away and hang him. String the koofer up, first offence, hang some sense into him'. I can see it now".

Steonberg sniffed, "When you're out of your depth Osbourn, you always resort to silliness don't you".

"Just letting off a bit of steam, my Dear, to relive the tension we don't want the engines to blow do we"?

"If you won't ask Crach to open that trunk and prove he really is a book dealer and not the Callisto Beast – I will do it myself".

"I don't actually know what is going on in that grey maze between your ears, Kym but your mind does not work like mine. You only have a suspicion. You also have no authority over Crach. If he tells you to *sod off*, then you will look pretty dumb won't you"?

"All right, Osbourn, in the morning I'll ping Inspector Staenhause at the Mój-głowa station. My pad can just about reach that far on the infra-web. I'll present him with the simple facts and let him decide whether he wants to come and interview Crach".

"I can live with that, Kym. Well, the radio's busted, fancy an early night"?

##

Curiosity is an attribute with two qualities. It can lead to a healthy pursuit of knowledge or it can lead to danger. It can be the catalyst of understanding or it can be a terrible agitation. To succumb to it in the wrong way can lead to disaster. Look what it did to the proverbial cat?

"Do you think he's up yet"?

"How should I know, I don't have supersonic hearing do I. We're two floors away from him remember".

"Right then", she decided, "I'll take his breakfast up".

"I'm not sure that's a good idea".

"He paid for the arrangement and I'll ask him about the radio and judge his reaction".

"I thought you were going to ping Staenhause"?

"Oh, I will if I'm not satisfied with Crach's answers. We're out a good radio and I want to know who will pay for its repair".

"Maybe I should come with you".

"That could actually lead to violence worst case scenario. No, Osbourn, I'll go and talk to him from the jamb".

Steonberg heated some oats in milk. Added juice, a flask of lichen-coff and two rounds of toast and after covering them placed them on her tray. Then with a purposeful tread that belied her timorousness, she made for the lift. While it hummed mechanically upward she kept bunching her free had over and again into a determined fist.

The doors hissed open and down the corridor she went, pausing only to dim the lighting with the dimmerswitch. Not that any useful illumination came through each window at either end of the corridor. The sky was always black on Callisto. She finally reached room 23 and hammered on it with her brave little fist. With the force of it, she actually pushed it opened. The door had been ever so slightly ajar. In anticipation of her arrival no doubt.

Crach was seated in the wicker chair that was the bedroom's only piece of furniture that allowed him to be seated. He was reading one of his so-called antique pieces, made from wood-mulch and bound with something that looked like dull neoplas but probably also came from a tree. Momentarily distracted from her purpose, she asked as she set the tray down,

"Is that a book, Mister Crach".

"You can call me Dahrah, Kym. Yes, it is do you want to hold it"?

As he held it out she could see he was wearing curious white gloves of fine linen.

"Are they to protect the book"?

He nodded, "They will be too big for your little hands, but I would be grateful if you put them on. You see there is acid in our sweat and it will damage the pages given enough time".

He peeled them off after placing the book on the bed. A bed already made up, he was tidy at least, was Crach. She took them from him and placed her own pudgy little hands inside the gloves. It surprised her that they were cool to her touch. Had Crach no heat in him?

Gingerly she picked up the collection of wood mulch and examined the cover. There was a font on it, etched into it in silver, never to be erased, cut or pasted. How permanent that was. The book could never be abridged, expanded, altered in any way. No mistake within it could ever be corrected. No statement that proved inaccurate by the passage of time could be updated. How did the ancients ever keep accurate records when nothing could be changed once it had been marked on this strange flimsy material called paper.

No wonder the Roman Empire had been destroyed by Billy the Kid and Wild Buffalo West. Their mistakes were permanent immutable and inflexible. It had happened more than once in ancient times. Had not the terrible reviews of I'm Camp by Adolf Hitler began to spell the end for the Nazi's of ancient Eurosia. It had been a simple illiterate farmer called Rasputin who had finally burned the book and caused Hitler to hang himself at the Nuremberg Literary Society. Then there was the infamous case in the twenty-third century when the writer Scene

Beanniss had written the expose of the affair of the Lady of Chatterley entitled 'D.H. Lawrence of Arabia'. He had faced the firing squad when it turned out after the investigation that Scene Beanniss had based the story on his own refused attempts to have an affair with the lady. She subsequently had successfully sued him for libel and won a capital punishment for the author and all the books burned.

Steonberg read the black marked words on the first leaf of the book, 'Remember Next Week by someone called Major Roxbrough' he was remembered well enough, but in history, not next week. She bet he wished he could come back from death and amend his title.

She heard the gravelly tones of Crach then,

"Look at the little black words, Steonberg", his command dripped shafts of absolute frigidity once again. "Do not take your attention from anything but them. Lock onto the words with all your concentration. Look harder. See how they begin to dance like tiny ebon figures, see the essence of the writer's quiddity. That's right keep looking. Keep listening to my voice. All that exists are you and I. There is nothing beyond. We are all. Outside of this area, we inhabit there is nought but void. You are filled up with it. You are consumed by it. It wearies and taxes you. You want to rest now for only in sleep can you feel any opportunity for calmness a chance to repose and let yourself go. You and all your inhibitions, all will fall from you leaving you……..".

Steonberg was suddenly back in the corridor. This time there was an unpleasant taste in her mouth. A slightly salty, slimy taste. A taste she was disgusted to recognise. For once in their sexual past. Osbourn had not kept his promise to pull away from her oral pleasuring if he felt himself beginning to climax. She had punched him where it hurt the most for breaking that promise. Now that familiar piquancy was once again in her mouth. Someone had raped it!

Retching she rushed for the bathroom and tried to hurl down the pan. All she managed though was a small dribble of congealed phlegm and semen. Horrified she realised she must have swallowed the rest. It had to be Crach, that villainous misbegotten imperfection was a rapist and a murderer. She rinsed her mouth out several times with Yummifect an oral mouthwash from Orang-U-Can. Now she was determined to ping Staenhause.

She ran down the stairs and found Stoff.

"I'm going to ping the comb-men", she told rather than asked him. "He wrecked the radio and I think he's got the missing girl's body in that trunk. There is only one sensible way to find out and that's with the law involved".

Stoff while shocked, saw the sense of at least consulting the Inspector so he nodded gravely.

Inspector Staenhause was as tall as a tree and with a body that might have been a trunk. His voice was impressively baritone of timber. He wore the unofficial uniform of a detective. Long raincoat, dark trilby the cigarette dangling idly out of the corner of his mouth. Inside that coat, he also had a needle gun nestling against his ribs. With a thunderous tread of his booted feet, he stomped purposefully down the corridor to the door marked 23.

"This is the right room"?

"Yes Inspector, the room that contains the trunk and your suspect".

Staenhause raised a quizzical eyebrow wondering when Crach had become *his* suspect.

"A big trunk", Steonberg repeated, "Big enough to fit a dead body inside"!

The Inspector hammered purposefully on the door. With a fist the size that he possessed, it was a commotion cacophonous enough to raise the very dead.

"What is it"? An angry voice demanded from behind the neoplas.

"Open up, Mister. Comb-man".

There were footsteps and then a contrite Crach asked in a mollified tone, "What is the matter, Officer"?

"Your names Crach"? Staenhause demanded in staccato fashion.

"Yes", came the tacit response.

"When were you in Gunter Tarrata last"? Staenhause's style was direct and accusatory.

"I passed through it on the train journey to here".

"There's the trunk. Look at the size of it, Inspector". Steonberg interrupted

Staenhause abruptly pushed past Crach to examine the item of luggage in question.

"Now just a minute, Officer you might be able to barge into a hotel room that belongs to this nosey woman here. But messing with my private things is illegal unless you've got a search warrant".

"You're familiar with legal proceedings are you, Crach and it's not officer it's inspector".

"I'm a law-abiding citizen of Callisto and other worlds, In-spec-tor and I know my rights that's all".

Very well, Crach. You can cooperate and let me have the combination of those three locks or we can drag you and the trunk down to the station and you can sit in a cell while I get a search warrant. The choice is yours. I'm not bothered which I get paid by the hour".

A look of cold fury appeared on Crach's face. Yet even then, he resisted, "You'll take me down to the station. What charge are you arresting me on then, Inspector"?

"Assaulting a comb-man in pursuit of his duty".

"I've not laid a finger on you, that's an outright lie"!

Staenhause grinned, "No but you will when I start beating on your sorry ass. Now undo those padlocks before it all gets a bit ugly and you end up with a few lumps".

Crach walked slowly toward the trunk and asked, "You'll see nothing but rare paper books inside. I ask you to stay by the doorway so as not to get any foreign material on them, they are very delicate and very very old".

"Foreign material"? The Inspector mused.

"Tobacco smoke, perspiration, saliva all contain harmful chemicals to the paper. If I cooperate, then I ask you to reciprocate please".

Steonberg was shocked. She had never witnessed such politeness from Crach before.

In a softer tone, the comb-man nodded and said, "I can see well enough form here, so quit stalling and open the damn thing".

The duo in the doorway waited while Crach turned nine tiny wheels releasing three padlocks with combinations. Then as he opened the trunk he said to Steonberg,

"I'll sue you for this. For defamation of character. I will not be treated like a scuffer, a guy who doesn't play it straight and gets away with it".

The two of them craned their necks to peer over the lip of the trunk and saw.... Books!!

Neat rows of books on two shelves spines outermost, covered in cling film sheeting. The plastic covering caught the room's overhead LED's and sparkled their defiance at the disbelieving duo.

"Would you do me a personal favour now, Inspector", Crach growled as he slammed the lid of the trunk back in place.

"What is it". Staenhause asked woodenly.

Would you get the koof out of my room"?

##

The train ground to a halt with a hiss of steam that drifted immediately upward through the thin atmosphere. It was dark of course, but the station platforms provided travellers with little pools of illumination. Cones of brilliance in a contrasting picture of the Jovian moon. Kym had her small outdoor mask over her nose and mouth. Her goggles over her eyes. That was all she needed since the terraforming had been underway. No longer did everyone travel everywhere under tubes, or if going outside in spacesuits. Yet the mask subsidised what meagre oxygen the still thin coating of air provided.

Kym had an address and it was not far from the station. Nowhere on Callisto was far from the railway station. The network connected every town to every other, few people other than those who made their living transporting produce and other goods used moon-buggies. Due to the ravaged nature of the moon, the most pitted in the solar-system moving from one place to another was a slow and painstaking process. In short, the train was faster. Huge trails of goods vehicles did most of the heavy haulage for the mines and a fine service they provided. On Callisto the Iron Horse was king.

Kym had come to Guntur Tarrata to pay her respects to the parents of Senia Lofton, she was only eighteen standard years old. It seemed her parents were absolutely heartbroken Senia Lofton, had only been eighteen standard years of age. Even so, a conversation with them might prove useful. It might provide her with clues. She had their address and the distance was well within the capacity of her mask, there and back that was. After an uncomfortable walk beneath the cold stars, thankful for the thermal quality of her poncho and hood. She arrived at the property and knocked on the airlock door.

"Who is that", the voice was metallic in the tinny speaker beside the aperture

"Kym Steonberg", she removed her mask momentarily to reply.

"Just one minute Kym" in the area of the Polish sector everyone knew everyone else. The metallic clunk of the electronically controlled lock released and Kym turned the lever to the release position. Stepping gratefully inside. She had not been in the thin atmosphere of the outside of the planet for quite some time. It was still an unsettling experience. A tall pale woman was in the hallway to greet her. At her shoulder just behind, her slim husband. Neither of them looked as though they were enjoying time on Callisto recently, which was only to be expected.

"My most sincere commiserations for your loss", Kym began. "I have no possible conception of how you feel right now, I am very sorry".

"Gracious though", the woman observed, "Please come into the lounge we will have some beverage".

Kym waited respectfully while the woman whose name was Aimba pored some lichen-tea. She nodded to Drakoma her husband, who accepted the tacit greeting in the spirit in which it was offered.

"I came to do more than offer my condolences", Kym finally said whilst sipping her tea.   "Painful as it might be I came to ask you some questions about Senia's murder.

"Are you in the Comb Service now, Kym"? Aimba responded to that.

"I don't believe the comb-men are getting far with their investigations", Kym told her. "After all do we not have five victims of the Beast of Callisto? Another girl is also missing".

"True", Drakoma agreed with some venom. First Numi-Torum, then Orestheus, Lycaon, Lodur and now Guntur Tarrata".

"And has anything struck you about that progress",? Kym asked.

"What do you mean"? Aimba asked.

"The towns are in an order as if someone was following the Great Southern train line. Travelling from one town to another in search of his next victim. Now I believe I might know where the Beast is"!

"Tell me and I will go and kill him", Drakoma demanded.

"I'm sorry, Dear Friend but I only have deep suspicion on my part. Not enough to be certain without a doubt. What I need to do in order to discern some additional piece of evidence that creates that certainty is to ask you some questions about Senia".

"What do you want to know"? Aimba asked.

"Well, firstly what I find hard to believe is that in all the unfortunate happenstance to each girl there was no DNA to identify the killer. I'm sure you will have asked the comb-men just such a question, what did they reply".

"They believe the killer wore gloves of course and as for fibre transfer - they identified a second set of clothing identical to that worn at the other murders but none that have picked anyone out in the past. They believe the killer changes into the clothes to kill and then out of them as soon as he is away".

"That would explain no DNA transfer onto poor Senia's throat it there was none the killer might have access to a supply of latex. I wonder why the comb-men did not pursue that line of enquiry".

"Latex"? Aimba echoed

"Some tiny shreds would have been left behind in the struggle".

"Oh! I see what you mean. No, the vile demented creature used gloves but they were not latex".

"Some sort of pseudo-leather then".

"No, it seems the tiny fibres found on poor Senia's throat were of lint".

The floor seemed to suddenly disappear beneath Kym's feet. She felt weightless as though gravity no longer tugged even gently at her body. She also felt the absolute zero temperature of the vacuum of space. Finally, she managed,

"Was it white lint"?

"That's right they presumed the Beast was going to wrap Senia up as they used to in very ancient times. Finding it too much trouble he subsequently abandoned the task".

"They came to that bizarre conclusion when the lint was found on Senia's throat. Why not the more logical one that the beast wore lint gloves".

"I suppose because no one wears lint gloves. They would not serve the normal healthy purpose - that of warmth. Callisto's slim atmosphere would soon take the heat from one's hand if all that bedecked them were gloves of lint".

Drakoma added, "The only people who actually use lint gloves are those who don't want to transfer their sweat onto items of antiquity. Like numerologists and timbrologists".

"And bibliophile", Kym muttered beneath her breath. "She asked the grieving couple, "What of the poor nineteen-year-old, Lavim Marca? Has anything been found of her"?

"Nothing, the comb-men are not even certain it is the work of the same man. The beast has never abducted anyone before".

"I would tend to believe rather that he was interrupted in his vile activities and had to make haste his departure with the body in tow".

"Body. You don't believe she was abducted then"?

Kym shook her head, "She was either disposed of in some way or crated and transported with the Beast himself. We both know there are plenty of places to dispose of a body on this crater strewn moon, so the poor girl now lies at the bottom of one such".

"It seems the crazed and hateful savage will get away with it again and we wait for another victim to surface", Drakoma observed defeatedly.

"Perhaps not. If the body of the poor Marca girl was transported for a while and the Beast still uses the container, he might not have thought of wet-wiping all the DNA transfer from its surfaces. A simple drug-store kit would be enough to hang him".

Drakoma rose fluidly from his seat and knelt down disconcertingly in front of Kym. He put his hands on her pudgy shoulders. "We have answered your questions, Kym. Painful as they were to do so. Now it's time for you to tell me what you know. Is the Beast, or the man you suspect as being the Beast in your hotel this very day.? Yes or no"?

"I have scant evidence", she protested.

Drakoma felt so passionately though that he actually shook her by the shoulders he gripped, "Tell me"!

"I only have suspicions. I can prove nothing and even if I could then I would go to Staenhause with them. We cannot take the law into our own hands. The resultant punishment would be yet another victory for the Beast of Callisto".

"Kym! Tell us what you know"? Aimba asked much more quietly than her long-term partner.

"Very well. The day after poor Senia was killed and the Marca girl went missing we had a new arrival at the hotel. He had dark clothing and hat as though he desired to slip unnoticed through a crowd. Yet he professed after careful questioning to be an antique dealer. He would not sit with our other guests for dinner rather asked to have his meals brought to his room. He was curt to the point of rudeness but not without coins. So Osbourn chose to ignore his sharp manner. Then I mentioned our radio to him and he reacted most strangely and the next day we found it vandalised. As though he wanted to cut the hotel off from the outside moon. These things would have been strange on their own but for two other matters which add to my unease about him".

"And what might they be"?

"He had with him a huge chest shaped travel trunk. Large enough to hold a body. The area of his collection was the ancient wood-mulch books, the method of recording before calculators, mobile telephones and now the pads we all take for granted every day. When he showed me one he bid me wear his lint gloves so as to not contaminate the mulch with my skin or perspiration"

"It's him"! Drakoma was convinced. "Take me to him, Kym and give me ten minutes alone with him".

"Kill him and you'll hang", Kym observed, Crazy as that sounds it is still the law, taking of life is punishable by death no matter what the provocation happens to be. You know that. On the other hand, if you beat him you'll do a lengthy term of enforced retribution service in one of the mines for GBH [grievous bodily-harm]. Would ten minutes of bruising your fists be worth it, Friend"?

"You presume that I'm going to get caught by the ever incompetent comb-men", Drakoma decided. "As you said, Kym. He has a huge trunk and there are thousands of craters on Callisto. Some of them are very deep indeed".

"You would descend to his level and destroy a human life"? Kym demanded of him.

"I would see justice done and execute my daughter's murder". Drakoma returned. "Please wait for me until I get my needle gun".

Throughout the exchange, Aimba had said nothing. Once Drakoma had hurried from the room Kym asked her,

"Do you approve of what your partner plans? Could you live with your guilt for the rest of your life Aimba"?

"I would embrace the justice of it and celebrate it", Returned Aimba frostily.

Drakoma returned presently and Kym asked of him, "Please assure me that you will not lay a finger on him until the DNA kit confirms that the Marca girl was definitely in the trunk at one time. Otherwise what we have is not enough to kill a man"?

Drakoma nodded grimly. He pulled a mask and goggles from his pocket, "Come we must hurry the drug store in Tarrata Guntur closes early today".

Feeling as though she had lost an element of control of the sequence of events, Kym followed the grieving man to the door. He bid his partner a tearful farewell and the strange duo sprinted out into the night. The drug store was only two streets away. Guntur Tarrata only possessed three anyway. The rain station was on the edge of the last of them. They had the kit courtesy of Drakoma's thumb and were on the platform with five minutes to spare.

"Don't do anything to threaten your own future will you"? Kym had a chance to ask through her mask as they were standing on the edge of the platform.

"Whatever happens the Beast tried to harm me firstly all right? It was self-defence".

"And if it wasn't"?

"It was".

"You'd put me in that position"?

"You were Senia's friend"?

"Of course, you know that it was so"?

"Then you do it for her, for the memory of Senia".

Kym whined, "That's not fair of you, Drakoma".

"Just as the foul creature the press have named the beast was unfair when he strangled the life out of a beautiful young woman".

Kym thought back to her two periods of blackout. Her inexplicable amnesia that led to being sexually violated twice and decided.

"You're right. If he's guilty he dies and you can have the privilege of being his executioner".

No further talk was possible for the whistle that proceeded the noise of the great iron train steaming its way into the platform. It was half empty the hour was 18:10 the commuters of various sorts had been on the earlier express. So they took a double seat and barely exchanged two words on the way back to Hoenir. As they disembarked at the sleepy little village, the long-legged Drakoma made to rush to the hotel, but Kym cried,

"Slow down Drakoma. My little legs can't keep up with your ground eating strides. Anyway, you don't want to get to confront our suspect all hot and bothered and looking like you want trouble do you".

"Oh, come on", he returned unreasonably, "My heart quickens at the thought of retribution and vengeance".

'Dramatic but none the less true', Kym thought to herself but refused to trot to keep up with her friend's father.

When they reached the front of the hotel he had to wait for her to make up the gap and key in the code to the airlock's lock before he could spill into the reception. Stoff was behind the desk,

"Kym! Where have you been. Ah, hello Mister Lofton. Can I offer you my sympathy for your loss"?

"Which room is he in", Drakoma demanded impatiently and somewhat rudely.

"Kym"! Stoff began, "What have you been up to"?

"I've merely told Drakoma of my suspicions and learned a new piece of evidence that also points to his guilt. White lint found on Siena's throat. Crach has some white gloves, he wore them for touching his books. Even loaned them to me to do the same. We just want to question him further.

"Well he's gone", the news shocked the couple. "He left this afternoon, booked out and went for a train".

"He obviously realised yo was closing in on hi", Drakoma noted to Kym. "Which train did he take Osbourn"?

"I never asked him. What do you intend to do? You're not a comb-man. If you have some new evidence take it to Staenhause".

"While the Beast get farther and farther away? No! I'm going after him, what time did he leave? I can check at the station and find out which train he got on".

"Kym"? Stoff asked with menace, you don't intend to go with him do you"?

Kym stuck out her lower lip in defiance of her boyfriend and confessed, "I want to see this thing played out to the end. I can't explain everything, Osbourn, but it's become important to me".

"While I continue to look after the guests on my own"?

"Thank you".

"It wasn't a statement, Kym. It was a question", Stoff was getting understandably annoyed.

"In that case, my answer is – yes, please. Now tell us if you know, what time did Crach leave the hotel"?

"About 14:30 I think. Give or take".

"Osbourn, let me do this, please?!, she asked. Drakoma was already making for the door.

"If it's so important then go and be careful", he finally conceded.

She hurried after the grieving father. "Drakoma, we're a team, wait for me"?

"Well hurry up then", the older man fumed.

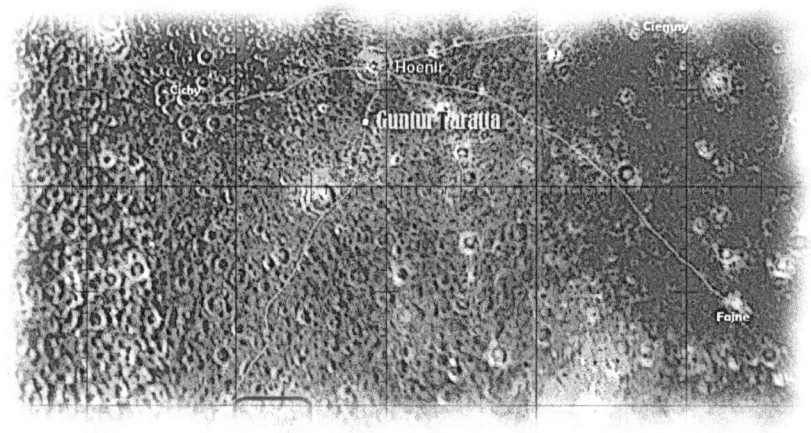

"When we get to the station there's no way of knowing which train the Beast was on if there were several in and around that time", she objected.

"I have a way around that", he smiled grimly, "Now hurry up".

Once they reached the station they quickly consulted the local map and rail-network from Hoenir. Crach could have jumped on one of four trains. Doubling back to Guntur Tarrata, cutting south-easterly to Fajne, North-easterly to Ciemny or west to Cichy.

They looked at the timetables next. At the train destinations for around 14:45. There were two the 15:02 to Ciemny and the 15:15 to Cichy.

"There's no way of telling which train he picked", Kym moaned through her mask. "We could end up going in totally the wrong direction".

"Come we with while we get the next train ticket to one of them", Drakoma sounded confident.

"But which one"? She objected.

"You'll see".

They went to the ticket office and stood in front of the glass counter, "Where to sir", the male-configured Android asked Drakoma who was standing foremost".

"Can you tell me if we can still get trains to both Ciemny and Cichy"? He asked.

From memory, the Android returned smoothly, "The next train to Cemny is the 19:23, arriving 19:20, it is on time. The next train to Cichy is the 19:37 arriving 19:34 it is on time. Which do you wish to go to, Sir"?

This afternoon a tall man dressed in dark clothes and hat got on a train. He was pulling along with him a rather large trunk, I would like tickets for the same destination as him".

"The android regarded then with an unblinking stare, noting, "That is a most unusual request, Sir. Why would I give you that information, when you might be planning to do the earlier traveller injury"?

"He's my Uncle", Kym said, "He asked us to follow him on a later train when I wasn't ready to leave the hotel. Just tell us where he went please, Albert"?

"I'm very sorry, Miss Steonberg, but I cannot discern your intent toward the man. I'm afraid...".

"Albert is it"? Drakoma cut in.

"That is my designation, Sir".

"And you're a what a grade three"?

"I am a grade two, Sir. I am yet able to...".

"How would you like to receive modifications that brought you up to the specification of a grade three then Albert"?

"I would like that very much, Sir. However on my pay grade, it would take me...".

"Just tell me how much the parts are, Albert"?

"I believe the retro-fittable upgrade kit would be four shillin and ten sestertii, Sir ".

"Tell me which train the man with the trunk was on and I will give you five shillin right now. You can become a grade three".

"The man with the trunk was on the train to Ciemny, Sir", Albert had considered the proposal and found it preferable in a millisecond, his hand had come out at the same instant.

"Two tickets to Ciemny, please, Ticket-master"? Drakoma asked, dropping six shillin into the Androids hand. For his change he received only two sestertii.

"Is it wise to carry such a vast sum about your person, Drakoma"? Kim asked. By way of answer, the older man smiled and replied,

"It comes in useful at times to have a bit of coin in hand".

"It will take me three months to pay you back for...".

"Nonsense, the decision and bribe were all my doing and I don't begrudge you a rail ticket".

"Then let me buy you tea from the buffet car, once we're aboard"? Kim asked, "It's the least I can do".

"All right. If it will make you feel better and look here's our train".

The huge metal beast of iron and plastics thundered into the station belching steam like an angry cornered predator. Drakoma opened a carriage door the instant it came to a halt. No one seemed to be getting off and they were the only two embarking, so it pulled it on time. This phenomenon was not unique to Hoenir station. It was said that one could set their wrist-chrono by the train times, so efficient was the service.

Kym led Drakoma to the buffet car and they enjoyed Labeef sandwiches and lichen-coff while the train tore over the surface of the moon. The genetic combination of lamb and beef created a wonderful full flavoured meat that could be enjoyed in a multitude of ways.

Once back in their compartment Drakoma began to talk about Senia. Kym let him, letting him get his sadness out of his system. He must have read her mind as he confessed to her.

"Thank you for being so kind and supportive today. Kym. I feel the sorrow begin to drain from me as time passes. I don't want to feel sorry for myself. That would be indulgent. What remains in my heart now though is a hard jet-stone of cool fury. If we catch the Beast on a lie, I will kill him and rely on you to lie to save me from the gallows".

"I've already promised you I will. I won't go back on my word Drakoma, have no fear".

"We must decide where to start looking once we reach Ciemny"? He proposed.

"It is no larger than Hoenir, so there can only be one logical place unless he lives there which I doubt".

"The hotel. Do you know the name of the place"?

Kym nodded, "It's called the Fajny Ziemniak. I know the proprietor vaguely from S.W. transmissions".

"The Nice Potato", Drakoma smiled, "What brilliant imaginations these Poles have".

"I don't know", Kym chuckled, "I rather like potatoes. Mashed with butter, or scalloped".

"In historical times the ancients cut them into oblong boxes, fried them in sunflower oil and served them with fish", Drakoma demonstrated his historical knowledge.

"They sound like the fries you get at Stu4gutz, those slim things they serve with burgers".

"These were much thicker and more succulent in the middle. You should try doing them that way at the hotel".

"It's worth thinking about. Ah, the train is slowing. Let's go to the doors".

Affixing masks and goggles they waited for the train to jerk to a halt and disembarked. Just like Hoenir they were the only people to be abroad at that hour. Because it was perpetually night-time on Callisto people tended to get in from work and stay in for the night. In the cities in the German Sector, they had the solar web to amuse themselves with and all the entertainment it provided. In the backwater towns of the Hoenir area, it was e-write on pads and shortwave radio. This led to the rise of other pastimes; numismatics, timbrology, writing and cards. Neighbours might visit one another in their homes never venturing out of their own street, however. This was the perfect killing ground for the Beast of Callisto. Practically deserted streets, those who ventured abroad masked without it drawing any suspicion and the odd young girl rushing to a friend's. It was too easy for he of the diseased and insane mind.

"Have you any idea which way the hotel is", Drakoma demonstrated his provincialism.

"East over that way", Kym knew without orientating herself by the stars. "I've visited once several years ago. I know for a fact that it has changed hands since though and I've not met the new owners. We go further north for supplies into the city at Mój-głowa".

"Then it will be quite the adventure for both of us", he offered Kym his hand. She knowing he was probably suffering from the daughter-figure syndrome, placed it in his without hesitation. "We are advised not to let them know of our true identity", he added.

"I see your purpose in that", She agreed, "If you decide who we are I will play along with it once we are at reception. No here is the Fajny Ziemniak".

Pressing for admission to enter the hotel airlock - a voice asked who was without.

"Pan Eślicz and his córka – Ziładzi, travelling through the Polish Sector for sightseeing, do you have two singles Please".

The inner lock clunked back and they entered the reception hall. Removing his mask and goggles Drakoma went to the desk. A pleasant looking young man was waiting to greet them,

"We can book you in, Sir, as long as you do not want the rooms adjourning, we are quite busy at present. Welcome to the Fajny Ziemniak".

"Thank you. I will scrawl for both of us if that is all right".

"The young man nodded turned the pad and stylus over to Drakoma. Undoing two buttons on her blouse Kym went over to him careful to dip slightly allowing him a sight of her generous decollete.

"Tell me, Young Sir, what are the sights worth seeing in this region"?

While the inexperienced and callow youth spent several moments talking to her breasts, Drakoma flipped the pad back a page and learned what he sought. Then he returned it to its previous position.

"I'll pay for the first night and meal now". Drakoma then told the young gentleman who reluctantly put his eyes back into his head and took one shillin and eight sestertii from him.

"The restaurant closes at 22;15 so you would be advised to eat before you unpack. Are your cases in some sort of buggy outside".

Blanders is following on with them on a later train", Drakoma lies smoothly, "Which way to the restaurant then please".

The young man showed them through and as Kym passed the desk her hand whisked over the edge and she hastily slipped a swipe card between the mounds that had distracted the young man so.

They were allowed to dine together even though Drakoma would be on the second floor and Kym on the first. The instant they were seated their order was taken by an Android being urged to get dinner over with by a human cook no doubt. Once they were sipping their drinks, Drakoma asked urgently in a lowered voice.

"Do you see Pan Widmo".

"Mister Spectre"! Kym translated from the Polish, "Really"

"Already dined"?

"Or had his meal delivered to his room for extra coinage, as was the case at our hotel".

"Listen then this is the plan. We go to our respective rooms and wait till all is quiet. Then you come to me. I am in 210. We go to room 23 and pay, Mister Widmo a little visit. When I got the DNA kit form the drug store I also bought two pairs of latex gloves, so we will leave nothing for a subsequent investigation to find".

"And how were you planning to get into Crach's room"?

"I'm going to sneak down to reception and pilfer a cleaner's passkey, once the place is all to their beds".

"No need", Kym was pleased with herself, "I already have one concealed in a place the young man found most fascinating".

"You did rather inflame his young hormonal balance somewhat", Drakoma chuckled, "But it got us all we require so thank you for letting him gobble you up with his eyes".

They finished their meal and Drakoma gave Kym the swipe card for her own room. They agreed to meet in 210 at 01:00. Kym went to her own single which was 121. Once inside she decided to freshen up. Using the complimentary toiletries pack she bathed, cleaned her teeth and put on fresh deodorizer and then lay patiently on the bed to patiently wait of two-and-a-half hours to pass. She could hear the sound of other guests retiring after a cocktail in the bar. Like most good Calliston however, they knew when to quit and by 01:00 it was as silent as the grave in the Fajny Ziemniak. Kym slipped out of the door, using the back stairs to reach the second floor. Drakoma was already outside his own waiting for her but impatiently. He already had his latex gloves on. So as she hurried after him, she slipped on her own with some difficulty. For though powdered, her palms were sweaty with a combination of nervousness and grim anticipation.

They reached the door of room 23. How like a serial killer to observe a ritual of always selecting the same room number. Another piece of evidence building up against Crach. Drakoma swiped the card and it softly clunked open. Then everything happened in the space of two seconds before Kym could comment. Drakoma slipped through the neoplas doorway and drawing a needle-gun with a single fluid movement shot the sleeping figure on the bed in the neck.

"What have you done"?! She hissed with alarm.

"Relax", his answering grin was vulpine, "The dart was a level one, he'll be out for a few minutes nothing more. Now, is this him"?

Kym looked down at the drugged features of her double rapist and shuddered a nod.

"Help turn him over and then tie-wrap his ankles together while I attend to his wrists".

"You were quite the consumer in the drug store weren't you"?

The two of them secured the Beast of Callisto with nylon wraps that no man had the strength to break. Drakoma then tied a kerchief over a pair of trollies that he'd stuffed into the supine Crach's mouth. He could neither move or call out. He was effectively at their mercy. Drakoma went to the digitally controlled lights and turned them to full illumination. He then whispered to Kym,

"Now for a proper look in this drań' trunk".

Of course, it was locked with three combination-wheeled padlocks. To Kym's consisted surprise the older man had planned for that contingency too. From yet another pocket of his boho jacket, he pulled forth a tiny plastic bottle. Even with latex gloves to protect his hands he carefully snapped the seal on the pipette-shaped top of it and then let three drops of the liquid inside drip onto the shanks of the locks.

"Chemical grade acid", Kym mouthed, "The sort you can only buy from a chemist".

The first shank fizzed to nothing and fell undone. The second edge one soon followed suit. The one at the centre which was twice the mass required another three drops of the H_2SO_4 before the steel also fizzled away completely dissolved.

"Would you like the honours"? Drakoma enquired graciously. Kym nodded thinking she deserved to see what the rows of books could reveal. She lifted the very heavy trunk lid and carefully let it swing to its most open position. Inside were rows of books just as before. Nothing could be behind them, for the perspective showed they were at the base of the trunk with nothing above them.

"There may be further clues within one of these tomes", she told her co-conspirator in the abduction and other crimes. Reaching down her hand passed through them, they were not of actuality!!.

"What"? Was all she managed.

Drakoma bent closer and his gloved hands felt around the edges of the trunk until he smiled and threw a tiny hidden switch.

What happened then caused Kym to stuff her fingers into her mouth in order to stifle a scream of pure horror. For Drakoma had turned off the holographic projection of books. An image designed to give the impression of perspective, showing the books deeply within the base of the trunk. Once that image was no longer there, the decomposing corpse of Lavim Marca was revealed. It showed grizzly evidence that when mankind had come to Callisto, he had inadvertently brought the bluebottle with him. For maggots wriggled in and around the corpse's nostrils, eye-sockets and mouth. Marca had been placed in the trunk after death. Because of Kym's attentions toward Crach though, he had not enjoyed the chance of dropping her corpse into a remote cater. The evidence of his grizzly murder remained with him hidden beneath a holographic projection that would fool casual inspection.

Quickly, Drakoma turned the projector unit back on and the image of books hid the terrible corpse. The image of her had burned into Kym's retinae though. She would never forget the sight she saw that night, ever!

Suddenly a grunting noise caused the two of them to turn toward the trussed up serial killer.

"Father", Kym hissed urgently, continuing to play her role lest circumstance prove it circumspect. "Let us alert the comb-men to what we have uncovered this night. He will be hanged for certain and we will see justice done without the threat of jeopardy to ourselves"?

"You would rob me of the pleasure of seeing vengeance enacted for your sweet sister", Drakoma ginned malignly. Enjoying his role in the brief tableau the tow of them were playing out

Crach meanwhile strained against his bonds in total futility, The effort causing his muscles and veins to bulge but all to no avail.

"Then how", she asked, seeing the grip of his resolve. "Do you have level two darts? Or perhaps enough Ones to stop his heart with over-dosage"?

"Neither and neither would be appropriate nor quick enough. No, he must choke as he choked the life out of your poor sister and my daughter".

Drakoma produced a knife, appropriated from dinner and hissed, "We will cut up the sheets of the bed and make a rope. That beam overhead is supported by yonder stanchion, it will be rightly fit for the purpose".

Crach suddenly hurled himself upward, despite his arms and legs being held securely. Drakoma's needle-gun crashed against his temple, however, it put paid to further struggling for the moment.

So the couple stripped the bed and with great difficulty and much patience cut it into strips and plaited them, making then strong enough to hold the Beasts weight, which was not great in the poor gravity of the moon.

Crach was coming to as the loop was placed over his head and the length of the rope was thrown over the beam. Drakoma savoured his victory and the moment by asking in a whisper,

"Have you anything to say in your own defence, Beast? Before this court passes sentence of death over your miserable hide"?

Crach nodded vigorously. Hoping he would be given chance to call out and raise the alarm. Obviously, he would rather hang later than sooner. Life was a sweet journey that none of us is hasty to conclude.

Drakoma pantomimed listening to a non-existent voice tilting his ear to Crach's gagged mouth, before answering,

"Get on with it. I embrace death! Very well then base malefactor, we shall conclude execution".

Kym went to get hold of the rope. Drakoma took her hands off it though, "I alone will be guilty if we are apprehended. You were asleep in your room, I acted alone", he grinned maliciously before adding,

"On my own, he will be raised slower, the end will be more tortuous, it suits my purpose".

With deliberate and slow hauling movements Drakoma hoisted Crach from the bed by his neck. The grizzly result was that the amount of oxygen heading to his brain was immediately cut short. His neck did not snap immediately and he began to gasp pathetically around the gag. Trying desperately to gasp for air. He was in the throes of brain ischemia. All his veins and arteries that carried blood to his vile and insane brain was being blocked. Crach was dying, slowly, lingering in the agony of brain ischemia. The blood from his carotids that would typically be en route to the brain suddenly had nowhere to go. So the pressure mounted. It continued to mount. Finally, when that blood was so backed up that it had nowhere to go, the capillaries in his face and eyes burst.

Kym could face no more of the horror. Even for one such as Crach, the slow and agonising end was not something she desired to witness.

He was not done yet!

Crach's brain was slowly dying from a lack of oxygen, but what was going on below his neck? His Vagus nerve, which aids in the control of the heart (among other things), sits at the base of the cranium. When Crach's brain started to swell due to lack of oxygen, it pushed downward triggering a Vagal reflex, which caused the heart rate and blood pressure to plummet. There was still one more major organ that was struggling, making Crach's suffering even worse. Crach's brain was dying, blood pooling under his skin, his heart barely puttering along, and blood pressure being basically non-existent. Slowly and in terrible pain, he was asphyxiating because the noose was crushing his trachea. He writhed in torment and phenomenal agony finally coming to a twitching end - heart, brain, or lungs had failed firstly.

"Six minutes", Drakoma had actually timed the process and recorded it on his pad. "He really suffered, I hope Senia lost consciousness before she died that way. "So we leave and in the morning the staff will find the Beast Of Callisto, overburdened by guilt - hung himself. It's unlikely the comb-men will think of any other solution as they will be pleased the Beast has come to an untimely end".

"Come", Kym entreated, "Let us get away from this horrible scene. Can I sleep with you tonight"?

Drakoma nodded, "You mean sleep"?

Kym nodded, "Yes. I fear it would not come to me if I was alone".

"In the morning we must breakfast and check out as though nothing is amiss. That way the comb-men will be forced to consider the entire guest list suspect, should they decide to pursue such a line of enquiry".

"I agree with you", Kym said satisfied it was all done. "The comb-men will be relieved to see the demise of the Beast of Callisto".

Echo of The Flesh

MAJOR ROXBROUGH

One

Dak Rambo realised he was a man with only a problem. One that presented with a single solution. The problem was his wife. The solution - murder. He was not a vindictive man. So he wanted her removal, though permanent, to be with neither pain nor suffering. He certainly did not want to be caught, though. On Venus, in the Anglo-sector, where Rambo lived capital punishment was practised. He did not desire to feel the hangman's noose tightening around his neck.

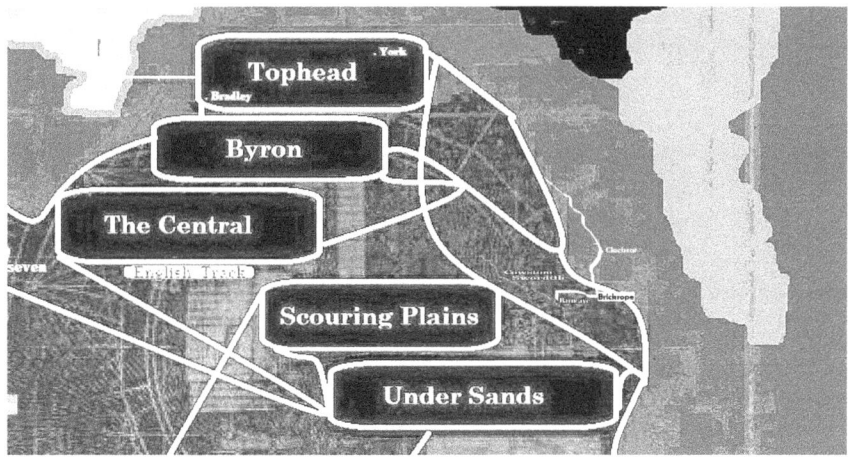

If only Monique would simply walk away from the marriage, she could live. As it was, the greed but obtuse mare would want half of everything. He could not afford to divide their flat in Clockcar. The sleepy little and provincial town lay north-easterly of Scouring Plains, on a spur of the main line. Property values were not modest, split them in half and they made no sort of deposit for a new place.

Rambo had loved his wife when they had first married, of course, he had. So when she had insisted upon the outmoded contract he had agreed without hardly any reservation. Everything had been going so very well. Monique was blonde, shapely, she gave head whenever he asked her to and her other positions were willing and very satisfactory. It was not until they had been together for several months, that he discovered her single dreadful weakness. Monique was unintelligent. Worse than that though, she complacent about her lack of intellect and this made her dull. If he could have helped her with education tapes, they would have provided one solution. She had no application though. No desire to be anything other than what she already was.

Rambo should have discovered this terrible short-coming before he had agreed to marry her. The truth was, he had spent most of their courting trying to get into her pants. Endlessly. Time had crept by. They had been living in Clockcar for twenty months. She was entitled to half. Half of all he possessed.

She was not going to get it.

She had to die!

One tiny detail. One fly in his ointment, though an imaginative man, Rambo had no idea how to kill someone. Even less how to do so and evade the long arm of the law. There was always the web. Risky though. The comb-men might use the same sites as he thus detecting his modus operandi with consummate ease. No point in selecting a fool-proof plan, if some officer of the law recognised the method at once. He needed to get out of the flat and think. So he jumped on a train, at the local station.

'This can't be happening', Stallone thought, *'The parallels between my own quandary and the lead character of this last story are so similar as to beggar belief'*. Yet he was sufficiently fascinated to continue reading, even though the tale seemed an impossibility.

The first train to pull into Cowstone was going south, to a little place called Brickrope. No prizes for guessing what was manufactured there. Most towns in the north-east of Venus were equally uninspiring. Rambo watched the landscape jostle past, through the special Energisave glass of the windows. A dull plain of scarred rock, eaten away in many places by the years of sulphuric-acid rain. Now the lichen-furs and other hardy plants were continuing to terraform the second planet from the sun. The satellite reflectors kept the world at a constant 292.039 degrees Kelvin. Mankind had come out from under the early domes. Though it was not easy to breathe without the new, slimline respirators even then.

There was constant wind. Infrequent rain. The planet could not be easily tamed. There was also the Venuser. Those being who had lived in disembodied form beneath the ravened surface. There they had lain dormant. Waiting. Waiting for the time when creatures they could inhabit arrived to be taken over. The first settlers had been prepossessed to a man. Only a biotron and android had managed to avoid the invasion. The internal invasion. Times had changed. The Venuser now agreed to reanimate only the dead. It was easy to see why they were evaded, circumvented. Yet they were not a warlike species. Ironic. They were also immune to Scaqualies. When the plague ravaged the human population of the world, not a single one was Venuser. Scaqualies, or to give it its full name Scapedic Qualito Iesthemia was a disease which was feared throughout the Solar System.

It attacked the immune system with startling rapidity. No amount of antibiotics were able to help rebuild the white cells which the disease destroyed. They were exploded from the inside out. Once the suffer was thusly debilitated, the slightest infection of any other sort was fatal. People died of colds, influenza, pneumonia septicaemia. They all had the same thing in common, firstly they had contracted Scaqualies.

Dak Rambo (named after the sepia-toned silent-movie star of the ancient cinematic times) deliberately missed the stop at Brickrope and instead climbed off the train at Barncave, casually gazing about him. He managed to breathe without his mask for a while. The nose filters doing a perfectly adequate job. He doubted that the provincial back-water hamlet could supply him with an answer to his conundrum. Who knew though? Fate had brought him here. Was it for a reason?

Reaching into his thermojacket, he pulled out a pair of Jean-Claude Schwarzenegger optic protectors. The bar rested on his ears. The lenses protecting his eyes from the harsh ultraviolet at such proximity to the sun. The town looked even more depressing through the filtration. Could such a place have any clue that would aid him in his quest? It seemed unlikely in the extremis. Shrugging his shoulders, he assumed the gallump. The special gait that any born off-world used when perambulating on mankind's newest world.

The Athenaeum on the edge of town took Rambo's breath away. It was huge. The sheer scale of it was not what he had ever witnessed before. It dominated the frontier town of Barncave. The instant he climbed down from the carriages, it hovered over the town like some monstrous beast of stone and glass. As he walked toward it, Rambo felt humbled. Mankind, in the past, had aspired to such monuments of grandeur. On Venus though, all was squat and airtight by necessity. It had come down to the diminutive Venuser, the ancient race of the formerly acidic world, to create such a work of sublime beauty.

Had Rambo not been alone he would still have approached the museum in awed silence. He did so at its only visible entrance. It was the airlock at the base of the grandly-domed cupola. The interior ceiling was terrific arch. It was supported by large stone columns. The lower floor contained an army of shelving, filled with actual books. Above it, a railed mezzanine mirrored it in size and content. For a few moments, Rambo simply craned his head back and drank in the visual feast. He suddenly became aware of the presence of someone else. Looking in the direction of the slightly wheezing sound he found himself face to face with a Venuser. The Custodian of the Athenaeum was not human. Why should he be?

"Good day", Rambo began, "I am a casual tourist and would take a tour of your museum".

The mustard-hued smile was nodrasic, "Right place you've come, museum many has treasures. Art, weaponry, books".

Books. Rambo had heard of them. Ancient i-Pads made of paper which he thought he recalled was a sort of mulched wood, the leaves of these were stitched together and then bound with animal hide or some material he could not remember the origin of - called cardboard. On the leaves, or pages data was pressed with ink and once it was done the page could not be erased or cut and pasted. It all seemed dreadfully permanent. Then a notion struck Rambo and he turned his attention back to the curator

Though the body was old the Venuser had not inhabited it for long. The speech was still newly mastered.

"I am Dak Rambo, pleased to meet you".

"I, likewise. In particular, anything? Venta is my name"?

"Yes. Fiction. Murder/mystery".

Rambo found himself speaking in clipped fashion as well. The Custodian waved a mustard-coloured and slightly shrivelled hand. "Please to follow".

As they trudged the stairs to the mezzanine, Rambo felt obliged to ask,

"So what are the duties of an Athenaeum Custodian, Mister"?

"Core Duties and Responsibilities: Monitor building upon entry and contact Director or designated contractors regarding problems. Coordinate with contractors doing on-site work as needed. Clear all entrances and walkways of snow as needed. Remove debris from grounds as needed. Maintain lichen shrubs. Clean, disinfect and re-supply bathroom. Vacuum tiles, swiffen all wood and dilurlleum floors. Clean main entrance Energi-glass doors. Remove all trash. Polish furniture and woodwork throughout the building. Check lanterns and replace wicks and oil as needed. Keep Custodian's area orderly". had memorised his responsibilities by rote it seemed.

"Murder/Mystery section here is. I leave".

"Thank you and yes. I'll browse and call you if I need any help".

"Do".

Then the little figure was gone leaving him alone.

He gazed at the rows before him. Roving them appreciatively. Until his eye caught one volume, the title of which, seemed apposite.

It was a blue book. As Rambo lifted it from its niche he felt the texture of the binding. It was from the skin of a real cow! Almost caressing it with his fingers he opened the book. The fusty smell was intoxicating. The row of dark ink on the yellowed page:

Murder Museum.

edited by Cardy Nodras.

Rambo was trembling with anticipation. He took a seat on one of the provided sofas. Unable to resist reading the first short story in the book in one go.

Two

It proved an intriguing read. One which hinted at the level of quality to come. Rambo wondered if there was a borrowing service. He tucked the book under his arm and carefully strode downstairs.

Venta was still at his desk. The two of them still the only current occupants of the building.

"May I borrow this book please, Mister Venta".

"Library it is". Came the clipped reply. The Venuser pulled the book from Rambo. From inside the front flap, he drew forth a slim foil slip. In an indentation on the desk, he carefully fed the foil. Somewhere in the bowels of the Athenaeum, the metal click of relays could be heard. Venta placed the slip into a box. The container had been empty before that.

"Days of twenty-seven, may you loan. Fine after that there will be".

"Plumb", Rambo acknowledged understanding and pleasure. "I'll be sure to bring it back before the forty-eighth of the month. Thank you for your help. Good day to you, Sir".

"Also to you", came the polite response.

Rambo walked thoughtfully out of the impressive structure. Murder Museum could well prove to be his textbook. Thank the stars for Cardy Nodras.

It grew heavy in his hands. Its weight increased in his mind burning his brain. On the homeward train, he could not leave it closed. He had the irresistible compulsion to read the second story. It caused him to almost miss the stop at Cowstone. The second story had thrown up a possibility. The only trouble with it was he did not think Monique possessed enough wit to go insane. In order to lose one's mind, one firstly had to be in possession of one. He punched in the combination to their flat and discovered she was home.

"Where've you been"? She wanted to know. Her voice contained no hint of accusation. Just simple curiosity.

"Why"? He countered. He did that quite a lot recently. It seemed to stump her.

"No reason, have you had any tea"?

"No".

"Want something zapping in the hypa-wave"?

This was the level of most of their intercourse recently. Not exactly intellectually stimulating. He reasoned aloud,

"I can do that".

"I'm going to shower then and then watch Celebrity Parts".

Celebrity Parts was mind-numbingly plebeian. He had not the faintest interest in it, he opened the frifreezr and looked at the array of gaudy cartonettes that promised, 'A nutritional and delicious meal in just twenty seconds (neoplas fork supplied in - carton)'!

After a shower, he decided to do a little work. His office was in the apartments. Being a bottle designer he rarely had to travel into head office. He usually pinged his latest creation digitally. Shampu4yoo headquarters were in Scouring Plains so only a short train journey even if he needed to go in.

Three

Something was different about her husband and Monique could not fathom out exactly what it was. He seemed dissatisfied. She aimed to please at every turn though. Her cooking was not dire, she was careful with money and in the bedroom, despite their being married she still went down on him whenever he asked her to. She turned off the tri-vid and tried to think. It was not easy for her, the application did not come naturally, but she reasoned that his change was recent and therefore the cause of it must be so too. She fixed herself a filtered-gin and lit a cigarette. The proper tobacco kind that was fast losing popularity. As the blue smoke drifted slowly toward the ceiling Monique actually cooked up a plan. She would watch Dak carefully. Like in the spy movies. She would discover what exactly was going on and then work out how to solve it. Satisfied that she had, at last, a strategy, she turned Celebrity Parts back on.

'Thank goodness for that', Stallone thought at that point. *'For a few minutes, I thought the book possessed some sort of inexplicable foresight. Now the story diverges to the wife. She certainly has more about her than Madchen. Hmm, let's read some more'.*

The following morning as the two of them ate their Whee-ties in thoughtful silence, the amazingly delicious and nutritional bite-sized protein and vitamin-packed parcels of pure wheat did not keep Monique quiet for long.

"Roxanne Jossa has finally had her baby".

"Really, subnormal was it"?

"That's not a nice thing to ask". Why did Dak have to be such a donkey-cavity about such important matters?

"I was just thinking of its chances as determined by its genetic pool that's all".

Monique bristled, "That's not fair, her husband who's Boreanaz Hasselhoff actually has degrees".

"That's true", Rambo was beginning to enjoy himself, "But only when having his temperature checked ha ha ha".

"I won't tell you any more of the news if you're going to ensnare the ordure".

"Sorry! So how is the Venuser-Earth political situation, are relationships still tense"?

"Oh you know I'm not interested in that dry stuff. I like reading about real people, not politicians".

She smirked, she might not be the sharpest knife in the drawer, but her point was valid on that score. He had finished by then. Excusing himself he went into his office, disappearing for the rest of the morning. At lunchtime, he precluded it with a walk giving her chance to commence her spying activity. His latest bottle design was on his P.C. she stared at it in horror, was he losing the plot? It was totally hideous. No one would buy shampoo that looked like it was being aimed at Zombies. In the ultimate scheme of things would Dak Rambo bottle designer be revered as a great man who should be committed to history.

She tried to imagine the advertisements that would accompany a shampoo bottle strangely distorted and created from black plastic.

Just because you are dead it doesn't mean your scalp should be too. Tired of your hair having that lifeless look to it? Sick of the last minute rush to look just right before you go out to rip the throat out of your latest victim? Well here at Orang-U-Can we've listened to over 20,000 living-dead and we've gone back into our super expensive laboratories in search of a solution just for you. After months of industrious research, we've found the answer…

It's a new shampoo called Valde Malus. One wash with Valde Malus and you'll immediately start to realise the benefits of continued use. Yes! By the time you're on only your third ergonomically designed squeeze-eezi tube, all your problems will be gone. No more bad hair days.

No more having difficulty rinsing out the blood and brains from your victims No more expensive and time-consuming trips to the barber. Your hair won't grow, because you're dead Buddy. But that doesn't mean what you've got shouldn't look it's darkest greasiest best!

Then, of course, the fine print. There was always fine print tucked away on the back of the tube so that the average consumer would never read it:-

Any connection to use of this product and the high incidences of complete decomposition of the head and brain is vehemently denied by the makers of this specially tested preparation. The corporation of Orang-U-Can exhaustively field tested Valde Malus on over 1000 specially selected dead molluscs prior to release. Not one of them has complained of so much as an itchy scalp never mind problems of concentration. Remember to do a scalp test on your own head before using this executive action shampoo. At the first sign of dead skin falling from the scalp, crumbling of the bone in the skull or searing agonising pain seek the brain of a living person and devour it - at once. Do not attempt to do a brainectomy yourself or you will negate your rights to a full refund.

Though fun, this was getting her nowhere. Her husband was not working not using his time constructively. Plainly he was not in the mood for serious work. She glanced about her to see if she could find a reason for his distraction. Her vision caught the edge of some strange artefact that looked incongruously out of place in the modern office. She picked it up. The item was made of a metal she had never seen the like of before. It was warmer and softer to the touching and it had a curious aroma. There seemed to be no lock on the device, no catch to open it. Monique lifted the top of the item and it yawed open on a silent hinge. Inside were words, yet the box had no apparent power source. The page of the pad-like box was white instead of grey and the words black instead of white. Yet she could still read them as they were in standard:-

Murder Museum ed Cardy Nodras.

The box contained information on how to conduct a murder! Monique felt fear grip her vital, cast an iron ring of frigidity about her heart. How many reasons could there be for her husband to be researching an ancient artefact in the art of homicide? What was the one that immediately sprang to mind? He was going to kill her.

Stallone grinned. This was getting amusing. In the story, the wife then knew the husband was going to attempt to kill her. No chance of that happening to him,

Madchen was far too dumb. He settled back in his chair and continued to read, the end of the book was in sight.

She went into the main part of the apartment to fix herself some lunch. Of her murderous partner, there was no sign. A bottle designer was on a pretty good salary - fortunately. At least she could go into scouring plains and do some therapeutic shopping to ease her fractured nerves.

She realised when she thought about it that the two of them did nothing together any more. They shared no interests. While he liked to collect ancient coins, she found it dreadfully dull. She was more interested in fashion and the continued improvement of her appearance. She possessed dozens of pairs of shoes, over a score of hats, handbags in their multitude. Her section of the fitted wardrobe they shared grew progressively greater. Dak dressed like a slob most of the time, happy to be in pullover and crumpled slacks. He did not even bother to put all his belongings in the wardrobe. Some of his soiled items were carelessly tossed into various recesses of his office.

She realised why he wanted to be rid of her. He could not live up to her high standards of personal care and appearance any more. He simply could not keep up to her standards. Of late he only spoke to her in a sarcastic fashion. The only time he was satisfactory was when they were fluttering and even then he did not always wait for her to climax. Maybe he hoped one of those yarns in that strange box provided him with evil inspiration for his planned crime? Time for some food. She felt herself getting an understandable tension headache. There was a surprise in store for her upon entering the kitchen. A tall handsome figure was at the rear airlock ringing the request for entrance. Monique recognised at once who it was. Her husband's brother Diesel. Monique punched in the security code that released the airlock and smiled at her brother-in-law. "Diesel! How are you, it's good to see you. You don't visit often enough".

"I mean to", he laughed but you know how it is, Sis, always something to be done".

"They heard the front airlock open and close. She told the tall handsome man, "That will be your brother, he just went out for a short while and is back now"

"Diesel's here, just arrived. I was going to shout you. I'm just making him a sandwich and some bits. Do you want the same"?

"That would be great. Thank you", he replied and went into the lounge to see his brother. Diesel was Dak's younger brother by four years, they were close, as a result, visits by each were frequent.

They hugged without speaking, then asked how each was. Monique became the perfect hostess. Silent, subservient and disappeared to allow the two men to enjoy guy talk.

Four

Finally, he managed to put the damned book down and then his i-Pad lit up again. He had a ping from the office. What did they want? Shampu4yoo headquarters were in Scouring Plains so only a short train journey. Even so, it was most unusual for them to ask to see him in person. He tended to work almost always remotely.

Don't say he was going to get the sack over that black shampoo bottle, the idiot had not handed it in had he? All she could do was wait and see what he said when he returned. Slipping into his office she discovered the box full of leaves gone. He had taken that with him to the office. Why? What on Venus could he want such a strange contraption with him for? It was a long and uncertain day for her. She had yet to come up with some strategy to save herself. All she could do was wait and see how events played out.

She heard the airlock before he called to her and then joined him in the lounge. His features possessed a strangely remote joy upon them. She could not fathom for the second what had happened and what he was thinking. With his hands on her arms he asked her,

"You know I work for a company called, Shampu4yoo, don't you"?

"Yes of course. I know what you do for a living Dak".

"And I've told you my bosses name is Vemmer, a German. He answers to the CEO Danvers the grandson of the entrepreneur who had originally set up the company".

"I met him at one of your yuletime bashes if you remember, Dak. Your immediate supervisor is the thin and balding Vemmer. A fair man in his dealings with his staff. Softly spoken and well-liked for the gentle way he goes about supervising some you. Vemmer's boss is another matter entirely, you remember you told me? Thick-set sandy-haired Danvers as you rightly told me just then is the grandson of the entrepreneur who had originally set up the company. He's well spoken and educated, but ruthless when it comes to hiring and firing. He's known for his quick temper which he often regrets afterwards and then profusely apologises for. You're never sure how to take the man due to his mood swings. You find it best to be as firmly entrenched in your own opinion as Danvers, who then frequently changes his mind backing down from his original position. You've not fallen out with him and gotten yourself fired have you, Dak"?

For the first time in quite a while, Dak smiled at her then and declared, "Quite the opposite, Monique, in fact, I've just been promoted".

"Promoted! Darling that's tremendous"! She cried throwing her arms around him. He said quietly into her ear,

"There's just one little problem".

"What's that then"? She felt her joy dissipate like smoke on the wind.

320

"The office I'm to run is in Gravelcaves".

Monique blinked, "Gravelcaves over to the west? Is it on the Scouring Plains line? How will you commute"?

"No it's on the Under Sands line and would take two connections for me to reach twice daily", he confessed. "If I except the promotion it will mean me moving firstly to Gravelcaves. To a flat say, then when we have the chance, moving you to a new home over there".

"A flat"! Monique could not keep the suspicion out of her tone. She went on, "Tell me Dak, will Camena be going to this new office by any chance.

"Camena"? Dak asked managing to keep a note of bemusement in his tone. He was an excellent liar was Dak.

"She of the auburn hair, beautifully creamy complexion and straight but purposeful nose. She who has thirty-eight Es and whom I caught you in a clinch with at the party I mentioned. You must remember her throat, Dak. You had your tongue firmly enough down it when I caught you"?

"Oh"! Dak actually slapped his own temple, "The redhead. I'm not certain she even works for the firm any more, Monique".

'She koofing well does and I saw her the other day at the reception desk', Stallone smiled to himself. The description in the book had been a perfect one of Ariel, the girl whom might very well replace Madchen in his bed once he had gotten rid of her. How could this story in an ancient book be so like his own experience? Was he asleep and reading this last yarn? He did not know but was intrigued to read on.

"I see. Well, even so, it's a lot to take in, Dak. But I'm pleased for you obviously and I know you'll make an excellent manager". Monique managed. She made him some dinner and then he disappeared into his study, with the box of ancient writing.

'Tomorrow I have to start finding out what exactly is going on otherwise I'm going to wake up dead one morning', she thought as she retired for the night.

Five

Monique Rambo could think of only one place where she might get some answers to her problems with her husband. She too had to journey to Barncave and find the Athenaeum - Dak had been to. She had found the train ticket stub in his scruffy coat, the day she had picked it up to launder it. As was her usual habit, she went through the pockets before hanging it in the chemical tank for cleansing.

With these thoughts filling her head, she hopped onto the train at Cowstone. To her dismay, she found herself opposite a strange little man in clothes so ragged that they contained holes and frays. His hair did not look like he had shampooed it for months, his long greying beard was straggly and yet in his eyes burned a fierce intelligence fuelled by the need to impart some sort of message.

"You're going to the Athenaeum, over in Barncave", he stated without the faintest notion of mistake. Incongruous to his appearance his breath was minty.

"Excuse me", Monique said politely, doing, "But I'm not really feeling in the mood to chat. Would you mind awfully if we journeyed in silence"?

"There is something you must know though", the tramp persisted, swaying backwards and forwards due to the motion of the train".

Monique opened her handbag and reached into her purse. "Look here's a couple of sestertii, go and get yourself a drink and something to eat at the buffet carriage. You'll even get centisestertii in change. If you don't I shall be forced to call out for a conductor".

"Do that and you will never know your fate, Miss Monique Rambo".

"How on Venus do you know my name? Have you been spying on me"?

"You could say that, although it was actually your husband that I was watching for the main part".

"Then tell me your message and be done with it, Sir. I really am disquieted by you".

"Very well. It is this message. Go to Athenaeum as you plan and once there seek out the aid of the librarian. A Venuser named Venta. Tell him of your suspicions, ask him for aid and it will be given, for you are innocent in your heart of dark movements and mysteries".

Monique nodded, not understanding the ramblings of a man who was possibly demented anyway. "All right, Sir. Now you've warned me, thank you. Now! Please take this money and go and get yourself a hot drink and something to eat. I will heed your words".

The tramp smiled and his rheumy eyes filled with tears, but he nodded and pocketing the money left her carriage so that she was alone for the rest of the journey.

'How strange', Stallone thought. *'When reading a story obviously written by a mare, the story has one actually rooting for the woman. In many ways Monique is like Madchen, but with far more about her. Madchen would never*

think to spy on me, she is happy with her tri-vid and the occasional meal while she does her costly on-line shopping and slowly loses her looks and figure. This Monique, she has given her dilemma thought and taken it to purpose. I can't simply hand the book in unfinished, I must get to the end before I take it back to the Athenaeum'.

The iron train ground to a shuddering halt and Monique daintily alighted onto the platform. No sooner was she walking through ticket check than a flitter-cab driver stopped her progress.

"Do-ya need a taxi Ma'am"?

"Possibly", Monique admitted, "Although I can see the Athenaeum from here. It's only a walk in actuality".

"With mask and goggles", the taxi driver persisted, "Over uneven ground. You might turn an ankle, maybe even break a leg. I can get you to the building unharmed. How about it"?

"How much then"? Monique felt her resolve to weaken.

"Six sestertii"?

"Make it five and five centisestertii and here is the coin ahead of the journey, My Good Man".

"Deal, Ma-am".

It was agreed and Monique arrived at the base of the vastly impressive structure in the same condition as when she had alighted the train. There could be no turning back now. Swallowing down her unease she alighted the stone steps leading to the front doors and pushed them open with a hiss of escaping air. The public buildings had *unlocked* airlocks, but they still had airlocks.

Monique glanced hither and thither and then, upward and was awed by the splendour of the interior she found herself within. So breathtaking was her surroundings that she failed to notice the approach of a diminutive and mustard-hued little figure. He who approached was an aborigine a Venuser.

"Hello", he began, "Custodian of Athenaeum am I. To you greetings and wishes of good health I give".

"Thank you", Monique returned. You're Venta aren't you"?

"Name was given and name is kept. As you suggest, so is true". The curious Venuser conceded. "Looking for what may I ask. Art to appreciate. Weaponry to examine. Or book to read"?

"None of those", Monique replied, "I come for your help, Sir. My husband is reading one of your books in the hope that it will contain a method he can employ to take my life".

Venta nodded slowly and with a wisdom in his eyes that went beyond understanding. He observed,

"Real name Stallone is he".

Stallone almost dropped the book from numbed fingers. Though the temperature in his office was unchanged he found that perspiration was running down his face. It was the sweat of terror.

How could this be?

How could he be reading about himself?

How was *he* - part of the book? He was not a character in a long forgotten book. He lived. He thrived. He was a real person. He felt dread grasp his chest and lungs tightly as he read on.

"Yes. That is correct. Dustin Stallone, I am his wife Madchen. Can you help me Loog"?

Slowly the Venuser waved one of his stunted mustard-hued hands, "Please to follow".

Madchen followed the Venuser around the back of the desk and into a small chamber beyond. Inside was a large machine. The working of which was a mystery to her.

"In the hurøøk, your husband goes, if pressing this lever I do". Loog stated.

"Hurøøk"?

"Apologies. Venuser word I use. Loop dear lady. I throw switch and machine activates. Aim at Dustin I shall, for the only way to stop him in his ambitions is to see that the day he plans to kill you never comes".

"It won't hurt him"?

"No pain, no demise, either for husband or for you".

"Then do it, please. Throw the switch......."

Stallone dropped the book. He let it rest on the floor where it had fallen. Instead, he hurriedly gathered up his mask and goggles, threw on a jacket and raced out of the house. He dashed to the train station. He had to get to the Murder Museum and as quickly as possible. He did not know what fate Loog had in store for him. All he knew was that he did not want it!

Buying a ticket waiting for a train going east, everything took far too long. He was in the agony of anticipation of events he could not fathom. He wanted to reach the treacherous little Venuser and get his hand s around his throat and....

The train arrived and Stallone was the first to jump on it. The next three minutes were as a century each. Finally - it pulled out. Just as it was moving a dishevelled tramp climbed into the compartment and seated himself opposite Stallone. He had a huge unkempt beard, long greasy hair that needed a good sudsing in valde malus. He was none too fragrant. In his rheumy eyes burned a fierce passion for who knew what.

"You're not real", Stallone said. "Either that or I'm not, I'm not so certain any more".

"Why so"? The tramp was tacit that day.

"You was on the platform at Scouring Plains, but you were also in the book. Both cannot be true can they"?

"Can a book not contain accounts of real people"? The old man argued.

"This is making my head hurt", Stallone confessed. "I suppose you are right, but I took the book out before …. When I took out the book, allegedly written many years past, I was not even born. Then I find myself described in inexplicable detail and yet I was not born when the book was written.

"Let me examine it"? The man requested not unreasonably. That was the moment Stallone realised he had left it behind. So eager had he been to get to the Athenaeum, he had left the book behind.

"It doesn't really matter all that matters is that the machine cannot do anything to me. Cannot disrupt my plans, will not change anything".

"All is change, all temporary", the man said vaguely. "Without change, we would endure stagnation".

"I want the changes to be my own", Stallone argued fiercely. "I don't want to read about myself in an ancient tome. I just want to...".

"Just what to what, Sir"?

"Never mind". Stallone was struggling to think straight. "It's my stop in a second and then I'll get to the bottom of this and put things how they're meant to be".

"I think perhaps how you want them to be", the tramp observed reflectively and with an inexplicable sadness, "I'll see you later then".

"Not when I've moved to another town a good distance from here", Stallone promised with projected certainty.

The tramp merely repeated, "I'll see you later".

Stallone had never been so glad to jump from a train. He was first in the ticket check and the instant he was through a flitter-taxi driver barred his way.

"Yes I want a taxi", Stallone barked quickly, "Get me to the huge museum on the edge of town and I'll give you a shillin".

The generous payment assured Stallone of the swiftest transfer possible. As he dived from the flitter he threw the coin to the driver and proceeded to vault up the stone steps three at a time. He hurled himself through the air-doors and was once again in the Athenaeum.

"Hello", he cried out. Of Loog, there was no sign. Nor of Madchen. Or was that Venta and Monique and if it was who was he. He could feel lunacy nibbling at the edges of his brain, "Hello for Venus' sake".

From behind the counter, the diminutive form of an aborigine appeared. Stallone gazed at him keenly, all Venuser looked alike to him. He was forced to ask,

"Are you Loog"?

The custodian of the Athenaeum nodded uncertainly, "Loog my name is. Met have we, Sir"?

"Yes, last week. Don't you remember (or was it next week he was asking him to remember)? I took out a book, borrowed it to read".

"I do not remember", Loog confessed. Problem it is not. Many books have we. Library this is in addition to...".

"I know it's a library and an art gallery and an exhibition of weapons through the ages because I've been here before. Last week. You and I met. You must remember"?

The annoying little base-born shook a head that still managed to remain atop the scrawniest of necks. Stallone could wrap his hand around that windpipe and squeeze and squeeze...

"Look in your records", he tried. "You'll see I took out a book called Murder Museum edited by Cardy Nodras. No1 Wait it minute that's not it. I remember now, it was called Murder through the Ages edited by Darcy Sardon".

"Which was it, Sir"? The amnesiacical librarian desired to know".

"Venus in the heavens, just check your records you, Little-shrivelled Frenger", Stallone exploded, "How many books did you loan out last week anyway".

"The book, Murder through the Ages edited by Darcy Sardon still on the shelves it is". Loog had grown frosty, not wishing to hear the profanity.

"I don't really care about the book. I want to know about the loop machine what it does, how it stops me achieving my ambitions. I..., just a moment? You say the book is still on the shelves. How many copies do you have"?

"We have but one, Mister Stallone".

"Now I know you're lying you, Shrivelled-little-worm, because the book is still in my....you called me by my name too. I never gave you my name. You are caught in a web of deceit you little koof zoid. Now take me to the machine".

"If to borrow the book you wish I will for you fetch it. Loog offered, "Machine, have me none".

"All right"! Stallone barked, "I that case what's this"? He promptly vaulted over the reception desk and plunged into the small room beyond.

It contained nothing but books some old painting and a couple of arbalists.

"These items waiting for restoration they are". The annoying Venuser remarked behind Stallone.

"You didn't have time to move it", Stallone muttered. "Even if you knew I was coming, which you didn't because I only read it in the book".

"Book, Sir, fetch I will", Loog chirped and trotted off while Stallone remained standing in the room gazing about him in a combination of confusion and disbelief.

Slowly gathering what was left of his wits, the designer of shampoo bottles wandered back out to the desk and rounded it absently. Above him and at either side the huge domed roof was as ever magnificent. The hall must have contained thousand upon thousand of paper-books. It was a Venuser marvel. Columns held up the banked rows of shelves and a tiny mustard-hued figure was currently in the 'M' section.

326

Stallone collapsed on a couch. An indeterminate time later the Venuser was once more before him. He smiled a yellow smile and held out a single volume,

"Murder through the Ages edited by Darcy Sardon it is. Sir would like to borrow for 27days".

"Yes", muttered the totally defeated figure that was the would-be murderer. "I'll read it on the train on the way back home to my wife".

"Remember days of twenty-seven though, Sir. Or fine you will pay".

"I won't forget", Stallone returned woodenly, "I'll never forget".

"The upon return next book you can take", Loog promised.

Stallone knew he was once again deceiving him however, he would take the same book out again. Over and over he would borrow it. Time and again he would read it. He remembered what he had read the Venuser had told his wife,

'The only way to stop him in his ambitions is to see that the day he plans to kill you never comes'.

It never would, the day never would.

Lightning Source UK Ltd.
Milton Keynes UK
UKHW040611190919
350067UK00001B/32/P